VAGABOND SQUADRON

VAGABOND SQUADRON

ROBBIE MACNIVEN

BLACK LIBRARY

A BLACK LIBRARY PUBLICATION

First published in 2025.
This edition published in Great Britain in 2026 by
Black Library, Games Workshop Ltd., Willow Road,
Nottingham, NG7 2WS, UK.

Represented by: Games Workshop Limited – Irish branch,
Unit 3, Lower Liffey Street, Dublin 1,
D01 K199, Ireland.

10 9 8 7 6 5 4 3 2 1

Produced by Games Workshop in Nottingham.
Cover illustration by Vladimir Krisetskiy.

This is a work of fiction. All the characters and events portrayed in this book are fictional, and any resemblance to real people or incidents is purely coincidental.

See Black Library on the internet at

blacklibrary.com

Find out more about Games Workshop
and the worlds of Warhammer at

warhammer.com

Printed and bound in the UK.

———————————

To Dad, who I can never dedicate enough to.

For more than a hundred centuries the Emperor
has sat immobile on the Golden Throne of Earth.
He is the Master of Mankind. By the might of his
inexhaustible armies a million worlds stand
against the dark.

Yet, he is a rotting carcass, the Carrion Lord of
the Imperium held in life by marvels from the
Dark Age of Technology and the thousand souls
sacrificed each day so his may continue to burn.

To be a man in such times is to be one amongst
untold billions. It is to live in the cruelest and
most bloody regime imaginable. It is to suffer an
eternity of carnage and slaughter. It is to have cries
of anguish and sorrow drowned by the thirsting
laughter of dark gods.

This is a dark and terrible era where you will find
little comfort or hope. Forget the power of technology
and science. Forget the promise of progress and
advancement. Forget any notion of common
humanity or compassion.

There is no peace amongst the stars, for in the grim
darkness of the far future, there is only war.

'We carry the God-Emperor's vengeance.'
– Motto of the 901st Imperial Navy Tactical Wing

'We're the God-Emperor's very own drop-off and
pick-up service.'
– Attributed to Flight Lieutenant Hal Vaughn,
901st Imperial Navy Tactical Wing

IMPERIAL NAVY COMBAT ROSTER G874/X, BATTLEFLEET AJAX, SUB-SECTION 2-12

VAGABOND SQUADRON, 901ST IMPERIAL NAVY TACTICAL WING

[Roster taken post ushen insertion, during the first tour of Kanai Tertius]

VALKYRIE PRIMUS, CALL SIGN: *VAGRANT*

    Pilot: Captain Cassandra Elza

    Co-pilot: Flight Sergeant Melisa Korrie

    Gunner: Corporal Solaris Ezekiel

    Gunner: Aviator Wilbe Platz [replacement]

VALKYRIE SECUNDUS, CALL SIGN: *ROGUE*

    Pilot: Flight Lieutenant Hal Vaughn

    Co-pilot: Flight Sergeant Xijen Lei

    Gunner: Corporal Xo Holsten

    Gunner: Aviator Arran Macks

VALKYRIE TERTIUS, CALL SIGN: *PAUPER*

    Pilot: Flight Sergeant Miken Cobb

    Co-pilot: Corporal Zats Akoi

    Gunner: Aviator Verren Skerry

    Gunner: Aviator Isiah Weets

VALKYRIE QUARTUS, CALL SIGN: *SCOUNDREL* [ADDENDUM NOTE: DESTROYED PRIOR TO OPERATIONS IN THE EJI VALLEY]

    Pilot: Flight Sergeant Eleanor Vaughn [KIA]

    Co-pilot: Corporal Zicks Marsten [KIA]

    Gunner: Aviator Gorg Sprats [KIA]

    Gunner: Aviator Dieter Fellows [KIA]

VULTURE GUNSHIP, CALL SIGN: *RUFFIAN*

Pilot: Flight Sergeant Emmi Konstantina

Weapons Operator: Corporal Erik Straks

GROUND CREWS

Enginseer Matriculate Zorn-Five

Tech-Adept Kravia Three-Six

18 Departmento Munitorum menials

14 servitor units, inc. maintenance, repair and haulage classes.

PART ONE

CHAPTER ONE

Four grunts were being flogged as Cass and Orlov passed by on their way to Suchen Palace.

They were Hyrkans, and their comrades were being made to watch. The battalion, roughly four hundred strong, had been drawn up in two ranks on three sides around the parade square. They were in full kit, and were visibly sweltering in the afternoon heat as the punishment played out. Tripod frames had been constructed from the hafts of the ceremonial spontoons carried by Hyrkan sergeants, and the guilty had been stripped of their upper fatigues and strung up to them by their wrists.

The battalion's drummer boys were administering the sentence with electro-flails. The wicked cracking sound of each strike cut the humid air like a knife. The bared backs of the four were red-raw.

'Thank the Throne the Navy doesn't flog pilots,' Orlov said to Cass.

'We're too valuable,' she responded, morbid fascination holding her attention as she and Orlov crossed around the edge of the parade's open side, headed for the palace's main gates beyond.

A Hyrkan sergeant major was calling out the number of each lash. Next to him, the regiment's senior commissar was watching to ensure the drummers weren't going easy on their comrades, or that their arms weren't starting to tire. There were several more junior commissars prowling like black-clad predators along the front ranks of the onlooking battalion, watching the faces of the men. They were making sure none averted their eyes, and hunting for any hint of a venomous glance cast at either themselves or the regiment's officers.

The guilty four had been given leather bits to chew down on, but one had lost theirs, and they began to cry out with each shivering blow. Cass saw several onlookers wince. She wondered how many lashes they had been sentenced to.

'I wonder what they did,' Orlov mused.

'Probably tied their boot laces the wrong way,' Cass said.

One of the junior commissars looked at them. Cass held his gaze until they had passed round the rear of the ranks drawn up immediately in front of the gates.

There were two Tempestus Scions guarding the doors, big brutes in the red carapace armour of the Alphic Hydras. They checked the ident-tags of the pair of aviators, before banging twice on the entrance. With a rusty squeal, the heavy doors began to part. Cass and Orlov stepped through, leaving the wicked cracks and agonised crying behind.

Suchen Palace had once been the residence of the High Charag, the local title given to Kanai Tertius' Imperial commander. It was just one of a number of royal residences dotted along the Eji Valley. In centuries past, the planet's ruler would have spent time touring between them, overseeing the implementation of the Imperium's authority. Nowadays, palaces like

Suchen were relics of a bygone era, uninhabited for almost a century.

That was, until the Guard had arrived.

The palace complex was walled, an inner courtyard in front of the primary residence with lower secondary and tertiary wings flanking it. The walls had been white once, but were flaking and discoloured with age. The roof in particular looked as though it had once been magnificent, a sweeping five-ridged hip construction made from layers of ruddy ceramic tiles, though many of the layers were missing, and avian nests bristled in the cracks. The remnants of the regal silhouette had been further broken by the installation of a vox-mast and an augur dish.

Still, there was a certain faded grandeur to it all. In a sense it reminded Cass of parts of her home, on board the Emperor-class battleship *Mandatum Divinum*.

The courtyard's centre was dominated by an elaborate stone fountain, carved like a nine-headed dragon. Once, Cass assumed, water would have spurted from each of its open maws, but it had long ago dried up, its basin cracked and baking in the sun. The bestial statue still glared across the courtyard with eternal, stony rapprochement. A pair of Guard staff officers were lounging alongside it, sharing a lho-stick. Both barely glanced at the new arrivals.

Cass and Orlov passed them on the way to the central building. Outside the heat was brutal enough to leave Cass' dark blue flight suit plastered to her body, but inside the courtyard's confines it was downright oppressive. Intense temperatures tended to bring on migraines, and she could feel one beginning to throb in her temples and behind her eyes. Pilots who had been operating planetside since the beginning of the invasion nearly two years ago said the weather should have shifted to wet and humid with the onset of the rainy season, but there was no sign of that yet. The last precipitation had been over a month ago, Terran standard. Good for flying, bad for existing, at least outside of a cockpit or hab-tunnel benefitting from air recyc.

Another Scion was on guard at the main door, but merely eyed the pair of Navy officers as they went through. There was little in the way of relief inside – a sole stuttering recyc unit that looked as though it had been stripped out of a cabin from one of the ships in orbit had been set up just inside the doorway, battling to make the space feel like anything other than a furnace. Cass resisted the urge to linger in front of it.

Suchen's entrance hall matched its exterior, flaking walls and a tiled floor littered with broken plaster and vermin droppings. A few old tapestries were still hung up, hunting scenes interspersed with beasts from Kanai's mythology, all faded almost to illegibility.

There was no one else present, and – besides the air recyc's wheezing – no sounds save for the clipped footsteps of the two pilots on the bared floor and the buzzing of the gangly insects that seemed to infest everything in this region of Kanai.

With Orlov taking the lead, they mounted the double staircase at the far end of the hall and turned right along the landing. They passed several rooms on their way to the east wing. Doors had been replaced by reinforced flakboard, but most had been laid aside so movement in and out was unobstructed. Whatever fine furniture and royal dignitaries the chambers had once played host to were now gone, replaced with stacks of Munitorum-stamped crates being catalogued by a few robed clerks, silently assessing stocks on dataslates. None looked up from their labours as Cass and Orlov went by.

A man was waiting for them at the door to the east wing, ruddy-faced and perspiring in the olive drab uniform of the general staff. He saluted Orlov and introduced himself.

'Wing Commander Orlov, my name is Lieutenant Rask. Lieutenant General Havali is expecting you.'

'Lead on then,' Orlov said, returning the salute. 'I wouldn't want to keep the general waiting.'

Rask took them through into another corridor. Here, the palace left behind its air of regal abandonment and dilapidation. The rooms they now passed were busy with the hustle of the Imperial war machine's command elements. Signals operators sat working at chattering vox-banks in a communications hub, while Cass caught a snatch of briefing cant from a strategium, along with a glimpse of senior officers gathered around the green glow of a holofield in a shutter-darkened room. They passed more hurrying staffers and aides carrying sheaves of documents or dataslates bearing tactical and strategic readouts, muster rolls, message chits and orders-of-the-day. Eji Valley might only have been the tertiary of Kanai's three main battlefronts, but the Suchen Palace headquarters was still responsible for the upper-level coordination of well over four hundred thousand men and women of the Astra Militarum.

And Cass was being taken to the heart of it. She had tried interrogating Orlov – her wing commander and immediate superior – on the way from Barduk Airbase West, but he had pled ignorance. All he claimed to know was that the summons from General Havali had something to do with Army Group Centre. That alone sounded bad to Cass.

They reached a reinforced doorway at the end of corridor, guarded by another Scion, who nodded them through. Rask took them inside, and swung the door shut behind them. The noise from the corridor was abruptly cut off.

Cass had met Lieutenant General Havali before, but only tangentially during senior briefing congregations, and never in what she assumed was his personal office. Whatever old furniture it had once possessed had been stripped out in favour of the familiar, utilitarian furnishings of the Imperial Guard. A heavy command desk, replete with its own inbuilt, purity-seal-studded power generator for a miniature holo-display, occupied the far end of the room, in front of a set of windows which Cass assumed looked out over the inner courtyard, but which had been largely covered up with flakboard and sandbags. A huge map dominated the right-hand wall, displaying in detail Eji Valley and the great river that ran through it, along with the two sprawling population centres, Ushen and Torr City, that lay on the plateaux to the river valley's east and west. The map bristled with different-coloured tacks, and Cass' gaze was instinctively drawn for a moment to the tight cluster of blue north of their own location, further up the valley and on the other side of the river. Army Group Centre, cut off beyond the Eji.

There were three figures already in the room, waiting for them. One was a staffer like Rask, loitering off to one side. Another was Lieutenant General Havali, standing behind the command desk. He was from Tallarn, and still wore the uniform of a senior Desert Raider, a dusty yellow desert smock with voluminous sleeves and a pale blue-coloured *shemagh* headscarf. His body was stout but was starting to ripen out into fat. He had an impeccably oiled white moustache, a contrast to his dark face and the livid pink scar that ran down his left cheek.

The third figure in the room was Air Marshal Jakyra, as gaunt and unsmiling as ever. She had been standing facing the map on the wall with her hands clasped behind her back, but she turned as Cass and Orlov entered.

Cass felt her mood plummet at the sight of her. If the commander of the entire Aeronautica Imperialis effort on Kanai Tertius had been called downstairs from her strategium on board the *Mandatum Divinum*, that meant whatever they were about to become party to was beyond serious.

'Welcome, welcome,' Havali said amiably, returning their salutes.

'Stand easy. It's good to see you again, wing commander. And this must be Captain Cassandra Elza. I recognise you.'

'From the last general briefing, sir?' Cass asked.

'And because I make it my business to know who I have under my command, especially when it comes to a decorated unit like the Vagabonds.'

Cass offered a smile, but said nothing. She hadn't left Barduk West to exchange pleasantries, but Havali was known as a man who liked to give his commands a veneer of personability.

The same couldn't be said of Jakyra. Cass felt her gaze as the general spoke, but refused to meet it. Now was not the time for a confrontation.

'Air Marshal Jakyra here informs me your squadron is still refitting, after that debacle over Ushen,' Havali said. 'Nasty business. You lost a warbird, didn't you?'

'Yes, sir,' Cass said, wanting to talk about anything other than the Ushen insertion. 'But we are almost recovered. Refits have been proceeding well, and my crews are eager for action. Another forty-eight hours standard and my squadron enginseer informs me the last of his repair-benedictions will be complete.'

'You might not have that long, captain,' Jakyra said from in front of the map.

Cass finally met her gaze. She was tall and aquiline, not unlike Cass in fact – they were supposedly very distant cousins, not an unusual fact among the ranks of the *Mandatum Divinum*'s pilots. She was dressed in her full air marshal's uniform, a deep blue jacket faced white, with chainmail epaulettes, the golden crest of the Aeronautica Imperialis – a winged, stylised 'AI' – pinned to her chest. She must have been infernally hot, though she gave no sign of it besides a slight redness to her pale cheeks.

'We are at your disposal as ever, air marshal,' Cass said to her, before looking back at Havali. The general smiled warmly.

'That is just one of the reasons why Vagabond Squadron possesses the reputation it does,' he said. 'And your pilots shall have the assignment they crave!'

The general moved out from behind his desk to stand next to Jakyra, in front of the map, while Cass tried not to think about how almost everything she had just said had been a lie.

'You are aware of the situation currently facing Battle Group Centre?' he asked.

'Broadly, yes,' Cass replied, using the clipped, succinct tone she had learned across a lifetime of briefing exchanges. 'The attempt to open a third front up the Eji Valley to split ork efforts at captured Ushen and Torr City has been halted. Army Group Centre is currently cut off and pocketed beyond the Eji River. Besides that, I'm not up to speed on recent tactical developments.'

'Strategos estimates show that Army Group Centre will be overrun within the next week, at the most,' Havali said, his tone turning dark. He indicated the desperate huddle of blue tacks that Cass had already noted on the map. They were surrounded by a sea of green, with the Eji River to their back.

'There are no viable crossings?' Cass asked. 'No way to get them over the river?'

'All destroyed, mostly through aerial strikes. Ork air presence is potent, as you well know. The only positive is that Army Group Centre's resistance is drawing xenos strength from the cities, but I had hoped to achieve that without the annihilation of nearly two hundred thousand men and war machines. Sadly, that is the reality we now face.'

Cass was tempted to ask if there was really no hope of going on the offensive and breaking the trapped army group out, but she held her tongue. It wasn't her place, and besides, Havali would surely have already considered such an operation. For whatever reason, it was seemingly impossible.

'A bad business, sir,' Cass said instead, knowing it hardly did any of it justice.

'It is, and I am going to ask you to become a part of it, captain,' Havali said.

This was the moment Cass had been dreading. She kept her expression composed and her eyes on the general, even as she felt her insides turn to ice and her hands, clasped behind her back, clench.

'I have spoken with senior aides and the air marshal here, and we have agreed that an airdrop into the pocket would be of strategic value,' Havali said, slipping even further into briefing-cant as he said something he clearly knew Cass would not like. 'Vagabond Squadron in particular would be the optimal choice. We would run you in under a decent amount of air cover. A simple drop-and-collect, in and out. If you depart tomorrow morning, you'll be back at Barduk West before midnight local time.'

'I see, sir,' Cass responded, trying and failing to keep the coldness from her voice. 'We're only deploying Vagabond Squadron and our air cover?'

'Yes,' Havali said, then answered the obvious question before she could ask it. 'Now, you're probably thinking that a single supply run by one Valkyrie squadron isn't going to be sufficient to keep the pocket intact, and you'd be correct. I'm afraid the problems faced by Army Group Centre go beyond logistics. But an elite unit such as the Vagabonds being seen to provide aid to our embattled troopers, all captured with a few good pict snaps – that has a value all of its own, both to the men there and the men here. I'm sure you understand the importance of morale, especially at a time like this. We can't be seen to abandon the forces beyond the river.'

Even though you are abandoning them, you callous bastard, Cass thought. She recalled the floggings happening outside, and found herself wondering just what those men would say about morale.

'Do we have landing zone coordinates, a flight plan?' she asked, trying to vent her anger on operational specifics. 'Supply manifests? Fuel and munition passes? The latest call signs and data-handshakes for Army Group Centre?'

'Those will be supplied in the next few hours,' Jakyra put in.

'Who's providing the top cover?'

'Bix's Thunderbolts from the Nine-Hundred-Eleventh Wing, the Cloud Knights.'

'Have you briefed her yet?'

'She should be on her way as we speak.'

Cass took a moment to master herself before she exploded. Perhaps sensing how close her veneer of discipline was to cracking, Havali began to speak again.

'You might be relieved to know there is more to this undertaking than an exercise in propaganda, captain. I have a second set of orders, an objective that won't appear on your noted instructions, but which should be considered as important as the offloading of your supplies.'

Havali waved at his aide, who scurried over and proffered a dataslate. Cass braced herself. What madness were they going to ask of her now?

She took the slate, read it, then reread it.

It was worse than she had feared. She felt an upwelling of pure revulsion.

'Are those instructions clear, captain?' Havali asked carefully.

'I believe so, sir,' Cass said, just about managing to swallow her disgust.

'You are to impress on them that these orders come direct from central command,' Havali said. 'That they are to be obeyed.

These aren't only my instructions. There are other forces at work here.'

'Am I to treat these orders as the real reason my squadron is being sent across the Eji, sir?'

'Yes, captain. They are also to remain an absolute secret, code-crimson. Keep that slate, in case you need to use it as proof that you carry my full authority, but until the time comes you are to share it with no one. That applies to your crews as well. You will not inform them of these instructions until you touch down. As far as they are concerned, your only objective is to offload the supplies, and to be seen doing it.'

'I understand,' Cass said, slipping the slate into her flight suit.

She wanted to say more. She wanted to tell the general that he was a fool and Jakyra that she was going to get them all killed. She wanted to damn them for their cowardice. She wanted to ask them how she was supposed to tell her crews what they were really there to do, what they were truly risking their lives for, when the time came.

She wanted to beg them not to go, not to send her out. Not again.

Instead, she saluted.

'We'll get it done, sir,' she said.

'That's why I called on Vagabond Squadron,' Havali said, with a smile that spoke of relief. 'Jakyra will make sure a full briefing packet is delivered to your section at Barduk by this evening. Any further questions?'

'No, sir.'

'Then you're dismissed. May the God-Emperor speed you on your way, Captain Elza.'

'Jakyra wants to get me killed,' Cass said venomously as she strode back into the palace's inner courtyard, Orlov in tow. 'She probably came up with this whole idiotic plan herself.'

'I doubt that,' Orlov said, his tone conciliatory. 'By all accounts, Havali is distraught about the situation with Army Group Centre and desperate for anything that might take the sting out of his defeat. Apparently the situation in the pocket is a nightmare. Throne, the offensive has cost over a hundred thousand lives, and that was just in the opening few weeks. This smacks of trying to save face in front of high command at Ushen, before they pull the plug on him. As he said, there are other forces at work.'

He didn't specify what he meant by 'other forces', and Cass knew not to press him, at least not here, at headquarters.

'So my crews and I are going to die so the general can make a play at saving face. Has he considered how his image with senior command will suffer when he gets his best Valkyrie squadron reduced to burning wreckage along the banks of the Eji?'

Orlov said nothing, and Cass knew he was letting her vent. He had been her wing commander since she had been a junior side gunner, and was everything Jakyra was not – when he gave orders they were clear and considered, not delivered as ultimatums as though she and her pilots were a platoon of Guard grunts. As the wing's most senior captain, Cass was closer to him than anyone else under his command, and she appreciated his style of leadership. She knew other wing leaders on board the *Mandatum Divinum* thought him too lax, but they weren't in charge of the capital ship's Valkyries.

'Why not send someone else?' Cass asked him, her tone still heated. She knew she shouldn't be asking that sort of question, but after her restraint in front of Havali, she couldn't help but bite back now at the unfairness of it all. 'Jakyra knows what happened over Ushen. It was barely a week ago. Isn't she tired of getting my pilots killed?'

'They asked for you specifically,' Orlov said. 'You know how these things work.'

'I do,' Cass admitted bitterly.

Out beyond the gate, the Hyrkans were being marched off the square. As they filed past, the victims of the punishment parade were cut down from the spontoons. Two of them were unconscious, and the other two were unable to stand unaided. Their backs had been reduced to red ruin.

It looked as though one of the drummer boys had also passed out, either from the heat and exertion, or the brutality of the punishment he had been forced to inflict. The regimental commissar was pencilling notes into a small, black-bound book, standing to one side as the medicaes worked on getting the fallen up, like carrion waiting for the opportunity to feast beneath the burning sun.

'Still glad you're a Navy pilot who'll never know the lash?' Orlov asked with the barest hint of humour. Cass grimaced.

'I'd rather that than dying for a general's vanity,' she said. 'The worst part is going to be telling my crews.'

'They're on stand-down just now, aren't they?' Orlov asked.

'They are. When they find out about all this, we might end up having to petition the Navy to introduce pilot flogging just for Vagabond Squadron.'

Orlov let out a humourless chuckle. 'Lieutenant Vaughn's going to take this the worst, isn't he?'

'Let me worry about Hal Vaughn,' Cass said darkly.

CHAPTER TWO

Blood flew, a sudden red mist that glittered in the harsh light of the lumens, there and gone again in an instant.

The crowd roared and the Zenonian reeled, his nose broken. His opponent, a Thracian corporal, followed up with two short, hard jabs to the gut. Even over the tumult, Wilbe Platz heard the thumping sounds of the two impacts. He couldn't help but wince.

'Don't just stand there, you useless bastard,' Flight Lieutenant Vaughn was screaming, gesticulating furiously at the Zenonian. 'Get your hands back up! Block him!'

But the Zenonian was done. A final haymaker to the face bounced him from the ropes of the sparring ring and sent him clattering to the floor, barely conscious. The crowd's baying had reached fever pitch, and a scuffle appeared to have broken out between the observing factions of the Zenonian Free Company and Thracian Guard on the opposite side of the ring.

'Pay up, star-boy,' snarled the Varakian Deeper who'd been

wagering against Vaughn all night, baring his rotting teeth. 'That's double you owe me now, and don't think I'll let you stake it all on the next one!'

It was fight night at Camp Yuzen, and it seemed as though half the base had packed themselves into one of the disused vehicle hangars. Normally it served as a crude gymnasium, but tonight its boxing ring was acting as centre stage for the biggest event in the camp's calendar of illicit gatherings – a night of bareknuckle boxing with little in the way of rules and plenty in the way of Militarum disciplinary code violations.

It seemed like every regiment on the base had at least one contingent present, not that Wilbe Platz was able to identify most of them. It was his first time down in amongst so many grunts. They, and their raucous sport, reminded him of the lower decks of the *Mandatum Divinum* – they were stinking in their sweaty fatigues, wild-eyed, baying, animal-like, penning in the half-dark surrounding the jury-rigged lumens that were spotlighting the ring. Yet these were the people he was expected to sacrifice himself inserting and extracting from the most deadly and desperate warzones the galaxy over.

'Give me the karking money, you pox-faced voidborn bastard,' the Varakian shouted in Vaughn's face.

Vaughn punched him.

'Oh, Throne,' Platz exclaimed.

He had feared the worst since leaving Barduk Airbase West. He had joined the squadron less than a week before, arriving with a consignment of repair parts from the Old Mother, as the aviators called the *Mandatum Divinum*. It had been less than a month, Terran standard, since he had passed the last of his flight examinations.

Platz already knew several of Vagabond Squadron by sight. He had grown up around his father's Thunderbolt wing, but the Vagabonds were the most senior of the *Mandatum Divinum*'s Valkyrie squadrons, and the most decorated. Platz hadn't been able to contain his excitement when he'd been informed he was being assigned to them.

His father had said nothing when he'd told him, not a single word. Platz knew he was thinking about the strained conversation they had shared when Platz had first told him he was applying to be a Valkyrie aviator, rather than joining the Old Mother's fighter wings. Aeronautica Imperialis casualty rates in any given warzone tended to hover around one-in-three for the fighter wings, but for the Valkyries and their Vulture gunship twins, losses averaged at half of all air crews engaged.

Platz hadn't cared. He was going to be a Vagabond.

He had expected slick Navy proficiency when he joined the squadron. They would also be guarded, he had no doubt. He was a newcomer, young and unproven, and this was an elite outfit. It would take time to earn their trust, but he was certain he would. He had top-scored in his shipside classes, and he prided himself on being a quick learner.

His first interaction had been with an aviator named Skerry, who had been the only squadron member present on the lines – the rows of prefabbed hab-tunnels on Barduk Airbase – when he had arrived. Platz had accidentally rousted him, dishevelled and glaring, from his bunk bed. He had told Platz to get lost, his breath stinking of alcohol. When Platz had insisted that he had been assigned to join the squadron, Skerry had insisted all the bunks were accounted for, and that he'd have to sleep on the floor.

That didn't seem true – there were a number of beds that were stripped and empty. His first mistake had been trying to claim one. Most of the rest of the squadron had got back that evening and one, who Platz had later discovered was Flight Lieutenant

Hal Vaughn, had slammed him up against the wall and had to be restrained from beating him. That particular bunk bed apparently belonged to his sister.

Platz had been brought before the squadron leader, Captain Elza – who the rest of the squadron seemed to refer to as either 'Chief' or 'Cass' – and received a terse series of instructions that boiled down to 'say nothing, do nothing unless ordered to, and keep out of the way'. When Platz had mustered up the courage to ask about Vaughn's sister, he'd been told nothing more than she had been killed recently, over Ushen.

The next few days had been a nightmare. Platz had spent his life around pilots, so he understood their camaraderie, especially when on leave. But this was something else entirely. The indiscipline, insubordination and general slovenliness of Vagabond Squadron would have shamed one of the *Mandatum Divinum*'s lower-deck work gangs. Even accounting for the fact they had seemingly just endured a difficult and costly operation over Ushen, there was little sign of the dedication and professionalism he had expected.

Finally, four days after his arrival, there had been what Platz had thought was a breakthrough. Up until then the other pilots had either ignored him, or taunted and belittled him – 'Fledgling' appeared to be his new name. Only one, a fellow gunner named Weets, had been willing to have any kind of conversation with him, and that was only because Platz reminded him of his teenage son back on board the Old Mother. But then, late one afternoon, as Platz had been about to head to the mess block, Vaughn had accosted him and asked him to be part of his crew, for one night only.

'Tonight's fight night, and you're coming with us,' he had said. 'That's an order.'

Platz hadn't known what 'fight night' was, but it had quickly become apparent that he had been added to the other avia-tors of Vaughn's Valkyrie, *Rogue*. There were the two gunners, Holsten and Macks, and his co-pilot, Xijen. A hanger-on from another of the squadron's four warbirds – Skerry from *Pauper* – had completed the impromptu crew, and they had bundled into a cargo-6 requisitioned from the airbase motorpool. Platz's mumbled question about whether this was going to be a viola-tion of regulations had just drawn derisive laughter.

They'd driven off-base, to Camp Yuzen, the primary Guard muster south of the Eji. Since the debacle of the offensive across the river three weeks earlier, most of the units that hadn't been cut off with Army Group Centre were festering on stand-down. The orks were all to the north, beyond the river, assailing Army Group Centre, and it didn't look as though Lieutenant General Havali had plans to go to their rescue any time soon.

The aviators had dismounted and approached one of the camp's hangars, Platz's guts squirming with nervousness. He had mustered the courage for one final protest.

'What if the captain finds out?'

Vaughn had laughed.

'Cass was called to headquarters at Suchen this afternoon, probably for more medals and tanna.' The final words were said with a particularly bitter inflection. 'We won't see her for the rest of the night.'

There were Guard bruisers on the hangar doors, Catachans. They eyed the six Imperial Navy pilots with undisguised dis-dain, raucous noises from beyond the entrance spilling out into the humid night.

'You star-hoppers lost?' one of them drawled. 'Barduk is back east of here.'

Vaughn did the talking, and they'd eventually been admitted on the conditions that when it came to wagers they paid up front with proper Imperial creds – 'none of those worthless local coppers, and none of your ship tokens' – and 'didn't start any shit.'

The interior of the hangar was overwhelming. Platz stayed in the midst of the pilots and tried his best to avoid eye contact with the horde that was mobbing the place. It only took seconds before they began to attract attention – various different groups of off-duty Guardsmen accosted them on their way ringside, most apparently taunting them or trying to start bets. Platz barely understood some of them, their slang wholly different from the Navy jargon he'd grown up with.

Vaughn fielded them with brash confidence. They ordered drinks from the big ogryn lumbering around the hangar with a keg strapped to his back, then started placing bets. Platz had been hustled into parting with a dangerous sum of credits by Vaughn's two gunners, Holsten and Macks.

They continued to draw attention, not least of all because they were wearing the dark blue flight suits of the Segmentum Pacificus branch of the Aeronautica Imperialis. On their arms were a trio of signifier patches – the sigils of the Aeronautica Imperialis, the *Mandatum Divinum*'s ship's crest, and the rearing hippogryph of Battlefleet Ajax. There was no chance whatsoever that they wouldn't be identified as pilots rather than ground-pounders, and that was apparently part of Vaughn's plan.

'Never hide your colours,' he told Platz when he had pointed out that they were making potential targets of themselves. The lieutenant tapped the final signifier, sewn into the breast of Platz's flight suit – the wing's numerical designation '901' alongside the squadron's hooded, grinning skull symbol.

'We're not just Navy Tactical,' he said. 'We're Vagabonds. Best of the best. Tonight is about getting you used to that. And making sure you deserve it.'

Platz had settled into watching the bouts in the ring, and was almost beginning to relax, mesmerised by the raw violence on display. Then Vaughn punched the Varakian.

Platz had never been in a fight in his life, at least nothing beyond childhood scraps with the semi-feral bands of deckhand offspring who had sometimes dared venture up from the lower decks and into the aviator quarters on board the *Mandatum Divinum*. He simply stood, frozen, as carnage broke out around him, fists flying.

It only lasted a few moments. There was a bout of furious shouting, and hands snatched at the nearest Guardsmen going for the pilots, hauling them back, restraining them. The Varakian Vaughn had cracked had to be pinned by two of his comrades, but he settled down when he saw who had curtailed the skirmish.

'Do we have a problem, gentlemen?' demanded the ringmaster, the crowd parting for him as he made his way to the little band of aviators. He wore a pelt cape and cloth forage cap, and had the nasal voice of a Ronarkian. 'And there was me thinking you'd promised there would be no incidents tonight.'

The final accusation was directed at Vaughn.

'Just a misunderstanding,' the flight lieutenant responded, flashing a dangerous smile. 'We've no intention of interdicting your fun, ringmaster.'

'You Navy boys and your funny words,' the Ronarkian said, drawing growled laughter from those around him. 'There'll be no "interdicting", but it seems like what we call "restitution" is in order.'

'He won't pay up,' the restrained Varakian snarled. 'Typical star-hopper!'

'He wants double what I really owe him,' Vaughn lied.

'Unfortunate,' the ringmaster said, spreading his arms with a shrug. 'But I believe we can find a compromise. A happy medium. Are the Navy and the Guard not the left and right fists of the God-Emperor Himself? Let us have no division here. No scraps, just an honest bout. A prize fight, between one of you fine gentlemen, and one of ours. How about you, sir?'

To Platz's utter horror, the Ronarkian looked past Vaughn and pointed at him. He opened his mouth, but no sound would come out.

'Or…' The Ronarkian paused, and offered the most unfriendly smile Platz had ever seen. 'We can make sure there's no further *interdiction* of tonight by ensuring debts are paid, and then removing your good selves from the venue. Physically.'

There was growled agreement from the mob.

'You'll match your last bet with my friend here,' the ringmaster went on, gesturing from Vaughn to the Varakian, who had finally stopped struggling and was now grinning instead. 'And then we can carry on with the evening's entertainment. Is that understood?'

Platz found himself praying Vaughn's makeshift crew chose the path of greatest resistance. Instead, he heard Vaughn agreeing to the ringmaster's terms, their voices now sounding surreally distant. Vaughn turned to him as a cheer went up from the onlookers, and threw an arm around his shoulder.

'Now's your chance, kid,' he said, tapping his chest with his free hand. 'You're a Vagabond, remember. That means flying into hell, without hesitation. When they order you to take your warbird up, you only ask them, "How high, sir?"'

Platz mumbled something, he wasn't even sure what. His mouth was suddenly so dry he could barely swallow, and his legs had gone weak. Vaughn began to steer him through the crowd towards the ring.

'Remember, best of the best,' he said, voice almost lost in the frenzy of the mob as the ringmaster began using his repurposed laud-hailer to announce a special prize bout, Guard versus Navy.

'What do you want me to do?' Platz found himself blurting out, knowing it was a stupid question. Vaughn grinned at him – the smile never quite seemed to make it to his eyes – and smacked him hard on the back before hoisting up the lowermost rope of the ring.

'Just keep your fists up,' he said.

Platz found himself clambering up into the ring, feeling like he was dreaming. The noise of the onlookers had melded into a background roar, a continuous thunder that he could feel vibrating through his body. The spotlight was blindingly bright, reducing his world to a square of dark blue canvas underfoot. It was just him, standing in the eye of the storm. Him, and his contender.

It was a Catachan and, in that moment, he looked like the biggest man Platz had ever seen. He pulled himself up lithely, almost casually, onto the platform and began tying a sweat-stained red bandana around his shaven scalp, glaring at Platz as he did so. He had a sergeant's chevrons tattooed on both massive arms. He reminded Platz of one of the grox bulls kept in the *Mandatum Divinum*'s livestock holds.

The Ronarkian was calling out the bout's rules from somewhere in the frenzied, stinking darkness surrounding them, but Platz wasn't really hearing him. He realised abruptly that he was going to die. There was almost a strange relief in the certainty. At least it would all be over.

A bell sounded. The Catachan sergeant began to advance while Platz stayed where he was, in one corner, simply staring up at him, engulfed by the sound and fury.

The snap-crack of a laspistol ended it all. Platz tore his eyes from the Catachan and turned, squinting in the light suddenly pouring through the half-open hangar doors. He saw a figure shoving her way through the press to the ringside, sidearm raised.

It was Captain Elza. Her Valkyrie's big co-pilot, Flight Sergeant Korrie, was at her elbow, her expression stoic.

'Get down from there,' Cass snapped up at Platz as she reached the ringside, glaring at him. He felt as afraid of her as he was of the Catachan.

'Bets have been placed, so the boy fights,' the Ronarkian said, trying to interpose himself between Cass and the ring, but finding himself blocked by Korrie.

'Unless you're planning on taking his place?' he added with a leer.

'There'll be no more bets, and no more fights, at least not tonight,' Cass snarled back at him. 'My crews are coming with me, right now.'

'Your flyboys are going nowhere,' the Ronarkian responded with equal vehemence. 'Not until we've had our fun.'

The Guard had closed in firmly all around Cass and Korrie, as well as Vaughn's little band. None seemed especially intimidated by Cass' drawn laspistol. They were a hair trigger from throwing themselves at the pilots.

'I'll fight,' Platz spoke up, hardly believing he'd actually uttered the words. He didn't know why he had said them, besides the desire not to see his new commander beaten because of his cowardice. There were cheers and jeers from the crowd.

'No you won't,' Cass snapped. 'Now get down here right now or God-Emperor help me, by sunup you'll be out of my squadron and back on board *Mandatum Divinum* cleaning latrines for the rest of your pathetic little life.'

Platz snatched a glance at the Catachan sergeant, whose frown seemed to imply the big brute was struggling to process exactly what was happening, then ducked under the ropes and dropped down next to Cass and Korrie. Vaughn and his crew had joined them as well, a little knot hemmed in by the beastly mob.

'You really think we'll let you walk out of here just because you've got a captain's aquilas on your shoulders?' the Ronarkian sneered, getting up in Cass' face. 'I think it's about time we showed you star-hopping Navy boys and girls just how we do things in the Guard.'

Platz braced himself for the brutality he was certain was about to be unleashed, but Cass' words gave the mob pause.

'Anyone who doesn't want to face charges, I'd suggest you leave now.'

'What, you going to take us all in by yourself?' The Ronarkian laughed.

'No, but the provosts will.'

'The provosts won't touch a night like this.'

'They will if someone informs a senior member of the Commissariat about what's happening in here. Which I did' – she paused to pull back her cuff so she could consult her bulky aviator's chrono – 'about twenty minutes ago.'

Perhaps that was a cue, or perhaps it was just luck, but none of the illicit assembly had time to respond to the claim before there was a crash from the hangar doors.

'*This is the Commissariat!*' roared a vox-amplified voice. '*Stay where you are! Resistance will meet with the full weight of Militarum law!*'

Bedlam gripped the hangar. With a roar of pure anger, the Ronarkian ringmaster swung at Cass. The blow never landed, caught by Korrie, who stepped in and delivered a straight-armed jab to the centre of the ringmaster's face. The Ronarkian dropped like a sack of spudroots.

The rest of the Guard threw themselves against the Valkyrie crews. Platz didn't have time to so much as think before he took a fist to his face. His vision flashed white for a moment, and then, finally, the adrenaline hit him.

He struck back, though against what he had no idea. The blow hurt his fist, but he swung again, then kicked out, feeling a satisfying connection with his boot. A second blow cracked his cheek, knocking him into Korrie, who had a different Ronarkian in a headlock and was using his bent-over body to drive more of the baying Militarum grunts back.

That was when the mist really descended.

His face ached, and he could taste blood – his own. It drove him. He swung hard, felt the satisfaction of his knuckles meeting someone's jaw. He kicked, screaming, vaguely aware of one of the Guardsmen going down in the press under him. The fight swallowed him up and he lost himself, giving as good as he got, everything forgotten besides the raw exhilaration, the wild thoughtlessness of it all.

Then his fist hit something hard. His knuckles crunched and he recoiled, the sharp pain lancing his fury.

He realised he'd just tried to punch an aquila-stamped riot shield, held in the grip of a towering, armoured provost trooper.

'Ah,' Platz had time to say. Then the provost's baton put him down.

He stayed on the ground, his vision swimming, defiance evaporating beneath the force of a follow-up boot to the ribs. He curled into a foetal position, expecting another blow at any moment, but instead what he got was a hand under his arm, hauling him back up.

He whimpered at the pain in his head and ribs, and discovered it was Vaughn who had helped him back to his feet. Despite the carnage all around them, the flight lieutenant was laughing.

'You're a wild little runt, huh?' he said with a split-lipped grin.

Platz tried to respond, but gagged on blood from his burst nose. He spat it out on the floor and groaned.

Cass had remained seemingly untouched in the thick of the

melee, presumably thanks to Korrie's presence. She was now surrounded by a phalanx of provosts, shields locked and batons ready. Beyond the cordon, more provosts were subduing those spectators who hadn't yet managed to successfully scatter. Platz saw the Ronarkian ringmaster on his front on the ground, still struggling even as a provost knelt on top of him while another mag-cuffed his hands behind his back.

The cordon parted, and Platz felt a chill descend as he saw the figure the provosts were admitting between them.

'Lord Commissar Vasquez,' Cass said. 'I didn't expect you to grace us with your presence tonight.'

Vasquez grunted. He was short and solid, and though he wore a lavishly brocaded jacket with the heavy black coat of the Commissariat draped over one shoulder, it did nothing to hide the fact he was physically almost the equal of the Catachan sergeant Platz had squared off with. He had scars on his face and on his fists, and his dark eyes glared out from under the polished visor of his peaked cap, sweeping the pilots like the master of an abattoir surveying livestock.

'You went in early, Captain Elza,' he said, not looking at Cass, but at each pilot in turn. Despite his best efforts, Platz found himself inspecting his scuffed boots rather than meeting the man's gaze.

'I wished to put a stop to these flagrant breaches of discipline as swiftly as possible, lord commissar,' Cass responded levelly. 'Besides, I brought my own backup.'

Platz's heart was racing, and his legs felt as though they were about to give way beneath him. They had been caught in the act. Pilot privileges only extended so far, and Platz found himself in a panicked review of the punishment that might await them. Incarceration in a penal legion? Servitor lobotomisation? Or even the firing squad, as an example to others? Maybe they'd be taken back on board the *Mandatum Divinum* and subjected to the traditional Naval method of execution – ejection from an open airlock.

'You brought your own pilots to try and disperse this… circus of iniquities?' Vasquez asked coldly.

'Yes,' Cass said. 'My crews always have my back.'

'And they arrived with you, then? All of them? None of them were already here… partaking?'

'Of course not, lord commissar. This is Vagabond Squadron. I would hope our reputation precedes us.'

'Vagabonds,' Vasquez said slowly, stepping in amongst the bloodied little formation of pilots. 'An interesting name to take pride in. The connotations it conjures are not flattering, not to a man such as I.'

The lord commissar reached out and gripped Platz by the chin. Platz cringed away, then froze, obeying the slight but firm touch. He found himself gazing into Vasquez's black eyes, unable to look down any more, beginning to tremble. He felt like one of the Old Mother's rodents caught in the glare of the hypnotic reptilian slipskins that hunted them through the ship's old metal guts.

He was acutely aware that blood from his nose was running onto the commissar's fingers, yet Vasquez made no attempt to remove his grip, saying nothing, continuing to hold Platz in place.

'Vagabonds have their place,' Vaughn offered, causing Vasquez to look away and breaking his spell. He let go, and Platz almost collapsed again.

'Everyone loves a rogue,' Vaughn added, grinning unabashedly at the commissar. Vasquez's scarred lips twitched, the barest hint of disgust breaking through his soulless expression.

'I will of course be carrying out interrogations of those we have seized tonight,' he said, finally looking at Cass. 'In order to more accurately ascertain all those present, and ensure that none escape justice.'

'I would expect nothing less, lord commissar,' Cass replied.

Vasquez stared at her for a moment longer, then nodded.

'Thank you for your assistance in exposing these crimes,' he said. 'The Commissariat will not forget you, Captain Elza.'

Without another word, he turned on his jackbooted heel and stalked away, barking orders at the provosts. The hangar had nearly emptied, the last of the captives being hauled out, the sudden silence a shocking contrast to what had come before. With a *thunk*, the primary lumens came on overhead, making Platz squint.

'Walk to the main doors,' Cass muttered to them all. 'Straight through, and don't look back.'

'I can't believe I missed all the fun,' Flight Sergeant Konstantina, the short, ferocious commander of the squadron's Vulture gunship, exclaimed as Vaughn's misbegotten expedition filed back into the squadron lines. 'Hal, you're an ass for not inviting the Ruffians.'

'Vaughn, my office, now,' Cass snapped at the flight lieutenant before he could respond to her. He made a crude gesture at Konstantina as he passed her bunk, and she jeered after him.

Cass slammed the door to her office behind him. The space was a cabin appended to the end of the hab-tunnel, little more than a prefab box with a desk plus a campaign cot in one corner. It wasn't so different from her cabin on board the *Mandatum Divinum*, but without the familiar, ever-present throb of the old warship's engines and support systems.

Vaughn stood nonchalantly while Cass stalked around him. He smirked at her. She managed to stop herself from hitting him, narrowly. That wouldn't have been what her father would have done, back when he had been squadron leader.

Vaughn's smirk became a bitter glare. Hatred, Cass realised, as she returned his look. He hated her. She could understand why.

'You're drunk,' she told him. It was a statement, and he didn't bother to reply. 'And you sent my newest aviator up to get mauled by a Catachan,' she pressed on. 'What in the God-Emperor's name were you thinking?'

'Actually, I was hoping the extreme violence would provide enough of a cover to get the rest of us out,' Vaughn admitted.

'And I take it he was a willing volunteer in this plan?'

'Of course.'

'You're full of crap, Hal.'

'It was a bit of fun,' Vaughn said, his voice low and dangerous. 'A chance to forget the shit you've put us all through. And don't act like you haven't had a wild one off-base before.'

'You tell me first,' Cass growled. 'Those are the rules. You *tell me* when you're going to raise hell. And I say, "Give them one from me." But you tell me first!'

'Maybe I would have if you weren't off fraternising with the brass at Suchen,' Vaughn responded.

'Don't make excuses,' Cass snapped. 'Once some incarcerated grunt spills that you were there to Vasquez, you'll be lucky to escape charges.'

'That's grox crap,' Vaughn said with an exasperated wave. 'Vasquez won't want to put out the Naval Commissariat's noses, so he'll route any charges to Polkov on board the Old Mother, and he'll ping us a sternly worded communique from upstairs and leave it at that. We're too valuable to them, you know that.'

He was right, though not for the reasons he thought. Cass knew she couldn't put it off any longer.

'We're flying out,' she told him. 'Tomorrow. The whole squadron. I was at Suchen because I was called in for a briefing with Havali, and Jakyra.'

Vaughn's expression changed from anger to disbelief.

'Where?' he demanded. 'Where are they sending us?'

'The pocket,' Cass said.

She watched the colour drain from his face. He sat heavily on the edge of her desk, gripping its sides, staring down as he tried to compose himself.

'Are they renewing the offensive?' he asked eventually. 'Or trying to break Army Group Centre out?'

'Neither,' Cass said. 'It's just a supply dump. In and out.'

'A supply dump conducted by a single squadron?' he asked.

'It's a picter run,' Cass elaborated uncomfortably. 'Morale booster. The best squadron planetside lending a hand. Trying to convince the rest of command the general hasn't given up on everyone still north of the Eji.'

'He wants us to die for a few bastard pict snaps?' Vaughn snarled, surging up, ruddy anger gripping him.

Cass was ready for it. She raised a finger, checking him, letting anger of her own resurface to match his.

'Don't think I'm happy about it. I know it's madness.'

'But did you protest?' Vaughn responded, eyes furious as he held Cass' gaze. 'Did you tell command you think it's madness?'

The demand caught Cass off-guard. She looked away, shook her head.

'I told you, Jakyra was there. Orlov too. There... was no room to manoeuvre.'

Vaughn spun to the side, raging, kicking the foot of Cass' cot.

'You've killed us, you've bloody well killed us!' he snarled. 'Wasn't Ushen enough? Wasn't my sister enough? You should have stood up to them then! You should have told command that insertion was a death sentence! Now you've done it again. You've let them send us out to die.'

'You think I have any say in these sorts of operations?' Cass shouted back, letting loose – the proprieties of rank hadn't meant much in Vagabond Squadron for a long time. 'What do you want me to tell them?' she hissed. 'Sorry, sir, we don't much fancy that one, give it to Shadow or Nemesis Squadron. We can't go to active, because my pilots are out getting grox-faced and starting fights with grunts in illegal gambling dens for the rest of the week. Maybe next time!'

Cass thought he was going to give it right back to her, but instead he just slumped against the desk again, head bowed. She noticed his hands were shaking. To her surprise, he let out a dry laugh, speaking without looking at her.

'So that's why you're in such a foul mood,' he said. 'There was me thinking you'd finally found some spine and decided to start commanding this squadron properly.'

Cass didn't take the bait. She felt suddenly tired, too tired for any of this.

'They want us in the air at oh-seven-hundred local,' she told her second-in-command. 'I've already spoken to Z-Five, he's working through the night to make sure everyone is flightworthy.'

'Not like his kind need sleep anyway,' Vaughn muttered.

'Fuel and munitions should be arriving round about now,' Cass said, ignoring the jab at the squadron's enginseer. 'The cargo will follow in the next hour, but the ground crews and the servitors will deal with it. That'll give you about four hours sleep. I'm ordering you to take it. With a bit of luck everyone will be sober by the time we're actually across the Eji.'

'I'll tell them,' Vaughn said.

Another surprise, giving Cass pause. She hunted for a hint of mockery, but there was none.

'You're tired,' he carried on. 'And I'm your secondary. I'll see they don't mutiny. Convince them I'm on their side. Damn you to the seven hells and back, like I need any encouragement to do that. And make sure they get some sleep. You should do the same.'

Cass nodded warily, daring to hope they'd found some neutral ground, for the good of their crews, while trying not to think about the weight of the dataslate Havali's aide had given her, resting inside her flight suit's inner pocket.

'In and out, like you said,' Vaughn declared, standing up and stretching. 'What could possibly go wrong?'

CHAPTER THREE

In the end, Vaughn didn't sleep. He pulled out the pict he'd kept in his flight suit for the past week and lay on his back, staring up at the bunk above him, the little square of image-paper lying on his chest, invisible in the dark.

His anger simmered, hot and slow, like good recaff. It would keep him sharp, he hoped. Keep him and the crew of *Rogue* in one piece. Other Vagabonds might put their hope in the captain, or in the machine spirits of their warbirds, or their own little charms, or the God-Emperor Himself, but privately, Vaughn had learned not to trust any of them. He'd put his faith in his anger, and damn the rest.

The other crews had taken the news that they'd received a new assignment pretty hard, as he had expected. His offer to Cass had been genuine – he let them sound off to him. He even defended her, up to a point. They all knew how this worked, he said. Elite they may be, but in their own way they were still just grunts in the great Imperial war machine, only fractionally less expendable than the newest ground-pounding conscript with an old lasgun and some ill-fitting flak plate. The worst of the grumbling had gradually subsided, and he'd ordered them to get some shut-eye. Then, when things were finally quiet, he'd fished out the pict and had lain still for as long as he could stomach.

Eventually, it was too much. He got up, dressed in the dark, and stepped out. Dawn was a few hours away still, and the temperature was almost tolerable. The airbase was still, the loudest sounds the humming of the perimeter defences and the *tick, tick, tick* of insects hitting themselves against the lumens.

It had been this way since the Vagabonds had got back from that ill-fated operation over Ushen. By then, Army Group Centre's push up the Eji Valley, an attempt to open a new front and split the ork forces attacking Ushen and Torr City, had already gone to hell. The Aeronautica were running interdiction now, and not much else. *Don't poke the beast* seemed to be command's current mindset. Let them focus on chewing up the remains of the offensive cut off across the river.

If Vaughn listened hard enough, he could hear the sounds of that struggle, the rumble of artillery, playing out night and day. Or perhaps that background noise was coming from the fighting in Ushen to the west, or Torr to the east. For a short while it had felt as though Vagabond Squadron had finally been deployed somewhere where the fighting wasn't happening. More fool him for thinking that would last.

He smoked a lho outside the prefab tunnel door, then set off for the squadron hangar, opposite the lines. Its main doors had been rolled back and its spotlights were on, casting their fierce white glow out into the night. Vaughn paused on the edge of darkness and took in the hangar's interior.

Vagabond Squadron's four warbirds sat like unsheathed blades beneath the light. There were three Valkyrie airborne assault carriers – Cass' *Vagrant*, Cobbs' *Pauper* and Vaughn's *Rogue*. Off to the right was the squadron's fire support, Konstantina's Vulture gunship, *Ruffian*.

There was a space on the hardpan next to *Rogue*, room for one more. Vaughn's gaze lingered on it.

Despite the earliness of the hour, the hangar was busy. Munitorum workers were filling the holds with the supplies they were supposed to be lugging over the Eji, while the squadron's Adeptus Mechanicus enginseer, Zorn-Five, was fussing around the fuel intakes and the weapons systems, accompanied by a coterie of servitors and his sleepy-looking, russet-robed young tech-adept.

Vaughn strode over to *Rogue*. Spotting him, Zorn moved to intercept him, his augmetic lower limbs clunking on the rockcrete.

'You are e-e-early, Lieutenant Vaughn,' the enginseer said, trying to get between him and his warbird. His voice was a machine whine that buzzed from the vox-plate that made up the lower half of his face. For some reason there was a glitch that caused him to stutter over every word beginning with 'e.'

'Pop the hatch,' Vaughn ordered, waving him aside.

'You are not scheduled to–'

'Just pop it, please,' Vaughn hissed, unwilling to offer any kind of explanation while doing his best not to snap at the Martian priest. Zorn unintentionally blurted something in binharic before gesturing at his adept to complete the rite that would allow *Rogue*'s primary cockpit hatch to be levered open.

Vaughn walked around the flier's nose as he did so, reaching a hand out and running it over the fore plate. He had preferred the paint job from their previous campaign on Sallic, over a year ago – classic Navy matt grey, rather than the olive drab she'd been coated in when they'd first arrived above Kanai Tertius.

At least Zorn had done a good job repairing the damage done

in the last outing. Vaughn's hand paused against the fresh pla-steel moulding added where hard rounds had punched into the prow. He remembered the sounds of the impacts, how they'd made him flinch, how they'd battered and cracked the cockpit shield – now replaced by a fresh sheet of armaglass.

He remembered how he'd thought he was sure to die, how his legs had given out under him the moment he'd clambered out of the cockpit and onto the hardpan. He'd been sick there, on his hands and knees, as it had all hit him, all at once. Not just the jagged draining after repeat surges of death-defying adrenaline, but the realisation that he was now suddenly, irreversibly alone.

Face set, he mounted the short ladder leading up the flank of the Valkyrie's nose and threw a leg over, dropping down with a lifetime's experience into the worn leather of his flight seat. He fished in his breast pocket, ignoring Zorn and his maintenance crew as they hung around nervously below, knowing they were trying to work out what he was doing, and if it would in any way insult or compromise the hallowed machine spirit of the airborne assault carrier.

He drew out the pict capture, then used a bit of plas-tape to stick it with great care to the top of the flight control panel, just above the auspex screen.

The image showed him and his older sister, Eleanor Vaughn, standing in their flight suits, beaming in front of the same set of Valkyries in the hold of the *Mandatum Divinum*. It had been taken the day they had discovered they'd been assigned to Vaga-bond Squadron, the day they'd known they were going to get to stay together in service to the God-Emperor. The day they'd sworn they'd never risk being parted again. Nine years ago now, though it felt like it had been a hundred.

Eleanor had rediscovered the pict and given it to him just before the Ushen operation.

'For luck,' she had said. *'And because mam and da' told me to keep an eye on you.'*

Vaughn had never had lucky charms in *Rogue*'s cockpit. Cobb had his flak shard, Konstantina had the razor wing tip from the Archenemy Hell Talon she had torn from the sky, her first kill in command of *Ruffian*. Even Cass had her father's old tags and helmet. Vaughn had scorned all that. Until today.

'Never flown without you, sis,' he murmured, touching the pict briefly before climbing back up out of the cockpit. 'Won't change that now.'

Platz wondered if he had died during the fighting at Camp Yuzen, and this was the hellish dimension the *Mandatum Divinum*'s preacher had regularly spoken of during his sermons.

Everything hurt, his face most of all. Macks had, after a cursory inspection, claimed his nose wasn't broken, though he wasn't sure. He'd quickly been forgotten by the other pilots when Vaughn, fresh from storming out of Cass' office, had delivered news none of them had anticipated.

They'd be flying out not long after dawn.

There had been disbelief and anger that Platz feared bordered on insubordination. Seemingly they were expected to deliver a supply drop to Army Group Centre, embattled across the river to the north. Eventually the squadron had settled, and exhaustion had got the better of them. Platz had experienced a sudden bout of nervousness when he had realised that, in just a few hours, he'd be flying his first sortie. Sleep had remained elusive, but at some point he'd drifted off.

The next thing he knew, the commander of the squadron's Vulture, Konstantina, was screaming at him.

'Get up, Fledgling,' she shouted, yanking his itchy, Munitorum-issue blanket away. 'You're late! They're taking off without you!'

'Oh, Throne,' Platz yelped, trying to sit up and cracking his already aching head on the top bunk. He scrambled groggily out of bed, casting around for his flight suit and helmet, and only then realised that Konstantina was laughing at him.

'I'm kidding, you skinny little wretch,' she said, shoving him by the chest so he fell back onto the edge of his bunk. 'We've got an hour, though Cass will want her crew loaded up before everyone else. She's a bastard like that.'

Platz didn't think a flight sergeant calling her captain a bastard was particularly appropriate, but then nothing he had witnessed of Vagabond Squadron so far had been appropriate. He held his tongue, and focused on his own misery, sitting on the edge of his bunk and carefully probing his tender face.

'You look like grox dung,' another pilot, a burly flight sergeant called Cobb, said as he walked past, spooning pallid nutrient paste from a mess tin into his maw. He paused to cuff excess from his stubbly jaw, then, to Platz's surprise, shoved the tin into his hands.

'Eat,' Cobb said.

'I… can't eat your rations,' he said, unwilling to admit that he felt sick – whether from the previous night or from his mounting nerves, he wasn't exactly sure.

'Everyone eats, even if it's just lho-sticks,' Cobb said, apparently joking. 'We could be in the air for the next thirty-six hours, and you're a door gunner. You'll end up passing out and slipping right out the hatch. If you do, pray we're high enough up for you to go splat, because if you survive the landing, the orks might get their paws on you.'

Cobb laughed – apparently that had been a joke too – and slapped him on the shoulder before wandering off, leaving the tin in Platz's hands.

He forced himself to eat. In fairness, the slop was no worse than what he was used to on board the *Mandatum Divinum*, and the stodgy taste went some way to helping him forget his aches and pains.

A shadow loomed over him again, and he looked up to find himself gazing at Cass' big co-pilot and navigator, Flight Sergeant Korrie.

'Time's up, Fledgling,' she said as he scrambled to get up and salute, narrowly avoiding spilling the last of the nutrient paste. 'The captain wants to speak with you before we mount up,' she went on, a ghost of a smile on her lips. 'Follow me.'

Cass met Major Bix on her way to the squadron hangar.

'Lovely day for it,' Bix quipped, her tone relentlessly cheerful.

'As good as any other,' Cass said, trying not to sound too morose. She'd slept for perhaps an hour before being woken by the noise of Zorn test-cycling the engines. After that it seemed like there was no more point in trying, so she had walked through the lines and out onto the hardpan, hoping to catch the last of the night's coolness before the sun was properly up. The rest of the squadron, those not still asleep, had acknowledged her about as readily as she had expected.

She'd spent a little time out at the airbase's perimeter fence, looking north, then had turned back and bumped into Bix on the way to her own unit's hangars. The two now walked side by side, flight helmets cradled under their arms. Even this early, the skies were clear and the sun was beating down. The rockcrete was starting to cook under their boots.

Bix was the commander of 911th Wing, one of the *Mandatum Divinum*'s coteries of Thunderbolt and Lightning fighter outfits. It was her own Thunderbolt squadron, the Cloud Knights, who would be providing top cover during the mission.

Like a number of senior fighter officers, Bix was ex Schola

Progenium, the orphan of a Navy frigate captain who had ended up finding her way back to the fleet, rather than joining the Commissariat or the Tempestus Scions. She was cultured enough to hold her own in the *Mandatum Divinum*'s lieutenant's mess, discussing matters of philosophy, history and literature, a far cry from the rougher mid-deck upbringing that Cass and many other pilots had experienced.

Cass didn't have a problem with that – the Vagabonds had been an anomaly since their inception, given they had never had any former progenia in their ranks. She had flown alongside plenty in other squadrons, and had always found they had their fair share of good aviators and bad. Bix, in her experience, was one of the former.

'How's it looking up there, across the river?' Cass asked her as they walked.

'A bloody mess,' Bix said without hesitation. 'I've managed to authorise a few sorties with my wing and Karro's Lightnings, but command won't allow anything like enough air cover to protect the pocket. The orks are hitting them hard, from the ground and the air. How they haven't folded yet is beyond me.'

'As long as you think you can get us through,' Cass said.

'Aerial threat is minimal south of the river, and once you reach the Eji it's a short hop over. You'll be running the gauntlet, but if anyone can make it, it'll be the Vagabonds.'

Their walk had brought them to the entrance of the Vagabonds' hangar, and Cass found herself gazing on the four remaining warbirds of her squadron. The ground crews were busy overseeing final checks on the exteriors as the pilots arrived and began to mount up.

'Good luck, Cass.'

She looked at Bix, and realised she was proffering a hand. She took it and shook as the Thunderbolt commander continued.

'See you back here in a day or two.'

'Safe hunting,' Cass said, that old Imperial Navy refrain, nodding to Bix as the major turned and carried on towards the hangars used by the 911th.

Rather than head in and board *Vagrant*, Cass remained outside the main doors. She had seen Korrie approaching, with the boy hurrying to keep up.

The sight of Wilbe Platz filled Cass with trepidation. The squadron couldn't afford any liabilities, not where they were going. He didn't look old enough to shave, yet she was supposed to believe he was suitable for the Vagabonds, that he had been selected on board the *Mandatum Divinum* to join them.

She supposed she had barely been any older on her first sortie. She remembered too what the boy had said, when he'd been standing looking like a lost pup beneath the harsh brilliance of the spotlights in Camp Yuzen's fighting ring. He had offered to see out the bout when it had seemed like refusal to do so would see his new comrades take a beating. He had spoken without thinking, instinctive sacrifice.

Perhaps that wasn't a good thing. Hadn't there been enough sacrifices lately?

'Good morning,' Cass said to Korrie and Platz. Korrie saluted, and Platz hurried to imitate the motion.

'Get the systems up and running, Mel,' Cass told Korrie, then gestured to Platz. 'Walk with me.'

Platz followed Cass in Korrie's wake, into the hangar. Engines were still cycling, and their screech battered at the cavernous interior. Platz resisted the instinctive urge to stoop, as though walking into the teeth of a storm, and maintained the relaxed, upright posture of the aviators and ground crews going about their business.

Cass stopped in front of what he assumed was her warbird, *Vagrant*. It was Platz's first look at the flier he had been assigned to. He had seen plenty of Valkyries on board the *Mandatum Divinum*, had trained on old, decommissioned ones as well as inside the simulation crypts, but he still experienced a moment's thrill as he looked up at the proud machine, with its broad, downswept wings, high twin tail and lowered, raptor-like prow. He noted the squadron's hooded, grinning death's-head sigil, alongside prow artwork – a cartoonish depiction of a stubbly-faced, winking pilot with a smoking lho-stick clamped between his jaws. Part of the design had been painted over with the flier's drab green camo scheme, and he realised it looked as though that part of the fuselage had been riddled with hard rounds, the wounds hastily patched up and repainted. Whoever the squadron's artist was, it seemed they hadn't yet had a chance to touch up their original piece.

'What is this we're looking at, pilot?' Cass asked him over the sound of *Ruffian*'s preflight cycling. Platz glanced at her, smiling sheepishly, wondering if he was about to be the butt of another joke.

'Something amusing, pilot?' Cass snapped, her expression stony.

'Ah, no, sir! It's a Valkyrie, sir. A Valkyrie airborne assault carrier.'

'I hope you can do better than that, Mister Platz,' Cass said. 'Give me specs.'

'Voss-class,' he said, pursing his lips as he looked with renewed intensity at the flier, trying to recall everything he'd spent years memorising. 'Mark… eight. Transport capacity, ah, varies depending on loadout, but typically averages at twelve fully equipped Guardsmen, plus an infantry heavy support weapon. Armour is three inches across the airframe, mostly plasteel and ferroplate.

Armaments in this case are a nose-mounted Hell-Hammer-pattern lascannon and two side hatch Solar-pattern heavy bolters.'

'Ammunition quantities?'

'Standard is one thousand rounds for each Solar and one hundred and fifty bolts from the lascannon's power pack, on average energy output.'

'Engines?'

'Two F75-MV afterburning vector-turbojets. Maximum speed, six hundred and ninety miles per hour. Range is one thousand two hundred miles, under standard atmospheric and gravitational conditions. Operational ceiling is forty-two thousand feet.'

'Weight without crew and cargo?'

'Approximately thirteen tons.'

'Weight with crew and cargo?'

'That… depends on how much cargo we're taking on, sir.' Cass grunted.

'Tolerably textbook,' she said. 'But what you're going to experience over the next day and a half will not be. Are you ready?'

'Yes, sir,' Platz said, and knew he was lying.

Cass looked at him, and he struggled not to back down. Did she want the truth? That his guts felt like a liquid mess and his hands were clasped tight behind his back so she couldn't see them shaking? He had dreamed of this day, had lain awake in his crib on board the *Mandatum Divinum* riven with excitement as he had imagined his first flight as part of his very own squadron. A lifetime's expectation hung on the next few hours. But the Vagabonds had eroded it. This was nothing like he had imagined his first mission, and they hadn't even left the rockcrete yet.

'We'll see,' Cass said. 'Go and mount up.'

* * *

Konstantina walked under *Ruffian*'s wings, getting a close-up view of the weapons hardpoints prior to final flight checks. They'd been configured at the start of the campaign on Kanai for killing orks, be they airborne or on the ground. Two lascannons gave the gunship the firepower it needed to knock out aerial threats, while a pair of rocket pods covered the anti-personnel side of things. The warbird's underslung prow heavy bolter completed the array, able to pump out the kind of firepower that could rip apart the toughest xenos mobs or turn their junker vehicles into proper scrap.

All the wing hardpoints were fixed position, but the heavy bolter was on a drum pintle. Konstantina had her gunner and co-pilot, Erik Straks, work it from his aft cockpit, checking it had its usual full range of rotation and depression. Of all the weapons wielded by *Ruffian* – and Konstantina did love them all – the heavy bolter was her favourite.

'Anything to report?' she called to Zorn-Five as the enginseer hurried past, trying and failing to avoid her. Konstantina teased the tech-priest relentlessly, and she was fairly sure he despised her, though Straks joked the machine-man's awkwardness – even more pronounced whenever she was around – was due to his secret feelings for her.

'The blessed war e-e-engine is at full functionality,' he stated hastily, looking up at the Vulture rather than its pilot. 'All diagnostics are within correct parameters and the machine spirit is fully awakened and e-e-eager for battle.'

'That makes two of us,' Konstantina said. 'It's about time we got back up there.'

She allowed the enginseer to hitch his red robes and scurry away while she paced round to the gunship's front.

'Looks good,' she called up to Straks over the rising noise of the engines filling the hangar. He gave her a thumbs-up in return. He'd been her co-pilot for nearly five years and her lover for four, though that latter relationship had been on and off, and lately more off than on. Some Aeronautica outfits forbade liaisons of any kind, but Cass had upheld the Vagabond tradition of not caring one whit, so long as it didn't compromise operational efficiencies. And letting relations get in the way of purging xenos was very much against Konstantina's style.

She patted the side of the fuselage where her kill tallies were painted, as she always did before lift-off, then clambered up into the forward cockpit and sealed it.

'Weapons systems look fine from the outside,' she confirmed to Straks on the intercom, adjusting her helmet mic. Unlike the Valkyries, the Vulture only had two crewmates, its lack of side doors making the need for secondary gunners obsolete.

'Think we'll get much chance to use them?' Straks asked. *'This is just meant to be a supply drop, right?'*

'Hope and pray, flyboy,' Konstantina said. 'Hope and pray.'

Before she climbed on board, Cass called Zeke over. Her starboard gunner was passing by, lugging a fresh crate of heavy bolter rounds towards *Vagrant*'s starboard hatch. He changed course, planting the crate on the hangar floor before saluting.

'All set?' Cass asked him, returning the gesture.

'As He wills,' Zeke said, his stock response.

'Try and keep an eye on the kid,' she told him, glancing towards the opposite side of the Valkyrie, where Platz was pulling himself up to his station in the port hatch.

'He'll be in my prayers,' Zeke responded.

From anyone else in the squadron, Cass would have assumed he was being facetious, but not Zeke. He was the son of the *Mandatum Divinum*'s ship's deacon, and as far as Cass was concerned, was even more pious than his father. He kept a pocket-book-sized copy of the Imperial Creed in his flight suit's breast, and spent much of his down time writing out litany scripts on long, slender scrolls of parchment, which he then bound around his forearms before heading out on operations. With his straggly, balding pate, hatchet-lean face and fierce blue eyes, he looked every bit the firebrand. The rest of the squadron had mocked him when he had first joined, not long after Cass, but his zeal had become a fixture of the Vagabonds' collective personality. He had practically assembled his own congregation – Cass knew Akoi and Weets on Cobb's warbird, *Pauper*, now wrote their own litany scripts, while Konstantina would sometimes ask him to bless *Ruffian* before a combat operation, as though he were the squadron's ordained Imperial preacher.

Cass was never dismissive of faith, but what really mattered to her was that Zeke was also an excellent side gunner and a reliable crewman. That was why she felt more reassured knowing he would be in the hold with Platz.

'Just do what you can for him,' Cass said. 'But nothing crazy. I've lost too many good crewmates to swap one for an untried fledgling.'

'As He wills,' Zeke replied.

Cass allowed him to go back to his loading and, after one more glance at the other crews, climbed the ladder into *Vagrant's* forward cockpit.

She settled into the worn leather seat and, without thinking, brushed her bare knuckles against her father's dog tags, wrapped around the grip of the centre stick. Then she strapped herself in, tugging on her flight gloves and resp-mask and pulling on her helmet. It was a big, bulky thing, with inbuilt comms and an adjustable visor shield that could link via hardwire connection with *Vagrant's* systems. Such means of interfacing were rare and precious even among elites such as the Valkyrie pilots, usually reserved for wing leaders only.

It was old, too. Its edges were scored and scarred silver, and its original chin clip had snapped long ago, replaced by one Cass had cut and repurposed from a spare Munitorum rucksack. The digits '901' and the slogan 'Chief Vagabond' were stencilled along its sides.

It had been her father's helmet before it had been hers, and that made it more valuable than any new marks of cranial protection.

She lowered and sealed the cockpit shield, partially shutting out the din filling the hangar. Everything was happening on automatic now, preflight checks she had run thousands of times before, since she had been small enough to sit on her father's knee and help him do the same in the simulation rigs on board the *Mandatum Divinum*. She checked the fuel level gauge, performed comms tests through both *Vagrant*'s intercom system and the wider squadron vox-net, scanned engine pressure and temperature and toggled weapons systems on and off. She performed a full run-through of the blessed avionics, before jacking her helmet's hardwire cable into the dataport under the control panel and slotting the down visor over her face.

There was a moment's lag before the helmet accepted the interface. Cass' vision fuzzed, then numbers began to blink up, zeroes that sluggishly ticked upwards until they properly reflected the data being transmitted from the warbird's systems.

As the old helm finalised its connection, she ran through the final system initiation ritual, murmuring the Pilot's Benediction as she did so. Zorn had already done the heavy lifting in that regard, performing the esoteric machine-communing that Cass didn't dare try to pretend she understood, nor imitate.

She lifted the small plastek protector covering the final initiation switch and flicked it. The engines ignited fully, their vibrations thrilling through the airframe around Cass, their roar kept at bay only by her helmet's ear baffles. She pressed the intercom button for the aft cockpit.

'All set back there?'

'Cosy as ever, Chief,' Korrie's voice ticked back. She was immediately behind and above Cass in what was called the aft cockpit, essentially wedged in behind Cass' seat and between the twin primary rotor fans. The confined space combined with Korrie's solid build made it less than comfortable for her, but Cass had never heard her navigator complain. She had been watching over Cass' shoulder since her very first pilot sortie.

'Excited to be back up?' Cass asked her, the question only part rhetorical. Unlike some of the other crews, Korrie never displayed any dismay or trepidation when they were given a new assignment, simply accepted it with her admirable brand of stoicism. Cass knew Korrie had her back – often literally – and that was the reason she was the closest thing Cass had to a genuine friend.

'Best thing for it after a bad flight, Chief,' Korrie said, doubtless thinking of Ushen. *'Good to get airborne again as quickly as possible. Stops things festering.'*

Cass supposed there was truth in that. It was certainly one way of putting a positive spin on what they were being asked to do.

She thought again about the orders on the dataslate, still resting in her pocket, but forced them from her mind. It was too late for doubts.

She checked the rest of *Vagrant's* intercom, getting positives back from Zeke and Platz, then sent status pings to the other three warbirds, making sure the intra-squadron vox was also fully up and running. Final comms checks complete, she called for the others to sound off.

'Rogue *ready*,' came Vaughn's voice.

'Pauper *is set*,' Cobb said.

'Ruffian *ready and willing*,' said Konstantina. *'Throne, I can't wait to knock some xenos scrap out of the sky.'*

'And what a sky it is, still not a cloud in sight,' Cobb observed. *'How long has it been since it last rained?'*

'I'm not complaining,' Konstantina growled.

'Well, the Guard out there on half water rations might,' Vaughn said.

'Focus up,' Cass ordered. 'Follow my lead. We'll climb to ten thousand once we're out and circle east before picking up the course, then swing low.'

She switched channels, contacting Barduk West's control spire and receiving the all-clear for lift-off. She fed more power to the engines and settled her grip on the stick, flexing it briefly around her father's service tags. Then she applied pressure, alternating lightly between the pedals at her feet that controlled the angle of the tail rudders.

No matter how many times she did this, and no matter how desperate the circumstances, there was still a thrill to those first few moments of flight, to the miraculous way in which a leaden thirteen tons suddenly felt lithe and weightless at her fingertips.

The main doors to the hangar had been rolled fully back. The ground crews had retreated, the roaring of the engines shaking the whole structure. Cass eased *Vagrant* towards the opening, nose dipping fractionally. On, out into the sunlight, her visor dimming slightly to compensate for the sudden glare. They were out and turning to starboard, climbing, up towards the great blue, to the heavens of another world they had been called upon to preserve from the ravages of mankind's enemies.

The rest of Vagabond Squadron tailed her out, rising in her wake until they levelled out at ten thousand feet and began to circle. Cass scanned the horizon, then the small, scarred auspex plate that formed part of her control panel. The skies were clear, apart from Bix's Thunderbolts, already high above and circling back on themselves.

'*Good to see you up, Vagabond Leader,*' Bix's voice crackled over the vox. '*All quiet up here, for now. Expect that will change soon enough.*'

'Keep us in the loop, Cloud Knight,' Cass said. 'I can already feel the cargo slowing us. If there's any trouble coming our way, we'll need all the forewarning we can get.'

'*Don't worry, we'll watch your top,*' Bix replied. Cass closed the channel and settled in, scanning the perfect azure, and wondering just what was waiting for her beyond the horizon.

CHAPTER FOUR

Vagabond Squadron made for the Eji, flying low and hard.

Cass slipped into the tunnel vision of an active operation. The fears and doubts were shut out, the uncertainties at what they had been ordered to do momentarily forgotten. Her focus was on her instruments, and the clear blue above, and the greenery and the dirt scudding by below.

Strategic orientation briefings they had received when they'd first arrived in-system six months earlier had described the tithe grade of Kanai Tertius as 'Civilised'. It was an Imperial world, the system capital, a focal point of stability and productivity in a subsector that had suffered as badly as any other in recent years. That was, until the orks had come.

They had initially struck the neighbouring system, Eclopia, but the hive and garrison worlds there had been ready. After almost a year of brutal warfare both sides had settled into stalemate, but the xenos hadn't been content to grind themselves to nothing against the hive-citadels. A breakaway force – estimated by Imperial strategos to belong to an ork seeking to rival the main warlord with exploits of its own – had swung spinwards and crashed into the Kanai System. Over the past six months the three habitable worlds of Kanai had gone from the secondary to primary battlefront in the subsector.

The Vagabonds had missed the initial fighting at Eclopia, arriving after a torrid warp passage as part of the reinforcements that had initially been assembled from veterans of the Sallic Suppression with the intent of buttressing the new front. Now they were trying to hold the line on Kanai, and praying the latest ork offensive spent its momentum.

That was the strategic situation as Cass understood it. She tended not to worry about the bigger picture – even as the most senior Valkyrie commander in the battle group, it was well above her grade. Her daily duties were keeping her warbirds fit and ready, and trying to do the same with her crews.

And that had been much harder since Ushen, barely a week earlier. Both Ushen and its twin across the valley, Torr City, were pure meat-grinders, urban fights in the most brutal sense. Built-up combat zones were one of the deadliest environments a Valkyrie squadron could face, but Jakyra had ordered them into the midst of it, in a mission that Cass knew now she should at least have registered protest against, or made some effort to amend.

Just as she should have protested more firmly against this one. The orders might come from above, but she knew as far as the likes of Vaughn were concerned, she was the one responsible for the wellbeing of everyone in her squadron. If she didn't fight their corner, no one would.

'Vagabond Leader, this is Cloud Knight Leader,' Bix's clipped voice came in over the vox.

'Cloud Knight, this is Vagabond, go,' Cass replied, glancing instinctively up through her cockpit's shield, looking for the arrowheads of contrails that marked the passage of the Thunderbolt fighters acting as their top cover.

'Picking up hostiles to the east, heading our way. Suspect they've caught our scent. Will be forced to turn and engage in approximately three minutes.'

'Think you can handle them, Cloud Knight?'

'Affirmative, but you'll be without cover until we've scattered them. No promises on how long that'll take.'

'Copy that. We'll be fine. Give them hell.'

It wasn't as though Cass had much choice other than to accept her support's absence. Higher up, the Thunderbolts could see more, both on their scopes and through visuals. Intercepting the scatterings of ork air-mobs that prowled the skies this far south was what Bix's warbirds were up there for.

As for surface threats, there was nothing they could do about those. Officially, the orks weren't meant to have crossed over the Eji River yet, but there were plenty of rumours circulating among Barduk's pilots that the xenos had done just that. As far as Cass was concerned, they were now flying over hostile territory.

It would be easy to forget that, with cloudless skies above and a seemingly deserted agri-landscape of browns and dusty greens whipping by below. Kanai Tertius' main habitable continent was largely given over to agri-labour, though its cities were large and industrialised, and benefited from being the system's capital and administrative hub. But the Eji Valley, with its fertile tributary streams and scatterings of rural collectives, felt a world away from the war-racked urban hell the Vagabonds had experienced when they had been assigned to the Ushen front.

The ground scudded away beneath them. Cass was used to flying low – it was second nature to all Valkyrie pilots, a required skill. There was always a thrill to it, the sensation of raw speed and power that became lost whenever a flier climbed to a higher altitude. It also created a strange sort of intimacy with the ground they passed over. Not for them a distant patchwork of fields, forests and agri-collectives, but a close-in view of the world they were fighting, sweating, bleeding, dying to defend.

That revealed the realities that might have been lost higher up. The agricultural prefectures that made up the Eji Valley region had been almost wholly abandoned, both by the families of rural labourers that had worked them for generations, and the overseers and gentry classes that ensured tithes, law and order were maintained. Refugee camps crowded the southern outskirts of both Ushen and Torr, the conditions appalling. The fields had been left behind to rot and the collectives to fall into decay, inhabited only by a few desperate scavengers and squatters. As Vagabond Squadron passed over, Cass saw rice paddies dried up in the relentless heat, networks of empty ditches, and abandoned steadings falling into dilapidation. Smoke rose in pillars in the distance, too far east to be the fighting around Army Group Centre – Cass assumed a promethium station or a collective had caught fire and was going up.

The landscape lay deserted, and despite her best efforts, Cass felt some of the tension that had been building up since lift-off ebbing away. She could hear Zeke humming an Imperial psalm to himself, audible over the intercom. Korrie would call out occasional, fractional adjustments to their course as she navigated from the aft cockpit, which Cass passed on to the rest of the squadron. It was all a well-known rhythm, dangerously familiar.

Then, while they were still almost thirty miles south of the Eji, they started taking fire.

The first rounds took Platz by surprise.

He had been a bundle of nerves throughout lift-off, clutching the support railings in the Valkyrie's main hold, feeling the vibrations of the turbojets running through his hands and up through his boots. A sense of awe had started to take over, though, when the warbirds had risen, circling east from Barduk. He had got an aerial view of the airbase, with its rows of prefab bunkers and reinforced hangars, its control spire and Hydra nests, and the ruler-straight lines of the runways, grey against the baked browns of the soil. The view alone was incredible to a voidborn, to someone who had spent their life in the warren of cabins and corridors and walkways that made up an Imperial Navy capital ship. He had only seen vistas spread out below in pict and vid captures, or in the simulations.

Then they had dropped down to the recommended combat height on Kanai, hugging the ground. He'd experienced the thrill of rocketing over the agri-spread, the raw sense of speed and power. He did as he could see Zeke doing in the opposite doorway from his, and sat down on the edge of the hatch, his feet hanging in space, the wind whipping at him, the roar of the port-side rotors above him. All of it had caused him to forget his fears, to marvel in the exhilaration of the moment.

That was his first mistake.

He heard what sounded like a tapping noise, coming from the outside of the airframe, barely audible over the engines and the rush of the wind. He frowned, trying to identify it.

Then *Vagrant* pitched.

Platz was fortunate it went right – if it had rolled left, he would have been left dangling on the edge, restrained only by his waist strap. He grunted as it sawed into his gut.

'*Incoming, incoming,*' snapped Cass' voice over the intercom. '*Ground fire. I don't have eyes-on.*'

The Valkyrie pitched back to its regular angle, and Platz heard more tapping. He realised it was small-arms fire, hard rounds hitting the outside of the hull.

'Oh, Throne,' he said, yanking himself properly back into

the hold and onto his fold-down seat before heaving the heavy bolter out of the stowed position. He swung it round and down in its pintle clamp, hauled back on the lever action to chamber the first round, and snatched hold of the twin hand grips before angling down under the wing and starting to fire.

It was only when he felt the brutal kickback of the heavy weapon, bucking against its mount, and heard the battering report even over the noise dampeners built into his helmet, that he actually realised what he was doing – sending rounds in a blind panic, down into the terrain skimming by below.

'*Platz, do you have eyes-on?*' snapped Cass' voice over the intercom bead in his ear. '*Platz, respond!*'

'No,' he admitted.

'*Then what in the name of Holy Terra are you doing? You don't lay down blind fire unless I order it! I need eyes right now, not bruiser rounds! Engage your brain, and tell me where those shots are coming from!*'

Platz let go of the bolter's grips, at least remembering to hit the safety and lock the weapon in place before he leaned forward as much as he dared, getting a view of the ground beneath *Vagrant*'s port wing.

He saw nothing bar rotting fields. The sounds of impacts had stopped too.

'*Think they're port side, at our seven,*' Zeke said over the intercom.

'*Affirmative, Vaughn's got them,*' he heard Cass respond, the captain privy to the communications with the rest of the squadron, while the other members of *Vagrant*'s crew could only hear each other.

'*More at our two, brace,*' Cass went on, and Platz just had the chance to grip the overhead restraints as *Vagrant* bucked once more. He heard the thunder of a heavy bolter, Zeke's this time, as he returned fire, presumably at targets on the ground that he could actually see.

'So much for there not being any xenos south of the river,' Platz heard Korrie say.

Vagabond Squadron experienced four separate surface-to-air contacts in the space of just over two minutes. Cass got visuals on two of them, mobs of ork infantry seemingly roving the fields and ditches south of the river, blazing away at the passing Imperial aircraft with their crude firearms for the few seconds that they were in range.

They posed no great threat, but their presence on the near side of the Eji was a concern. Bix had claimed her wing had detected nothing crossing over from the north.

'Think they've repaired one of the bridges, or built a pontoon?' Korrie wondered.

'Surely air recon would have picked that up?' Cass said. 'I know command has been hanging Army Group Centre out to dry, but we can't be that blind.'

She had already called in the sightings, but Barduk had offered nothing more than confirmation that her message had been received.

The problem became somebody else's as Cass glanced at her console's auspex chart, and realised they were coming up fast on the Eji.

'Ten points to starboard, on my mark,' she ordered the squadron over the vox. Carrying on directly north would take them through a narrow defile called Kantu Valley, cut by a feeder stream that ran down from the flanks of the wider Eji Valley. Passing along it would be the quickest route to Army Group Centre, but it was, according to reports from the pocket, crawling with xenos. Strategos oversight had recommended circling east, and Cass had agreed with the assessment.

The Eji itself was soon beneath them, a broad band of muddy-looking water winding its way sluggishly through the wider valley floor. It had irrigated the crops of the region since the earliest days of settlement, though rampant agri development and the dumping of waste from both Ushen and Torr City had left it heavily polluted. Cass noted the dark markings on the river's banks – it looked like the water level had shrunk considerably, likely the result of the ongoing drought.

Vagabond Squadron used the river as a guide to turn east, their passage stirring the scummy waters. Their route took them over a rail bridge and then a highway crossing, both bombed out, their central spans now nothing but jagged nubs poking above the waterline like the broken bones of some great river monster's carcass. There was no sign that the orks had attempted any kind of repairs.

Cass received static-chopped confirmation from Bix that her Thunderbolts had dealt with whatever high-aerial threat they had detected, and were again overhead. Cass' relief was short-lived – barely a minute after ordering the Valkyries to swing north once more, they started taking ground fire again. This time, it was more than just small-arms.

System warnings blurted in her ears and amber flashed across her visor, and a moment later a rocket corkscrewed past, dangerously close to clipping the starboard wing. Cass growled and evaded as another slashed upwards from below and detonated above the flier's prow, sending shrapnel scalping off the cockpit shield.

'Engage, engage,' she ordered over the intercom, the words followed almost immediately by the thudding of the side hatch heavy bolters. She could see the enemy below them now, a mass of green interspersed with ramshackle structures and crude palisades. If this was what the alternative route was like, she dreaded to think what would have been waiting for them in Kantu Valley. That would have been a proper gauntlet run.

'We're going to have to punch it,' she said tersely to the other warbird pilots. 'Split spacings, and make fractional adjustments to your flight path so they can't ladder us. Clear?'

The affirmatives came back, and she opened the throttle and pitched *Vagrant* forward, into the fire, feeling the familiar pressures of atmospheric flight pressing hard against her.

It took perhaps three minutes to clear the worst of it. Three heart-pounding minutes, as she tried to keep an eye on the ground and the air simultaneously, her helmet's interfacing helping her track what was happening around the Valkyrie.

At one point the sky was smudged by bursts of dirty black smoke.

'They've got flak,' Korrie reported. *'At our three, almost under us. Turning now, but too slow.'*

'Doubt they were expecting to track anything so low and fast,' Cass said, knowing that speed and surprise were their best defences. More anti-air fire burst in the sky around them, but none came close to touching the Valkyries.

Bix came through over the vox again, more chopped than ever. Apparently ork fighters were scrambling en masse, and she couldn't hold the airspace above any longer.

'Don't worry, we're through,' Cass told her. 'Get out while you still can. I'll send word to command when we're ready for lift-off. Good hunting.'

Bix confirmed, pulling her fighters back as Cass double-checked the landing zone tags on the auspex and lined it up with what she was now seeing below her – trench lines, dugouts and defensive hardpoints, scarring Kanai's dry earth. They were passing over Army Group Centre, entering the besieged pocket north of the river.

Cass picked up the air control frequency being used by the defenders, warning them of their imminent arrival. They lost altitude as they circled in, numbers steadily dropping on Cass' visor as she lined *Vagrant* up with their destination on the auspex.

She picked it up visually a few moments later, a cleared square of packed dirt, hemmed in between what looked like a makeshift medicae station and a few ruined agri-buildings, plus an armour park. Artillery dugouts and Hydra anti-aircraft emplacements littered the core of the pocket, their elevated barrels catching the sun as the Valkyries passed overhead.

Cass swung them in and put *Vagrant* down carefully, checking her spacings – the landing zone was tight, and there was barely sufficient room for the four warbirds to make touchdown together. *Rogue* followed her in, then *Pauper*, *Ruffian* bringing up the rear, until the four fliers were arrayed in a diamond formation on the hot dirt.

Munitorum drones began to hurry towards the Valkyries from all sides. Cass sent a vox-message to the other pilots as she stilled the engines and popped the rear hatch.

'Help them get the cargo offloaded, make sure the pict servitors get a few good snaps. Hal, see someone about refuelling, we'll want more in the tanks in case anything goes awry. We've got enough to see us back to Barduk, but not if we have to alter course.'

As their affirmatives came back she uncoupled her helmet, undid her restraints, and unlatched and raised the cockpit shield.

The first thing she heard, as she clambered out into the oppressive heat, was the familiar *thud-thud-thud* of Hydra anti-aircraft guns. Bix had been right about the incoming ork wings. The air was riven with their scrap planes and smeared with dirty bursts of flak. If Vagabond Squadron hadn't put down when they did, they would have been caught up in the chaos.

She cast about for someone to report to, and saw a harried-looking lieutenant in the garish red-and-blue uniform of the Atraxian Zouaves hurrying towards her.

'You'll need to go as soon as you're unloaded I'm afraid, captain,' the lieutenant called over the thunder filling the sky. Cass frowned at him, uncomprehending.

'I'm not taking my squadron up into the middle of that,' she said. 'We'll wait until it's cleared. Besides, I have orders other than delivering the cargo.'

The lieutenant looked perplexed. 'But the landing zone here isn't sufficient for more Valkyries. I was told we made it clear to command that the supplies would need to be delivered in waves. You'll have to clear out to make room for the next drop.'

'This is it,' Cass said, realising where the man's confusion was stemming from. 'This is the supply drop. There is no more coming.'

The lieutenant stared at her, then looked at the fliers, as though he was struggling to count to four. The rear ramps of the trio of Valkyries were already down, and teams of Munitorum supply hands were hauling pallets out of the holds. The pair of pict servitors that had been strapped into the hold with the crates were lumbering about, twitching with nerve responses each time they took a snap using their cranial recorders, documenting the frantic offloading.

'This isn't enough,' the lieutenant finally exclaimed. 'Does… does command know what's happening here? We need rations, munitions, fuel… We barely have enough water to last–'

'I need to speak to your officers,' Cass said, trying to refocus the man's mind. 'Your senior commanders, all of them. Can you take me to them?'

The man finally tore his gaze from the warbirds, his expression now grim.

'Yes,' he said. 'I'll need to report this to them in person.'

Cass resisted the urge to tell the man to hurry. Every moment they spent on the dirt in the pocket was another moment they were vulnerable. She couldn't help but glance back at her grounded warbirds, then up at the burning blue sky, before striding out after the lieutenant.

* * *

Vaughn dropped down onto the dirt and accosted the first Munitorum officer he found, a clerk overseeing the hasty unloading of the Valkyries.

'Fuel,' Vaughn said to him. 'We need a refill. Promethium grade three if you've got it, grade one or four if you don't.'

'I-I would need regimental authorisation,' the clerk stammered. 'All the remaining fuel has been distributed.'

Vaughn growled and abandoned the man, heading instead to the closest Guard officer he could see. A Kantib captain was snapping at a gaggle of his exhausted-looking men – most of them seemingly walking wounded from the neighbouring medicae bay – to get up and lend a hand to the Munitorum drones working on emptying the Valkyries.

'My battalion doesn't have any fuel, not enough for your birds anyway,' the man said. 'You'll have to speak to Lieutenant Colonel Rekk. He's with the armoured division. They should have more stocks.'

He pointed across the landing zone at the sorry excuse for an armour park on the other side.

'Throne,' Vaughn swore under his breath, and hurried back past the Valkyries, weaving his way through the mounting mound of supply pallets being offloaded onto the dirt.

He eventually located a Kantib Armoured officer, a major who, going by the patch on her grimy tanker's overalls, was named Korix. Vaughn explained his request, and watched the woman's expression harden.

'You want to take fuel from my companies just so your birds can fly out of here?' she demanded.

'Flying tends to be what we do best,' Vaughn replied, trying to cover up how taken aback he was by the hostility.

'You'll address me as "sir", or doesn't the Navy respect the ranks of the Astra Militarum any longer?' Korix demanded.

Vaughn felt a sudden, burning urge to draw his aviator's laspistol and start waving it around. He was thankful Cass had ordered him to see to the refuelling – if she'd given the task to Konstantina, the little Vulture pilot would have started murdering by now.

'Apologies, sir,' he said. 'But we really need that fuel.'

Major Korix's expression darkened even further.

'And what do you suppose we're using it for? Training manoeuvres? We need every drop if we're going to keep fighting. Without armour, the pocket collapses. What little we have left we're stockpiling for a possible breakout. We can't dump it all in your Valkyries just so you can fly away. We'd be leaving ourselves inoperable. Dead. Besides, didn't you come here with enough prom to get you back across the river?'

'We did, but there's no leeway. If we need to detour–'

Korix scoffed. 'If you insist, I'll pass the request on to Lieutenant Colonel Mekin, but he'll tell you the same thing.'

'Can I at least speak to him in person?'

'You'll find him in the medicae bay. He lost both legs yesterday to an ork scrap tank.'

Vaughn clenched his jaw, delivered one of the finest Navy salutes of his life, and hurried back across the landing zone.

The Atraxian Zouave led Cass to the headquarters of Army Group Centre. It had been erected in what she took to be an agri-manor, the home of one of the provincial nobles tasked with overseeing production along this stretch of the valley. She assumed it had been chosen because it was one of the few stone buildings in the area, though little in the way of its whitewashed walls and sweeping terracotta roof were still standing. What remained had been buttressed by plasteel and flakboards.

They passed by a sandbagged Hydra emplacement on their

way to what was left of the front doors. The quad-barrelled anti-aircraft gun was battering away, sending ladders of flak stitching across the sky. The ork air assault didn't seem to be showing any signs of dissipating, and Cass caught sight of a clutch of crude fighter-bombers swooping down to the north, prow cannons blazing and rockets streaking away from under their wings. They were hit by more air defence fire, one ripped apart and falling in a hail of burning metal, but the others completed their dive and arced back up on dirty plumes of fuel smoke, chased by more flak.

'Are these assaults regular?' Cass asked over the Hydra's discharges as they reached the doors. The Zouave laughed bitterly.

'This barely constitutes an assault, captain.'

He led her into the ruins of the manor's entrance hall. There was no air of abandoned dilapidation here, no similarities to the headquarters at Suchen. Part of the space had been turned into a triage centre, blood-spattered medicae working to assess screaming, crying men and women hauled off the nearby trenches. A neighbouring room was acting as a comms post, a few signals officers shouting to be heard over the din as they tried to maintain the flow of reports between the front and reserve lines. If this wasn't a major offensive, Cass dreaded to think of the carnage when there was one.

The Zouave led her through it all, to a set of stairs going into the basement. It was packed with Munitorum crates, most of them empty. A hole had been drilled through the far wall. Cass pushed through the gas curtains and found herself descending again, into a dugout buried under the manor, its soil-packed walls and flakboard beams and balustrades lit by the dirty yellow light of jury-rigged lumens.

One thing Cass could never fault about the Guard was their ability to dig.

They passed a pair of grim-faced Mordian Iron Guard troopers who saluted the Zouave with a crisp click of their booted heels, and ducked through another low doorway to emerge into what Cass took to be the primary command space. It had been constructed from flakboard and sandbags, with a large, circular campaign table with an inbuilt holo-display occupying the centre. A generator in one corner of the room rattled unhealthily as it fought to keep everything running.

The dugout was packed with officers. It was infernally hot, and most had their uniform coats or jackets off, stripped down to their undershirts or more basic fatigues, all except a Mordian commander and his young-looking aide, who had refused to dishonour their proud blue frock coats by removing them.

'Captain Elza, of the Imperial Navy's Nine-Hundred-First Tactical Wing,' the Zouave announced to the room, before singling out one officer in particular, who was staring at Cass through the holo-display being beamed up from the table. The Zouave went to his side and muttered in his ear.

'What?' the officer barked, his eyes still fixed on Cass. 'What do you mean that's all?'

'Sir, if you'll hear me out–' Cass began to say, but it was clear the Zouave had already informed him there would be no further resupply.

'Damn Havali,' the officer snarled. He was tall and looked young for his rank, with a tousled mop of golden hair swept rakishly to one side. He was dressed in his undershirt, along with a tight-fitting set of black cavalry breeches and riding boots, and a black leather belt which held a scabbarded power sabre. Cass assumed the man had to be Brigadier General ven Weem Percivald of the 222nd Maelwych Lancers. According to the addendum information on the dataslate she'd been given, he had commanded Army Group Centre since its original senior officer, Major General Westlake, had been killed in the initial offensive.

'This is all we've been sent,' Percivald continued, addressing his assembled staff as he gestured angrily at Cass. 'Three bastard Valkyries. Enough to feed and supply one regiment for three days, at most. Havali has abandoned us, as I said he would! He's left us here to die!'

Angry sounds of disbelief filled the dugout. Cass spoke over them, addressing Percivald.

'With respect, general, my squadron didn't come here just to drop off supplies and be pict-captured doing it. I have other orders from command at Suchen.'

She pulled the dataslate from her pocket, feeling a sudden rush of revulsion. She forced herself through it. She couldn't disobey orders, not these ones.

She gene-activated the slate and passed it to an aide to give to Percivald, speaking as she did so.

'I have been instructed by Lieutenant General Havali to evacuate you, your staff and all senior officers, from brigade level upwards, out of the pocket. Throne willing, by tomorrow morning you will be debriefing at Suchen Palace.'

CHAPTER FIVE

Uproar filled the dugout.

It was ended by a bellow for silence, one which immediately quietened the assembled officers. They stood like pups chastised by a bull hound.

Cass realised it was a commissar who had barked the command. She hadn't noticed him until now – he had been lurking like a malignant spectre at the back of the dugout.

'Thank you, Commissar Vulkrov,' Percivald said tartly. He took the slate offered to him and began reading it. Pensive silence filled the sweltering space, disturbed only by the muffled pounding reaching them from the surface. Eventually he looked up, and spoke again.

'It seems you are correct, captain…' He glanced at the slate again. 'Captain Elza. These are signed orders from Lieutenant General Havali, requiring us to evacuate with you immediately.'

'That is outrageous,' said the ranking Mordian officer in the room. He was one of the oldest-looking figures present, and Cass noted that he was also the only one who looked as though he had been recently wounded – much of the left side of his face was plastered with anti-burn synthspray. The edges of the injury looked raw and painful, but he gave no sign of discomfort as he spoke.

'The lieutenant general is suggesting nothing less than the abandonment of the men and women under our command. It would be an unconscionable dereliction of duty.'

'Refusing a direct order would be even worse,' said another officer across from the Mordian, glancing at Percivald for support. 'I am sure it would not be… out of turn to state we have had many issues with Lieutenant General Havali's instructions lately, but we have followed them to the letter, and fought this hopeless fight. Are we now starting to pick and choose which directives we adhere to?'

There was a cautious swell of supportive murmurs, none of which had been present for the Mordian's words. Cass saw that most of the officers seemed to be looking to Percivald, waiting to take his lead, the green light of the holo-projection bathing their anxious features.

'It would appear that someone at command, General Havali or not, has remembered we exist,' Percivald said eventually. 'And not before time. Colonel Ziets has put it well. We have obeyed orders thus far, we will not stop now.'

'Commissar Vulkrov, surely you cannot permit this flagrant display of cowardice?' the Mordian snapped.

'The orders are clear enough,' Vulkrov replied coldly.

'How dare you accuse us of cowardice, Brigadier Felkin,' Percivald barked. 'We who have sacrificed so much!'

'Do not speak of sacrifice, not when our regiments are out there right now, bleeding and dying,' the Mordian – Felkin – replied, starting to go ruddy-faced. 'I am going nowhere, except out there, to the front. I am certainly not allowing myself to be… *evacuated*.'

He spat the last word like a curse. A few of the officers had the decency to look down, clearly mastering their own sense of disgust.

'Were it not for your exemplary service, I would have you up on charges, brigadier,' Percivald snarled.

'Do whatever you please, but you will hear me out,' Felkin said. 'You are not abandoning a doomed position, and you all know it. The pocket is defensible, and the river is fordable. We can still break out, to the south! Through Kantu Valley!'

'I will not repeat myself on this matter,' Percivald yelled, smacking a palm on the campaign table like a petulant child, causing the holo-display to momentarily distort. 'Three times, we have been forced to reduce the perimeter, and now the northern spur is almost surrounded. If it falls the xenos scum will be able to bring up their artillery, and that will put them in range of us, here. The heart of our defences. We will all be lost. So strike out yourself if you wish. Once we have departed, you will have command. But it will only hasten the inevitable. We were doomed the moment Havali failed to properly support us.'

'Continue to tell yourself that,' Felkin said. 'You had best pray high command sees it the same way.'

'That's enough, brigadier,' Commissar Vulkrov growled from the back of the room.

Cass was considering her options should the situation get any uglier, when the holo flickered again. This time, Percivald hadn't touched it. The lumens dimmed a moment later, and a shiver ran through the flakboard walls and ceiling, sending a cascade of soil down onto the shoulders of the assembly.

'Those are Renet's batteries opening fire again,' said one woman dressed in an artillery colonel's tunic.

Before anyone could elaborate, a signals trooper ducked in through the dugout door, message chit in hand.

'General, sir,' he said, saluting and passing the chit round to Percivald.

'What is it?' the general snapped without looking at the message. 'Out with it, man!'

'Colonel Ayubu's compliments, sir, but it seems another coordinated ground offensive is underway. They're coming at us from beyond the northern spur, as well as the ruins of the West Side agri-collective, and through Kantu Valley to the south. And the auspex station is picking up more fighter-bomber wings inbound from the north and west. It's another assault wave, much bigger than the last.'

'Damnation,' Percivald hissed. 'The whole line could collapse! We have to get out before it hits!'

Cass glanced at Vulkrov, but the commissar seemed happy to allow Army Group Centre's senior officers to flee. Orders were orders, she supposed. Vulkrov would assume Havali's instructions to the pocket's leadership had been cleared by Lord Commissar Vasquez.

'Go,' Felkin said to the assembled headquarters. 'Flee as fast as those warbirds will carry you. I will stay with my regiments.'

'The lieutenant general's orders were that you all come,' Cass said, knowing she had to at least offer protest to the Mordian's decision.

'I will sooner take a las bolt from the good commissar here, than abandon my men to the xenos,' Felkin told her levelly. To Cass' surprise, she saw his young aide look at him, mouth half-open as though he was about to argue with his commanding officer. Felkin cast him a warning glance, and he said nothing.

'We need to go now then,' Cass told the others. 'If the orks catch my warbirds while they're still grounded, nobody will be getting evacuated.'

* * *

Cass led the pack of officers out and across to the landing zone. Her dataslate had included a manifest stating which officers were to actually be evacuated, but it had a caveat that the information might not be up to date, Cass assumed because command at Suchen didn't know exactly who amongst Army Group Centre's leadership were still alive. When in doubt, seniority was to take precedence.

At that point, Cass didn't especially care who got on her Valkyries and who didn't. It was an ugly business, and she just wanted to get airborne and south of the river. Percivald had been right about one thing – if the xenos hit them while they were still lifting off, or worse, while they were still on the ground, nobody would be getting debriefed back at Suchen.

The nearest aircraft was *Pauper*. Cobb was perched halfway into his cockpit, bellowing at the last Munitorum drones to get away from the rear hatch. He paused to look down at Cass, before his eyes darted to the gaggle of officers trailing after her, clearly confused.

'Where's Hal?' Cass shouted up at him.

'Looking for someone to authorise the refuelling,' he responded.

'You mean we haven't taken on more promethium yet?' Cass demanded, dismay warring with a moment's panic.

'They won't surrender any,' Cobb replied. 'From what Vaughn said on his way past, they were refusing to give their reserves to us because we'd be flying out. Said they needed it for a breakout, and that we were abandoning them anyway, so it would be a waste.'

'Shit,' Cass hissed. They'd been running on lower tanks anyway, trading some of the weight for greater speed. They would still have enough to detour round Kantu Valley and make it back to Barduk, but that was all – they wouldn't be able to divert any further, and even complex evasive manoeuvres would risk shortening their flying time.

'We have more than enough authority to see you refuelled, captain,' Percivald said, stepping forward.

'It's too late for that,' Cass said, trying not to snap. 'If you're correct about a major assault wave, we need to get off the ground immediately. We run with what we've got.'

'Will that be enough?' Percivald asked.

'Yes,' Cass said, unwilling to elaborate. 'I suggest you board *Pauper*, sir, and strap yourself in.'

'I will only travel with you, captain, assuming you are in command of these transports,' Percivald said. 'As will the most senior officers.'

'Suit yourself,' Cass said. She told Cobb to get prepped, and hurried over to where she had spotted a thunder-faced Vaughn returning to the landing zone.

'The bastards won't give up their fuel,' he exclaimed, throwing up his hands in frustration. 'I asked them if they thought we'd be much use drawing our laspistols and getting down amongst the trenches with the grunts. They've sent me on a damned dance trying to find someone to overrule these grox-brained officers.'

It was only at that point that he seemed to notice the ones still trailing behind Cass.

'They're coming with us,' she told him. 'Orders.'

'Their orders?' Vaughn asked.

'No, from Suchen.'

'Did Havali vox you?'

'No, we've had these instructions since the start. Drop the supplies, airlift the brass.'

'And you didn't think to tell any of us?'

'I was directly ordered not to, by Havali.'

The anger that had animated Vaughn's face when he relayed the lack of fuel was nothing compared to the fury that transfixed him now.

'So what you're saying is we're here risking our lives so a few dozen privileged imbeciles can leave the men they led into this madness to die? That we've been reduced to glorified transports for Astra Militarum aristocracy?'

'By the God-Emperor, I've never heard such insubordination,' Percivald yapped, making to advance past Cass. Without thinking she put a hand against his chest, checking him. He blinked, seemingly never having had hands laid on him in his life.

'Enough,' Cass barked at Vaughn. 'We have our orders, and if you want to rant at me then you can do it after we're airborne and not under fire! You'll take a dozen of these officers and you'll make sure they're strapped in. There's another wave coming, and we've got to get out from under it on a minimum of fuel. So less talking and more doing, Hal.'

The flight lieutenant glared at her, then, without another word, turned on his heel and stalked towards his Valkyrie.

Cass led Percivald and the remaining officers to *Vagrant*, along with Commissar Vulkrov, who seemed intent on accompanying them. Korrie was just jogging round from the rear hatch, and came up short when she saw them.

'We've got company for the flight home,' Cass said. Korrie shrugged.

'Not a problem, Chief. The last of the cargo has just been hauled out. No fuel though.'

'So I've heard,' Cass said. 'We'll make do with what we've got. There's a major xenos assault underway, though, so it's time to mount up and get out.'

Cass directed Percivald and his staff in through the rear hatch, then hurried to the flier's prow.

'Chief,' Korrie called out, getting her attention from the aft cockpit before she could drop inside. The co-pilot gestured, and Cass saw two figures hurrying towards *Vagrant* from the direction of the agri-manor. It was the two Mordians, Felkin and his young aide.

'Throne damn it,' Cass hissed, spending a moment battling the temptation to simply seal the cockpit and ignore the Guard officers. Instead, she dropped back down into the dirt and saluted them.

'Had a change of heart, sir?' she asked.

'No,' Felkin said, waving his aide forward. 'Not for myself, anyway. This is Lieutenant Wellend Felkin. He's my son. Do you have space for him?'

'Probably,' Cass allowed, eyeing Wellend briefly. She could see the family resemblance now, though he was still just a slip of a boy compared to his tall, grizzled father.

'This isn't mere nepotism, captain,' Felkin said. 'I have given Wellend a dataslate with a download of the current tactical situation here. I believe Percivald exaggerates the grievousness of our situation. We are beset, it is true, but we can hold for some time yet, and there is still the possibility of a breakout. I want Wellend to argue that case with the lieutenant general, in person. I fear he is our only hope.'

'The Eji is impassable,' Cass said, not wanting to end up stuck in a debate with the Mordian, let alone instigate one back at high command. 'The bridges are down. It would take a week to repair even one.'

'The bridges are down, but the river isn't impassable,' Felkin said. 'It's fordable. The drought has caused its banks to shrink. How do you think the orks are able to attack us from the south, along Kantu Valley? Initially our defence was flush with the river because we thought, like command did, that it couldn't be crossed. But the orks used it to outflank us, and we were forced to pull further north to tighten the perimeter. I'm telling you, captain, it's fordable.'

Cass remembered the ork warbands roving south of the Eji,

the ones who had shot ineffectually up at them as they had passed by. That would explain how they had come to be on the south side of the river.

'We can make it across, with support,' Felkin carried on. 'The whole army group, or at least what's left of it. Tell Lieutenant General Havali that. Tell him not to abandon us. Tell him that the xenos are focused on our destruction, but once we are overrun, they will turn south in force, and the Eji won't stop them.'

'With respect, sir, strategic matters are above my station, but I'll make sure your son makes it to Suchen to state your case,' Cass replied. 'We really need to go now, though, or none of us will get through.'

She exchanged another salute with Felkin and mounted up. As she dropped into the cockpit, she saw the two Mordians face one another, father and son. For a moment Wellend wavered, as though he wished to embrace the brigadier. Then, what Cass took to be the old Iron Guard discipline asserted itself. They exchanged salutes and, after seeming indecision from Felkin too, he held out one hand, and they shook. Then Wellend broke off, and hurried for *Vagrant*'s rear hatch.

'Everyone strapped in, Zeke?' Cass asked over the intercom as she locked down the cockpit shield and began to run through system initialisation rites, gloved hands dancing across her control panel as the engines ignited and the primary rotors cycled up to a throaty whine. 'Tell them I won't be responsible for cleaning their brains off the walls if any one of them refuses to use the restraint harnesses.'

'*They're strapped in, Chief,*' the gunner replied.

'That's a good start, I suppose. Stow the bruisers and get your side door closed, tell the Fledgling to do the same. We need to minimise blueblood casualties.'

'Expecting to take fire, Chief?'

'Something tells me we might,' Cass said.

The auspex finished initialising, and immediately pinged with new alerts. Cass had to do a double take – it was even worse than she had feared. The Valkyrie's wideband scan was picking up dozens of hostile contacts incoming from the north and west, ragged formations of ork aircraft. Some were already over the pocket's front lines.

'We've got to get up there,' she said into the vox. 'Everyone good?'

The rest of Vagabond Squadron sounded off hastily.

'Lift-off, bearing forty-five degrees east,' she instructed, easing on the stick and the pedals simultaneously, feeling *Vagrant* responding.

Then, something hit the port wing, not the patter of small-arms they had endured before, but a solid impact that clanged off the airframe. A rocket, mercifully a dud. Ugly alert sounds blurted in her ears, *Vagrant* screaming a warning to her.

Incoming.

'Shitting Throne,' she snarled, and yanked the stick. *Vagrant* bucked but obeyed, yawing to starboard before swinging round. As it went, she saw the ground just ahead of the prow kicked up by a stitching ladder of hard rounds, as an ork fighter-bomber rocketed overhead, so close its passage caused *Vagrant* to rock from wing to wing.

'Break, break,' she instructed her pilots. 'They're on us!'

CHAPTER SIX

'Evading,' Vaughn snarled through clenched teeth, as he yanked *Rogue* to port. A flurry of hard rounds whipped at the warbird, the machine spirit's distress delivered via a strident series of alarm blurts.

'They're right on top of us,' Xijen shouted as a shadow passed over Vaughn, momentarily blotting out the daylight.

He looked up, and caught the tail end of a xenos fighter-bomber, just as the explosive that had been strapped to its underbelly dropped.

Vaughn didn't have time to evade, and by the Emperor's grace he didn't have to. The bomb plunged down ahead of *Rogue*'s lowered prow, so close he caught sight of the jagged black-and-white patterns painted on its muzzle and fins.

'Brace,' he managed to bark into the intercom just before the bomb hit the edge of the landing zone underneath them. *Rogue* was yanked to starboard, momentarily out of Vaughn's control, the air blast of the detonation causing it to buck and pitching him against his harness straps.

He wrestled with his stick, knowing that the slightest loss in altitude during lift-off would see them crashing into the ground. He managed to get *Rogue*'s nose back up, momentarily breaking formation with the rest of the squadron in exchange for not skiffing his warbird's underbelly through the dirt.

Not that there was much of a formation left. Cass was shouting at them to break over the vox, but all four fliers were already scattering. The orks were literally on top of them, scrap aircraft hurtling down from all angles, spitting hard rounds, launching rockets and dumping bombs. Only their inaccuracy had stopped anyone taking a fatal hit.

Vaughn jinked *Rogue* left and right, working the pedals as much as he dared while they were still so close to the ground, then opened up the engines. The acceleration pressed him back in his flight seat, and he heard Xijen curse instinctively.

No time for niceties, or for fancy flying. Every pilot in the squadron would be thinking the same thing – they had to get out from under the hammer. Another minute more and they'd all be pulverised.

'Not today, you green bastards,' Konstantina snapped, heaving back on her flight stick, the sudden angle making her stomach lurch.

The abrupt manoeuvre – more than risky given how little airspace was between *Ruffian* and the ground – gave the Vulture gunship an arc of fire up into the air, and into the storm of xenos aircraft.

'Frag them, flyboy,' she snarled at Straks, seated in the Vulture's aft cockpit behind her.

Straks didn't answer – he let *Ruffian* speak for him instead.

Two of the four weapons hardpoints on the wings, the twinned lascannons, spat.

An ork fighter-bomber was caught in the sudden fusillade as it came streaking down for what it must have thought was an easy kill on the near-stationary warbird, the Vulture's sudden, pinpoint turn meaning they were facing each other head-on. Konstantina laughed with vicious glee as she watched the twin streaks of las scythe off both its wings while the heavy bolter mounted on the prow's underside riddled its front grille, causing flames to engulf the cockpit.

The fighter-bomber's remains nosedived, becoming part of the deluge of metal and fire hammering the pocket.

'Em, this isn't the time or place to make a stand,' Cass' voice cracked like a whip over the vox, snapping Konstantina out of her bloodlust. *'Just get out of there!'*

As though to underscore her words, a burst of cannon shells beat against *Ruffian*'s right wing, causing the warbird to shudder as though in pain. Another fighter-bomber streaked across their bow, flak from a Hydra attempting to track it bursting in its wake.

'I know, I know,' Konstantina said, more to her own flier than to Cass. She shifted the angle to put her prow back down and heaved the stick, swinging *Ruffian* eastwards, after the rest of the squadron.

Platz grunted as he was thrown against his restraint harness by the wild pitching of *Vagrant*'s hold.

One of the officers strapped in across from him threw up all over his uniform's front, drenching his medals in bile. From the stench, it wasn't the only bodily fluid that had been expelled in the hold. Some of the Guard commanders looked as though they were screaming with terror, though between his helmet's ear protection and the howl of *Vagrant*'s engines, Platz couldn't actually hear them.

He had been confused and concerned when a dozen officers had filed into the hold just before lift-off. There had been no explanation from Cass over the intercom, besides the fact that these were now their passengers, and to make sure they were all strapped in.

Zeke had thankfully dealt with that, and the wisdom of the order was now apparent. The side hatches had been sealed, and Platz had found himself trapped inside a metal box that felt as though it was being jerked and shaken in the fist of some frustrated giant.

He could understand the discomfort of many of the senior officers – few of whom seemed to have ridden a Valkyrie in seriously contested airspace before – but this was something he had trained for. His stomach was still lurching and his body alternately pressed back in his fold-down seat or thrown against his harness straps, but he rode with the motions, keeping himself relaxed, at times closing his eyes and letting everything else subside. In a strange way, the terror of his new companions made him feel better about himself.

Perhaps he was supposed to be an aviator after all.

Vagrant took more hits. Cass had to put two hands on the stick to stop the warbird being completely thrown. She hit a switch that had been thrown back off to keep the engine airflow circulating, cancelled the latest rash of alarms, and checked the structural integrity display – the port wing had been clipped by another rocket.

'Damage report,' Cass said to Korrie, too busy yanking *Vagrant* into another evasive yaw to give the readout a proper assessment.

'*It detonated, but it was a glancing hit,*' Korrie responded. '*Some buckling on the slope plate, so you might notice a little more drag, but we've had worse. Much worse.'*

Cass wasn't sure it would stay that way for long. She was caught in a deadly dilemma, faced with the options of continuing to evade, or simply punching it.

Cobb had gone with the latter, and it looked like it was working for him – her helmet's visor display directed her towards *Pauper*, visible through the starboard side of her cockpit shield. Cobb was pulling ahead of the rest of the squadron, prow pitched forward in the familiar motion of a Valkyrie flying at full tilt.

Cass decided to do the same. The airspace above Army Group Centre's defences had descended into utter carnage, and they couldn't climb any higher. Doing so would leave them in the midst of the horde of ork fliers, not to mention the desperate defensive fire being churned out by the Guard's anti-air batteries. She witnessed a ladder of flak whip past, dangerously close to clipping *Vagrant*'s starboard wing. Ahead and above, an ork scrap-jet was hit, wing sheared off, plummeting down into a death spiral as flames ignited across its airframe and left it trailing a pillar of smoke. It fell directly ahead of *Vagrant*, in amongst the rear trenches of the pocket. The Valkyrie surged through the greasy black smoke left by its plunge, the stink catching in the back of Cass' throat as it was dragged in through the intakes.

They whipped through the smoke, and Cass realised they were hurtling out over the front line. A blizzard of las was being spat from the Guard positions into the rising wave of green thundering across no-man's-land towards them, a savage tide that, in just a few rapid heartbeats, Cass found herself flying over. 'More small-arms fire incoming,' she said, just before shots started peppering *Vagrant*'s underbelly, the orks towards the rear of the surging ground assault blazing wildly up at the Imperial fliers.

It was less concerning than the fighter-bombers with their hard-round cannons and missiles, but every pilot knew of aircraft that had been lost to simple 'metal hail'. Cass wanted to get them up, but the skies still weren't clear – the auspex was as jammed with returns as it had been above the landing zone. Worse, the angle the squadron had got out at was putting them too far south, too close to the ork emplacements along Kantu Valley. They weren't far enough out to detour back the same way they had come in.

'Can you see a break?' she asked Korrie. 'We need to swing further east before turning for the river.'

'That might be a problem, Chief,' Korrie said. *'There's inbounds all over the scopes. It looks like another wave, coming in from the east.'*

'Emperor's wounds,' Cass swore softly, snatching a glance at the auspex long enough to see that her co-pilot navigator's assessment was correct. The ork aircraft already throwing themselves against the pocket were only the first wave.

'There's a break to the north-east, between the stragglers from the northern wave and the vanguard of the one coming from the east,' Korrie said.

Cass jinked to port, avoiding a rocket-propelled grenade launched from the mobs whipping by beneath them.

'That would take us away from the river, not closer,' she said.

'It's the only way out I can see, Chief.'

Cass dared take her attention away from the fire coming from below to double-check the auspex screen, adjusting its dial to enhance the display being fed across her visor.

Korrie was right, as usual. The northern and eastern wings weren't joined up, whether by design or ork inefficiency. There was a channel of clear airspace between them. If they turned now, Vagabond Squadron could run it before the eastern wave hit, like a rapier sliding through a gap in plate armour.

Cass made her decision. She opened the vox-channel to the other three warbirds.

'Vagabonds, this is Vagabond Leader, come to new heading, twenty-three degrees north-east, on my mark. We're going to punch out through that gap. Form up on me, trail formation, level off at six hundred. That should get us away from the worst of that small-arms fire while we stay low enough to make a less tempting target for anything higher up.'

'*Cass, confirm that first part,*' crackled Vaughn's voice. '*That bearing will take us away from the river, and what about fuel? We won't make it back to Barduk.*'

'We'll think of something,' Cass said tersely. 'The only alternative is meeting that next wave head-on. I know you said I'm going to get you all killed, Hal, but I wasn't planning on making it that simple.'

CHAPTER SEVEN

Vagabond Squadron made a break for it, running hard north-east. For a while, Cass dared believe they'd make it. She had visuals on the wave coming from the east, a great mass of planes flying in what barely constituted any sort of formation, like some vast insect swarm. Their focus was on Army Group Centre, and as the Vagabonds left the pocket behind, they also left the fighting.

That was until Korrie, monitoring the auspex, warned her that they had company.

'Three hostiles, peeling away from the main formation, coming about on a northern heading,' she warned. *'Looks like they're making to follow us.'*

Cass cursed softly, flexing her stiff fingers on her stick, and her father's service tags wrapped around it. Apparently they had used up their quota of luck getting up and away from the landing zone.

'Estimated time to contact?' she asked.

'I'm going to say just under five minutes, on current headings.'

Cass checked the terrain below, looking for anything that might aid their escape. Sunset was drawing closer, the sky slowly turning a magnificent gradient of mauve, but it would be at least an hour before there was anything like enough darkness to hamper their pursuers. There was a ridgeline further east, which gave her some hope. She reassessed the chart display. Five minutes more would take them wide enough to swing back south again and make the run for Barduk, but that would then shorten the intercept course the orks were currently on.

They could keep running north-east and hope the xenos got bored and gave up the chase. Or, they could turn, and fight. She opened a link to Vaughn.

'Hal, you seeing this?'

'Just when our passengers were starting to get comfortable,' came the flight lieutenant's laconic reply.

'Think we can take them?'

'Doubt we have much choice. They're bearing down on us.'

She knew he was right. She switched the channel, addressing all three of her warbird pilots.

'We're going to take them, but to give ourselves a better chance we're going to split them. Em, I want you to break off, take up a new course heading south-east, forty degrees. *Rogue* and *Pauper* will carry on with *Vagrant*. Clear?'

'*Clear,*' Konstantina growled back over the vox, doubtless overjoyed at the prospect of fighting back.

'On my mark,' Cass said. 'Three… two… one… break.'

The Vulture gunship peeled away from its siblings. Cass gave Konstantina a thumbs-up from the cockpit, hoping she was doing the right thing. They had executed this kind of manoeuvre before, but it was always risky. And it was just going to mean more lost fuel.

'Hal, do you want to do the honours?' she asked.

'*With pleasure,*' Vaughn responded.

Cass began to bleed speed from *Vagrant*, Cobb doing the same on board *Pauper*. She kept her eyes on the sigils representing the incoming ork aircraft on the auspex. They were closing the gap fast now, easily capable of reaching speeds double that of the Valkyries.

'Watch for missile launches,' she said. 'Dump flares if you have to.'

'*You want us on the guns, Chief?*' Zeke's voice came in over the intercom.

'No. Maintain airframe integrity, I want complete control of our speed. Besides, we're about to start taking hits.'

Sure enough, the first burst of hard rounds whipped past the port side of the cockpit, under the wing, darts of red in the slowly gathering twilight. Cass swung to starboard, then immediately back to port, suspecting the xenos pilot would overcompensate to the right after their first salvo.

Rogue had a nice lead on them now, close to cresting the ridge ahead, dropping even lower towards the festering agri-fields blanketing it. Shadows were lengthening across the landscape under them. More shots laddered by, off to the starboard side this time.

'*Captain Elza,*' snapped a new voice over the intercom, so unexpected Cass blinked with surprise. '*This is Brigadier General Percivald. I need you to explain this outrageously erratic flying.*'

Cass realised the general was using the hold's intercom hard-point to contact her. This was the last thing she needed.

'General, please return to your seat and strap in,' she said. 'We are in a live aerial engagement!'

'*I don't think–*' Percivald began to exclaim, but Cass shook her head and cut the link.

'Got the numbers for me, Mel?' she asked Korrie, trying not to sound strained.

'Five degrees to starboard, and Hal needs to match that. Targets coming in at… fifty-one degrees. He'll have a bit under two seconds to adjust.'

Cass relayed the information to Vaughn, just as his warbird disappeared over the ridgeline.

'Copy that,' Vaughn replied. *'You'll have to count me in.'*

'Affirmative,' Cass responded.

It was going to take timing, precision, and a fresh, clean slice of luck, but then they were Vagabond Squadron – those were the three things they could usually count on.

'My one's on me hard, Chief,' Cobb's voice clicked. *'Not… sure I'm going to make the ridge.'*

'Bank to port,' Cass advised him, sitting forward as much as the cockpit would allow, trying to get a visual. Sure enough, Cobb's warbird had been hit – the right tail fin had been partially staved in, and it looked like a string of rounds had struck along the upper starboard side of the airframe, holing the engine – a slender line of black smoke was ribboning out behind the flier.

'Bank to port,' she reiterated. 'And as soon as I can break, I'll swing in behind him.'

'Copy that,' Cobb said, *Pauper* beginning to bank sharp-left, the manoeuvrability of the Valkyrie hopefully throwing its pursuer's aim.

'Raising the altitude,' Cass said, climbing higher as the ridgeline approached rapidly. 'You ready, Korrie?'

'Ready,' came the reply. Cass flexed her grip on the stick again, scanning her visor display, seeing more incoming fire. She held her course.

Now it was just a matter of trusting to instinct, and the God-Emperor's good graces.

* * *

'Come on, come on,' Konstantina muttered to the ork aircraft, eyes locked on her displays, grip tense on her flight stick. She was bleeding speed to a painful degree, dropping the throttle and flaring the air brakes, leaving herself an easy target. It felt unnatural, repulsive even, but it was all part of the act.

Another warning from *Ruffian*'s augurs, another deft twist and pressure to the pedals causing the Vulture gunship to jink, hard rounds spitting by. The xenos scrap-warbird was almost on top of her, and it was only her evasions – and perhaps the ork pilot's overeagerness to claim the kill – that was keeping *Ruffian* in the air.

It couldn't continue. Another few seconds and their pursuer would be so close it would be practically impossible to miss. Its hard rounds would shred *Ruffian*'s tail, riddle the wings and hole the turbojet.

Which was why the timing had to be perfect. But it was Konstantina, so it was.

At last, she felt the moment arrive. Teeth gritted against the velocity changes she knew were about to hit her, she redirected the engine to the lower-wing rotors and hit the thrust while hauling on the flight stick. The movement combined with the previous deceleration caused the Vulture's prow to buck upwards sharply while driving the angle of flight backwards, bringing the gunship to a sudden and complete halt and slamming Konstantina and Straks against their harnesses.

And just like that, the hunter became the hunted. The ork plane overshot them, rocketing straight over the top with a roar that rattled Konstantina's cockpit shield. Face set in a rictus of concentration, Konstantina kept applying plenty of throttle, and kept the prow up, her warbird's vertical lift-off and landing capabilities fully engaged.

That was the hard part. The easy part was locking on and

watching with a brief, vicious grin as Straks punched las into their former pursuer's tail, the powerful crimson bolts of energy searing right along the airframe. The xenos pilot appeared too shocked to even attempt to evade, likely still trying to work out where its prey had disappeared to.

The fighter exploded in mid-air, a fireball in the deepening twilight, burning debris raining down on the parched soil below.

'*Another notch for the cockpit tally,*' Straks said casually over the intercom.

Konstantina didn't reply. She was hungry for more, already hunting for the next kill. Her eyes darted between *Ruffian*'s auspex and the skyline, comparing readouts and visuals with an ease born out of lethal experience.

A few seconds more, and she had identified the optimal target. She swung *Ruffian* around and gunned the engines.

Zeke shoved the general down into his seat and fixed the harness over his chest, no easy feat given that, with the wild pitching and rolling of the deck, he could only let go of the ceiling's support bar for a second at a time.

The general, young and red-faced with rage, was shouting something at Zeke, but the din that filled a Valkyrie's hold during flight made it impossible to hear what he was saying. Platz was thankful for that, and thankful that it had been Zeke who had got up to wrestle the officer back into the seated position. He didn't want to do anything that might draw their ire, or risk a dressing-down once they got back to Barduk. A commissar had boarded with the officers back in the pocket, and had watched the whole interaction darkly from where he was strapped in at the hold's far end.

The political officer alone looked to be in a fit state to take names, ranks and numbers. All the others they'd picked up were dishevelled and sweating, and several had been sick. The one opposite, a portly woman in a dark purple uniform jacket trimmed with silver lace and epaulettes, had her eyes screwed shut while her lips moved – Platz wondered if it was a prayer or some sort of soothing catechism or half-remembered childhood lullaby from the culture of whatever world in the God-Emperor's domain she hailed from.

Platz found the extent of their fear and discomfort oddly reassuring, and had further doused his nerves by trying to guess at different regiments and ranks. The officer directly to his left on the port side of the hold he recognised as a Mordian. He also looked by far the youngest of the assembled staff – perhaps even younger than Platz.

The youth in question seemed to have gone into a panicked trance, just staring straight ahead, pale-faced, but when Platz glanced at him he looked back. Their eyes met. Knowing that, even sitting next to him, he probably wouldn't be able to hear him if he spoke, Platz just slowly raised a thumb, making a half-hearted attempt at reassuring him.

A spray of heavy-calibre rounds from the pursuing xenos aircraft hit the hold's topside. These ones penetrated, punching down into the decking plate between the occupants, all bar one, which ricocheted. It retained enough force to hammer through Platz's helmet, skull, and blow his brains out over the Mordian's shocked face.

'The Fledgling's down, repeat, the Fledgling's down,' Cass heard Zeke yell over the intercom. *'We've got hold penetrations!'*

No time for remorse, or even to demand more detail on the extent of the damage. One more burst like the last and they'd be blown from the sky.

Orks were predictable enemies, right up until they weren't, a tactical paradox that had been the death of many an Imperial aviator. Cass had to trust that their raw aggression would line them up for her.

The crest of the ridge was just ahead, sweeping closer at reflex-response speeds. Cass pulled on the stick one more time, desperate for a fraction more height, relaying Korrie's words to her via the vox as she did so.

'Cresting in three… two… one.'

And then they were over, chaff from the brittle crops on the ridgeline's top billowing and eddying around them.

Death passed them by, faster than thought.

Vaughn accelerated before he could see the target, and came over the crest of the ridge spitting las.

He had turned *Rogue* hard as soon as he had passed the eminence, making full use of the Valkyrie's manoeuvrability. It was, on paper, just a case of lining up on the coordinates Cass had given him cross-referenced with the auspex display, and getting the countdown right.

Vagrant, having climbed higher, ripped over the crest, going in the opposite direction. A few hundred feet lower and it would have collided with *Rogue*. As it was, Vaughn was under Cass and rising, the upturned angle giving him an arc on the xenos warplane hurtling after the squadron leader.

One moment, crystallised perfectly. A breath, a heartbeat, all he had to make sure the alignment was true and pray Xijen had timed it right as well. He had – he was Vaughn's co-pilot for a reason. He squeezed the trigger toggle. It was instinct more than anything, instinct and calculation, the two tools of a good aviator.

In that perfect, vanishingly eternal instant, Vaughn saw the xenos craft, as ugly an alien war machine as had ever taken flight. Its fuselage looked like nothing more than a conglomeration of jagged, red-painted scrap metal, upon which two wings had been bolted. Its prow was a broad, rusting engine grille. Coming up as he was almost from its underside, he couldn't see the cockpit.

Xijen hit the las. *Rogue*'s prow cannon discharged one, two, three times in quick succession, lancing beams of red brilliance up at the ork flier as it whipped overhead in its pursuit of Cass, not yet realising it was already dead.

The first two las bolts missed, angles and speed failing to match, searing up ahead of the target rather than spearing it.

The third hit. It drilled a hole through the prow's underbelly, flashing straight through and out the top of where Vaughn assumed the cockpit had to be.

Pilot kill-shot.

The aircraft was over and past *Rogue*, gone by before the effect of the las bolt became obvious. He twisted, just in time to catch an impression of it plunging away behind them like a leaden weight. Vaughn didn't see where it impacted down the reverse side of the slope, but he didn't need to.

'That's for my sister, you bastard,' he snarled. 'Good shooting, Xijen.'

Cass was sawing *Vagrant* to port as soon as she caught *Rogue* slashing past beneath her. It was partly to try and throw her pursuer if Vaughn missed, though Korrie, craning her neck in the aft cockpit, reported the manoeuvre had been a success – the xenos was down and burning.

The other reason for the port turn was to try and save *Pauper*. Cobb's warbird had been hit again, and Cass doubted he'd be able to evade for more than another minute. Sending him off in another direction had opened up an angle on his tail, but Cass needed to get *Vagrant* higher up and locked on.

She had already lost *Scoundrel* and Vaughn's sister over Ushen. It seemed she'd lost the Fledgling today. She couldn't lose Cobb and *Pauper* as well.

She heaved *Vagrant* up, Korrie offering her possible firing angles, nudging them via the shared system link into her helmet display. Too far out still. Cass heard a strangled cry over the vox, and saw the smoke plume from *Pauper* worsen. The warbird dumped flares, a glittering shower of luminance in the deepening twilight, causing a rocket that had been hounding it to detonate prematurely.

'Go low, Cobb, go low,' she urged. They were approaching the steep flank of the valley itself. The sudden adjustments necessitated by a climb would give the more responsive Valkyrie the edge, but first it would have to make it up through the ork's fire.

No target lock still. Cass began to shoot, unable to keep her frustration in check, seeing the prow lascannon bolts beam away, red wrath rendered impotent by angles and distance, twinkling away into nothingness in the growing shadows.

Then she saw *Ruffian*. Cass hadn't even been sure what had happened to the Vulture gunship – she had been too locked in her own personal duel. Yet Konstantina had clearly not only ended the threat posed by the ork aircraft that had been tailing her, but had spotted *Pauper*'s plight ahead of *Vagrant*, and was now gunning full throttle for the wounded warbird.

Ruffian had hung low after the first kill, but now rose up to cut along the flight path of the ork plane running *Pauper* down. Rockets streaked from under the gunship's wings, spears of light in the gloom, but none struck true. The xenos fighter was firing too, at *Pauper*, shots sparking off its airframe. A few seconds more and it would be gone.

Then, finally, *Ruffian*'s prow heavy bolter opened up. Straks tracked the stream of mass-reactive rounds ahead of the aircraft, tracers streaking away into the night, intercepting the ork flier as it thundered after *Pauper*. It flew into its own demise, its fuselage riddled, fire igniting from the holes punched in its big, blocky engine section.

It fell, slamming into the valley slope. *Pauper* was still flying.

Cass closed her eyes for a moment, feeling pure relief render her limbs weak.

'Good shooting, *Ruffian*,' she said into her vox-mic.

'Three kills on a supply run, not too bad,' Konstantina responded.

'I fear there'll be time for more yet,' Cass pointed out.

'As Zeke says, "as He wills",' Konstantina quipped. Cass smiled, her eyes passing from the burning wreckage of the ork aircraft to where *Pauper* was coming around to fall in with its three siblings.

'How's it looking, Cobb?' she asked.

'Still assessing,' his voice crackled back. *'Handling is alright, but the engine's definitely holed.'*

'Do you think you'll need to set down?'

'No, definitely not out here anyway. We'll be alright for now.'

Darkness had almost fallen. That alone felt like a blessing. Cass ordered her warbirds to climb to six thousand feet and, finally, wheel south.

'We need to get to the other side of the river before the tanks run dry, or we're as good as dead,' Vaughn said. *'Even if we do make it across, we know the xenos have a presence there as well.'*

'We switch speed for quiet,' Cass said. 'Keep climbing to maximum ceiling, instruments only, and hope we don't run into any more ork air-mobs. If we're lucky, we might meet Bix or another friendly sortie. Do you think *Pauper* can handle the ride, Cobb?'

'Don't have much choice,' Cobb replied bluntly.

'There's contacts down below,' Konstantina put in. *'Looks like an encampment. I'm guessing you're not going to let me take a passing shot or two, Chief?'*

'Negative,' Cass said. 'This is why we need to go higher. We're way beyond the river front or the edge of the pocket. Orbital scans show this area is infested with ork camps, all the way along the valley side. Nothing Imperial in our vicinity either, there's nothing up in support that we can call on. This area is a no-fly zone.'

'*But what about fuel?*' Cobb asked.

'I'm working on that,' Cass responded. 'I'll update you in a moment.'

'*At least the bluebloods don't know how karked we are,*' Vaughn said. '*Yet.*'

PART TWO

CHAPTER EIGHT

Vagabond Squadron shut down all but the essential systems and went dark, flying as high in the night sky as Cass dared take *Pauper*.

The xenos were looking for them, or perhaps expected some kind of retaliation following the day's assaults on the pocket. Search beams stabbed up at Kanai's heavens, roving unsteadily, creating pillars of illumination that slashed through one another like duelling blades. Thankfully the sky was not as clear as it had been during the day. There was a degree of cloud cover, which the squadron stuck to as best it could, though the turbulence didn't make the ride any easier for their miserable passengers.

Still, something must have caught the flicker of their underbellies or the roll of their engines echoing back from the valley's flank, because eventually an ork anti-aircraft gun began to hammer away. More took up the barrage, likely goaded into letting fly as much by the sudden wrath of the neighbouring batteries as by any suggestion that they had caught sight of Vagabond Squadron.

In a matters of minutes the sky, already cut up by search beams, was criss-crossed by ladders of tracer rounds and covered with flak bursts.

'Make for the valley sides,' Cass said, knowing the sheer weight of the indiscriminate bombardment meant there was a risk they'd start taking hits. A slight adjustment took them over the crest of the valley's eastern flank, leaving the worst of the hail of shot and shell to rumble away below them.

The movement meant they had swung further away from their objective, but Cass hoped to correct course when the xenos had settled once more.

Korrie found a possible solution to their fuel problem soon after. She had drawn out a pocket chart from her flight suit and was analysing it using the hooded red lumen lamp all pilots carried, its bloody illumination not running the risk of lighting up the cockpit at a distance.

'There's a promethium hub just south-east of our current route, on the far side of the river,' she told Cass. 'Looks like it's at the opposite end of one of the destroyed bridges, Highway Crossing Twelve-Seven.'

Korrie read out the coordinates and Cass cross-referenced it with her own chart. Her co-pilot was correct.

'It's no use to us if it's been drained, though,' she mused. 'And it would take us even further out of our way. If we put down and the wells are empty, we'd barely have enough left to get airborne again.'

'At least we'd be south of the river,' Korrie pointed out. 'Looks like it would be a… two-day trek to Imperial lines if we had to make it on foot. We've got just about enough water and rations to last that, and we should still have comms, so we might be able to arrange a pickup.'

All of that made sense, and there was the flipside – they simply weren't getting back to Barduk with what they currently had in the tanks. They were going to have to drop somewhere.

Cass relayed the plan to the other pilots. As she had expected, Vaughn was the first to find fault with it.

'We don't know if there's actually any prom there,' he pointed out. *'And there are xenos south of the river. They might have drained it already.'*

'It's out of the way for either side,' Cass pointed out. 'We're a good deal south-east of the pocket now, and still west of Torr City. If there are xenos there, they won't be numerous. Besides, I don't see how there's much alternative.'

'If we put down, we're sitting targets,' Vaughn said. *'If there are any orks up here tailing us, they'll be able to fall on us with impunity. We'd be vulnerable. I think we should push the warbirds as far as they will go, and only land when we're running on fumes. Then we trek the rest of the way on foot.'*

'That would mean abandoning Cobb and *Pauper*,' Cass pointed out. 'He's losing fuel, his range is now less than ours. If we run until we've got nothing left, Cobb will need to put down well before we do. So do we carry on without him?'

Vaughn was silent. Cass made her decision.

'Adjust course south-east by eight degrees, on my mark,' she said. 'Maintain formation, essential systems only. And keep up your visual scanning.'

They were flying for Highway Crossing 12-7.

The squadron continued to maintain as high an altitude as Cass dared while following the course of the valley's steep eastern flank. Eventually Cass caught slight, flickering illumination amidst the darkness yawning to her left, and realised she was looking at the edge of Torr City, the massive industrial sprawl that ended just short of the valley's eastern side.

That was where the heart of the planetary conflict was being fought, there and in Ushen to the west. Over eight million

Imperial soldiers were engaged fighting for the two megalopolises. As the third front the Eji Valley paled in comparison, yet it should have made the difference. Army Group Centre's drive up the valley should have cut the ork forces in half, separating both cities and allowing the Astra Militarum to concentrate, first against one, then against the other. Instead, Army Group Centre had been stalled and then pinned in place, and now it had been abandoned to its fate. Cass did what she had done since first reading her orders in Suchen Palace, and tried to avoid pondering what she had become a part of.

Torr City became a latticework of fire, lighting up the eastern sky with an ugly orange glow. Cass considered the fact that they had now drifted so far east it might be easier to make a run for Imperial forces fighting in the city than for those south of the river. She dismissed the possibility without voicing it to Korrie or any of the other pilots. By all reports, Torr was as much a mess as Ushen, a raw urban slugfest with no clear front lines, a meat-grinder that high command were happily continuing to feed. Ushen had taught Vagabond Squadron that death was everywhere in Kanai's cities, and Cass wouldn't be taking them over any of them unless directly ordered to.

The Ushen operation had been Jakyra's fault, or so Cass had told herself. Vagabond Squadron had been instructed to provide insertion for a Tempestus Scions platoon intent on striking down the xenos warlord leading the campaign against the city.

There had been warning signs right from the beginning. Intel on the ork commander's exact location had been scanty, as was knowledge about what exactly was protecting the xenos. There was little in the way of a solid extraction plan, and initially the Vagabonds had even been instructed to hold station over the drop zone while the Scions completed their mission, a command that even Jakyra had considered suicidal enough to eventually overrule. That was as far as her assistance had gone – it was clear the whole thing had been the brainchild of someone from the upper command echelons, rather than a proper joint Navy-Tempestus venture, and that had doomed it from the beginning.

Ultimately, Jakyra had wanted a victory for her Valkyries, with minimal recourse to the other wings. Her willingness to provide air support for the Militarum regardless of risk helped ensure the approval of the ground-pounder leadership and consequently strengthened her position as air marshal, at least for the duration of the campaign. Both the warbirds and their crews were currency to be spent. Cass supposed her willingness to do that was why Jakyra was air marshal, and the likes of Orlov continued in the role of wing commander.

Yet Cass had been the one who agreed to it all. She hadn't voiced more than token complaints, even though she suspected the plan was far too risky. She should have pushed for more intelligence gathering, for more top cover. They had ended up losing a warbird, *Scoundrel*, and four good aviators – Marsten, Sprats, Fellows, and Vaughn's sister, Eleanor, killed when a flight of xenos deathkopters had struck while they were pulling back from the objective. Eleanor had died protecting Vaughn's flier, and his anger and sorrow in the aftermath of her loss had been terrifyingly raw. He had made no secret of the fact he blamed Cass for letting them fly against such long odds. She hadn't known how to react to that without simply falling back on rank and authority. Privately, she hoped Vaughn forgave her, but feared that he never would.

Such morose thoughts haunted Cass as they carried on southeast, grazing the valley's edge. She experienced the strange, quiet loneliness of night flying, twinned with the tiredness that came on after a fraught combat experience. The temptation was to stop scanning, stop checking visuals, to fly on autopilot. She knew she couldn't afford to do that. They were still far from safe.

She busied herself by sending an emergency alert to Barduk, requesting top cover and warning of the ork presence south of the Eji, but she wasn't sure if it went through. Signals were badly chopped up along the valley side, and she couldn't tell if it was simple atmospherics, or the work of ork scrambling devices in the sprawling encampments below. Perhaps it was both.

'*Chief, the general's getting pretty insistent back here,*' Zeke's voice ticked in Cass' ear. '*He says he's ordering you to turn the hold intercom back on.*'

'Tell him it's broken,' Cass said, too tired to want to field what she was sure would just be more complaints and ill-conceived commands from Percivald. 'Tell him a hard round blew it out earlier.'

She doubted that would be enough to placate him, but she also trusted Zeke to remain unfazed by his wrath.

They caught sight of the Eji not long after. It was a silvery ribbon in the darkness, strung out below them. Its appearance sent an unexpected surge of relief through Cass. Even knowing the orks were capable of crossing over, it still represented progress on the way to safety. They were about halfway there.

On Korrie's advice Cass had the squadron adjust course slightly, following the waterway a short distance while beginning their descent. Korrie spotted the bridge they were looking for, or rather what remained of it, debris choking the river. The water foamed and glittered around the nubs of its central pillars. The Marauder bombers of 899th Wing had done their work well when they had wrecked the Eji's crossing points, after it had become clear the offensive had failed and a counter-attack was a real possibility.

Vagabond Squadron's new objective lay directly on the far

side of the bridge, a refuelling hub that would once have serviced ground traffic heading south along the valley floor. Cass' rising hopes plummeted again when she caught sight of what she had feared most – there were lights among the buildings and promethium well stacks.

'Throne damn it,' she muttered, reinitialising the auspex and reviewing its finding across her visor. It took a moment for *Vagrant*'s senses to reawaken fully, but when they did they showed several dozen living returns in and around the hub.

'*I knew it,*' came Vaughn's voice, having presumably done the same thing as Cass. '*I told you the xenos would have occupied it.*'

'*Could those be Imperial?*' Cobb wondered.

'I didn't think there were any outposts this far east, or this close to the river,' Cass admitted. 'We're going to have to clear it.'

'*You want us to go in hot on a promethium hub we need in order to refuel?*' Vaughn asked disbelievingly.

'*It could also be locals,*' Korrie pointed out. '*Scavengers.*'

'*They've probably drained the well stacks anyway,*' Vaughn carried on.

'No sign of any intact vehicles,' Cass pointed out. 'If it's xenos, I doubt they've been able to ford the river with any yet. This area has been no-man's-land since the start of the invasion, so chances are the stacks shouldn't be too heavily depleted. Konstantina, run a pass on the hub and see what you can pick up. If it's orks, they'll let us know soon enough.'

'*Affirmative,*' Konstantina said.

'And weapons off, for now! We don't want to turn that place into a fireball.'

'*Understood.*'

While the rest of Vagabond Squadron peeled off and began circling at mid altitude, *Ruffian* continued to descend, swooping down from out of the night sky. Cass leaned over in the cockpit, keeping an eye on the buildings as the Vulture gunship swung by. After a moment, she caught the telltale flare of muzzle flashes from amongst the structures.

She closed her eyes, feeling a moment's plummeting despair as Konstantina's voice came back.

'*Oh yeah, it's xenos alright!*'

'*We can't engage them in a firefight, not where they're camped out,*' Vaughn said. '*And we don't have the numbers or portable fire-power to disengage and attack on foot.*'

Cass spent a second assessing their options, then spoke to Konstantina again.

'Em, can you put a few rounds over the roof? Make sure you're shooting above the wells. It might flush them out.'

'*Glad you trust me not to light the whole place up,*' Konstantina said, before Cass caught the flare of heavy bolter fire, and the slashing luminance of tracer rounds arcing dangerously close over the top of the hub. The Vulture had swung round and gone into hover mode, pounding the air above the promethium stacks.

'*This is madness,*' Vaughn said, but Cass ignored him. Konstantina came back to her again a moment later.

'*Some of them are making a break for it,*' she said, sounding exultant. '*Wrong move, you little xenos beasts!*'

Ruffian swung up over the buildings and began to blaze into the ground on the far side without orders, presumably mowing down those who had been unwise enough to attempt to flee from the hub's protection. There was no longer any sign of any return fire, and mercifully, no indication of any rockets or any other projectiles being launched against *Ruffian*, at what would have amounted to point-blank range.

'*They're the small ones,*' Konstantina said, Cass able to hear the rhythmic background thudding of the Vulture's prow heavy bolter over the vox. '*What do they call them? Grots!*'

That made sense, Cass supposed. According to her *Imperial Aviator's Uplifting Primer*, the smaller breed of xenos were often employed in scavenging duties, and were typically altogether more cowardly than their ork masters. Cass noted that all but one of the auspex returns had disappeared beneath Konstantina's barrage – the sole survivor was still holed up in the main hub building. Presumably, that was the ork who had been directing its smaller cousins.

'I'll come around and put down, flush the last of them out on foot,' Cass decided. '*Vagrant* and *Pauper*, keep circling until Korrie or I vox that it's clear, then bring yourselves down as close as you can to those promethium stacks and get them hooked up.'

She waited for the inevitable complaint from Vaughn but, for once, he held his tongue. Cass switched channels so she was only addressing Konstantina.

'Em, I swear to the God-Emperor if you engage again when I explicitly order you not to, I'm going to be asking Jakyra for a new gunship pilot.'

'*You're welcome,*' Konstantina responded, and Cass could picture the grin on her face as she spoke.

CHAPTER NINE

Ruffian continued to hover above the hub, acting as overwatch, like some great, menacing insectoid whose engine rotors beat at the night air. Cass landed *Vagrant* in a field about one hundred and fifty yards west of the buildings, across the highway. She killed the engines and spoke to Korrie.

'You okay with this?'

'The auspex says it's just one xenos. I reckon we can take it.'

'Not often we get to act like grunts,' Cass said, checking her laspistol. She realised her hands were shaking. She closed her eyes, breathed out, then uncoupled her helmet, undid her harness, popped the cockpit and dropped to the dirt.

The night was cool, a blessed contrast to the intense heat of the day. The air was shuddering with the rhythmic beating of *Ruffian*'s rotors, echoing back from the surrounding fields as it held station above the hub. There was no illumination coming from any of the buildings now.

'Tell Em to stab-lumen it,' Cass called up to Korrie before

her co-pilot exited the aft cockpit. She wanted as few surprises as possible.

Korrie got on the vox, and a few seconds later a spear of white light lanced the central building of the station, centred on its front door.

'Em's asking if she can open up on the main structure,' Korrie called back down. 'Says it's far enough away from the prom hubs not to be a risk.'

'Tell her no, and if she does I will personally shove her head through *Ruffian*'s rotors,' Cass snapped.

Her grip on the laspistol was made clumsy by her flight gloves, so she pulled them off, finding her palms cold and sweaty. She was still shaking, and her throat felt painfully dry.

She had conducted ground operations before. During the Dagoran Repression, three years earlier, *Vagrant* had been clipped by anti-air and forced into an emergency landing. Cass, Korrie, Zeke and their other gunner at the time, Marwell, had retreated to the hold and manned the heavy bolters, holding the recidivist scum at bay until the Guard had arrived and driven them off. On Holdmire's World, years before that, Cass had briefly fought a kroot xenoform, during a deadly night-time raid on an airbase. It had been her first face-to-face encounter with an alien. Korrie had shot it before it could gut her with its long, broad-bladed knife.

None of those experiences meant Cass was looking forward to what she was about to do.

'Wait here for a moment,' she told Korrie, making a decision. She reached back into the cockpit to disengage the rear hatch, then went round to the tail of the Valkyrie.

The interior of *Vagrant*'s hold was in a sorry state. Platz's corpse was still strapped to his side gunner's seat between the officers, the side of his helmet staved in. Half of his face was corpse-white and peaceful-looking, but the other half was covered in a sheet of drying crimson. More of his blood had splashed across the deck and spattered the surrounding officers, as well as the pict servitor still clamped and inactive against the far wall.

All of Army Group Centre's evacuees were dishevelled, pale-faced and exhausted-looking, none more so than Percivald. At the sight of Cass in the hatchway he threw off his restraints and rose unsteadily, as though still struggling with the pitching of the Valkyrie's deck.

'Where are we?' he snapped, grabbing the hand railing along the roof and approaching the hatch. 'Is this Suchen?'

'It is not,' Cass said stonily, anticipating what was coming next. 'We're just south of the Eji, well short of our own lines still. Because your troops refused to resupply us, we've had to make an unscheduled stop at a promethium hub to refuel.'

'We're still in hostile territory?' Percivald demanded.

'It was that, or fly until we drop out of the sky. If everything goes according to plan, we'll be underway again soon enough. We can have you at Suchen by midday tomorrow. But first we need to clear the hub.'

'You mean it's occupied?' Percivald said, looking increasingly alarmed.

'More or less. My Vulture gunship has already cleared out most of the xenos. It was just a few scavengers who had strayed south of the river, but it looks like there's at least one remaining. We can't just blow the main building for fear of igniting the promethium wells. So we're going to clear it out on foot.'

'I hope you don't intend to simply abandon us while you do that,' Percivald said.

It took a great deal of control for Cass not to snap at him that he was supposed to be a soldier in the Astra Militarum, and that fears of being 'abandoned' shouldn't even register in his thinking.

'My gunner, Ezekiel, will remain with you,' she said instead. 'But I would appreciate your assistance in ensuring the station is properly cleared before we begin refuelling. I'm asking for volunteers to join my navigator and I.'

'You have more pilots! Why not take them?'

'I don't want to land at a distance from the wells, dismount, take control of the hub, then have to remount and bring my Valkyries into refuelling range,' Cass said. 'That would lengthen the entire operation, expend further fuel, and risk one of my warbirds that has already taken damage. The less it has to touch down and lift off the better. That goes for your fellow officers it's transporting too.'

Percivald looked set to reply, but Cass carried on over him, speaking to the other passengers instead.

'Are any of you who are armed able to assist us in clearing the hub?'

'I will,' said a voice. Cass thought for a surreal, heart-stopping moment that it was the corpse of Platz that had uttered the words, before realising it was the bloodied figure strapped in beside him who had spoken.

It was the young Mordian, Wellend. He freed himself and stood, looking no more stable on his feet than Percivald, but when he spoke again his voice was full of conviction.

'I will come with you,' he said, then drew his sidearm, a las-pistol, and showed it to Cass, as though she might think he was lying. 'I'm armed.'

'He will not be the only one,' said another voice from the back of the hold.

Commissar Vulkrov had stood up, his deathly stare not upon Cass but upon the two rows of officers that had remained seated.

With icy slowness, Vulkrov unbuttoned the flap of his las-pistol's holster.

'I'll go,' the man nearest to him, a Ventrillian, declared, rising too. His expression was more determined than afraid, as though disgusted that he had initially hesitated.

'That's probably enough,' Cass said, deciding that if something went wrong, she didn't want to stand accused of having put too many officers in harm's way.

'I will accompany you as well,' Vulkrov said.

'As you wish,' Cass said, before speaking to Zeke.

'They're all yours.'

The gunner rolled back the side door and swung down the heavy bolter, while Cass beckoned Wellend, Vulkrov and the Ventrillian down out of the flier. She led them a few paces away, joined by Korrie from the prow, before pausing to address them, speaking to Wellend in particular.

'How old are you, lieutenant, Terran standard?' she asked him. To his credit, Wellend frowned.

'With respect, sir, I'm not sure that's relevant. I have a side-arm and I'm capable of using it.'

Cass laughed without really meaning to.

'That's good enough for me, Mordian,' she said before he could take offence, then gestured at Korrie, introducing her to the little gathering. 'This is my co-pilot, Flight Sergeant Korrie. You might be thinking she could wrestle an ork and win, and you'd be right. If she tells you to do something, do it. Understood?'

'Understood,' Wellend said.

'I'm Major Marquen d'Kato,' the Ventrillian declared with a guarded nod to Cass and Korrie. 'I was aide-de-camp to General Westlake before his death. I'm sure, if the good general were still with us, he'd have volunteered as well.'

'I'm sure he would have,' Cass said, turning her attention to Vulkrov. The commissar seemed to have nothing to add but, with a whisper of steel on leather, he drew the sword he carried at his hip.

'I wouldn't want to be within stabbing distance of any xenos in there,' Cass pointed out, eyeing the blade.

'That is why you are not in the Imperial Guard, captain,' Vulkrov said humourlessly. 'Come. Let us be about our duties.'

'I'll take point,' Cass said. 'Follow my lead, and stay close.'

'Sure I can't go first, Chief?' Korrie asked.

Cass would have loved to let her lead the way into the hub, but she knew she couldn't. Not in front of the Guard. She forced the temptation from her mind.

'Can't have my aft cockpit navigator in front of me,' she told her. 'It wouldn't feel natural. Follow.'

Cass set off towards the hub, which stood brilliantly illuminated in the surrounding darkness. She had to clamber over a pair of highway barriers, one on either side of the roadway, her boots briefly pounding on the rockcrete surface between them. She could see details she had overlooked from higher up, burned-out groundcars and agri-haulers heaped along the side of the roadway, rusting. They had presumably been abandoned at the start of the invasion and then bulldozed out of the way during Army Group Centre's initial advance north, before the bridges had been blown.

It was strange how utterly different existence was from ground level. She would have barely noted the wrecked trail of vehicles while flying above them, but now spent what felt like an age having to negotiate a path through them on the far side of the highway, trying not to lose her footing in the dark. The hub ahead, with its promethium stacks looming in front of it, seemed like a towering citadel, filled with terrors that could not have troubled her when she was in the safety of *Vagrant's* cockpit.

She told herself she was being an idiot. She couldn't even be completely certain the Valkyrie's auspex had given her an accurate return. Perhaps there were no xenos left in the main building.

Or perhaps there was more than one.

Heart pounding, she sprinted into the spotlight being thrown down by *Ruffian*, feeling the beating of the gunship's single F200-KW4 vector-turbojet vibrating the air and making the few remaining intact windows ahead of her rattle in their frames.

She half expected fire to blaze from one of them, for one of the xenos brute weapons to cut her down before she reached the main doors. Instead, she banged against them without incident, and was about to kick them in when a voice hissed behind her for her to wait.

To her surprise, it was Wellend. She came up short, and the Mordian pulled her and Korrie to the side of the doorway, d'Kato and Vulkrov on the opposite side.

'Don't run straight in,' he said, keeping them close so he didn't have to shout over the noise of *Ruffian* holding station above them. 'You'll silhouette yourself against the light. Easy target for anything inside.'

Cass felt foolish – pilot she might be, but like all Imperial Navy aviators she had been trained in basic infantry drills. In her headlong rush, partly in an attempt not to think about what she was doing in case she faltered, she had totally neglected even the most basic principles of close-quarters combat. It had taken a Guard officer, no matter how young, to remind her.

'Stack up,' she instructed, getting the other two against the wall behind her, Korrie's hand on her shoulder, while she faced d'Kato and Vulkrov. 'Wellend, Korrie and I will go left, Vulkrov and d'Kato, you go right. Ready?'

'Ready,' came the response.

Cass kicked the door in and swung to the left, laspistol up, wishing she wasn't still half-dazzled from the stab-lumen. The darkness beyond the light spearing through the open doorway was overwhelming.

She crouched, sidearm poised, heartbeat pounding a tattoo in her ears as she braced for a blow or shot that didn't come.

Her eyes adjusted to her new surroundings. The left side of the hub building's interior was taken up by a bank of promethium assignment counters, where petitioners wishing to draw from the wells could state their case and offer payment. The right side had consisted of racks packed with foodstuffs that could be purchased alongside permission to use the wells, though most of them had been overturned and their contents devoured or left littering the floor. The room had the stale stink of the xenos about it, but nothing moved.

Cass dared snatch a glance over at the others, and nodded Korrie and Wellend towards the counters on their side of the room. They advanced warily, Korrie moving to outflank the stands while Wellend swung his laspistol over their top.

'Clear,' he said, voice a dry rasp.

Cass pursed her lips and picked her way towards the fallen racks Vulkrov and d'Kato were securing, wary for anything that might be lurking among the detritus. Konstantina had said the targets she'd mown down as they tried to flee from the far side of the building had been grots. By all reports they were small and cunning, the opposite of the orks that ruled them. The last thing Cass wanted was for one of the creatures to ambush her from amongst the few racks that were still standing.

'There's a vox-booth back here,' Korrie called softly from behind the counters. 'Clear as well.'

D'Kato reached the far side of the room. 'Got a door,' he called out softly. 'Sign says prom assigners and maintenance only. Probably just a storeroom.'

The door exploded outwards with a crash, followed by a shuddering roar.

Something came charging out, hunched forward but still towering over every human in the room. Cass got an impression of gaping tusks around a stinking, open maw and small, piggy eyes, surging towards her with terrifying speed.

D'Kato was the closest, and didn't have a chance to get a shot off before the beast hit him, moving with terrifying speed and aggression.

The fine burgundy-and-white uniform turned dark crimson as a single blow from the great cleaver the brute was wielding bisected General Westlake's former aide, chopping him in half as easily as one of the Munitorum cooks back at Camp Yuzen might have cleaved a large fruit in two.

The beast swatted aside the gory mess with another bellow. Cass brought up her laspistol, heart hammering, hands shaking, but Vulkrov was in the way. The commissar brandished his sword.

'For the Emperor,' he shouted, and lunged.

The sword plunged through the ork's midriff, its keen point driven by Vulkrov's strength through leather and dense musculature.

The ork stopped, and so did everyone else. It looked down at the sword, then at Vulkrov, who seemed frozen in his moment of victory.

Then, it punched the commissar.

The side of Vulkrov's head caved in and his neck snapped. The ork clutched the brass hilt of the sword and simply snapped it, leaving half the blade still buried in its torso. Then, it lunged at Cass.

She yelled, tripped and fired, all at the same time. Her first las bolt punched into the ceiling and blew out an inactive lumen bar in a shower of sparks. The back of her heel had snagged on one of the fallen racks, and she went down on top of it with a clatter, trying to roll desperately away.

The trip saved her life. The ork swung its massive cleaver,

but the butcher's blade of a weapon cut only air, and it was forced to arrest its headlong rush before it too fell over what had tripped Cass.

She scrambled arm over arm on all fours to get away from the monstrosity. Korrie and Wellend both opened fire over her, the *snap-crack* of discharges filling the confined space. The xenos bellowed. The combined firepower of the two pistols only seemed to make it angry.

Cass snatched at the next rack, this one still standing, and used it to haul herself up. Somehow she'd kept her grip on her own sidearm. She turned and loosed a shot off, seeing the crimson bolt of energy sear into one of the ork's trunk-like arms but seemingly do no more than singe it. She grabbed hold of the rack's side as it continued to come at her and hauled it down with a crash in the beast's path, catching it partly beneath the frame.

It beat its way through with another bellow, metal buckling in its fist and coming apart under a few chops of its cleaver.

Cass fired again, trying to hit it in the eye. Instead, the shot clipped the side of its head, deflecting off its thick skull and burning away one pointed ear tip. Now it was definitely angry.

It charged again, thundering at Cass like a bull grox. She found herself frozen, rooted to the spot.

Korrie slammed her aside and took the force of the impact. The navigator, big though she was, was flattened like a child by the alien, hitting the hub floor with a gristly crunch. The beast half trampled her, almost tripping itself again, and raised its brute weapon.

'No!' Cass roared, throwing herself at it and grabbing on to its arm. It shook her off with an animalistic snort, rounding on her, grabbing at her with its other hand. A grip closed around her throat, immediately shutting her airways, feeling like it would crush her spine.

Her finger clenched on the laspistol's trigger, emptying most of its power pack into the far wall. She stopped being properly aware of what was happening, able to think only about the desperate need to release the pressure around her throat. Blood pounded in her temples and everything started to ache. Blotches spread across her vision, her hands smacking and striking uselessly against the ork's solid body.

She didn't want to die. Not like this. Not at all. Please, God-Emperor.

Then the pressure was gone. It was replaced by a slamming impact against her forehead, but her flight helmet took the worst of it. The xenos had just cracked her head off the edge of one of the petition counters. She reeled back, gasping air down into her aching lungs, and found that the reason the ork had relinquished her was because Korrie, still pinned under it, was shooting her laspistol directly into its ankle.

Huffing with apparent annoyance, the beast kicked Korrie and reached down, snatching her by the collar of her flight suit. It hefted her up like she weighed nothing.

Cass fumbled for a fresh power pack, seeing that Wellend too was trying to reload, his hands shaking.

There was a crash like thunder, making Cass flinch. She thought briefly that *Ruffian* had just launched its rocket pods at the building, and that the ceiling was about to come slamming down and bury them all. Then she realised the ork's head had exploded.

Nightmarishly, even with blood squirting from the ruination of its neck, the thing still stood and maintained its grip on Korrie, as though the rest of its body was struggling to accept that it was dead. Then, as abrupt and heavy as a sawn-through rustwood, the alien's remains toppled, dragging Korrie down on top of it, spattered in its stinking, dark blood.

Cass looking at the doorway. A figure stood there, silhouetted by *Ruffian*'s light. They had a smoking bolt pistol still raised in one hand.

'Thank the Throne,' the newcomer said, stepping properly inside. 'I haven't used this bloody thing in so long, I wasn't sure if it still worked.'

Cass recognised another one of the Guard officers from *Vagrant*. He was heavyset and wheezing unhealthily, his starched uniform coat unbuttoned. He lowered the heavy pistol and exhaled.

'Carruthers,' Wellend exclaimed and dashed past Cass. For a moment it looked like the young officer was about to embrace the older in a wave of relief, but then propriety and discipline reasserted themselves. Wellend saluted hastily.

'Captain Elza, this is Colonel Vitkin Carruthers, Ninth Kass-andran Foot,' he said to Cass. 'He's in command of my father's division.'

'Formerly in command now, I fear,' Carruthers said, cuffing sweat from his brow. 'After leaving those good men to die. It was wrong of us. Of all of us, bar you, Wellend. You're at least trying to make a difference.'

Cass turned to help Korrie up. Her co-pilot was wiping rancid xenos blood from her eyes, her face pale beneath the sticky patina. She winced when Cass took hold of her.

'Where did it get you?' Cass asked.

'Ribs,' Korrie grunted. 'I'll be fine.'

Cass put her arm under Korrie's shoulders, supporting her towards the door. Wellend had moved over to Vulkrov, check-ing for a pulse, but he looked up at Cass and shook his head.

'My thanks, colonel,' Cass said to Carruthers, who holstered his bolt pistol and shifted to help Korrie from the other side. 'What made you decide to join us?'

'The last vestiges of a conscience, I suppose,' Carruthers said, casting a remorseful glance at the bodies of d'Kato and Vulkrov. 'I was a friend of our old commander, Lieutenant General Westlake. He was a good man, but too forgiving of the younger officers. He didn't play the game of high command well, and he allowed Percivald and his acolytes to take control. When he was killed at the start of the offensive, they seized power, and it's all been downhill since then. Myself and a few other good officers are culpable, we did nothing to stop it. Just as we did nothing to help Felkin when he tried to make a stand. I can only apologise for that, Wellend. Your father is a good man.'

'I know, sir,' Wellend said proudly.

'I also decided sitting back there waiting was probably even more painful than lending a hand,' Carruthers added. 'I should have come with you at the start.'

'Better late than never,' Cass said. 'Wellend, run ahead to *Vagrant*. Tell Zeke to get on the vox to the others and inform them the hub is secure. *Ruffian* should hold station for now and maintain overwatch, the other two are to bring their warbirds in as close as they can to those well stacks.'

Wellend hurried off. Cass, Korrie and Carruthers followed more carefully, squinting as they stepped out into the brilliance cast by *Ruffian*. Cass waved blindly up into the light, and the gunship switched its beam off and began to bank off to the side, shifting so it was holding station directly above the hub.

CHAPTER TEN

They got Korrie back to *Vagrant* eventually, negotiating the highway barriers with some difficulty. As they reached the field where *Vagrant* had been set down, *Rogue* and *Pauper* swooped low overhead, coming in to land on the rockcrete space adjacent to the promethium wells. Cass caught a change in the usual pitch of the engines, an ailing rattle that she attributed to Cobb's injured warbird.

Wellend and Carruthers returned to *Vagrant*'s hold and informed its occupants of d'Kato and Vulkrov's deaths, while Zeke helped Cass get Korrie up into the aft cockpit.

'Shooting the xenos was too easy, so she decided to wrestle it instead,' Cass said by way of explanation to Zeke. Korrie's laughter was cut off by a pained hiss as she settled down into her flight seat. Cass leaned in to help her strap up.

'Still up to being my co-pilot, flight sergeant?' she asked her.

'I can take over, if He wills it,' Zeke called up.

'Throne, no,' Korrie said with an expression that was half grin, half grimace. 'You'll have us charting a course to Holy Terra if you're left in charge of the navigation, Preacher. I'll be fine. You know I've flown with worse injuries, Chief.'

That much was true. Cass shifted her foothold over to the forward cockpit's ladder and climbed inside.

Vagrant joined its siblings on the rockcrete hardpan beside the wells. The stacks themselves were a series of great, rusting cylinders that would once have been attended to by the menials responsible for siphoning sanctified promethium into the vehicles lining up off the highway. They now stood abandoned. Cass just hoped they hadn't yet been looted of all their reserves.

Vaughn, Cobb and their crews had already dismounted by the time *Vagrant* landed again. It seemed as though they were in luck – there were lines now connecting the well stacks to the fuel tanks of the Valkyries.

Cass voxed for *Ruffian* to cease its overwatch and touch down too before dismounting, ordering Korrie to remain on board and monitor comms and the auspex.

Zeke uncoupled *Vagrant*'s fuelling lines and began refilling the tanks as the hold's occupants cautiously made their way out onto the rockcrete.

'I hear the station is secure, captain,' Percivald said, peering at the main building. 'At a cost.'

'It's secure,' Cass confirmed. 'Major d'Kato and Commissar Vulkrov died to ensure that. Their bodies are still inside. We won't be extracting them.'

'They knew the risks,' Percivald said with a haughty sniff. It took an effort for Cass not to reply that he had too, and he'd been too afraid to take them.

'There's a latrine closet in there for those who need it,' she said instead. 'And there looks to still be some non-perishables that the xenos haven't scavenged yet.'

The officers from *Vagrant* began to mingle with those from *Rogue* and *Pauper*. Cass went to the latter, finding Cobb up on one of the wings, inspecting the damage to the starboard turbojet and the rest of the battered warbird's airframe.

'How's it looking?' Cass called up to him, hands on her hips.

'Not ideal,' Cobb said, shifting onto his haunches and wiping greasy hands on his flight suit's front. 'One of the fuel lines is holed. So is the main engine block, though the tanks are still sealed. Pressure is good, but we'll be bleeding fuel from the line. I've tried to patch it, but I doubt it'll hold.'

'Think it's still airworthy?' Cass asked – that was the real question.

'I reckon we'll find out soon, Chief,' Cobb said, sliding down the wing and thumping onto the rockcrete next to her.

Cass noted that Percivald's officers were moving into the main building of the station hub. She made to follow them inside, but Vaughn intercepted her in the doorway.

'Is *Pauper* still viable?' he asked her.

'Cobb thinks so,' Cass said. 'Which will have to do, at least until we get back to Barduk and Z-Five can take a look.'

'If we get back to Barduk,' Vaughn pointed out. '*Pauper* will slow us down.'

'What are you suggesting?' Cass asked carefully. Vaughn at least had the decency to look momentarily shamefaced, before turning his ire back on Cass.

'We'd be quicker in the air if we didn't have full holds. Why does Havali want us to go to the trouble of fishing out these blueblood bastards anyway? By the looks of things, they've doomed their own commands.'

In truth, Cass had been wondering the same thing since her briefing with Havali. She assumed it once more came down to the politics of Guard headquarters.

'The general will save some face if he gets the top brass out,' she said. 'The likes of Percivald probably have connections among high command at Ushen. If they rescue the senior officers, maybe he'll be able to conceal the scale of the defeat.'

'Over a hundred thousand left behind to die, but it's all okay as long as a few dozen power-sword-wielding aristocrats are airlifted to safety?'

'Don't sound so surprised,' Cass said, glancing through the doorway to check they weren't being overhead. 'You know how all this works.'

'Doesn't mean I have to be happy about it,' Vaughn growled. 'We're expected to be efficient, professional, duty-bound, and then we get heaped down with bureaucracy, crapped on from above. Commanded to do the impossible or the unthinkable. And you just salute and say, "Yes, sir."'

'You've got complaints about the brass, take it up with the likes of Lord Commissar Vasquez when we get back,' Cass said, in no mood for another fight. Vaughn gave a hollow laugh and shook his head.

Cass felt a sudden urge to hit him. He seemed to sense it, looking at her keenly, goading her without saying another word.

She clenched her fist and held his gaze.

'Save your shit for after the mission, Hal,' she told him. 'Go and get *Rogue* refuelled.'

Vaughn saluted her and departed.

Cass told the other aviators she was going to try to use the hub's vox-unit to raise Suchen. As she had expected, the device itself was busted, useless, but it gave her an excuse to lock the door and sit alone.

The tide rose, engulfing her, and she wept.

She tried to stifle the tears, to drive them back, but they just returned, surging up with ever greater intensity, making her choke. She screwed her eyes shut, clenched her fists, sat shaking in the vox-operator's chair.

Then, as suddenly as it had struck, the storm passed. She cuffed tears from her face and looked down at her flight helmet, cradled in her lap. She raised it so she was face to face with it.

'Help me,' she whispered hoarsely, looking into the helmet's visor. It had a new, slight crack in one corner, presumably from when the ork had slammed her head off the petition counter. It had saved her life, not for the first time. But if it had any more help to give her, it wasn't sharing just then.

'I miss you,' she said aloud, to no one. To her father. 'I miss you and I don't know what to do.'

He would have known. He had commanded Vagabond Squadron at its height, when it had been considered the best part of the finest Imperial Navy Tactical Wing in the sector fleet. Cass' mother had died during childbirth, and Cass had spent her life looking up to him, dreaming of emulating him, of carrying on his legacy as part of the 901st. She had joined the Vagabonds while he had still been in command, but that hadn't been for long.

He had died on Morband, on Cass' second-ever operation. *Vagrant* had been reduced to scrap, along with every other flier in the squadron bar the Valkyrie she had been flying with at the time, *Pauper*.

There had been talk of folding the squadron, but Cass had begged for it to be maintained. The only child of Captain Elza still held some sway on board the *Mandatum Divinum* – the air marshal at the time, Ahng, had agreed to a full refit. New Valkyries had been supplied, given the old names and serial numbers the Vagabonds had carried since the squadron's formation almost four centuries before. New crews had been brought in, most of them even younger than Cass. In an unprecedented move, she had been given command. Blazing with pride and determination, she had been convinced that it was because Ahng and other senior Naval officers could see her potential, understood that she was a worthy successor to her father. It was only later that she realised it was more likely because the fleet was spread desperately thin, and didn't want to waste an experienced Aeronautica captain leading a squadron that was almost completely green.

She had tried to rebuild. For a while, she was certain she had. There had been victories, often against the odds. They'd maintained the premier reputation of the Vagabonds. But there had been losses amidst the triumphs – the pain of the death of Vaughn's sister was only the latest.

And it just didn't stop. It had been years now. Almost a decade. There was always another flight. Always another mission. Cass had dodged the odds too many times. All of them had. It couldn't last, and she couldn't keep going out. She didn't want to die.

How had her father managed it? Had he ever experienced these doubts? Had he ever gone away from the others and simply come undone, alone, ruined by loss and fear? She had only ever seen him smiling, confident, ruffling her hair and telling her not to worry before heading to the launch bays, or returning triumphant, the hero of the Navy's propaganda reels. She had never known him to weep.

She continued to stare blankly into the helmet, seeing her own reflection in the visor, distorted by the new crack.

'You didn't have a choice, did you,' she murmured. 'And neither do I.'

There was a knock at the door.

Cass cuffed her eyes again, feeling suddenly ashamed and angry, as though someone had caught her in some illicit act.

'Who is it?' she demanded.

'Korrie, Chief,' came the familiar voice from the other side. 'It's the Mordian. He says he needs to speak with you, in private.'

Cass considered telling Korrie to go away. But that would be unworthy. The same sense of duty that had seen her accept this operation in the first place wouldn't allow her to keep hiding.

She unlocked the door and pulled it ajar. Korrie looked at her levelly, her expression giving nothing away.

'I'll tell him you'll be a few minutes, Chief,' she said.

Cass wordlessly nodded her thanks, closed the door, and composed herself.

She couldn't lose it, not now. Not while they were still in the middle of a warzone, grounded in contested territory. She had to get the rest of them home. She had to prove Vaughn wrong. She wasn't going to get any more of them killed.

She made that promise to herself, even as she knew it wasn't hers to keep.

Wellend saluted her as she joined him behind the petition counters. The ork still lay where it had fallen, headless, its remains given a wide berth by the Guard brass – its stench made Cass grimace. D'Kato and Vulkrov also lay untouched. It seemed their former comrades were content to simply abandon their remains. The hub had mostly emptied, just a few of Percivald's officers forming a gaggle in the far corner, muttering among themselves and gnawing on scavenged ration bars. To Cass' relief, there was no sign of Percivald himself.

If Wellend sensed any indication of her earlier struggles, he gave no sign.

'Permission to speak freely, sir?' he asked.

'Out with it,' Cass said, trying not to let her impatience get the better of her. 'This isn't Guard headquarters.'

Wellend mustered himself before continuing.

'I wanted to ask you whether you'd speak in my favour when we reach Suchen. I'm going to put my father's case before General Havali, and advise him not to give up on the pocket.'

Cass sighed. 'I told your father, I'm only an Aeronautica captain. I'm not even a wing commander. I don't have a say with high command.'

'But with respect, sir, you're the leader of Vagabond Squadron. Your exploits are well known, even among the Astra Militarum. If I'm not mistaken, you were given this mission partly because of that. I think your opinion carries weight.'

Cass scoffed, though she knew the young Mordian had a point, one which she was trying to avoid.

'What would you even want me to say?' she asked. 'That the pocket is holding out just fine? From what I saw, it looked desperate.'

'Desperate but not doomed, sir,' Wellend said, and there was passion in his voice now, determination. 'I have seen the fighting there up close, at my father's side. The line holds. It will continue to hold for weeks, I believe. I have it all here.'

He pulled a dataslate from his uniform pocket and activated it to show Cass the information it contained. There were current unit strengths and dispositions, charts of the trench networks and their fire arcs and artillery coverage, even statistics on ammunition expenditure and the regularity and size of each ork assault.

'It shows that we can hold,' Wellend assured her. 'And most importantly, the Eji River can be crossed. As long as the drought continues, it remains at a low ebb, and becomes more fordable every day. With support, Army Ground Centre could still break out and fight its way south. It could provide vital forces to bolster the defences when the xenos inevitably strike across the river in force. We can turn the tide back in our favour.'

It all sounded too hopeful to Cass, but then she was used to Guard officers dressing up the borderline-impossible as probable.

'I haven't seen orks crossing the Eji,' she said, her last feasible fallback.

'But you've seen them south of the river! There's one lying right here! We know they're crossing over, and there are no intact bridges or any signs of river transports. So the river must be fordable. Will you at least confirm that to Havali for me?'

'I will consider it,' Cass said, unwilling to commit to anything more.

'The lives of many thousands may depend on your testimony, sir,' Wellend said gravely.

'Let's just hope we reach Suchen to make any report at all,' Cass replied.

'Take this,' Wellend said, proffering the slate to her. 'If something happens to me, at least you'll still have the evidence.'

Cass shook her head. 'Either we're both making it back, or neither of us are. You keep it, and I'll think about what I'll say if we reach Suchen. That's the only promise I'll make.'

Cass took the time to use the hub's latrine closet, then devoured a pair of ration bars that she'd brought in her flight suit. She returned to *Vagrant* as she ate, checking on the refuelling.

'It's prom two, so it'll wreck the engines if we leave it in for too long,' Zeke warned her from where he was standing under the primary coupling point in the Valkyrie's flank. 'It'll need to be purged when we get back, but it'll do us for now, if He wills it.'

'Z-Five will be furious,' Cass said wryly, lightly tracing a new, silver gouge running along the lower part of *Vagrant*'s port wing. 'How are we looking damage-wise? Anything that you think won't have shown up on the cockpit displays?'

'I'd say we're good,' Zeke said. 'The hold took some penetrations, but integrity is fine. What should I do with the Fledgling?'

Cass took a moment to understand what Zeke meant. Platz's

body was presumably still strapped up inside *Vagrant*'s hold. They could carry him back to Barduk, but there was little reason to bear unnecessary weight, not while they were still so far from home. She had ordered Vulkrov and d'Kato abandoned. She shouldn't show favouritism.

'Leave him,' Cass said. 'Make sure you take his kit, though. Anything personal too. Do you know if he had family back on board *Mandatum Divinum*?'

'I think he was Falco's sister's kid, one of that ex lower deck lot, anyway,' Zeke said with a small shrug.

'Well, pass anything relevant over to me when we get back to Barduk, picts or anything like that. I'll try and get them returned to whoever might want them when we head back upstairs. Oh, and say a few words for him?'

'I already have,' Zeke responded. 'As He wills.'

Cass called her trio of pilots together as the refuelling cycle continued.

'We need to get straight back up there,' she told them. 'There's every possibility there are more xenos in the area, and the dawn won't help us. I know everyone must be tired. If any of you need a break at the controls, tell me now and we can get your co-pilot in the hot seat. None of you are damned Astartes, so if you're flagging, don't endanger anyone else's lives by not saying so now.'

Nobody spoke up. Cass looked at Cobb.

'We'll go as easy as we can for as long as we can,' she told him. 'Whatever altitude you're most comfortable with. Let me know if you have any issues, any at all.'

'Has there been any contact with Barduk, or Suchen?' Vaughn asked.

'Nothing confirmed,' Cass said. 'I'm going to try again as soon as we're up.'

'What's the plan if we get bounced by more xenos?' Vaughn asked.

The thudding of boots on the rockcrete disturbed the little gathering before Cass could answer. It was Macks, one of Vaughn's gunners, who'd been put on lookout.

'Chief,' he panted as he ran up. 'There's movement out there, in the dark past the highway. Thinking it might be more of the little scavenger xenos.'

Before Cass could respond she heard Korrie calling across the hardpan from her open cockpit.

'We've got a problem, Chief! Multiple contacts on the auspex. Ground returns, but there are aerial signals inbound from the north-west as well!'

Cass cursed. She'd hoped they would have more time. What they had drawn so far from the wells would have to be enough.

'Disengage the fuel lines and prep for lift-off,' she told Vaughn, Konstantina and Cobb. 'I'll get our passengers back on board.'

The assembly broke up, and Cass strode over to Percivald and his coterie.

'Apologies, sirs, but we need to get airborne again. We have incoming hostiles. I need everyone back on board immediately.'

'Are your transports even airworthy, captain?' Percivald demanded imperiously. 'We will not risk ourselves in some flying bucket that has been shot full of holes.'

'The alternative is two days trekking back to our lines on foot, fighting your way through xenos scouting parties as you go. They're already just beyond the highway. I'm happy enough to report your deaths once I land.'

'There will be an inquest into all this when the time comes, captain,' Percivald responded. 'You have my word on that!'

'You are welcome to threaten me all you like, general,' Cass snapped, pointing at *Vagrant*. 'But for all our sakes, please do it from inside the damn warbird!'

There was a cracking sound that Cass realised was gunfire, followed by the chilling noise of hard rounds spanking off the frames of the nearest Valkyries. Vaughn's co-pilot, Xijen, was half standing in his cockpit, returning fire with his laspistol, sending bolts of red energy out into the darkness beyond the edge of the highway.

The small fusillade was answered by a rising series of roars, echoing through the night.

The sound of an impending ork assault motivated the officers the way Cass knew she never could. As they scrambled into the hold she hurried forward to where Zeke was still overseeing the refuelling.

'Time's up,' she shouted to him as she went.

'As He wills,' Zeke said, sounding utterly unfazed as the xenos howling grew more intense. 'We're almost three-quarters full anyway. Should be plenty.'

He began to unfasten the fuel line from under *Vagrant*'s wing, muttering what Cass assumed were benedictions towards the flier's spirit as he did so. The stink of promethium redoubled.

Cass jogged round the rear of *Vagrant*, and almost tripped on Platz's corpse. He had been laid out, presumably by Zeke, on the rockcrete behind the flier. His helmet, ruined by the shot that had killed him, had been left on, though Cass noted Zeke had taken his sidearm and stripped his flight suit's pockets of compact charts and ration bars. He had also left one of his litany scripts in the dead youth's cold grip, clasped over his chest.

Once it would have felt wrong to leave the body of a squadron member behind, but Cass had done it too many times now for it to register the same way it once had, especially given how little she had known Platz. He had just been unlucky, but that had made him a poor recruit for the Vagabonds.

She mounted up, snatching a glance at the roadway. There

were muzzle flashes from among the wrecked groundcars lining the side of it, more hard rounds zipping overhead. She could see shapes clambering over the obstructions too.

She swept through her preflight checks, feeling a moment's relief when *Vagrant*'s engines kicked in without issue.

'*It's going to be tight,*' Korrie said over the intercom.

'So I can see,' Cass said, throwing another glance at the highway.

'*I didn't mean the ground-pounders,*' Korrie said, and Cass realised she was referring to the returns on the auspex. The aerial contacts were closing fast. Another three or four minutes and they'd be on them.

'*They're charging,*' squawked Cobb's voice over the vox, forcing Cass' attention back to the road.

A xenos mob had broken from the dark and were now storming across the highway and into the light of the hub station, their roars reaching Cass even over the rising pitch of the engines.

'Zeke, hit them,' Cass yelled.

Thankfully, her side gunner had already anticipated the order and hauled the starboard hatch open.

A hail of heavy bolter fire from the flanks of all three grounded Valkyries ripped into the oncoming xenos. The heavy calibre explosive rounds tore the leading orks to shreds as they hauled themselves over the nearside highway barrier and the old, abandoned vehicles, drenching rockcrete and plasteel in dark, glistening blood. They came on into the concentrated barrage, heedless of the weight of Imperial firepower.

Cass heaved *Vagabond* up, the fire from Zeke never slackening. *Ruffian* was rising directly ahead, the Vulture's prow-mounted heavy bolter rotating right and adding its firepower, empty shell casings tumbling down onto the rockcrete in a continuous brass cascade.

'Starboard oblique, on *Ruffian*,' Cass ordered, snatching a look down at the roadway. Those orks not cut apart by the heavy bolters were onto the hardpan and closing the last few yards, but the Valkyries were rising up above them, remaining infuriatingly out of reach even as the side gunners continued to drill rounds down into the mob. Those orks with ranged weapons blazed away at them. Cass cursed as one brutal slug pranged off the side of the cockpit.

'*Contacts on my six, closing fast,*' came Cobb's voice.

'Climb,' Cass instructed. '*Rogue*, *Ruffian*, let *Pauper* past and form up to starboard. We're going south, and we're not stopping for anything. Understood?'

'*I can see those xenos off,*' Konstantina said.

'There's six of them, and more behind that,' Cass said after another glance at the auspex. 'We need to have a serious discussion when we get back to Barduk, Em.'

'*I just like shooting xenos,*' Konstantina exclaimed defensively. '*And blowing them up, and burning them, and–*'

Cass cut the connection and opened the throttle.

CHAPTER ELEVEN

Pauper led the Vagabonds out, but it was painful going. The warbird was still obviously struggling, and Cass knew Cobb would be pushing it as hard as he could. It just might not be hard enough.

'*They're coming up on us fast,*' Korrie warned. Cass could still hear the tension in her voice from the pain of the injuries she'd suffered in the hub.

'Hold course for now,' Cass instructed, thinking desperately. They weren't maxed out in terms of speed, because *Pauper* couldn't handle it, and Cass had refused so far to break formation.

The signifier indicating an incoming private transmission on Cass' control panel blinked. She already knew who it would be as she accepted it.

'*We have to leave him,*' Vaughn said.

'You want to abandon a Vagabond?' Cass demanded.

'*If we don't, we're all dead,*' he snapped back. '*Along with our precious cargos.*'

Cass said nothing, looking from the auspex to the horizon. Dawn was approaching, a sliver of pink driving out the deep blue from the edge of the world. The sky was clear, no hint of cloud cover. It would be another hot, dry day.

Lights twinkled past underneath them, in the darkness that still reigned far below, like a stray constellation of stars seeking to escape the coming sunrise. She realised she was looking at shots that had fallen beneath their target. The ork warplanes closing on them had opened fire, though they were still at extreme range.

'We've got incoming fire,' Korrie prompted. 'Contacts gaining.'

More shots laddered underneath, louder this time as the distance continued to close and the xenos adjusted their aim.

Cass knew there was no genuine hope of outrunning them, especially not if they continued to hold *Pauper*'s hand. But how could they just abandon Cobb? It probably wouldn't make a difference anyway – even at maximum acceleration, they would still be run down and savaged, like cervids hunted by bloodhounds.

She opened the vox, transmitting across all frequencies, looking into the strengthening dawn.

'This is Vagabond Leader to all Imperial call signs, repeat, Vagabond Leader to all Imperial call signs. We are under close pursuit carrying vital cargo to Barduk West,' she said, adding their coordinates and another plea for aid. Where in the God-Emperor's name was the top cover?

The answer, she suspected, was to the west. They had been thrown so far off course, and were coming in to Barduk way out of line compared to the route they had taken on the flight out.

She retransmitted their coordinates one more time. Vaughn came on again.

'For Throne's sake, Cass, they've got us in range!'

'*Let me turn and hold them off,*' Konstantina added.

'No,' Cass snapped. 'Maintain formation!'

'She's going to get us all killed,' Vaughn snarled into *Rogue's* intercom.

'*So you keep saying,*' Xijen responded dryly.

Vaughn looked right, at *Pauper*. Black smoke had started to trail from one of the engines, a smudge in the brightening sky.

What if he broke formation? Cass would have him up on charges back at Barduk, for sure, but then Cass wasn't going to make it back to Barduk if she insisted on dying with Cobb.

Besides, wasn't it his duty to see the mission fulfilled? To get Army Group Centre's commanders back to safety? Cass was failing in that. Her leadership was compromised. Dying for the Emperor was no excuse for not fulfilling objectives.

He tried to imagine saying any of that to the likes of Lord Commissar Vasquez. Then thought about his sister, tried to see if the anger and sorrow pushed him in one direction or the other.

There was one thing he was sure of – Eleanor wouldn't have abandoned Vagabond Squadron.

He held his course.

Konstantina flexed her grip on the flight stick, trying to channel her frustrations away.

'If we're going to die it should be facing the bastards, not running away,' she said to Straks.

'*You just want more kill tallies,*' he replied, sounding amused despite the circumstances.

'I want to die doing the thing I love most,' Konstantina countered.

Something streaked past *Ruffian's* port wing and away into the dawn, not hard rounds this time, but a rocket. Another one passed, corkscrewing wildly before detonating mid-flight,

Ruffian whipping through the smoke. More shots from prow and wing cannons followed, arcing just above the Vulture. It was time to start jinking.

'Evading,' Konstantina said.

'Leave us,' Cobb urged Cass.

She said nothing, teeth gritted. A warning pinged in her ears, followed by the rattling of rounds striking off the airframe. They were starting to take hits.

She rocked *Vagrant* as much as she dared without breaking formation, weaving to port, then starboard, then back again. They were running low, but their pursuers had enjoyed plenty of time to line up on their tails.

'We could split, try the same manoeuvre as last time,' Konstantina suggested.

'There's too many,' Vaughn responded harshly. *'We need to at least break formation!'*

More hits. Cass looked at the auspex. The xenos were almost on them.

'More contacts inbound, from the south,' Korrie interrupted urgently. Cass felt an overwhelming sense of despair.

Then, she realised just what that meant.

'We're with you, Vagabonds,' Bix's voice called over the vox.

Munitions tore past *Vagrant*, followed moments later by the warbirds firing them – Thunderbolts from the 911th Air Superiority Wing, Bix's Cloud Knights. One squadron came in low along the edge of the hard base, at almost the same height as the Vagabonds, roaring past them in the opposite direction as they met their pursuers head-on. A second squadron, Lightning interceptors, stooped from above, a pincer movement that seemed to catch the xenos completely by surprise.

Vaughn whooped over the vox as cannon rounds and las

beams carved up their pursuers. Cass found herself grinning, watching a clutch of enemy returns on the auspex simply cease to exist.

'*The Emperor protects,*' Cobb said, his voice audibly shaking with relief.

'*I think the Nine-Hundred-Eleventh might have a hand in it as well, but don't tell them, or we'll never hear the end of it,*' Konstantina added, sounding almost jealous.

There was a flash of light, the sound that accompanied it lost under the engine noise, but sudden and bright enough to immediately get Cass' attention.

And then, Cobb's warbird went down.

'*Starboard engine just gave out,*' he barked over the vox. '*I'm losing altitude, fast!*'

'Shit,' Cass hissed, straining against her harness to try and get a visual on *Pauper* from the cockpit. 'Can you reignite?'

'*Trying,*' Cobb's voice came through.

'*They're dropping too quickly,*' Vaughn said. '*Cobb, get your nose up!*'

Suddenly, there was no more time. Speed, altitude and gravity all asserted themselves with terrifying rapidity, and Cass saw that *Pauper* had passed the point of no return, beginning to spin to the right as its weight overcame the efforts of its remaining engine to keep it airborne.

The Valkyrie crashed into Kanai's soil. The area beneath was an abandoned rice field, baked hard by the unremitting heat. Cass saw *Pauper* plough nose-first into the dirt, slewing to the right, starboard wing crumpling beneath it as its momentum slammed it onto its side. Then, *Vagrant* was past, and she could no longer draw a direct line of sight on the crash.

'Cobb,' she yelled into the vox. 'Cobb!'

'*He's down,*' Konstantina said, bringing up the rear.

'Detonation?'

'Nothing yet. Smoke, but I can't see a fire.'

'We need to circle back, pick them up,' Cass said.

'We can't,' Vaughn snapped. *'Just look at what's happening back there!'*

Cass saw what he meant on the auspex. Bix's aviators were now playing out a ferocious low-altitude brawl with their former pursuers. The airspace was a mess of tangled dogfights, munitions and plunging wreckage. Banking around and back that way would bring them into the midst of it, and slowing to a near-hover and turning would take time, given how quickly they were flying. They'd then have to land and get airborne again, making themselves perfect targets.

'Throne damn it,' Cass shouted. She had thought they had made it. All of them. That they were through.

She smacked the inside of her cockpit shield in frustration, then bowed her head, trying to regain control.

'Looks like more contacts inbound from the north, Chief,' Korrie said quietly over the intercom. Before Cass could check, Bix cut in.

'We're going to need to break contact soon, I'm afraid, Vagabonds. We're heavily outnumbered up here, increasingly so. The rest of the wing is scrambling, along with Vivek's Nine-Hundred-Tenth, but I recommend you make yourselves scarce as quickly as possible.'

'Copy that, Cloud Knight,' Cass said bitterly. She tried Cobb's channel again. 'Cobb, for Throne's sake, respond.'

There was no answer, nothing besides the static.

She didn't have a choice. That was what she could tell herself later.

'Maintain course for Barduk,' she told Vaughn and Konstantina. 'Let's get this Throne-damned cargo home.'

The three remaining warbirds of Vagabond Squadron came in over Barduk airbase, setting down on one of the open hardpan landing zones at the northern end of the perimeter. Cass was trying to find the right words to use when she told Vaughn that they were going out again as soon as they had dumped their cargo and refuelled, to try and reach Cobb. Abruptly however, that plan was superseded by even more pressing issues.

The Commissariat was waiting for them at Barduk.

Cass only noticed them when Korrie pointed them out while she was cycling down the engines and opening the rear hatch.

'*Contacts at our nine, Chief,*' the navigator said quietly.

For a dreadful moment Cass thought the xenos had made it through and were intent on mounting an airstrike on Barduk itself. Then she realised Korrie was referring to the welcoming committee advancing from the landing zone's edge.

Cass knew immediately that something was very wrong. There were a trio of armoured Taurox ground transports parked up across from them, and a squad of Alphic Hydra Tempestus Scions, fully kitted out, were advancing from the vehicles towards the settling Valkyries. At their head was Lord Commissar Vasquez and a gaggle of black-clad aides and cadets.

'Now what?' Cass snarled, popping the cockpit shield and beginning to clamber out. She paused to help Korrie, then dropped to the hardpan and swept round to *Vagrant*'s rear, where the Scions had stopped.

They were hauling the officers out from the flier's hold. Percivald had already been apprehended, one particularly big Scion brute mag-clamping his hands behind his back as he shouted furiously at Vasquez, demanding an explanation. The commissar grimaced and turned, slapping Percivald across the face with one black-gloved hand. The general became abruptly silent, stunned as much by the act of having been struck as by the blow itself.

'What in the God-Emperor's name are you doing, Vasquez?' Cass shouted, striding up to him.

'Commissariat business, Captain Elza,' he said, barely sparing her a glance. 'I suggest you stand back.'

Another of the officers was on his knees at the foot of the hatch ramp, wide-eyed with shock as he was clamped the same way Percivald had been. Cass looked past him, at the other officers still in the hold. She made eye contact with Wellend. He beckoned her urgently, and she pushed through to him.

'Take it, please,' he hissed. 'It's in my left jacket pocket!'

At first she didn't understand what he meant, but then she remembered – his dataslate, the one showing Army Group Centre's order of battle and current disposition. Without thinking, she reached in and snatched the slate, stuffing it into one of her own flight suit's pockets.

'What was that?' one of the Scions barked, shoving the other officers out of the way and gesturing at her. 'Hand it over!'

'Quieten down, grunt-face,' Cass snarled at him, squaring up. 'And ask politely.'

The Scion snatched her wrist and she shoved him, shoulder driving into his carapace armour. It hurt her, but it was enough to force him back out of the hold.

More Scions closed in, but Korrie and Zeke were with her. She was reminded briefly of the scrum at Camp Yuzen. She realised she was grinning, about to vent her anger in the purest way possible.

'Cass!'

The voice of Major Orlov shattered the moment. The wing commander was forcing his way into the press.

'I'm sorry, Cass,' he said, grabbing her by the upper arm and getting between the aviators and the Scions. 'I didn't know, I swear to you. But now's not the time for a confrontation. Not here, and not like this!'

'They're going to shoot them, aren't they?' Cass snarled. 'The Commissariat's behind all this! They want to make an example, so they sent us out to play pickup for the condemned! One of my warbirds is down, one dead and four lost, just so they could murder everyone we dragged out of that hellhole!'

'I told you the Commissariat would remember you, Captain Elza,' Vasquez said with the barest hint of a smile. Behind Cass, Korrie started forward, the pain of her damaged ribs seemingly forgotten, but Cass blocked her.

'You're a bastard, Vasquez,' she spat.

'And you are a decorated hero who has just endured a particularly arduous operation, so I will overlook all this,' the lord commissar replied carefully. 'For the good of morale.'

Cass told him exactly where he could put his good morale. Orlov dragged her away and, after a brief resistance, she let him, Korrie and Zeke following.

'You really didn't know?' she demanded of her wing commander once they reached the shadow of the nearest hangar. 'Because if I find out you did, Orlov…'

'I didn't,' he said firmly.

'And Jakyra?'

'Probably. But that's a fight for another day. You're exhausted, Cass. For Throne's sake, get some food and some rest, and we can talk about this tomorrow.'

'How many of them will be lying cold in a ditch by then?' Cass demanded, nodding past Orlov at the officers. They were being frogmarched under Scion escort towards the waiting Taurox, presumably for transportation to Suchen. Most of them looked stunned, disbelieving. Wellend was among them.

'Are they even going to get a mock trial?' Cass went on. 'Or is it just a case of up against the nearest palace wall, in front of all the grunts?'

'Why do you care?' Orlov asked. 'It was a job, and it's done. By all reports they're a pack of cowards and incompetents anyway.'

'Not all of them,' Cass found herself saying. 'And we both know the Commissariat won't bother to differentiate.'

'I'm asking you to just leave it,' Orlov said. 'But I can also order you. I'd rather not.'

Cass glared at him in silence for a moment before speaking again.

'Cobb and *Pauper* are out there somewhere. I want a sweep to see if we can pick them up. He has another batch of officers with him too, so more red meat to satisfy Vasquez, if that's what you want.'

'You know if they're still alive?' Orlov asked.

'No. *Pauper* went down, but it was engine failure from earlier damage, not a kill-shot. I've seen survivors walk away from worse crashes.'

'I'll have Bix run a fly-past when she can,' Orlov said. 'There's a pitched air battle developing right now to the north. Jakyra is overseeing it from upstairs. We might need to scramble support from Ushen.'

'You want us back up there?'

'No. You need to refuel and rearm anyway, and none of you are in a fit state to fly again, not today.'

'The xenos are south of the river, not just in the air,' Cass said. 'On the ground too. The Eji is fordable.'

'So you said in your last vox-transmission,' Orlov pointed out. 'Does Havali know?'

'Go and sleep,' Orlov said firmly. 'I'll see about Cobb. I promise.'

Cass finally nodded. Adrenaline and anger had carried her this far, but now it was spent. She felt exhausted.

She exchanged salutes with Orlov, and he departed.

'What're we going to do, Chief?' Korrie asked.

'You're going to do what the major suggested,' Cass said. 'Sleep. But first you're going to go to the medicae and get those ribs looked at. That's an order.'

'Can you believe all this?' Vaughn said, striding over to her from *Rogue*, flight helmet cradled under one arm. Konstantina was with him too, and their crews – Straks, Xijen, Holsten, Macks.

'Vasquez has bagged the whole lot of them,' Vaughn said. He sounded more amazed than angry. 'Do you think that was their plan from the start?'

'Yes,' Cass said bitterly.

'Did you know?' Vaughn asked, looking at her sharply.

'Not this time. If I had, I wouldn't have done it.'

Vaughn's expression became disbelieving, but at that point, Cass didn't care.

'What about Cobb?' Konstantina asked.

'The major is going to have a flight swing by the crash site as soon as he's able,' Cass said. 'It's kicked off up there, apparently.'

'Think we'll be called on?' Konstantina asked, sounding almost hopeful.

'Better not be,' Vaughn growled.

'Just get back to squadron lines and get some rest,' Cass said, beginning to stride off across the hardpan.

'And where are you going?' Vaughn called after her.

'Suchen,' Cass said, without looking back.

CHAPTER TWELVE

Havali was summoned down into Suchen's courtyard from an overly long fleet strategic assessment update, delivered to Militarum command across Kanai via a holo-link with Admiral Byrak and Fleet Master Sorn. Relief at the prospect of leaving the meeting early was tempered by the obvious concern on the face of the aide who had interrupted him. He rapidly realised why the man looked so nervous.

Army Group Centre's command staff had returned, and Vasquez had already snapped them up. As Havali descended into the inner courtyard, he found a frightened-looking clutch of dishevelled officers being shoved and corralled against the western wall by a platoon of Alphic Hydras. The lord commissar was overseeing it all, accompanied by a flock of black-clad underlings. A unit of dusty Hyrkans were tramping in from the outer courtyard as well, presumably an execution squad conscripted by Vasquez.

'Lord commissar,' Havali said sharply as he strode out into the burning heat, tailed by more of his aides. 'A word, if you please?'

Vasquez glanced at him from under the gleaming visor of his peaked cap, then moved to meet him, accompanied by his own cadets.

'We discussed this, Vasquez,' Havali said as the two groups met near the drained dragon fountain. 'You promised me there would be restraint. Due process.'

'I decide what constitutes due process when it comes to these sorts of matters,' Vasquez responded.

'Charming as ever,' Havali muttered, his tone becoming more urgent. 'For Throne's sake, you can't shoot all of them. Two or three will be enough, surely? Think about the effect this will have on the rest of the officer corps! You've made your point.'

'They must be reminded of the price of failure,' Vasquez said.

'Enough,' Havali snapped, stabbing a finger against Vasquez's chest. 'I know why you demanded so much secrecy on this, and why you're rushing it through now. You won't get away with this if you do it by the book. You know there have been mutterings about failings in the Commissariat since the last offensive collapsed. Your superiors at Ushen are breathing down your neck and you're trying to show them you don't take prisoners. Literally. But I won't let you run roughshod over this front. These men are under my command. Shoot three of them, and that will be the end of the matter. You'll have reminded everyone of your authority and reminded the rest of high command of their duty. Your own superiors will see that you acted decisively. But if you kill all of them, they'll begin to think you're a butcher. And you know what happens to commissars who overstep their own authority. The same fate they mete out awaits them.'

'Do not threaten me, lieutenant general,' Vasquez growled but, to Havali's relief, after a tense silence he seemed to concede the point. Havali knew that for all the dread that surrounded the lord commissar, he had skewered the man with cold, sharp truths.

'Three will suffice,' Vasquez said. 'The senior, and another two, as the Emperor wills it. Their sentence has already been decided, and it will be passed immediately.'

'As you wish,' Havali said, turning to head back inside.

'You will watch,' Vasquez called out, making him pause.

Havali turned back, anger rising once more, but he knew from the hard glint in the commissar's gaze that he wasn't going to back down on this last point.

'Senior officers must bear witness to the wages of their subordinates' failings,' Vasquez said.

Havali bristled at the implied insult, but stood his ground.

'Get on with it, then,' he snapped.

Orders were barked, ringing back from the high walls. The Scions yanked three officers away from the line pinned up against the wall, one that Havali recognised as Brigadier General ven Weem Percivald, and two others seemingly at random – a silver-haired Logres Ice Worlder and a young Mordian. They were frogmarched to the dragon fountain and made to kneel in its cracked, empty bowl.

'General Havali,' Percivald cried out, finally finding his voice. The words came out as a dry, desperate croak. 'Sir, please! This isn't right! We haven't failed our duties! We did not retreat! The line still holds!'

'Silence,' Vasquez barked, causing several of Havali's aides to cringe. 'By the authority vested in me by the God-Emperor and the Officio Prefectus, I have judged you upon the charge of cowardice in the face of the enemies of mankind,' the lord commissar continued. 'You have been found wanting. In consequence of this, I hereby sentence you to death, the punishment to be enacted immediately. May the God-Emperor have mercy on your misbegotten souls.'

'You can't do this,' Percivald wailed, starting to weep openly.

Havali realised he was holding his breath as Vasquez stepped up to the fountain and drew his laspistol. It seemed the blood-thirsty bastard wanted to do it himself.

The first shot rang out.

Cass requisitioned a Munitorum groundcar from the airbase and ordered it to take her to Suchen. She abandoned it at the main gates, where the Tempestus Scion guards impeded her.

'I have vital intelligence for General Havali,' she told them after identifying herself, drawing out the dataslate she'd taken off Wellend.

'You aren't scheduled to visit headquarters,' one of the guards said. 'The inner courtyard is in lockdown right now anyway, by order of Lord Commissar Vasquez.'

'This intelligence is time-sensitive,' Cass said. 'And vital to the war effort. I'm happy for you to provide an escort, but I need to get this to the general.'

'I'll take it and give it to him immediately,' the other Scion said.

There was a sound from beyond the gates, the all-too-familiar crack of a lasweapon. Cass felt an unbidden surge of adren-aline hit her. If she wasn't already too late, she was about to be.

'No, you won't take it yourself,' she snapped at the Scion. 'It's classified. Vasquez is in there, right? How do you think he'd react if I made a report to the Commissariat stating you two impeded me in fulfilment of my duties? And who do you think will be the scapegoats when a thousand tons-worth of xenos air power comes crashing down on us here, and we're completely unprepared?'

She was completely winging it now, like any good Vagabond pilot. But she had dealt with enough Scions before to know where to press.

The pair exchanged a glance before one spoke.

'I'll take her,' he said to his comrade.

He banged on the gate, and it swung partly open. Cass followed him in through the arch, half expecting to hear another shot as she entered. Her heart was racing – she'd had minutes to come up with all of this.

It was a totally unnecessary risk. Why couldn't she just leave Army Group Centre's command to their fate? Most of them probably deserved what was happening to them. But she knew at least one who didn't and so, running on that frustration, she had decided to put her neck on the executioner's block, again.

She was still half convinced the pocket was doomed anyway. Getting the exact details of what was happening there wouldn't change things. Trying to save Wellend wouldn't guarantee the survival of those still fighting beyond the Eji. In fact, she doubted she could even secure Wellend's life. But she had to try.

We do our duty, her father used to say. *And great or small, that is always enough. You can always rest easy, if you know your duty is done.*

She walked into the heat and shadows of the inner courtyard, finding it almost full. The main body of officers taken from the Valkyries were stood to one side under Scion guard, while three appeared to have been singled out and were being held in the dried-up basin of the nine-headed dragon fountain. One, in the uniform of a Logres Ice Worlder, was already slumped over, dead, a wisp of smoke rising from a cauterised las wound to the skull. Vasquez was standing over him, while his subordinates watched like a flock of vultures from the other side of the small square, along with Havali and a few other members of the Suchen general staff. The windows of the palace's east and west wings were filled with faces, officers, aides and clerks snatching a moment to watch the macabre rite play out.

Wellend was one of the two remaining officers facing execution, along with Percivald. Cass had feared if only some were to be killed, the young Mordian would be an easy scapegoat.

Percivald was begging and crying as Vasquez shifted from the dead Ice Worlder to him and raised his laspistol again. The Alphic Hydra leading Cass had clearly expected her to go straight to Havali, so when she deviated instead towards the impending execution, he started after her, snatching her wrist.

'Let go,' she barked at him, yanking herself free before he could get a proper hold. She tried to call out, tried to reach Vasquez.

Too late. There was a second cracking discharge, startling a flock of flitwings from the ragged terracotta roofing. As they surged away in a flurry of beating feathers, Percivald slumped, a slender ooze of grey matter running from his nose – the las bolt had cauterised both entry and exit wounds, cooking his brain on the way through.

'Stop,' Cass yelled.

Vasquez turned as she came at him, and suddenly she found herself staring down the barrel of his laspistol. She froze.

'Seeking to inhibit the Commissariat in the performance of its duties carries an immediate death sentence,' he declared in his cold, unyielding voice.

'For Throne's sake, Vasquez, wait,' Havali called out, striding over from the edge of the square. 'I won't permit you to just shoot one of my best pilots out of hand!'

Cass experienced a moment of plunging terror as she tried to drag her gaze away from that yawning barrel, feeling the eyes of what seemed like the entirety of the Suchen headquarters on her.

'This can't go ahead,' she found herself saying, hearing the words as though they were being spoken by someone else, coming out as a dry rasp. She swallowed, spoke louder. She was committed now, as sure as a warbird plunging below hard base.

'These executions will harm the Imperial war effort on Kanai!

I have intelligence that needs to be reviewed, and it was delivered to me by this officer!'

She pointed past Vasquez at Wellend. He was pale-faced with fear, visibly trembling.

'Scion, remove this miscreant,' Vasquez snapped at Cass' guard, who had regained his hold on her. She pulled back, struggling not to be moved by the big brute while turning her attention towards Havali.

'I'm only asking for a stay of execution, until this officer can tell you what he knows! Please!'

Havali looked paralysed by surprise, but his expression hardened. He said nothing. The Scion hauled on her, forcing her to give ground.

'The Eji can be crossed,' Cass shouted desperately, looking up at the surrounding windows instead, her voice echoing around the sweltering courtyard. 'The drought has made it fordable! Army Group Centre hasn't broken yet, and there's still time to evacuate!'

'Enough,' Havali barked. 'Scion, hold her.'

The general closed the last few yards towards Cass and Vasquez, snapping at his aides to remain where they were as they started after him. He reached Cass, leaning in, his taller, broad frame suddenly threatening. She stood her ground.

'Throne take you, Captain Elza, this is neither the time nor the place,' he hissed, swatting the Scion who had been gripping her aside and drawing her by the elbow so she was facing away from the majority of the crowd, towards the back of the courtyard. 'What do you think you're doing?'

'I'm sorry, sir, but you need to see this,' Cass said, trying to show him the dataslate. 'This was compiled by that Mordian there. He's an aide to Brigadier Felkin, one of the officers who chose to remain behind in the pocket. The information he's collated shows the situation is more stable there than the likes of General Percivald has been making out.'

'You think I didn't know that?' Havali demanded, his tone low and dangerous. 'You think Suchen headquarters is completely blind? There is more at play here than you're aware of.'

'I would advise you to step away from her, general,' Vasquez said.

'Or what?' Havali said. 'Are you going to make me kneel in that fountain as well?'

'She is interfering with Commissariat business,' Vasquez snarled back. 'I suggest you allow me to deal with her, unless you want to be considered as aiding and abetting.'

'Give me a moment,' Havali all but shouted at the commissar. 'Stop straining at your leash. You've had two kills already, you bloodthirsty dog.'

Vasquez's expression was murderous, and he showed no sign of withdrawing, but nor did he say anything as Havali spoke again to Cass.

'You are meddling in matters you have little knowledge of, captain,' he reiterated, emphasising her rank. 'And now you've managed to force my hand. You've just told everyone at headquarters that the rumours that have been going around about the pocket being tenable are true. High command at Ushen will hear about it within the hour, and then I'll be hauled over there to explain why I've apparently left over a third of my forces to die.'

Cass didn't understand, and it clearly showed on her expression. Havali sighed, like a weary father dealing with his child's latest misdemeanours.

'Intelligence points to a major ork offensive being prepared to the north of us, higher up the valley,' he said. 'It seems as though they plan on doing what we tried, and failed, to do – drive through the Eji Valley and split Ushen and Torr City. I have been readying our defences here for that.'

'But wouldn't Army Group Centre be best used bolstering those defences?' Cass asked.

'They are, in their own way. They are forming a bulwark, a breaker against the coming xenos tide. I had hoped that by the time the orks were finished with them, we would be fully dug-in here.

'Of course, the alternative is trying to break Army Group Centre out. No easy thing to disengage, not when they're as hard-pressed as they are. Such an operation would be fraught. It would risk compounding the failure of the earlier offensive and wreck any chances we have for forming a coherent defence south of the Eji. I am not in the habit of reinforcing failure. That works for Guard commanders blessed by the Throne with greater resources and a disregard for the tools at their disposal, but it is not my way.'

Cass was beginning to understand. Army Group Centre had not been forgotten about; it was being consciously sacrificed. But not any more.

'You've forced my hand,' Havali told her. 'My intention to leave Army Group Centre in place was known only to a few of my most senior aides, but now the entirety of Suchen knows a relief operation is feasible. I now have to carry out that operation, or high command will deem me incompetent or a coward. They will think I have lost touch with my forces or that I have become paralysed by indecision. I have enough enemies among the Ushen echelons already, and they will be sure to take advantage of this. So I must act first. Congratulations, Captain Elza, on leaving me with no choice but to risk the entire front.'

'Success would reinforce the front,' Cass pointed out, her indignation flaring. 'Bolster the line, and bolster morale, far more than a few pict snaps of a worthless supply drop. We can get Army Group Centre south of the Eji and shore up the defences. Tens of thousands of lives depend on it.'

Havali scoffed. 'The risk outweighs the advantages, but don't worry, you've made your point.'

'You should still free him,' Cass said, nodding past Havali at Wellend. 'He's only a lieutenant, a junior aide. He's the one person we brought out of the pocket who doesn't deserve to be standing there. He only left so he could argue the case for a relief operation.'

Havali looked back at the shivering subaltern and gestured dismissively. 'I'm not the one who wants to make an example of them. Lord commissar' – the last words were directed at Vasquez, who looked pointedly at them both, still lurking nearby – 'it has come to my attention that the Mordian boy you've singled out holds valuable intelligence in the ongoing struggle against the xenos threat. Would you spare his life, at least for the time being?'

Vasquez grunted and gave a shrug. 'If you wish to preserve him, I will have another. Failure must be punished.'

Havali muttered something in a Tallarn dialect that Cass assumed was entirely non-complimentary.

'As you wish,' he added, more loudly. 'Take another then. Any of them.'

Vasquez snapped a finger at the Scions, and they hauled a new officer from among the prisoners, seemingly at random, and marched him to the fountain.

Cass recognised him. It was Carruthers. The portly Kassandran colonel's expression was set, and as he passed he made eye contact with Cass. She opened her mouth to say something, though she didn't know what – to plead for mercy a second time? As though the Commissariat would be dictated to twice in one afternoon. But Carruthers shook his head at her, and Cass held her tongue. She knew in truth there was nothing she could say. She had played her own hand, and in doing so had signed his death warrant.

She followed him to the fountain, neither Havali nor Vasquez's minions trying to stop her now. She pulled Wellend up and tugged on one of his epaulettes. He seemed to be in a daze.

'Come on, before they change their minds,' she hissed.

'I'm not afraid to die,' he blurted out, glancing from her to Vasquez, who simply glared at him.

'Then you're an idiot,' Cass told him. 'Now come on!'

She succeeded in getting him out of the fountain, his place beside the two corpses taken by Carruthers.

'I'm sorry,' Cass said to the Kassandran as they went past.

'It's no more than I deserve,' Carruthers said, his expression grim. 'I'm glad it's over. That's the truth. I won't have to be ashamed any more.'

Cass nodded and hustled Wellend off to one side.

Carruthers knelt beside Percivald's body. 'May the God-Emperor forgive us all,' he declared loudly as Vasquez stood over him and raised his sidearm.

Cass found herself glancing away.

The final shot rang out, cracking hard in the sweltering air. She was dimly aware of Wellend throwing up next to her. Without thinking she undid her canteen and passed it to him as he supported himself against the nearest, flaking wall.

'Drink,' she ordered him, looking warily at Vasquez and the Scions in case they decided to seize the young Mordian after all. The lord commissar had at least holstered his laspistol, while a section of the Scions clambered into the dry fountain to drag the trio of bodies out.

'Captain Elza,' Havali said, calling her over again.

'Stay with me,' she told Wellend, who managed to nod. He'd taken a swig of the canteen's warm water, and a little colour had started to return to his face.

Cass returned to Havali's side with Wellend. The general's mood didn't seem to have improved. He was snapping at members of his staff to get the gaggle of surviving officers inside the main building, and to find them something to eat and drink. Cass wondered briefly what he intended to do with them – scattered to minor postings out of the way of the front line, she supposed, or demoted and left languishing on the lowest rungs of the general staff.

'Thank you for volunteering,' Havali said as he turned to her, flashing a brief smile that she didn't particularly like the look of.

'Sir?' she asked, not sure if he meant the rescue of Wellend.

'We're going to need you for the offensive that's coming,' Havali said. 'The one you just left me with no choice other than to try and orchestrate. Vagabond Squadron, the best of the best, leading the charge to rescue Army Group Centre.'

The bitterness in his tone was now obvious, and Cass realised too late what was happening.

'My squadron has been reduced to almost fifty per cent of the strength it started this tour with,' she told him. 'We've just come back from a needless operation you sent us on, where at least one, and probably five, of my aviators have been killed and a warbird lost. And now you want us leading the line again?'

'Careful, Elza, lest the good commissar hear you,' the general said, looking back at where Vasquez was overseeing the clearance of the bodies. 'I assure you, his patience is far from limitless. Nor is mine, for that matter.'

'I didn't think you were a petty man, sir,' Cass retorted, letting her anger run its course. It felt good, at last, to be fighting back. To be taking a stand. 'That's what this is, isn't it?' she demanded.

'Pettiness. I've embarrassed you in front of your staff and the Commissariat. Now what? You want me to pay with my life? With the lives of my aviators?'

Havali's expression had darkened, his smile now long gone.

'I think you've forgotten who I am and who you are in this exchange, captain. Besides, there is nothing unreasonable about ordering the finest Valkyrie commander in the system to take leadership of the vanguard. After all, this operation is going to be vital. Tens of thousands of lives depend on it.'

'You're mocking me.'

'I am not. You are acting like a petulant child. Or do you think yourselves exempt from future duties because of the losses you have suffered? Will Air Marshal Jakyra find you non-operational? I doubt that. In fact, I can make sure she doesn't. And if you show any further insubordination, you will answer to Vasquez. I promise you, you'll have better odds of survival facing the xenos than you will the lord commissar. And likewise your crews. Think about that.'

Cass knew she was in no position to argue. Everything Havali was saying was true. She wanted to tell him that what he was doing was cruel, but the words died in her throat. She knew how foolish they would sound, how pointless. Childish even, as Havali had said.

'What do you expect from us?' she asked instead, trying to find any angle she could use, a point that might yet make Havali reconsider.

'That is yet to be determined,' the Tallarn general said. 'Numerous matters have to be addressed before a breakout operation can be deemed viable. But it is certain the Valkyries of Nine-Hundred-First Wing will have a major role to play. I may have twisted the knife, Captain Elza, but I mean no disrespect when I say we will need your Valkyries and your flying abilities if we are to have any hope of success.'

'When?' Cass asked coldly.

'Some days,' Havali said. 'These things cannot be done quickly, even if speed is of the essence. You'll have time to rest and recuperate, assuming the xenos don't mount any major sorties south of the river. I'll speak to your wing commander and Jakyra, and you'll be brought in on relevant briefings. Go back to Barduk for now, and sleep. You look like you need it.'

Cass glanced at Wellend, who was standing awkwardly beside her. Havali sensed her unspoken question, and let out a short laugh.

'Don't worry, I won't let Vasquez eat him.' He looked at the Mordian, addressing him directly. 'I'm glad Captain Elza spoke up for you, young man. If what she said was true, you're going to have an important part to play in the planning and preparation of what comes next. I'll have you quarters assigned here in Suchen, and you'll be brought in on the planning sessions. If all goes well, your father and the greater part of the troops still under his command will be rejoining us sooner rather than later.'

Wellend nodded, seemingly lost for words. Havali spoke to Cass again, holding out a hand.

'That slate you were waving about earlier. If it has intel on the pocket, you'd best hand it over.'

Cass hesitated briefly, then did as the general suggested. She forced herself to salute, then spoke to Wellend.

'If you have any problems, come and find me at Barduk,' she told him, before turning and striding from the courtyard.

The bodies of Percivald, Carruthers and the other officer were being dragged out of the gate by the Scion detail, and Cass had to wait until the way was clear.

'Where are you taking them?' she asked the brute in charge of the detail. He glanced at her briefly before answering, his tone reserved.

'The lord commissar wants them strung up outside the gates, where the Guard can see them.'

'I suppose plenty of ground-pounders would be happy to see their officers with a las bolt to the skull,' Cass commented bitterly. The Scion said nothing.

She walked out after them, wondering how she was supposed to explain what had happened to the squadron.

She looked up at the clear blue sky, and thought of the storm about to break.

And Vagabond Squadron would be flying into it.

CHAPTER THIRTEEN

Cass returned to the lines and, finally, slept.

It was the deep darkness of pure exhaustion, a welcome oblivion. When she woke, she briefly didn't know where she was. Then everything came flooding back, and she lay for what seemed like an age, weighed down by what had come before, and what now lay ahead.

She knew it would be dangerously easy to stay there as the hours dragged by, to ignore knocks at her door, pretend she was absent or busy. But that would do no good. That was how the rot set in.

Instead, she made herself get up, stretching the stiffness from her limbs, still feeling exhausted despite having slept. It was still early, and most of the others were in their bunks. Even Korrie was still asleep, her side strapped up after her visit to the medicae bay.

Cass padded through to the refectory room appending the prefab tunnel, scavenging the cupboards for recaff. She found a stash and brewed it up in one of the squadron's collection of mismatching mugs. It tasted foul and bitter, but she knew it would help kickstart her.

She knew what she had to do. Her biggest problem was trying to find the right words, the ones she would use when she explained to the remnants of the squadron that they had been assigned to spearhead a new offensive. The words that could accurately encapsulate why she had ensured they'd once again be fighting for their lives, just days after losing more of their number.

She sensed movement in the doorway and froze, as though caught in some illicit act, before turning and finding Konstantina entering. She looked as rough as Cass felt, but mustered one of her lean, deadly smiles.

'Morning, Chief. That smells good.'

'Smells better than it tastes,' Cass warned, raising her recaff in salute.

'Mind if I grab one?'

Cass made space for her at the counter, and the Vulture pilot busied herself making her own brew.

'Any news about Cobb?' she asked as she did so. Cass shook her head.

'No. I need to go and speak to Orlov, then see about doing a sweep back north. Nothing hit during the night, so I assume Bix's sorties were a success and the xenos air presence is back on the other side of the Eji.'

'*Ruffian* can head out just now,' Konstantina offered. 'Erik's awake.'

'Wait until I've spoken to Orlov,' Cass said. 'I'll need to get clearance.'

They settled into a brief moment of companiable silence, before Cass ruined it.

'Command wants us to go out again,' she said. She hadn't

really intended to tell Konstantina before the others, but she was here, and Cass suddenly didn't want to delay.

'Command always wants us to go out again,' Konstantina said with a cold laugh. 'That's the nature of the job. Go out again, and again, and again, until one day you don't come back.'

'How do you deal with that?' Cass asked, genuinely intrigued. It was the reality that few Aeronautica pilots liked to discuss, for obvious reasons – precious few grew old enough to reach retirement on board the *Mandatum Divinum*. Some received honourable discharges following crippling injury, but those were few and far between – most just didn't survive at all.

'I just delude myself, the same as everybody else,' Konstantina said. 'It won't happen to me, will it? Happens to the others, but won't happen to me! I'm the hero of this story. Besides, the God-Emperor likes what I do. He likes the number of His enemies I torch. So as long as I keep notching kill tallies up on *Ruffian*'s flank, He won't be demanding to see me in person anytime soon.'

Cass couldn't tell if she was being serious, or what Zeke might think about such theology.

'What about you?' Konstantina asked as the recaff pot began to bubble on the stove. 'How do you cope?'

She seemed wholly uninterested in the fact Cass had told her they'd been given a new assignment. That was part of the reason Cass liked her. She just didn't seem to care. Whether that was true or not, Cass didn't know, but if it wasn't then she respected the front.

'Same as you I suppose,' Cass told her. 'I'm a good pilot. I wouldn't be leading Vagabond Squadron if I wasn't. So the odds are better for me, because I'm good.'

She realised she was smiling, and Konstantina cocked an eyebrow at her as she poured out her brew.

'What's so funny?' the gunship pilot asked.

'It just sounds so stupid, saying it out loud,' Cass admitted.

'I've heard much worse, and I'm sure you have too,' Konstantina pointed out. 'Remember Sulla? Who thought he'd never die as long as he watched every sunrise during each new deployment? Didn't account for getting hit during night ops though.'

The memory of Sulla – cantankerous, crude, the best navigator in the squadron, and dead the past six years, brought a sad smile to Cass' lips as Konstantina carried on.

'And how many trinkets and lucky charms have we all got? All you can do is straighten it out in your own head. Or try not to think about it too much, though you'd have to be an idiot not to. Like Cobb.'

'Do you think he made it?' Cass asked, knowing she had to face up to the likely answer. Konstantina gave a shrug.

'From what I saw, probably not.'

Cass nodded, slipping into silence once more as she contemplated the loss, her own failure. She should have challenged Jakyra and Havali over the supply drop, over the evacuation, over anything at all.

'Vaughn is going to lose it,' Konstantina said. 'He's been bubbling over hotter than this recaff pot since Ushen.'

'Since Eleanor,' Cass clarified, daring to speak the name of Vaughn's dead sister aloud. 'That's my fault.'

'It's almost never your fault, Cass,' Konstantina said, voice taking on a stern edge. 'I would have thought you'd have that part of your conscience locked down by now. It can never be the captain's fault, or it would drive you mad. All these deaths. All this loss.'

'We just left the Fledgling back at that prom hub,' Cass said as she pondered Konstantina's words. 'He took a round through the hold while we were airborne. Zeke just dragged him out onto the rockcrete and we left him there when the xenos attacked. I barely even thought about it at the time. I barely cared.'

'I'm sure Zeke would have said a few words for him. What else did you want? I don't think they even have a mass grave here at Barduk. Not enough pilots make it back to make it worthwhile. He'd probably have just been incinerated.'

She thought about Platz lying there, the litany script gripped in his stiff fingers. The memory felt as much like prophecy as a guilty conscience. What if she was marked for death next?

She knew Konstantina would say she couldn't think like that, any more than she could blame herself for the squadron's inevitable casualties. Start giving into that sort of mindset and it would gnaw away at the bedrocks that held everything up – duty, courage, determination, comradeship.

She thought about Vaughn, about how he had demanded they give up on Cobb and run. Even in the midst of a developing aerial attack, that had surprised her. The Vaughn of a few years or even months ago would never have suggested such a thing, at least not out loud. But Ushen – Eleanor's death – and their ongoing desperate operations had changed him. Not so much changed, Cass realised, as eroded. Chipped away at the foundations. The edifice she could see now was close to collapse.

'You knew the odds when you joined up, Chief,' Konstantina said. 'Every Aeronautica brat does. How many of us have pilot parents who are still alive? I think there's two in the whole squadron. But it's all we've ever known. It's the life we've been given. We are the guardians of the God-Emperor's skies, the patrollers of His heavens, the lightning bolt that strikes down His foes. Or something like that, anyway.'

'You've been talking to Zeke this morning?' Cass asked, sipping her recaff.

'Damn right I have,' Konstantina said. 'Mad-eyed bastard has a direct link to the Golden Throne, and I need all the help I can get! Me and Erik.'

'How is Straks?' Cass said.

'Clingy.' Konstantina shrugged. 'I thought we had passed that phase, but I worry. I think he wants things to go back to the way they used to be. Serious.'

'That would be one way of getting out of the firing line for a bit,' Cass pointed out. 'Bringing the next generation of gunship pilots into existence. Then again, knowing you, you'd be eight months gone and demanding we strap you into *Ruffian* so you can pilot a bombing run on some poor xenos supply dump.'

'I wonder if I'd still fit into the cockpit,' Konstantina said with what sounded like morbid curiosity. 'Anyway, balls to that. Erik would be a crap father, and I'd be an even worse mother. Just don't tell him I said that.'

'Promise,' Cass said, draining the dregs of her mug and grimacing. Konstantina leaned over and punched her lightly on the arm.

'Don't let any of it get to you, Chief. It'll be back up to the Old Mother for tanna and medals soon enough. Another campaign badge at least. There's worse jobs in the Imperium.'

'Not sure there are many that are more lethal,' Cass pointed out.

'At least we get to take plenty of the bastards with us,' Konstantina said. 'Besides, would you rather be toiling on the Old Mother's gunnery decks, or down in the trenches of some benighted world with the grunts?'

Cass told her succinctly how little either of those options appealed, and Konstantina laughed.

'See? So that's how I deal with it. Now, tell me about this new, undoubted mess of an operation you've just volunteered us for. On a scale of regular karked to mega-karked, how karked are we?'

* * *

Vaughn did not accept news about the new offensive, or Vagabond's projected role in it, with the same good grace and humour Konstantina had displayed. He bowed his head when Cass told him, then asked to be dismissed.

Cass let him go. The hard part had been done, and she had no more detailed information for him yet anyway.

She watched him stalk out of the lines, slamming the door behind him. A few moments later there came a roar of rage from outside.

Rogue's other three crewmates had gathered around, and Vaughn's co-pilot, Xijen, put a hand out to stop Cass as she took a step towards the door.

'Best leave him, Chief,' he said quietly. 'We'll get him straightened out.'

'If he folds, you're flying *Rogue*,' Cass told him bluntly. 'I'll do what I can to protect him. Say he was injured in the last operation. But I won't lose a whole warbird because he can't handle it. How close was he to disobeying me and breaking formation after we left the prom hub?'

Xijen shrugged noncommittally and looked away. Cass knew she shouldn't be driving a wedge between crewmates or trying to have one inform on another, but she needed to know. Eventually Xijen answered, his tone guarded.

'Pretty close.'

'Well, you let me know if he's ever "pretty close" again,' Cass told him. 'Hal is a damn fine pilot and I respect him for it, but nobody's bigger than the squadron. Understood?'

'Understood,' Xijen said, meeting her gaze.

She returned to her quarters.

Vaughn's hands were shaking so badly he couldn't light his lho-stick.

He crushed it in his hand and threw it away in frustration, then squatted down in the shadow of the prefab unit and buried his head between his fingers.

He hated her. Hated her for what she had done, what she was still doing. He couldn't go out again.

He heard boots on the rockcrete, approaching him slowly. He didn't look up. There were tears in his eyes, but he blinked them back, swallowed the fear and loathing choking him.

'Did she send you after me?' he asked the newcomer, knowing it would be Xijen. The footsteps stopped, and there was a clicking sound.

Vaughn looked up, and found he'd been presented with a lit lho-stick. He took it, inhaled, and bowed his head. Then, after a few draws, he stood, slowly, stretching out before speaking.

'It's grox shit, Xijen, and you know it,' he told his navigator.

'I do,' Xijen agreed.

'I'm going to speak to Orlov,' Vaughn said, taking another drag.

'And say what?'

'That she's unfit for command. That we're unfit to… to go back out there again.'

'You're proposing we get pulled off the line?' Xijen asked. 'You know what would follow. Honours wiped. Squadron privileges revoked. Unless we give them a damn good reason.'

'They can go choke on their reasons,' Vaughn exclaimed, gesturing with the lho wedged between two fingers.

'If Orlov does pull us off the line, the whole squadron I mean, then we'll get worse duties on the next campaign. And if you ask for just *Rogue* to be pulled, we'll never fly with Vagabond Squadron again. We'll be reassigned to one of the other outfits, and we'll be given the same or worse assignments with less skilled pilots on our wings.'

Vaughn knew Xijen was walking him through it, as he always

did. He didn't appreciate it, not now, when he was trying to find the courage to make a stand.

'She won't stop until we're all dead,' he said. 'She talks about Em having a death wish, but she's no better. She's obsessed with living up to her old man, including the part where he got blown out of the karking sky!'

He knew Cass would tear into him if she heard him saying that. Perhaps that was the key. Perhaps he needed to pick a fight with her, get her to fly off. Hit him. Throne knew, she hadn't shown any reservations about doing that lately. Get her to assault him, then get the provosts and the Commissariat involved. Have her declared unfit for command, before it was too late.

Would Xijen back him if he did that? Once, he knew he could have counted on *Rogue*'s crew. Not any more. Every relationship in the squadron was strained. He couldn't trust anyone now that Eleanor was gone.

'You didn't answer my question,' he said to Xijen. 'Did she send you after me?'

'No,' Xijen said, finishing his own smoke and dropping it before stubbing it out under his boot. 'She was going to come after you herself. I said it'd be better if I went. We've got fighting aplenty to be doing without you two going at it.'

Vaughn exhaled a cloud of smoke and dropped his burnt-out lho as well.

'Cassandra wants to die a hero,' he told Xijen. 'And I'll raise a glass to her when she does. When I know she isn't going to get any more of us killed with her. Until then, she's as much an enemy of *Rogue* as the Throne-damned xenos. Don't forget that when we're next up there.'

Orlov visited the lines while Vaughn and Xijen were still outside. Konstantina heard his rap at the door to the hab-tunnel.

'Going to get that, Preacher?' she called over to Zeke, sitting on the bunk opposite hers. He was cross-legged, leaning forward, muttering to himself as he leafed through a dog-eared copy of the Imperial Creed. He appeared not to have heard either the door, or Konstantina.

Hissing with annoyance, she dropped lithely down from her bunk and headed out to open the door. She saluted Orlov and took him through to Cass' office at the far end of the tunnel, then made her way back to her bunk.

The squadron was in a dark, quiet mood, made even more desolate by the stark absence of Cobb and his crew. Cass hadn't been able to offer any news about whether they'd been recovered or not. Konstantina doubted they would be, but knew better than to voice that truth to the others, at least so soon after their loss.

It had been relentless, one blow after another, and after what Cass had done, it didn't look to be ending anytime soon. Konstantina felt she had learned to roll with the punches better than most, but there was only so much any of them could take. She was almost starting to understand how Vaughn felt.

She looked in on Straks, who occupied the bunk beneath hers. To her surprise she found him writing something on a sheaf of parchment.

'What're you doing?' she asked, sounding accusatory without meaning to.

'Nothing,' he said, her sudden appearance causing him to start and make a half-hearted attempt to conceal the length of paper. It was a prayer scroll, Konstantina realised. Straks had been roughly scribbling High Gothic words onto it with a stylus, copying them out from the pocket-sized edition of the Creed that each Aeronautica aviator was given when they first took their oaths.

'Not you too,' she groaned. Straks gave a defensive shrug.

'It can't hurt, right?'

Konstantina turned to Zeke, still on his top bunk.

'Congratulations on adding to your flock, Preacher,' she told him sarcastically. He closed his book slowly and looked up at her, pale eyes fiery behind his long, lank hair.

'The end is coming, Konstantina,' he said. 'You should look to the preservation of your immortal soul, before it's too late.'

Konstantina stared at him, then scoffed, doing her best to try and conceal the sudden chill his words had brought with them.

'You'll need to work harder to scare me into your prayer sessions, Ezekiel,' she told him, looking back at Straks. 'Don't expect me to wrap those things around my arms.'

'He's just praying you'll take him back, Em,' Macks called out from his bunk further along the line. Straks glanced away, looking more annoyed than Konstantina had expected he would from such a shallow jibe.

'Make your peace with each other,' Zeke said morbidly from his perch. 'We'll all be entering the fire together.'

Konstantina gave him a hard look before replying.

'This is Vagabond Squadron. I wouldn't have it any other way.'

'I heard about what you did at Suchen,' Orlov said to Cass in her office, his voice accusatory. 'What were you thinking?'

'I was thinking it would be a damned waste seeing a good officer shot for no reason,' Cass said.

'Since when did any of the evacuees become good officers?' Orlov asked, sounding dismayed. 'Did he save your life on the return run or something?'

'He tried to, which was more than most of the others did,' Cass said. 'Apart from the other one they shot. Carruthers. So I guess I let the Commissariat have that one.'

Orlov sighed and sat down on the camp chair across from Cass' desk, uninvited.

'I've been told you volunteered to spearhead a new offensive,' he said. Cass let out a short bark of laughter.

'As much as we volunteer for anything,' she replied. 'This warbird is fuelled by duty and not much else. Recaff, at the moment.'

'Havali isn't normally vindictive. You must have really pissed him off.'

'Calling him out in front of his general staff probably had something to do with it.'

'For Throne's sake. Don't expect me to dig you out of this one. I've already been ordered to provide an operational overview and complete combat roster by tonight.'

'Well, the sooner we get up there, the better,' Cass said. 'It's a hell of a siege that's playing out on the other side of the Eji. They should hold a while yet, but the xenos look to be on top of them, night and day. The aerial attacks are some of the most brutal I've ever seen.'

'So Bix has reported. She was in a tussle all day with the scrap you drew south after you.'

Cass looked at him hard. 'Does she have any news about Cobb?'

'One of her Lightnings did a low pass on the crash site,' Orlov said. 'Admittedly whilst getting tailed by a xenos fighter, but their under-recorder got a few automated pict captures. *Pauper* was burning, no signs of survivors. I'm sorry, Cass.'

Cass said nothing, wrestling with bitter disappointment.

'Marrand and Shadow Squadron are scheduled to go take a look in an hour, but the odds aren't good,' Orlov carried on.

'I really thought we had made it through,' Cass said eventually. 'I thought I was bringing everyone back, except the Fledgling.'

'He didn't make it?' Orlov asked.

'Hard round through the hold, right in the head,' Cass said. 'I'll file the report later today. Kid was unlucky.'

'At least it sounds like it was quick.'

Cass was silent again, thinking about that body laid out on the rockcrete, half the face serene, sleeping, the other half crusted red with ruination. Was he still out there, lying rotting on the hardpan? Or were xenos scavengers tearing him apart and devouring him?

She remembered Konstantina's words about not blaming herself, and tried to force it all aside.

'What time do they want me at Suchen?' she asked, assuming that was the real reason for Orlov's visit.

'Tomorrow morning, oh-nine-hundred local,' he said. 'I'll ride with you, since I'm attending too. Jakyra might even be back down as well.'

'She'll be delighted,' Cass said. 'Another suicide mission, and I brought this one on myself.'

'It isn't a damned suicide mission,' Orlov snapped, looking genuinely angry for a moment. 'The whole point of this is to save lives, not lose more. Throne knows, if the rumours are true about another ork offensive brewing to the north, we'll need every man and woman capable of holding a lasgun.'

'That was my thinking too,' Cass admitted. 'Havali took some convincing.'

'How about the rest of your squadron?' Orlov asked, trying and failing to avoid making the question sound pointed. Cass gave a little shake of her head.

'There won't be any trouble from the Vagabonds, Orlov. At least none you'll hear about.'

'I guess I should be thanking you then,' he said. 'I'll be here to pick you up tomorrow morning.'

'Orlov,' Cass said, checking him in the doorway. 'Let me know if Marrand finds anything? Anything at all.'

He simply nodded, and left.

* * *

Cass and Orlov arrived at Suchen Palace together the next morning. They were once more led into the east wing, though this time the aide took them not to Havali's office, but to the primary strategium. The chamber wasn't yet ready, so the two aviators joined the host of Guard officers waiting in the corridor outside.

'No Jakyra?' Cass asked Orlov as they waited, wondering whether her apparent absence was a good thing or not.

'There's a dogfight developing above Torr City, a big one apparently,' Orlov said. 'She's still upstairs helping to coordinate it. Last I heard Drusha's Thunderbolts were scrambling to lend assistance.'

'We're stretched thin,' Cass pointed out as she pondered the news. 'Do we even have enough aircraft in this sector to go on the offensive?'

Orlov said nothing.

A figure approached them from among the Militarum officers, and Cass realised it was Wellend. He looked as nervous as he had when he had been facing a firing squad, but nodded guardedly to her and Orlov.

'All ready then?' Cass asked him, trying to sound upbeat.

'I think so,' he responded, sounding anything but.

'Has there been any word from out of the pocket recently?' she went on. 'Since we pulled out?'

'I don't know,' Wellend admitted. 'Nobody will tell me anything.'

'Welcome to headquarters,' Cass responded, glancing ruefully at Orlov.

They didn't have to wait for long. Havali appeared from his office, trailing a wake of staffers and green-robed Munitorum logisticians. The officers, Cass included, saluted as he passed by and swept into the strategium. A few moments later those left outside were invited in.

The room was dark, lit only by the blue glow of the holotable projecting a three-dimensional, rotating Imperial aquila into the air above it. Havali had taken up position on the far side, and the officers present arrayed themselves around the table, taking post by seniority. As members of the Imperial Navy, Cass and Orlov stood out of order, on Havali's left. Wellend, the most junior officer present, stood across from the lieutenant general. Cass noted there was no sign of Lord Commissar Vasquez, or any of his ghoulish minions.

There was a thudding sound as the flakboard-reinforced doorway was closed and locked. The holo-display blinked and changed from the aquila to a chart showing the Eji River Valley and its environs.

'Greetings, soldiers and aviators of the Imperium,' Havali began. 'I trust you have all familiarised yourselves with the general order yesterday as well as the army-wide stand-to, so I won't delay things with any preamble. Suffice to say the rumours are true – we are shifting stance in preparation for immediate offensive operations.'

Silence greeted the official pronouncement. Havali continued.

'Over the past day cycle you have all provided me with orders of battle and combat readiness reports. I thank you for these. I've just finished meeting with Quartermaster Primus Almira, of the Departmento Munitorum, and she has assured me the stocks and reserves are there. We have the fuel, the foodstuffs and the ammunition necessary to renew active manoeuvres, albeit for a short period.'

Almira, standing with her logisticians away from the gathering around the holo, inclined her hooded head briefly.

'The primary operational objective is as follows,' Havali said. 'Link up with Army Group Centre and support their withdrawal south of the Eji River. I have already spoken with the divisions I intend to be directly involved, but it will require army-wide movement and support. This is going to act as an overview briefing covering preliminary outlines. You are welcome to ask questions. At this stage, everything is on the table.

'Kantu Valley is the key,' he carried on, highlighting the relevant part of the holo-chart, turning a small subsidiary valley digging into the flank of the Eji crimson. 'It runs directly from the southern edge of the pocket to the river's northern bank. If it can be secured, it will provide a channel for an organised withdrawal by Army Group Centre. The difficulty will be dealing with its current occupants. The xenos are present in force.

'Their exact strength is being tabulated, and an approximate estimate will be supplied to you all as part of an intelligence docket by this time tomorrow. I will speak openly though – exact figures are difficult to come by. Army Group Centre is under continuous, heavy assault, but the enemy's air cover and the stalemate in orbit means we're unable to locate and assess the enemy's reserves with any degree of certainty.'

'There are rumours of an extremely substantial xenos force massing further up the Eji Valley,' an immaculately attired Ventrillian colonel interjected. 'How true are they?'

'That is conjecture, based on a few long-range picts and reports from Ushen and Torr City regarding the movements of the ork forces there. Regardless, we must treat this intelligence as viable, which is part of the reason an effort must be made to relieve Army Group Centre. We must retake the initiative before the xenos strike. There is no indication they are yet in a position to counter a push over the river.'

Cass wondered how many of the officers present really believed the enemy's unpreparedness was truly the cause for the sudden, new operation, but none moved to cast any aspersions on Havali's claim.

'The most important feature of Kantu Valley is its agri-collective, which lies on this spur of ground here, at the valley's northern entrance. It is currently infested with xenos, and is acting as a centre for their control over the valley and a base for their artillery, bombarding the southern side of the pocket. Capturing it is vital. I am therefore proposing that it be the target of an initial, airborne assault. Once it is taken, it should be possible to link up with the southernmost units from Army Group Centre. Then it will be a case of pushing across the river and effecting a full link-up, clearing the rest of the valley as we go.'

'How can any of this be practical when the river lies between us?' a Zenonian Free Company colonel asked. 'Haven't all the crossing points been destroyed? Surely it will take too long to construct a pontoon, especially as it's likely to come under immediate artillery and aerial attack.'

'The river is fordable,' Havali said with a finality that sounded like the pronouncement of a death sentence. There were murmurs around the table.

'Even to heavy armour?' an Alban tanker asked.

'That is still being assessed, but we have good reason to believe certain stretches are.'

'What is this intelligence based on?' the Alban pressed. 'How can you be sure it's crossable at all?'

Cass thought Havali was about to make a target of Wellend, and perhaps in doing so deliberately undermine the whole proposed offensive. She was impressed, however, when the lieutenant general shielded him instead, keeping the matter vague despite the obvious unrest of several of the officers.

'It is based on assessments by Army Group Centre,' he said.

The silence indicated the assembly was dissatisfied with the answer. Cass hesitated, then spoke up.

'I can confirm it, at least in part,' she said, feeling every eye suddenly on her. 'There are certainly xenos present on the south side of the river, which implies it can be crossed. In our recent mission into the pocket, my squadron experienced brief contact with ground forces approximately here, and here.'

She raised her hand into the holo to highlight sections along what had been their flight path, then added a section of the river to it.

'We followed the course of the Eji on two occasions, here and here, and I saw no boats or water transports being used, or any sign of such things on either bank. The numbers that have crossed over are not inconsiderable, even if they have not yet formed a unified threat. But I don't see any other way they could have made it over unless the river is fordable. Certainly its banks look far lower than they once were, which makes sense, given the lack of rain.'

The silence she had interrupted returned. She wondered if she should have held her tongue, glancing at Havali, who finally took her lead.

'Even if the river is not entirely fordable right now, if this weather continues it may soon become so. The dry weather has caused its banks to shrink a great deal, and unless the rainy season arrives in the next few days we won't be able to afford to leave it unguarded. At the very least, advancing to the Eji is now a strategic necessity. It should have been done weeks ago.'

Nobody pointed out that it was Havali's orders – or lack of them – that had kept Imperial forces well south of the river up until now.

'Stratego Eblin agrees that an aerial insertion into Kantu agri-collective will not only deprive the xenos of their strongest point in the valley, but will also further draw their attention away from the river,' Havali pressed on, trying to regain momentum as he switched the highlighting on the holo to a more detailed over-view of the settlement. 'He has assessed that serious resistance to a crossing is unlikely, and I am in agreement.'

'Because the orks will be too busy attacking the poor bastards we've dropped in the agri-collective,' a Hyrkan divisional commander observed. Cass wondered whether he would have made such a bold assessment if there had been a commissar in the room.

'The initial moments in the collective will be fraught, yes, as all such airborne insertions are,' Havali said patiently, clearly trying to keep as many officers engaged with the idea as possible. 'But resistance will not last long. As soon as Kantu Collective is secured, Brigadier Felkin will begin pushing troops south to link up, while the main body of our relief column begins to cross the river. The xenos in Kantu Valley will be pincered and destroyed in short order.'

'And what of those outside the valley, attacking the pocket along its other fronts?' the Hyrkan asked. 'Surely as soon as they learn of the attempted evacuation, they will mount an all-out assault.'

'They will, but strategos analysis estimates they will struggle to reach that level of coordination. We should have the better part of the day to begin mobilising the pocket. Army Group Centre is aware of the difficulties that will be involved. Casualties will likely be high.'

'How high?' someone asked.

'Possibly around fifty per cent,' Havali said.

Expressions grew grimmer, and Cass found herself wondering how brutal the true figure would be, if that was the one Havali was admitting to.

'Isn't there a risk of destabilising the entire front for minimal potential strategic gains?' the Alban tanker pointed out. 'Has there been a proper value assessment? If this goes wrong, Army Group Centre might be wiped out, and we will have expended crucial resources ahead of a potential major xenos offensive.'

'The risks have been weighed,' Havali said. 'And Ushen has given its blessing. High command wish to see action taken, and all the tests we have undertaken have indicated the likelihood of victory falls within acceptable marginals.'

The general had slipped into 'headquarters speak', and Cass didn't like it. He was obfuscating, deliberately keeping details at bay. She doubted many of the other officers around her were fooled either. Had he just tried to imply the impetus for the whole operation had come from high command at Ushen, rather than his own desire to save face?

'How capable will the pocket be of coordinating with us?' the Ventrillian who had spoken before asked. 'Is their command structure still intact after the evacuations? Are their communications open?'

'Comms with the pocket are patchy, but I was able to speak with the current field commander of Army Group Centre, Brigadier Felkin, for a short while this morning. He was made aware of the shift in strategic priorities and the preliminary plans to come to his aid. He agreed that the operation is viable and that he expected Army Group Centre can continue to hold for another week standard before lack of supplies and mounting casualties risk a total collapse. I informed him that I would update him with a more detailed plan at the conclusion of this session.'

'What's the aerial situation over Kantu?' Orlov asked.

'Challenging,' Havali replied, which almost caused Cass to let out a bitter laugh. 'Xenos artillery includes anti-air, all along the valley sides. Flying low will be a safer option than attempting to stay high or coming over the ridgelines. That's why we'll need your Valkyries, major. Not only the Vagabonds, but Shadow and Nemesis Squadrons as well.'

'That represents this front's entire complement of fliers,' Orlov pointed out.

'I am aware,' Havali said. 'I have already spoken with Air Marshal Jakyra, and she has cleared a full deployment.'

Of course she has, Cass thought. Jakyra was never one to hold back when it came to putting her pilots in harm's way.

'Speed, aggression and the application of overwhelming force remain potent buttresses in the architecture of victory,' Havali said, now reduced to just quoting scripture-strategy from the *Tactica Imperialis*. 'I intend to make use of all three here. We shall storm Kantu Valley and remind these xenos monstrosities of the weight of the Emperor's wrath.'

There were murmurs of support, but nothing more. Cass' focus was on the holo's ill-defined representation of the agri-collective at the northern end of the valley.

'Do we have details about ork dispositions in the settlement itself?' she asked. 'The locations of anti-air batteries there? They'll be far easier to silence if we know where they are before we go in.'

'What scans and picts we have are still being examined, but you will have an update on that soon,' Havali said.

'Is that headquarters speak for "we don't know", or will there be genuine, actionable intelligence forthcoming?' Cass asked, not caring if she sounded insubordinate.

'There will be more,' Havali said firmly. 'I cannot yet speak to its level of detail.'

'I will hold a further briefing with the air marshal and my other squadron leaders, and we'll assess all this and come up with a viable tactical report,' Orlov said, trying to defuse the moment.

'You will have to do so quickly, major,' Havali urged. 'I plan on beginning forward motions towards the river within the next three cycles. Battlespace shaping is already underway. The Terrifern Light Division began engaging the xenos scattered south of the river this morning. The pocket may be holding, but it cannot do so indefinitely. We must move with alacrity.'

Cass suppressed the urge to point out that it was only the threat of being hauled before high command that had generated this sense of urgency in Havali. They were all committed now.

'The briefing will be held later this afternoon, and I will have a full assessment to you by this evening,' Orlov confirmed. 'Fuel and supplies are already being massed at Barduk West. I'm sure the air marshal will be able to furnish you with more specifics.'

'Who will we be carrying?' Cass asked. 'Who's forming the spearhead?'

'A mixed strike force,' Havali said. 'A platoon of Alphic Hydras and a company of Harakoni Warhawks.'

As he spoke, he indicated officers in the livery of the two forces, standing across from him. Cass exchanged a brief nod with them.

'Will it be enough to hold the ground if we take it?' she asked, not intending any insult, but likewise no longer willing to simply accept the assumptions of her superiors.

'You should have immediate support from the southern end of the pocket,' Havali said. 'I expect the greater part of the relief column to have arrived to reinforce the vanguard at the collective within two hours of insertion, and that's without counting on further assistance from within the pocket itself.'

'I request I be allowed to accompany the airborne assault, sir,' a voice cut in. It was Wellend. 'I know the terrain and dispositions, sir,' he said, standing firm under the sudden attention of the room. 'I believe my own regiment, the Mordian Five-Fiftieth, currently hold the line closest to Kantu Collective. I can provide liaison and get the pocket moving, especially if comms are unreliable.'

'As you wish,' Havali said. 'I'm sure Captain Elza can find a space for you on board one of her transports.'

Cass wanted to tell Wellend that going in with the spearhead meant almost certain death, but she suspected he knew that already.

'I assume my squadrons won't be expected to remain on-station above Kantu once it is captured?' Orlov asked. 'Xenos air presence will have scrambled by then.'

'You will have as much top cover as can be spared,' Havali said. 'But you will be expected to remain flexible, either in supporting the defence of Kantu and the southward movement of the pocket, or assisting the movement across the river to complete the link-up. I will inform the air marshal of those priorities.'

Another lack of reassurance.

Havali fielded more questions from his Guard commanders, allaying concerns about supplying the offensive and contingencies in case the pocket collapsed. The dry weather was mentioned, and the lack of supplies, especially water, in the pocket, as well as the possibility of the rainy season finally arriving. The mood of the gathering didn't seem good to Cass, but no one made a stand against the overall plan. Havali had either strong-armed the naysayers in private already, or they understood that speaking out against making an effort to rescue the remains of Army Group Centre risked the same sort of censure Havali was currently trying to avoid.

'Three day cycles, local,' he reiterated as he brought the general briefing to a close. 'Local objectives and order priority lists will be circulated to corps commanders tomorrow, to be disseminated to their divisions. I will also contact the relevant officers undertaking the agri-collective insertion for a more detailed planning session tomorrow evening. For now, are there any further questions?'

There were none, at least none anyone was willing to voice publicly.

'The Emperor protects,' Havali said, and dismissed the meeting.

* * *

'I don't like it,' Cass said as she and Orlov took an open-topped Munitorum groundcar back to Barduk.

'Nobody does,' Orlov said. 'I'm going to speak to Havali and Jakyra in private before the next major briefing, try and pin down some firmer details. Get Marrand from Shadow Squadron and Sergios from Nemesis Squadron involved too, so the whole wing is represented.'

'Do you think it's realistic? Going on the offensive, I mean. Breaking the pocket out.'

'You're the one who's flown it already. You tell me.'

'It will be rough, as far as the aerial side goes. We were told to avoid Kantu, now we're flying down its throat. Every wing will suffer, whether it's top cover or us flying the hard base. And that's before the orks begin to scramble. The fighter squadrons are going to have a hell of a fight on their hands.'

'From what I've heard, they're ready for it,' Orlov said. 'The likes of Bix don't appreciate being stuck out on the tertiary front. Get high command to take note and they could be shifted in the next strategic reshuffle, to Ushen or Torr City.'

'Throne knows why anyone would want that,' Cass said coldly.

'It goes for Jakyra too. She wants this to succeed as much as Havali. A win on the tertiary front while Ushen and Torr are deadlocked would boost her standing in the fleet. And those rumours about a major ork concentration to the north aren't going away. Hitting them first may take the sting out of whatever they're planning.'

'Or provoke them,' Cass said. 'Do we really have the numbers to follow this through?'

'Looks like we'll find out soon enough.'

'And none of it would be happening if I hadn't made Havali aware of the possibility,' Cass went on, unable to hide her frustration, or the sense of regret stalking her.

'You had your reasons,' Orlov said. 'What's done is done. Vagabond Squadron is going up again, Cass, and we all need your head in the game if we're going to make it through this one, let alone win it.'

Cass brought her aviators together when she returned to the lines. Korrie, Zeke, Vaughn, Holsten, Macks, Konstantina and Straks gathered in her office, most of them looking grave. Cass laid out what Havali had said, using a flight chart spread out on the desktop to illustrate the plan as it currently stood.

'So it's a gauntlet run?' Vaughn asked. 'Figures.'

Cass was in no mood for her flight lieutenant's attitude, but refused to take the first bait he threw out.

'We should be able to fly below the worst of the flak curtain, at least on the way in,' she said. 'And we'll have the element of surprise.'

'How can we be sure of avoiding the flak if we don't know where their batteries are emplaced?' Vaughn asked.

'I've been promised more detail.'

'Well thank the Golden Throne for that.'

'And they want us to stay on-station?' Korrie said.

'They want us to be "tactically flexible". But if they're not specifying then no, we won't be staying above the collective if it's under serious fire.'

'What about enemy interdiction?' Vaughn asked.

'We'll have the whole of Barduk up watching our topside. There's no doubt it'll get messy, but we'll have support.'

Konstantina gave a little shrug of her slender shoulders. 'At least there'll be plenty to shoot.'

'For about three minutes, before we've all been blown out of the sky,' Vaughn said.

'If you have alternatives I can take to the general before the rest of this plan is locked in, I'd love to hear them,' Cass said, eyeballing the lieutenant.

'What do the other squadron leaders think about it?' Vaughn asked without offering any suggestions.

'I don't know, I haven't had a chance to speak with them yet,' Cass said. 'There'll be another briefing tomorrow that will include them, the Scions and Harakoni, and maybe Bix and the other top cover commanders. We'll know more about where we stand then.'

'What're we supposed to do until then?' Konstantina said.

'Relax and enjoy life,' Cass responded. 'While you all still can.'

'What about Cobb?' Vaughn asked. The question caught Cass off-guard. She shook her head.

'No news.'

'Has anyone actually been looking?'

'A Lightning swung over the crash site, but reported no signs of any survivors. *Pauper* was burning.'

'If that's the case then we're going into this operation with barely fifty per cent strength,' Vaughn pointed out.

'Which is why we're all going to need to be at the top of our game,' Cass replied. 'No excuses from here on in. Is that clear, lieutenant?'

Vaughn looked at her venomously, but held his tongue.

'As soon as I know more about anything, be it Cobb or the operation, I'll let you all know,' Cass promised. 'Right now we're in a waiting game, and all of us know how to play it. Do whatever you have to do to keep your head square on your shoulders, and if you have any issues, come speak to me in private.'

That evening Cass made contact briefly again with Orlov, asking him about the possibility of another warbird, and pilot replacements. He headed her off with news that he had already made the request, but had been told the *Mandatum Divinum* had nothing to spare. All but a few mothballed fliers from the Old Mother's full Aeronautica complement had now been committed to the war on Kanai Tertius, and even the most advanced of the new trainees still had weeks before their final exams. They could prove more a liability than an asset if drafted early into a unit like the tactical wing.

The best Orlov could do was the offer of a repurposed combat servitor for *Vagrant*, to man the bruiser slot left vacant by Platz's death. Cass almost refused, knowing how little Zeke liked servitors, but at that moment she was willing to take anything she could get.

After the talk with Orlov, she went to bed. Sleep was fitful, and she woke sometime around dawn.

She lay on her back in the dark, listening. The lines outside her office were quiet, the rest of the squadron presumably still asleep. She had woken up with her hands resting together on her chest, and as she shifted, she discovered something was pinned between her fingers.

She frowned, lifting it before her eyes, peering at the faint glow beginning to spread in through the prefab room's half-closed blinds.

It was one of Zeke's litany scripts, a strip of parchment with the Imperial prayers for the dead inked on it. The same strip Cass had seen clutched in Platz's dead grip after Zeke had pulled him out of *Vagrant* and left him on the rockcrete at the promethium hub.

Hands starting to shake violently, she threw the scrap away, and only then did she wake up properly.

There was no script. She had been dreaming, at least in part. Sunlight was beaming in through the blinds.

The experience left her cold, but she tried to shrug it off, to forget the memory of how they'd simply abandoned the Fledgling's body. She couldn't afford those sorts of distractions, at least until the operation was over and they might be able to afford a few precious moments of introspection and memorialisation. If they were going to keep living, they had to forget the dead.

Later that morning, after Cass had washed and dressed and was reviewing fuel and ammunition rosters at her desk, there was a knock at the door. She bade whoever it was enter, and found Korrie ducking inside.

'You wanted to see me, Chief?' she asked, closing the door behind her.

'Just briefly,' Cass said. 'How's your side holding up?'

'Just fine,' Korrie said with a broad smile.

'Am I going to have to go to the medicae and ask to see your report, or are you going to tell me the truth?'

'It's a couple of minor fractures,' Korrie said, looking a little shamefaced. 'So like I said, just fine.'

'I want you to stay grounded for the next one, Mel,' Cass told her. 'Zeke will take the aft cockpit, and we'll run *Vagrant* with servitors for gunners. We've done it before.'

'Not a chance, sir,' Korrie said immediately.

Cass tapped her desk. 'Don't forget who's in charge of this squadron, navigator. Don't think I won't order you.'

'Please,' Korrie said, looking far more distressed than she had after she'd been trampled by a rampaging ork. 'Don't do this, Chief. I'm fine. You can't ground me with everyone else going up. And with *Pauper* gone surely we need everybody?'

'If I was a roughhousing kind of officer I might get up at this point, shove you, test to see if it really hurts,' Cass pointed out. Korrie smiled again.

'Pretty sure I can still take you, Chief.'

Cass sighed, resting her hands on the table. 'I don't want to go up without you,' she admitted. 'Throne knows, I don't want to go up at all. I've got… a bad feeling about this one.'

'All the more reason for me to be with you, Chief. It's just sitting in a Throne-damned chair, after all.'

'Are you on morphia?' Cass asked.

'A little. Not enough to impair me, I swear. Just enough to take the edge off.'

Cass looked her old friend up and down, and gave in to her own fear. Conscience had demanded she tried to save Korrie, but what she had told her was true – she would feel much better with her in the aft cockpit, injured or not.

'Have it your way,' she said. 'Go get some rest, while you still can. Dismissed.'

CHAPTER FOURTEEN

The next three days were the worst kind of Aeronautica experience: briefings interspersed with interminable waiting. Cass tried to keep a handle on her own emotions, all the while worrying that the squadron was on the brink of breaking point. She feared that there was now little more than unit pride keeping the Vagabonds on a steady course.

Matters came to a head on the morning of the day before operational launch. Cass had just got dressed after a short spell under the icy blast of the squadron's shower block when a knock came at her door. She opened it to find Korrie on the other side. She knew immediately from her expression that it was bad.

'It's Vaughn, Chief,' she said. 'You'd better come right away.'

'What's the idiot done now?' Cass breathed, following Korrie through the lines to the main door.

To her surprise, she found Bix waiting for her just inside. The fighter commander looked apologetic.

'Sorry to come knocking, Elza,' she said, returning her salute.

'But I think I've accidentally picked up something that belongs to you.'

She moved out of the way so Cass could see through the door. There were two pilots standing just outside, aviators from one of the 911th's Lightning squadrons. They were supporting Vaughn between them. *Rogue*'s pilot was barely conscious, and Cass could smell the stink of alcohol even from inside the doorway.

'Throne damn it,' she growled. 'Where did you find him?'

'He broke into my liquor cabinet sometime last night,' Bix said. 'How he managed it without waking me I've no idea, but this morning he stumbled into Reaver Squadron's bunk room. I thought I'd better bring him here before the provosts or the Commissariat got a hold of him. Not the sort of problem any of us want to be dealing with on the eve of an offensive.'

'I'm sorry, Bix,' Cass said, feeling a rush of embarrassment. 'I had no idea he'd do something like that. Has he said anything?'

'Nothing that bears repeating,' Bix said. 'It's lucky he picked me to rob.'

'I'll restock you once we're upstairs,' Cass promised. Bix waved her off.

'Don't worry about that. Just be careful. If you need any help with anything, let me know. The Nine-Eleventh always has your back.'

Cass thanked her again and got Vaughn inside. Bix and her pilots departed, leaving Cass glaring at her most senior pilot in the entrance to the lines. He was barely aware of her, slumped against the wall.

'Hal,' she snapped, shaking him by the collar of his stained flight suit. 'Wake up.'

He grunted and looked at her blearily. There was a moment of horrified recognition, and he groaned.

'You're a disgrace, Hal,' Cass growled under her breath. 'A Throne-damned disgrace!'

To her surprise, he burst into tears.

As she tried to find the right words, she heard movement behind her, and turned to find Xijen emerging from the main body of the hab-tunnel. He looked from Cass to Vaughn, his expression grim. Cass wondered if Korrie had gone and found him.

Macks was behind him, and wordlessly the pair moved past Cass and got a grip on Vaughn. He snivelled, but made no effort to resist as Macks moved him further inside.

'Wait,' Cass ordered Xijen. He stayed behind as Vaughn was helped away.

'He's gone too far this time,' Cass told him. 'He's lucky Bix brought him back. Breaking into another squadron's lines, stealing, insulting a senior officer, intoxicated while on standby, and all right before an offensive. He'd be lucky not to face execution, either here or back on board the *Mandatum Divinum*. Stripped down to the rank of gunner, or thrown out of the Aeronautica entirely. He'd be pressed into the Munitorum as a menial or end up with the lower deck work gangs on the Old Mother.'

'I know,' Xijen said. 'And with respect, sir, I don't think you believe he deserves any of that. He's cut up inside. He needs time off, away from the front, so those cuts can heal.'

'We're flying into what might be the hardest operation of this tour tomorrow, and you're asking me to sideline my best pilot?' Cass demanded. 'Are you ready to fly *Rogue* in his stead?'

'Yes,' Xijen said without hesitation.

'I doubt Orlov will approve his rotation off the front, not with the Commissariat sniffing for blood right now.'

'You know there are other ways he can avoid this, sir,' Xijen said.

That was true. Temporary injury would take Vaughn out of the firing line, and stop him being Cass' problem for the time being. But wasn't that another example of taking the easy path? What did it say about her leadership?

'Are you doing this because you want to try and spare Hal?' Cass asked. 'Or because you genuinely think he's incapable of leading?'

'A bit of both, I suppose,' Xijen answered cautiously. 'You said yourself, he's the best pilot in the squadron. But everyone can see he's been pushed too far for too long. Give him some time out, sir, and I'm certain he'll be back to his old self.'

'So indiscipline at best, and a terrible influence on other members of this squadron at worst,' Cass said. Xijen smiled.

'It takes all sorts to fly a Valkyrie, captain.'

'I'll think about it, Xijen,' Cass said eventually. 'Just get him in his bunk, and make sure he doesn't disturb me, or anyone else, for the rest of the day.'

Cass went and found Vaughn in the early evening, prior to the final tactical briefing. She had given him long enough to sleep it off, but he still looked awful – he rose from his bunk like a revenant from their tomb, gaunt and unshaven, hair tousled, stinking even more than he had when Bix had brought him in.

'I'm pulling you off the line,' Cass said, not even bothering to haul him through to her office before telling him. Most of the squadron's remnants already knew anyway.

'What do you mean?' Vaughn demanded.

'I mean you're not flying out tomorrow, or anytime soon,' Cass said. 'Xijen will pilot *Rogue*. I've already spoken with him.'

'Has Orlov okayed this?'

'Not yet, but he will.'

'I doubt it. The offensive begins tomorrow.'

'He won't have much choice once you've broken your arm. You can do it yourself, or I can get Korrie to do it. Your choice. We'll say the bunk above you collapsed.'

Vaughn slumped back into his crumpled sheets, his expression smouldering.

'What?' Cass snapped. 'Didn't you want this? Hadn't you had enough? That's what you've been telling me, what your crew's been telling me! I'm going to get you killed? Well, not any more.'

Vaughn closed his eyes, saying nothing.

The final briefing ran without a hitch. Afterwards, Cass made sure everyone had eaten, then did her best to sleep. The lines were quiet – it would be hours yet before even Zorn began doing his checks.

She slipped into a fatigued state, half awake, half asleep, until she moved her arm and hit her hand on something near her head. The pain against her knuckles jolted her awake. She reached up groggily, peering at what she had hit, finding her fingers probing something. Flesh, and something wet – blood. Platz, lying next to her, half his face a sheet of crimson, his skin cold, dead. She'd struck her hand off his helmet.

She cried out and scrambled out of bed, but the body wasn't in her bed – she was tripping over it where it now lay on the floor, the way she'd almost tripped over it behind *Vagrant*. She yelled, snatching for the lumen switch, flinching in the sudden, harsh light.

Nothing. There was nothing there. No corpse, in her bed or on her floor. No dead Fledgling. She had simply rapped her knuckles against the wall and been woken by the pain.

She made it back to bed, sweating and shaking, and lay awake watching the unblinking red glow of her chrono until she could no longer stand it. Then she rose, dressed, and ventured out to the squadron hangars.

Cass wasn't the only one who couldn't sleep. Zorn and the ground crews had only just started their checks, but half the squadron were already up and running their own assessments on their warbirds. Zeke accosted Cass almost as soon as she entered the echoing hangar.

'They've given us a dead-eye,' he said, looking downright distressed. 'To replace the Fledgling.'

'Orlov mentioned it,' Cass said. 'Is that going to be a problem?'

Zeke's silence combined with his expression implied it would most definitely be a problem, albeit not one he felt comfortable complaining outright about.

'Where is it?' Cass asked.

'Already mounted up. The ground crews brought it and Zorn activated it. Freaking bastard thing.'

Cass walked with her gunner to *Vagrant*. The Valkyrie was sitting hunched and still partly clad in a tarp under the hangar's half-active lumens, looking like a predator poised to strike from the pre-dawn shadows. Sure enough, a figure was already sitting strapped into the fold-down port gunner's seat in the flier's open side hatch. It was a combat servitor, the living, lobotomised remains of a large man, clad in a dark blue Navy jump suit and a brass interface cuirass that was studded with tubes and cables worming their way into the thing's body. Its shaven head was part crude augmetics and restraining bolts, part slack, expressionless flesh. It showed no indication of any awareness of its surroundings, staring off across the hangar bay unseeingly.

Servitors fulfilling actual mission roles as opposed to just supplementing the ground crews weren't unheard of in the Aeronautica Imperialis. There were even some specialised enough to act as co-pilots, but their presence was much rarer among the tactical wings, where the need for skilled and experienced fliers precluded what could be programmed into a near-vegetative brainpan by the strange tech-rituals of the Adeptus Mechanicus. Among many other pejoratives, aviators tended to call them dead-eyes, not because they were good shots, but because their expressions, regardless of the circumstances around them, were almost always corpse-like.

Zeke got up cautiously next to the servitor and waved a hand in front of its face – sure enough, there was no reaction. It just continued staring dead ahead. It would do so until relevant battle stimuli intruded into its base consciousness and triggered preset combat responses. That, at least, was the theory.

'We're going to need both bruisers in action for this one,' Cass told Zeke. 'Even if one of them is being manned by a servitor. It's better than nothing.'

'We're carrying Scions, aren't we?' Zeke asked. 'I'd rather one of them took the port side.'

'If everything goes to plan, we won't have cargo for long. You're just going to have to put up with it.'

'It's a bad omen,' Zeke said darkly. 'We shouldn't be carrying dead things on board.'

'I've got enough to worry about without adding omens to the list,' Cass said, rapidly losing her patience. 'It's flying with us and that's the end of it. It could save our lives.'

Zeke was wise enough to let the matter lie for the time being. Cass heard her voice being called over the engine cycling. She broke off and strode back out in front of *Vagrant*.

Orlov had arrived.

'Thought I'd come and see you in person before lift-off,' he said, looking almost sheepish as he glanced around at the activity filling the hangar. 'Wish you good fortune and the Emperor's blessings.'

'Well, a bit more of those sorts of things can't hurt,' Cass said, trying her best to sound upbeat. 'How're things looking back at command?'

'Pensive,' Orlov admitted. 'As you'd expect. Havali is risking it all on this.'

'Tell me about it,' Cass said humourlessly. Orlov glanced away, then looked back at her, seemingly finding the resolve to say what he had actually come to say.

'I requested I be given the lead of this one, in person. It was denied by Jakyra.'

Cass felt a moment's surprise. Going by the normal hierarchy of the Aeronautica Imperialis, as wing commander of the 901st Orlov would usually have been expected to lead the day's operation himself. But that wasn't how the Imperial Navy's tactical wings functioned. Valkyrie wing commanders were typically considered an elite asset of greater use at headquarters, overseeing what were typically complex and fraught operations. Orlov's own warbird, *Wrathbringer*, was among the reserve craft mothballed on board the *Mandatum Divinum*, and Cass doubted he had led an operation since his promotion. She had never assumed he would be required to take the lead in the push north.

'You didn't have to do that,' she told him truthfully.

'It felt right,' he said. 'Havali forced this on you. It shouldn't be your burden to bear.'

'He gave me an order, and I'm obeying,' Cass said. 'Nothing I haven't done a thousand times before.'

Orlov looked as though he wanted to say more, but couldn't find the words.

'I'll be fine,' Cass told him, privately amazed to find herself trying to console him, and not the other way round. 'This won't be worse than Ushen. It can't be. Besides, I'd rather have you in the operations room making sure things run smoothly. Better you than Jakyra.'

'She's expected to be there as well,' Orlov warned. 'Her shuttle's currently inbound from the Old Mother.'

'But you'll still have the tactical lead?' Cass said, hoping she was right. Jakyra assuming command of the situation once it started to develop certainly wouldn't improve their odds.

'I will,' he confirmed, to Cass' relief. 'Don't worry. I'll get the green light to get you out of there as soon as you drop your cargo, if you need to.'

'We'll see,' Cass said, not wanting to ponder the idea of trying to remain on station above Kantu.

Orlov held out his hand. She took it, and shook.

'You're a damn fine pilot and a damn fine squadron leader, Cass,' he told her, his tone fierce. 'Trust your instincts up there, and the Vagabonds will win another victory for mankind.'

Orlov was good enough to briefly mingle with the other crews, but he had barely got into the staff groundcar taking him back to Suchen when the sound of heavy boots ringing in unison from the rockcrete caused Cass to abandon her final checks of *Vagrant*'s exterior.

She turned and found a wedge of Alphic Hydras approaching her. A moment's instinctive concern was replaced by the realisation that her cargo had just arrived.

All of the Hydras had their dark red carapace armour on, but they had not yet connected their hellguns to their power packs, and their helmets still hung from their belts, replaced for the time being with maroon berets. The individual leading them was even taller than the ones following him, a slab of a man with a stubbly, square jaw and livid burn scars down the left side of his face. He looked as though he had just come charging right out of a Militarum recruitment poster.

He saluted Cass, and she returned it.

'Lieutenant Stryk, Eighty-Fifth Alphic Hydras,' he said in a deep, growling voice. 'Your squadron will be providing transport and aerial support for my platoon.'

'So I hear,' Cass said, remembering Stryk from the final tact-briefing they had undertaken the day before. 'Let us hope for a swift and uninterrupted flight.'

'As the Emperor wills,' the big man declared, reminding Cass of Zeke. 'I'm told you'll be able to remain on-station once we deploy?'

'If the situation demands it,' Cass said, trying not to let her reluctance show. 'But I can't make any promises. It depends how hot it gets up there. If the airspace remains unsecured and they're hitting us with anti-air, holding station would be a death sentence. At least you might be able to use our wreckage as cover.'

'Affirmative,' Stryk said. To Cass' relief, she realised he was agreeing with her.

'We'll play it by ear,' he carried on. 'Top cover would be appreciated, but I accept you'll likely be needed elsewhere, back south at the river. Either way, the Hydras will get the job done.'

Cass heard the clicking of running steel-heeled boots, and the Hydras parted to admit Wellend, face flushed, cramming his Mordian cap onto his head as he came. He looked small and slender compared to the hulking, armoured bulk of the Scions he passed between.

'Am I late?' he asked, glancing nervously between Cass and Stryk before remembering to salute.

'No,' Cass reassured him before making introductions. 'Lieutenant Stryk, this is Lieutenant Wellend Felkin, Mordian Five-Fiftieth. He's accompanying your platoon today and assisting the link-up with Army Group Centre.'

'I'd been told we'd have liaison on the ground,' Stryk said, looking Wellend up and down as he spoke. 'I wasn't aware he'd be so... young.'

'Lieutenant Felkin was fighting in the pocket only a few days ago,' Cass said, feeling an unexpected desire to defend the

Mordian. 'He has seen action alongside the men and women we're going there to get out, and he knows the ground. I'm sure his contribution will be invaluable.'

'It's going to get hot once we reach Kanai,' Stryk said to Wellend, ignoring Cass. 'Stay with my platoon, but don't get in the way. When we have need of you, we'll let you know. Is that clear?'

'It's clear, lieutenant,' Wellend said, and Cass was glad to hear some iron in his voice as he held Stryk's gaze. The big Scion grunted, then smiled.

'Just get us to that agri-collective, Captain Elza, and the Alphic Hydras will do the rest.'

The 901st Wing's preacher, old Ionicus, came to bless them before lift-off. Cass joined the rest of her crews as well as the Scions in kneeling on the rockcrete, arrayed in a semicircle around the holy man. He had been the caretaker of the wing's spiritual needs for as long as Cass could remember – Throne only knew how old he actually was. Dressed in the deep blue, white-trimmed robes of a formal Imperial Navy pastor, he raised his aquila staff in benediction over them, his droning voice calling for the God-Emperor's blessings, for His protection and, above all, for His favour in smiting the foul and perfidious xenos. Cass tried not to let her mind wander, tried not to consider the carnage and the death that no doubt waited for them. She fought to find some solace in faith.

Ionicus spoke the *Ave Imperator* at the end of his prayers, and Vagabond Squadron and the Alphic Hydras echoed it, the final benediction ringing back from the high vaults of the hangar. Ionicus then wetted his fingers with blessed water from the bowl being carried by the pale-faced, robed boy who followed him, and stooped with some difficulty to anoint the brow of each soldier and aviator in turn. Cass, as squadron leader, received the blessing first, fixing her gaze on the golden aquila topping the preacher's staff.

'May the God-Emperor's grace be with you,' Ionicus mumbled as he brushed his forefingers to Cass' forehead. She smelled the mustiness of his robes, felt the slight, senile tremor behind his touch.

'And with you,' she replied, realising how dry her throat had become.

Afterwards, Ionicus switched to blessing the aircraft themselves. His young assistant in tow, he went from one to another, dashing holy water from an aspergillum against the prow of *Vagrant*, *Rogue* and *Ruffian*.

Cass caught sight of Zorn watching on from the hangar's edge. The red-cowled enginseer had already said his own benedictions to the warbirds, anointing them with the sacred oils used by the Martian priesthood. Cass suspected he would scoff at this display of the Imperial Creed, perhaps even consider it blasphemous, but he also knew better than to attempt to interrupt it. It would do good for pilots like Zeke to know their flier had been blessed by an Imperial preacher, and not just the arcane, unknowable machine rituals of the Adeptus Mechanicus. Cass had found Zeke spending the last few moments before lift-off gingerly wrapping fresh prayer litany scripts around the servitor's forearms.

'If I'm going to share the hold with it, I'm going to make sure the God-Emperor is keeping an eye on it,' he had said defensively.

Before embarking, Stryk paraded his Hydras in front of the Valkyries. Cass paused to watch the Scions as they went through some sort of pre-combat rite of their own. Stryk barked phrases at them in High Gothic – which Cass didn't understand – and they shouted them back, the call-and-response of the martial-sounding declarations ringing through the hangar. At the end of it, they beat their gauntlets against the breastplates of their butcher's-red carapace armour, then removed their maroon berets and pulled on their helmets and visors. Combat gear donned, they then linked the leads of the power packs strapped to their backs to the connection points of their hellguns. The whine of the weapons charging in unison was audible over the rising sound of Valkyrie engines.

Cass was just climbing up into her cockpit when Korrie called to her from the aft seat.

'*Rogue* might have a bit of a problem, Chief,' she said.

Cass didn't need to ask. She dropped back down and rounded *Vagrant*, hearing raised voices over the engines. Sure enough, Xijen was having an altercation next to *Rogue*.

Vaughn had come back. He looked bedraggled, but he was fully kitted out and was already half into the forward cockpit, with Xijen seemingly trying to convince him to get back down.

'Hal, what in the Emperor's name are you doing?' Cass snapped as she approached.

'What does it look like?' Vaughn snarled back from his perch.

'We talked about this,' Cass said. 'I've spoken with Orlov! You're off the damned line!'

'We didn't talk about shit. You told me not to fly. I never agreed to anything.'

'You realise where we're going?' Cass demanded. 'You realise the odds?'

'I'm not going to hide in the lines while the rest of my crew go out there,' he responded. 'And it's a damned disgrace you ever thought I would.'

'You think you're in a fit state to command *Rogue*?'

'Never felt better.'

'And you're going to follow my orders once we're up there?'

'When have I not? You act like I'm nothing but a liability. I'm not. I'm the best damned pilot in the best damned squadron in the fleet.'

Cass glanced at Xijen. He simply nodded.

'If you'll excuse me now, captain, I've got preflight checks to run,' Vaughn said, pulling on his helmet.

'I'll speak to you up there,' Cass said, relenting. 'Until then, just follow my lead.'

'All set, big boy?' Konstantina asked.

'Looks like it,' Straks responded from the aft cockpit, the shields still raised as he ran through weapons checks.

'I was talking to *Ruffian*,' Konstantina quipped, reaching out from her own cockpit and affectionately banging its flank, where the kill tallies were notched. 'I've got a good feeling about this one.'

'*Glad someone does,*' Straks said as the shields began to lower, switching to intercom.

'I've never seen the squadron in such a crap mood,' Konstantina agreed.

'*Might have something to do with the fifty per cent casualties we've suffered over the past month.*'

'Well, that's the average isn't it? So no more deaths scheduled for the rest of the tour! Happy days!'

Straks mustered a dry laugh, and Konstantina lowered her helmet's visor and pressed two fingers against the shard of blackened steel she'd taped to the bottom edge of her flight control panel. It was a fragment from her first kill, an Archenemy Hell Talon she'd tagged during a wild dogfight above Mariena Dax.

'God-Emperor, see us through,' she murmured, closing her eyes. 'And if our time has come, let us take plenty of the bastards with us. Ave Imperator.'

'*Ave Imperator,*' she heard Straks mutter in agreement.

She opened her eyes and ignited the engines.

Vaughn finished strapping himself in, closed his eyes, and tried to stop shaking.

He felt like he was about to be sick, but he ended up just dry-heaving. He was fairly certain he'd expelled all his bodily fluids over the past cycle. He gritted his teeth and made himself take a sip from the tepid water in his canteen before fastening his resp-mask.

Get it together. Focus. You chose to be here. You had an out, and you threw it away.

Why? He wasn't sure, besides the fact he knew he could never look the rest of his crew in the face again if they went up this time and he didn't. Not that it would matter, because none of them were coming back, not from this one.

He tried to drive out such thoughts. They were false. His fate wasn't set. The odds of survival weren't nil.

But at this point, it felt as though they couldn't be far from that. He'd been lucky to make it out of the pocket the last time. Cobb hadn't. And now he was running those same odds again, except this time it wasn't some supply dump or asset evacuation, but a full-scale insertion. He couldn't avoid it, though. He was second-in-command of the most successful Valkyrie squadron in the fleet. This had been his fate since the day he had signed his name on the *Mandatum Divinum*'s enlistment ordinance and sworn his oaths to the Imperium and the God-Emperor in the ancient warship's primary flight bay, in front of the ranks of gleaming Aeronautica aircraft.

And what were the alternatives? Even if he avoided formal punishment for his absence, what would happen when operations on Kanai Tertius were over? He'd return to the Old Mother, shorn of any pride and honour, a shadow of his former self who was spurned by his fellow pilots. He'd rather be demoted to Munitorum menial and spend the rest of his days scrubbing the flight decks than face that kind of shame.

'Hal?'

Vaughn finally noticed Xijen addressing him over the intercom. He surfaced from his morbid reverie, wondering how long his co-pilot had been trying to get his attention.

'What is it?' he snapped.

'Zorn said there was a slight cyclic delay in the port primary rotors. He said he believed he had cured it, but I thought you should know, before we head up.'

'Copy that,' Vaughn said brusquely.

'The cargo is also outside waiting for the rear hatch,' Xijen added, as though that important point were an afterthought.

Vaughn disengaged Rogue's ramp, and looked again at the pict of his sister, stuck to the top of the control panel.

'I won't let you down,' he said, reaching out briefly to touch her smiling face. 'Emperor willing, I'll see you soon.'

The Scions trooped onto the fliers, and Cass closed Vagrant's ramp. She tried not to think about the sickness in her stomach, the fear that felt as though a clenched fist had just pounded into her gut. She latched her focus on to the familiarity of the checks and the comms tests, letting her mind run on autopilot, knowing that if she considered what they were about to do, she might freeze up.

Systems looked good. The vox was loud and clear. Zeke confirmed that their cargo had strapped themselves in. All set.

The hangar doors yawned ahead, the pallid pink glow of dawn beginning to seep through from outside. Cass eased Vagrant up off the rockcrete and nosed out into the strengthening light.

CHAPTER FIFTEEN

Vagabond Squadron rose with the dawn over Barduk, leading the rest of the 901st Wing out.

Cass had commanded the entire force only once before, on Dagoran. It was a responsibility she tried not to think about, unwilling to add its weight to the concerns already crushing her. *Vagrant* was at the front, and as the flight began to circle north around the airbase she leaned forward against her harness, looking back at the arc of Valkyries and Vultures rising in her tail from their hangars, the sunlight glinting from their wings and cockpit shields. For a short while, she allowed herself to feel inspired by the sight.

Then she found herself wondering how many of them would make it back again at the end of the day.

A flight of Lightnings roared past, so close Cass caught a glimpse of the nearest one's pilot. The wicked little interceptors were heading north as well, climbing to combat altitude and joining the rest of the 911th and 910th Fighter Wings. Bix and the commander of the 910th, Kobe, were already up and circling – Cass could see the clusters of Thunderbolts and Lightnings overhead framed against the dawn glow, re-forming around a great phalanx of heavy Marauder bombers that had lumbered up ahead of the Valkyries. They were forming a strike group, with the Thunderbolts splitting into four protection teams around them and the Lightnings acting as the lead group and top cover. The Marauders would deliver their payload along Kantu Valley just ahead of the Valkyrie insertion before turning for home, while the fighters engaged the inevitable xenos reprisal.

'*That's the last of them up,*' Korrie said. Cass glanced at the auspex and saw that the rest of the 901st was now in formation behind her, strung out in echelon. They had completed their turn around the airbase.

'Form on my heading,' she instructed the entire wing as she eased on the stick, lining up in the same direction as the Marauders overhead. 'Echelon left, extended flat.'

'*Look below,*' Korrie added as the wing formed up. Cass glanced down. From the height the Valkyries had reached she could see Camp Yuzen and the other main cantonments in the distance. The roadways and tracks between the Imperial lines were dark and flooded with vehicles and infantry, like lifeblood flowing through a network of veins and arteries. They'd started moving to their muster points during the night – Cass knew she was just seeing the rearguard, and that as they flew they would pass over the main columns. The Astra Militarum was on the offensive once again.

The trio of Valkyrie squadrons finished falling into formation and swept north, towards the Eji, and Kantu Valley.

Wellend forced himself not to clutch on to his restraint harness, or close his eyes. He stared dead ahead, at the Valkyrie gunner sitting opposite him – Zeke, he thought his name was.

He wouldn't show the fear he felt, not to the aviator, or to the Tempestus Scions seated around him. He would do his father, his regiment, and his home world proud.

'*You are Iron Guard,*' he remembered Felkin telling him on the day he had passed out of the Vanandra Officer Corps Academy, back on Mordian. '*That means not a step back. Not a moment's hesitation. Your duty to the God-Emperor is the first, the last, the only consideration. That's how it has been with our family for fifty-three generations, and may it be so for fifty-three more. Do you understand?*'

Wellend had, and still did. He had been inducted into the ways of his people since birth. No hesitation. Not a backwards step.

But fear was always there. The galaxy had been torn in half, and Mordian was lost, subsumed beyond the God-Emperor's light. Like all Iron Guard regiments cut off from their home world, those on Kanai Tertius had continued to do their duty with firmness and exactitude. The fate of Wellend's mother, of the rest of his family, was unknown, and that terror was a burden in itself, but he was thankful he still had his father. He was his certainty, the living memory of home he clung on to in the midst of the storm.

At first, he had also struggled with the fear that he would fail in his duties when he finally saw combat. Kanai Tertius was his first major deployment, after many months of arduous warp travel, and he had dreaded the thought that he might freeze up, falter, or worse, show cowardice when called upon.

Memories of the offensive along the Eji Valley and its aftermath were now just a blur. He recalled his first action, during the river crossing, and then not much after. It had turned into a disaster, and then a nightmare as Army Group Centre had been encircled and besieged. His father had kept him close, but Felkin still led from the front whenever he could, and Wellend had plunged into the carnage with him time and again, father and son fighting side by side.

The desperation of the past few weeks had melted into a continuous parade of blood, mud, exhaustion and horror, but he knew he hadn't faltered. He had followed his father's orders. He had fought alongside the men and women of the regiment. At times he had been shaking so badly he could barely reload his sidearm – as had happened when faced with the bestial xenos in the promethium hub, when Captain Elza's Valkyries had been refuelling – but he had not frozen, or fled. He had not brought shame on his family or the regiment.

Now, his fear of what was to come was subsumed by his fear of showing any sign of weakness to those around him. He knew what they thought. He knew he was young, that he must seem like little more than an unblooded boy. But he was more than just that. He was Iron Guard. He would prove that to them, and when he was reunited with his father, he hoped he might even have made the old man proud.

The first thing the xenos infesting Kantu Valley knew of their coming destruction was the low, deep rumble of quad J79-CS afterburning ramjet engines, rolling across the skies like a constant, rising thunder.

Sirens and alarm squigs began to wail as orks poured from their crude huts. Overseers beat grots towards anti-aircraft artillery, loading the conglomeration of different-calibre weapons and ratcheting their mismatching clusters of barrels up to face the dawn sky.

In ramshackle airbases along the northern end of the Eji Valley, ork pilots broke off their carousing, fighting, and tinkering with their aircraft and began to scramble. Xenos planes roared along their runways and raggedy formations began to coalesce as they turned south on interception headings.

They would be too late to stop the Marauder squadrons of 899th Wing from delivering their payload. The phalanx of bombers opened their munition bays, one squadron after another, as the ork defences along Kantu's sides began to blast up at them.

The bomber formation had split down the middle so they were dropping across the valley sides, rather than into its bottom. A tide of massive detonations started to hammer along the slopes, a bow wave of destruction that obliterated entire mobs of xenos, demolished their encampments and pulverised their defences.

The bombing did not go unanswered. Orks were anything but accurate, but the nature of anti-aircraft gunnery and the sheer weight of artillery bristling along the flanks of the valley meant they did not have to be. Within moments of arriving above the southern end of Kantu, the Marauders were flying through flak, dirty smears smudging the new day.

The commander of the Annihilators, 899th Wing's most decorated Marauder squadron, was among the first to die as his bomber was riddled with shrapnel, killed alongside his servitor co-pilot as their aircraft was shot to pieces. The Marauder plummeted out of formation before exploding spectacularly halfway towards the ground, its primary bay still half full when one of its bombs went off.

More losses followed. Another of the Annihilators, *Grinning Reaper*, had a whole wing shorn off by a pair of strikes, and corkscrewed down into a fiery detonation in the valley's depths.

One Marauder from the following squadron, *Scarlet Imp* of the Red Fiends, had one of its two starboard engines shot out. As the ramjet began to burn and flames spread along the wing, its pilot, Flight Sergeant Chul, realised he couldn't maintain altitude, but he still had enough control to direct the bomber's descent. He angled it towards a battery of ork anti-aircraft guns, the weapons swinging to face him as his intention became obvious. They hammered

Scarlet Imp bloody, ripping away its plasteel armour, holing its other engine, shattering the reinforced cockpit shield to pieces, shredding the airframe, but they could not stop its plunging descent.

Chul and his co-pilot and partner, Kyong, were dead long before their plane impacted, but their duty was done. The Marauder struck the battery like a blazing comet, wiping it from existence and gouging a vast crater near the crest of the valley's western slope.

The 899th Wing held its course. Marauder casualties rarely fell below the brutal losses suffered by Valkyrie pilots – on operations such as these, flying into the teeth of the foe and dealing destruction to the enemy's fastness, they could even exceed them. The 899th delivered their payloads, then turned for home, up and over Kantu's western sides.

The 901st came in low and hard, right on their heels. Cass had been concerned that a gap between the bombing run and the airborne insertion would give the xenos time to prepare for them. She pushed the Vagabonds, keeping almost beneath the 899th as they began their final approach towards Kantu. Doing so meant the bombs were dropping dangerously close, but Cass trusted herself and Korrie to get the speeds and timings correct, and that would in turn keep the following Valkyrie squadrons right.

As the wedges of Marauders began to bank away just ahead and above of them, *Vagrant* screamed through the smoke and the dust of the bombing raid, causing the rising pall to shiver and eddy in the aircraft's wake. *Rogue* and *Ruffian* were with them, on the left in echelon, closed up now to tight formation. Briefly, Cass felt her fears and regrets melt away. There was no force in the galaxy she would not face when the Vagabonds were on the hunt. The thrill of it caused her to grimace, a fiery determination supplanting her uncertainties.

They were going to win today, and add another victory to the Vagabond roll of honour.

'*Taking fire,*' Korrie warned. Cass became aware of it moments later, as she saw points of light dart through the smoke ahead, followed in another few heartbeats by the familiar smacking sounds of shots hitting the airframe.

'Hold course,' she ordered. It was small-arms or low-calibre anti-aircraft, nothing to be concerned about, yet.

They surged through the fire and smoke churning from the Marauder that had been brought down in the valley's depths, flying so low *Vagrant*'s systems actually pinged her a heat warning from the wreckage.

She snatched a glance at the auspex. Almost halfway. There was no indication that any of the Valkyries following the Vagabonds had been hit yet. So far so good.

'Prepare to adjust altitude on my order, fifteen degrees,' she instructed *Rogue* and *Ruffian*. They were coming up on their objective – the knoll at the north end of the valley, where Kantu agri-collective was perched. At current altitude they wouldn't actually clear it, but Cass wanted to keep them running as low and fast as possible for as long as possible.

The fire being directed at them intensified. The orks manning the anti-air guns had been forced to decrease elevation after initially bringing their guns up to hit the bombers high overhead, but now they were beginning to track the targets arrowing between them. There were orks along the valley floor as well, more clustered towards Kantu's northern side, blazing indiscriminately at the aircraft roaring overhead.

A marker representing one of the following Valkyries from Shadow Squadron blinked from green to amber. Another followed seconds later. Then, one of Nemesis Squadron turned abruptly red. Kill-shot.

'Throne,' Cass hissed into her resp-mask, teeth clenched. Fire was whipping at them from all sides now, shredding the smoke cover around them, beating at the fliers as they drove on through the worsening storm.

'Ten seconds,' Korrie warned.

'Zeke, get on the bruiser,' Cass said, giving the gunner permission to roll back the side hatches. *Speed* was about to be relegated to second place on the Vagabonds' list of priorities, below *firepower*.

The cloud of ash and dust parted briefly, and she saw the knoll's slope dead ahead, rushing up on them.

She held a fraction longer, then eased back on the stick, resisting the urge to snatch at it, speaking into the vox-mic as she did so.

'Climb, climb, climb.'

Rogue and *Ruffian* mirrored *Vagrant*, the manoeuvre executed to perfection. The three warbirds came surging up over the crest of the knoll, just high enough to clear the buildings crowning it, the change in velocity making her stomach lurch and pressing like a firm hand against her chest.

Cass suddenly found herself above Kantu agri-collective. She looked down at a settlement of timber and rockcrete, simple prefab homesteads and the domes of grain silos and livestock pens interspersed with older structures with whitewashed walls and terracotta tile roofs.

She and the rest of the airborne operation had been furnished with maps and old picts of the little settlement during the briefing session, but Kantu now bore only a passing resemblance to any of those. Much of it was ruined, shelled by the southernmost artillery of Army Group Centre. The xenos had infested its remains, adding their own ramshackle structures made from rusting plasteel and dung. They were swarming below the trio of Valkyries, orks great and small as well as hordes of their diminutive grot slaves pouring out into the detritus-littered knot of streets and alleyways.

'Objective sighted, dead ahead,' Cass relayed via the intercom to Stryk and his Hydras. 'Fifteen seconds to touchdown. The landing zone is hot, repeat, the landing zone is hot.'

That almost went without saying. The dedicated anti-aircraft fire had slackened as they had hit the end of the valley, but a hail of small-arms shots were battering at the Vagabonds. Cass caught the drumbeat of Zeke's and the servitor's heavy bolters engaging, accompanied by the powerful *crack-whine* of Scion hellguns as they added their firepower from *Vagrant's* side hatches, las bolts flurrying down onto the nearest rooftops and into the streets.

She ignored both the incoming and the outgoing for the time being, zeroing in on the landing zone that had been picked during operational planning, all the while praying desperately that it was still viable.

Vagrant, *Rogue* and *Ruffian* swung in unison over the collective's centre. Korrie called out as Cass jinked to the right to avoid heavy weapons fire coming from the roof of the remnants of a silo building.

'That's the square, just to starboard.'

Cass stole a glance and saw, to her relief, that there was still an open space at the heart of the settlement. Once it had been the location of weekly markets and livestock fairs. Now it was just hardpacked dirt and littered refuse, the ground scarred and scorched by shell strikes.

It was an ideal landing zone, and an optimal point for the Alphic Hydras to secure in the midst of the enemy's defences while the Harakoni platoons with Shadow and Nemesis squadrons hit the eastern and western ends of the collective. Ordering *Rogue* and *Ruffian* to stick with her, she swung out over the square before levelling to start her descent, under fire the whole time.

'We're set to drop,' Stryk said to Cass over the intercom.

'Negative, negative,' she responded over the sounds of more hits against the cockpit. 'Less danger if we put down. The airspace here is on fire. Prep for rear hatch disembarkation.'

'Copy that,' Stryk responded.

Cass flicked a pair of switches and eased up on the stick, rerouting engine power to the vertical wing rotors and engaging hover mode. She began to bring *Vagrant* down on the north side of the square, rear hatch facing in towards its centre, kicking up dust from the ground beneath. She threw a glance over her shoulder as she did so, checking the other two warbirds were settling without incident. She saw sparks bursting from *Rogue* as the other Valkyrie was pounded, but it completed its descent below rooftop level, and the fire finally began to slacken.

'Touchdown in three… two… one,' she said into the intercom. 'Ramp away! Go, go, go!'

Wellend had never been part of an airborne combat insertion. Besides rudimentary training during his youth at Vanandra, the only experience he had of it was the evacuation from the pocket. That had been a nightmare of twisting, jolting, and of course the horrific death of the young gunner who had been occupying the space next to him in the hold. Despite his exhaustion, on the first night after making it to safety, after Captain Elza had arrived at Suchen and pulled him out from in front of the firing squad, he hadn't been able to sleep at all. It wasn't how close he had come to death, either at the hands of the orks or the Commissariat, that kept him awake, or wondering about how his father and the regiment were faring, still beset beyond the Eji. It had been his mind's absolute refusal to stop replaying his core memories of that moment when the aviator had been killed.

He had been smiling at Wellend. He remembered that smile.

Then a loud bang and a crack and the sensation of something warm and wet on his face, making him jump with alarm. He hadn't known what it was at first.

He'd found the aviator still looking at him, but he wasn't smiling any more. Blood had run down one side of his face, a sudden, crimson half-mask, and Wellend had realised that what he was tasting was the young gunner's brains.

He'd seen those sights, tasted that horror over and over in the days since, irrespective of whether he was awake or asleep. He wanted desperately to be free of it, and feared he never would be. But in those moments, as the heavy bolter on the right side of the hold began to hammer and the Scions around him undid their harnesses, he finally forgot about it. There was no time for other nightmares while he was in the middle of one.

The worst part of it was the noise. It was making his ears ache and shuddering through his diaphragm, beating away hard and irregular in his chest like a madman's drums.

His father had told him there was nothing that could prepare him for the sound of war. It could be described, it could be simulated, but it could never be properly replicated. Its wrath was too great, its chaotic nature too unpredictable, too untameable. Small-arms, heavy weapons, artillery, air strikes and bombing runs, orbital bombardments and atmospheric insertions, screams, crying, shouting, orders, pleas, curses, words on the vox and in the ear, bellowed point-blank yet still going unheard. It could drive out reason, Felkin had told his only son. It could remake brave men into cringing cowards and drive cowardly men insane. None could understand it without first experiencing it. None could adequately describe it to those who had not known it. None who had yet to endure it could know for sure how they would react when they finally did.

Wellend had discovered that his father's words were true in Eji

Valley, and he was reminded of them once again as the Valkyrie alighted, the landing made with the easy grace of an experienced pilot, even as all around was riven with chaos.

The Scions were already up. Wellend could hear nothing of any orders being issued, nothing at all besides the engine-scream and the hammering of impacts on the outside of the hull.

He fumbled his harness off and got to his feet, relieved to find his legs didn't simply give way beneath him. The gunner opposite was still manning the heavy bolter, the noise of its firing punching Wellend's ears. Through the hatch he could see the vague outline of ruins and movement, flashes of green amidst the smoke and disorder.

More light poured into the thunder-filled, claustrophobic metal box the hold had become. He realised the rear ramp had just dropped, and the Scions were exiting.

Wellend dragged his laspistol free from its holster, selected the energy output and eased the safety off. He was at the back of the two files, and he found himself having to endure one final wait as those in front swept out. Then, at last, the broad, armoured shoulders of the Scion ahead of him were moving forward, and he was able to follow, out into the light and the steel, the fire and dirt.

Not a backwards step.

Vaughn slammed *Rogue* onto the earth, the touchdown so rough and ungainly it sent a jolt of pain up his back.

He swore vehemently. It had not been a landing worthy of a Vagabond pilot, but they were on the ground and somehow in one piece, and at this point that was all he cared about.

'Macks, tell me when the grunts are all out,' he ordered. 'We're going straight back up once they are.'

As Macks acknowledged, the beating of his heavy bolter providing a backdrop over the intercom connection, he switched to Cass' vox-channel.

'Ready for immediate lift-off,' he told her.

'*Negative, negative,*' her strained voice came back. '*We're staying grounded for now.*'

'Are you mad?' Vaughn snapped. 'We're sitting targets here! I'm taking fire from all sides!'

'*Less than you would be if you were fifty feet higher,*' Cass pointed out. '*The whole collective is crawling with contacts. The minute we rise up again we'll be target-locked by every ork in the street or on a rooftop. There are far fewer angles on us down here. Once the Scions and the Harakoni start securing the rest of the settlement we'll be able to get back up and the airspace won't be so full of metal.*'

'They'll be ready for us by then, back along the valley,' Vaughn pointed out. 'And what about xenos aircraft? They'll be scrambling here from all over!'

'*That's why we've come with a whole lot of top cover,*' Cass said. '*Where their anti-air is concerned, they're ready for us now anyway. Sit tight. That's an order.*'

Vaughn cut the connection and slammed his hand against the inside of his cockpit shield.

'*Take it we're not going straight back up?*' Xijen asked.

'She wants the collective secured first,' Vaughn growled, patching in Macks and Holsten.

'Keep it up, boys,' he told his two gunners. 'Seems like we're not going anywhere.'

'I can help them secure this place,' Konstantina said to Cass over the vox. 'I'm packing as much firepower as half the rest of the wing combined!'

'*You'll wait for me to receive notification of any viable priority targets from the Scions or the Harakoni,*' Cass responded firmly.

'*You,* Reaper *and* Doom Hound *are all on standby for target acquisition.*'

'As long as I get priority,' Konstantina grumbled.

She craned in her flight seat, hunting for targets amidst the surrounding ruins, hungry for kills, even if they were just ork foot-mobs. The Scion platoon's two squads were sweeping out from the holds of *Vagrant* and *Rogue* and spreading out to the left and right. They conducted close-quarters battle drills as they advanced on the buildings looking onto the square, the eye-achingly brilliant energy bolts from their hellguns making Konstantina glad of the tinting of her flight helmet's visor.

The Scions and their two Valkyrie fliers were securing the northern, eastern and western sides of the square, but its southern arc was *Ruffian*'s kill-ground. Orks started to pour from the broken and gutted buildings directly in front of Konstantina. The sight made her grin from ear to ear.

'Let's get purging, flyboy,' she told Straks. 'Just the bruiser for now though, unless it starts looking like they're going to mob us. I think we'll have better targets for the rocket pods soon enough.'

Ruffian's prow heavy bolter lit up, tearing into the first orks to come charging out into the square. Konstantina leaned forward against her harness, drinking in the sight. Being on the ground made for an unusually stable firing platform, and it was rare that she got to see the work of her warbird's weaponry so up-close. It was a treat.

'*There's another mob breaking round to our port side,*' Straks, with a slightly higher view in the aft cockpit, warned. Konstantina snarled, realising the xenos were trying to outflank them, getting out of the Vulture's static firing arcs. The Vagabonds had performed similar grounded or extremely low-level point defences before, but normally there had been at least four or five warbirds in action – being reduced to just three made it more difficult to cover all the angles.

She hit the vox and patched through to Vaughn.

'Hal, your starboard gunner got a line on that mob circling to my left?' she asked. The reply came back moments later.

'Macks is on it.'

Konstantina twisted in her seat, catching sight of the orks Straks had warned her about being caught in a burst of mass-reactive bolts from the side of *Rogue*. Those not blown open and scythed down broke off, scrambling back into the cover of the nearest buildings.

'Good shooting,' Konstantina told Vaughn. 'Now, how much longer do we have to keep this up?'

CHAPTER SIXTEEN

Wellend ran out into the storm, following in the wake of Stryk's Scions. The squad that had been on board *Vagrant* were driving hard for one side of the square, spitting a blizzard of hellgun las into anything that moved in the buildings ahead.

Wellend kept on their heels and gained the nearest alleyway with Stryk and two others. He stepped over the twitching bodies of felled orks, cauterised las wounds bored through their tough flesh, their insides liquified.

He felt painfully underequipped compared to the Hydras in their hulking carapace plate and with their hyper-charged lasweapons, but he was just glad they were spearheading the assault. Stryk swept down the alley, punching las bolts clean through another ork that loomed, roaring, at the far end before reuniting with the rest of the squad on the other side. They had secured the ruins to the left and right, their hellguns possessing the penetrative power needed to put down even the larger members of the xenos mobs.

The Scions parted again into two fire-teams of five, the comms they were sharing between them behind their helmet visors audible to Wellend only as the odd crackle and click. He stuck with Stryk's team as they pushed into a wrecked building that had been partially reconstructed by the xenos invaders, patched up with rusting metal and repurposed lengths of flakboard. It stank like an animal pen, and Wellend did his best to avoid tripping on the unidentifiable refuse and crusted dung heaps that littered the floor.

Orks flung themselves, howling, at the Scions, and the Alphic Hydras put them down with controlled bursts of point-blank hellfire. The stink of burned flesh and melted innards overcame even the reek of the xenos nest, and Wellend pursed his lips and tried not to retch.

The fire-team was half out of the building when shapes loomed in the shattered window on its left, and a blaze of hard rounds slammed indiscriminately through it. Wellend flinched, hearing shots whip by and crack off the wall beside him. The Scion in front stumbled before return fire slashed at the opening, blindingly bright. There was a bellow, sounding more like rage than pain from the shooter.

A heartbeat later and something else came flying through the las-scorched window, bouncing amidst the detritus on the floor.

Wellend realised he was looking at an ork stick grenade.

'Down,' the Scion alongside him bellowed, and slammed into him. He fell, and the grenade went off.

Wellend's ears burst, and his lungs filled with dust. He choked, pinned, momentarily blind and deaf. He expected a great, overwhelming pain to strike, maybe from an arm or leg, or in his side, but there was nothing.

He clawed at his eyes and managed to open one, feeling the pressure that had felled him vanish. The Scion that had brought him down was clambering back up, caked in the dust filling the remains of the room. The grenade had flung the rubbish into the corners and left a scorched blast mark across the floor. That, and blood. The Scion ahead of the one that had flung Wellend aside had taken the worst of it, and his left leg and side were now a mangled mess, his carapace cracked open like an insectoid's broken shell. He slid down the wall as Wellend stared, and slumped to one side.

The one who had saved him barked at him, gripping an epaulette and hauling him back to his feet. He dragged in air, coughed, and whimpered as his hearing returned with a painful pop.

'Move,' the Scion was shouting at him. 'Karking move!'

He shoved Wellend, and he finally responded, stumbling over the dead Scion and getting out the door. He'd barely gone a few paces into the sunlight before he was yanked unceremoniously to the side once more.

More gunfire battered at Wellend's ears, rounds kicking up dirt from the open space he'd just been hauled away from. The rest of the Scions were in cover on either side of an alleyway, seemingly pinned in place. As he'd exited the building behind them, Wellend had caught a glimpse of a tall structure commanding the alley's far end. A grain silo, repurposed now as a xenos strongpoint.

He spotted Stryk and hunkered down behind him as the Scion pressed a finger to the side of the vox-set incorporated into his helmet, transmitting a message.

'Strike target acquired,' Cass' voice clicked, making Konstantina sit up straight. The xenos ahead of *Ruffian* had been thoroughly suppressed and the prow heavy bolter had been reduced to firing the odd warning burst to conserve ammunition. Considering

how potentially fraught the insertion had been, things had started getting boring fast.

'Let's hear it,' she said eagerly.

'*Agri-silo, immediately north-west of our current position,*' Cass said. '*It's fortified, and it's causing problems. Scions are painting it.*'

'Copy,' Konstantina said, already adjusting the engines. 'You'll be able to hold here without me?'

'*I'm not planning on staying much longer,*' Cass said.

That was welcome news as well. Konstantina took *Ruffian* back up, hard, her stomach plunging and her heart racing fast once more as the thrill of flight and thoughts of more kills took hold. The fire that they'd taken on the way in had slackened now considerably, and she noted that the other two Vultures from the sister squadrons were up and striking targets as well, presumably called in by the Harakoni securing the collective's eastern and western ends.

She immediately located the structure Cass was talking about. It looked as though it had once been a domed grain silo, but the xenos had made their usual modifications, daubing it in their crude symbols, and bolting on glyphs and rickety platforms bristling with weaponry. It acted as a stronghold near the collective's centre, and without heavy weapons or armoured support the Scions had clearly decided they needed something else to clear it.

They had tagged its front with a las marker, and Konstantina locked on to it without difficulty. She was almost oblivious to the shots that had starting lashing at *Ruffian* as soon as the Vulture swooped up above the level of the remaining rooftops. The silo was a prime mark, and she was going to wreck it.

'Light it up, flyboy,' she instructed Straks, already anticipating the coming devastation. 'All hardpoints.'

The xenos scurrying across the gantries and decking plates

around the structure's shell had been firing down at the Scions in the narrow streets and lanes below, but as *Ruffian* rose up before them they switched targets. Shots started to crack against the Vulture's prow.

Ruffian answered their aggression. The lascannons spat first, drilling brilliant beams of light through the structure and cutting down any xenos caught in their path.

Then the rocket pods launched. A blizzard of explosive warheads hammered the silo's flank, a rippling wall of smoke, flame and shrapnel demolishing part of the structure and its defensive additions. The prow heavy bolter was just overkill.

'Save some rockets,' Konstantina told Straks, resisting the urge to unload completely on the target. 'Adjusting to port.'

With *Ruffian* still hovering face-on to the silo, she swung the Vulture left, clearing the smoke and allowing Straks to drag his bolts and las along the structure's curvature, hitting parts untouched by the initial fusillade. Konstantina grinned as she watched orks blown apart and cut through with las, several choosing to leap from their makeshift gantries rather than be butchered at point-blank range.

They completed a full circle of the silo, leaving it partially caved in and leaning dangerously, crowned by a great plume of smoke. Konstantina voxed through to Cass.

'Make sure you remind the Scions of this when we're back on the ground.'

CHAPTER SEVENTEEN

'Go,' Stryk shouted.

The Scions broke from cover and moved down the alleyway, reaching the base of the agri-silo and advancing past it. Wellend went with them, finding himself hurrying over the broken and torn remains of orks thrown down amidst the silo's partial destruction. A Vulture gunship – the one Wellend recognised from Vagabond Squadron – had come sweeping overhead and hammered the structure, staving in part of it and riddling the rest with las bolts and hard rounds. The deadly aircraft was still on-station, covering the Scions as they advanced past the silo's remains, in case anything still lived within the ruins. The downdraught from its under-wing rotors snatched at Wellend's cap as he passed beneath, forcing him to grab hold of the hat with his free hand.

They reached another narrow street in the agri-collective's twisting, broken warren. The tone of the Vulture's engines changed as it shifted rotors and swept away, pursued in vain by the twisting contrails of several rockets launched from else-where in the settlement.

Suddenly, it seemed a lot quieter. The walls of the hab build-ings pressed in around them, muffling the sounds of the fighting happening nearby. They were prefab units, tall and unlovely, more modern than the traditional plaster and terracotta-tiled structures once inhabited by the farming communities of Kanai Tertius.

The two Scion fire-teams had reunited again into a single squad. They'd made it a little over halfway down the street when someone called a halt. Wellend copied their movements, get-ting off the walkway and into the nearest doorway.

'Contact at our six,' he heard the Scion he was hunched next to call out. The squad immediately inverted, and Wellend twisted in his shelter to discover what the rearguard had spotted.

He heard what he at first mistook for a bestial, animalistic growl, before the wall of one of the hab units they'd already passed further back down the street came crashing inwards in an avalanche of crumbling rockcrete.

A monstrosity forced its way through the ruins, engines snarl-ing. Wellend realised he was looking at a xenos scrap tank. Once it had been a Leman Russ, but its familiar outline was now defiled and twisted by ork modifications. Extra, ablative armour had been bolted to its flanks and a jagged dozer blade to its front, while glyphs and trophy poles hung with rotten remains decorated its front glacis and turret. The sight of it sent an instinctive thrill of revulsion through Wellend.

It burst out into the street the Scions had already advanced down, collided against the wall of the silo opposite, and remained wedged there as, with a screech of unoiled gears, its turret cannon began rotating in their direction.

'Break, break!' Wellend heard Stryk shouting. He had the

presence of mind to throw himself through the doorway he'd been crouched in and into the building itself. Its rear wall had been blown out, and he found himself in the neighbouring alleyway almost before he realised where he was, stumbling on rubble.

The scrap tank fired. Wellend actually heard the whickering noise of the battle cannon shell as it whipped past and down the street, followed by the detonation. The doorway they had just passed through collapsed in the blast, rockcrete and plasboard crashing down. Wellend caught himself against the pauldron of a Scion who had followed him through, choking and coughing on the surge of dust and smoke that swept over them.

He became totally disorientated. Another pair of Scions barrelled past him, knocking him onto his knees. He tried to rise, still choking on dust. The one who had arrested his initial fall put a hand on his shoulder again, preventing him from rising.

'Stay down,' he barked, voice turned into a distorted crackle by his visor's vox-vocaliser.

Wellend realised the Alphic Hydra was clutching a melta bomb. He turned and vanished into the haze after the first two.

Wellend had dropped his laspistol, and fumbled for it amidst the rubble, finally managing to find it. He shoved it back in its holster and unhooked his canteen from his belt, getting the cap off and taking a swig of the tepid water. He gagged, but it cleared his throat of the dust and killed the coughing fit threatening to incapacitate him.

He'd barely managed to take a breath before there was a monstrous detonation from ahead. Fire surged along the alleyway's entrance, and there was a clattering noise that he realised was the sound of debris cracking into nearby walls. Terracotta tiles cascaded from the rooftops around him, shattering in the rubble.

He regained his feet, ears ringing, returning the canteen to his belt as he caught sight of two Scions re-emerging from the smoke.

Neither bothered to tell him what had happened. He could only assume the threat of the scrap tank had been dealt with.

He fell back in as the squad reunited in the street, briefly occupying the smoking crater the battle cannon round had ploughed up in its centre. Wellend glanced back. Sure enough, the scrap tank had been reduced to a blazing wreck, its dishonourable enslavement at the hands of the xenos brought to an end by the 85th Alphic Hydras.

They pushed on, then halted again by an agri-machine shed at the far end of the street. Wellend realised Stryk was motioning for him to move up to the front of the formation. He hurried forward and crouched beside the Scion officer, leaning in to hear him over the cracking of hellgun discharges as a scattering of orks emerged back the way they had come, bounding down the street after them.

'This is the northern end of the collective. I need you up here with me once we move out, so you can guide us to the Imperial lines along the south of the pocket. Clear?'

'Clear,' Wellend responded, snatching a glance round the corner of the machine shed.

Stryk was correct – the only buildings beyond them now were a few partially demolished outhouses, and a handful of old stone shepherd's huts. The ground sloped downwards towards the valley's end, where it opened up into the zone occupied by the southernmost trenchworks of the pocket. Between them were fields and fences, as well as the Kantu streambed. There were also massing mobs of xenos, pushing into no-man's-land.

'They're already trying to encircle the collective,' Stryk said. 'We have to keep moving.'

He issued a curt series of signals to the rest of his squad, and they rose as one and began to move out beyond the last of the collective's habs and silos. Wellend went with them, but they didn't get far.

With a roar of engines, an ork war buggy streaked round the nearest buildings to their left, taking the turn so sharply it almost careened over onto two of its four fat tyres. The open trailer that formed its rear was laden with bellowing orks, and they began blazing away at the Scions or leapt from the flatbed before the bouncing, rattling transport had even screeched to a stop.

The Scions immediately started returning fire. The squad's hotshot volley gun blazed a hail of las through the buggy's windscreen and chassis, lacerating the driver and causing it to lurch violently to the right. It hit one of the tool sheds, crashing through its last remaining wall before overturning and detonating in a spectacular fireball. Wellend felt the heat prickle his skin.

Orks came stumbling from the smoke and ruins, ablaze from head to foot but still roaring and trying to get at the Scions. Stryk's team gunned them down along with the ones who had already leapt from the speeding transport, barely pausing their advance.

Wellend did his best to keep up. He retched on the stench of burning xenos. One ork he passed was still struggling to rise, flames licking at it, but the last Scion put a boot on its shoulder and a las bolt through its skull.

They were on the downward slope. A wire fence lay between them and the pastureland beyond, but the Scions kicked down its posts and strode onwards, hellguns swinging left and right as they sought targets. The slope had been used as grazing ground for livestock, but the death or departure of the animals had left the grass to grow tall in places – in some parts it had been trampled by the passage of ork mobs and vehicles.

Hellguns whined and snapped, these ones off to the right. Wellend looked, and realised the second Scion squad that made up the platoon were breaking from the cover of the collective, moving down the slope to link up with Stryk's team. They paused only to cut down a rush of orks pursuing them out of the ruins.

Stryk signalled a halt in the lee of a rough shepherd's hut to allow the second squad to reach them. They crouched in its shadow, every angle covered as Stryk signalled for Wellend to get up next to him once more.

He scrambled to do so. The style of fighting the Scions practised – rapid, fluid, brutally efficient – felt very different from the slow, uniformed, methodical combat doctrines of the Mordians. There was no denying its effectiveness though.

The second squad of Alphic Hydras joined the first, and they divided into four fire-teams that began to leapfrog one another down the slope. Wellend stuck to Stryk's side, crouching every time his team took up new firing positions and opened up on the xenos mobs closing in around them, then running with all his strength during the sudden, ferocious bursts of speed the Hydras put on when they repositioned under the covering fire of the other teams. Despite being unencumbered by the heavy carapace armour, hellguns and power backpacks worn by the Scions, Wellend still found himself struggling to keep up.

They reached the bottom of the slope. There was a dip in the ground ahead, and as Wellend dropped down into it he realised it was the remains of the Kantu, the stream that ran through the small subsidiary valley. The drought had dried it up entirely, leaving a shallow gully of dust and stones fringed by tall, brittle grass.

The Scions followed the streambed's course, out into the flatland just north of the valley. Now, two fire-teams took to the gully's sides and laid down fire while the other two pounded between them in double file, before they in turn split and acted as the covering force. They moved with speed and assured, controlled aggression, their small-unit tactics made even more impressive by the fact Wellend couldn't hear their comms – they seemed to act with instinctive fluidity, like a pack of bonded predators.

He focused on sticking with Stryk. The southernmost trench-works couldn't be much further. He remembered his time on that part of the line, snatching glimpses of the entrance to Kantu Valley and the agri-collective on that knoll through trench peri-scopes or while repelling an attack, remembering the shells that had fallen among the defences from the xenos batteries sited up next to the settlement. Those guns were now spiked and burning, courtesy of the Harakoni company that had gone in either side of the Scions, but either there were other ork long-range pieces covering no-man's-land, or the flurry of activity had prompted a Guard artillery officer to instruct their batteries to join the fight – shells started screaming down from out of the sky, pounding the ground to the left and right of the streambed and showering them with clods of dirt.

'That's danger close,' Stryk complained over the sudden thunder. 'Or they haven't realised we're out here!'

The Scions didn't have a means of contacting the pocket prior to actually reaching the trench lines. This part of the operation was every bit as fraught as the contested landing. If the orks were able to muster a wider assault on Army Group Centre's southern defences, they could find themselves trapped in the crossfire.

The streambed ahead had been gouged and torn up by pre-vious artillery strikes. They were moving over corpses now, stinking xenos remains in various stages of decomposition, rotting in the heat. Just as the Scions were now doing, they had attempted to use the gully as cover while approaching the trenchworks. Army Group Centre's solution had been to simply destroy the streambed with close-range artillery fire.

Wellend halted with Stryk again, more nearby detonations shaking the sweltering air. The ground just ahead was a morass of steel-scarred dirt and unidentifiable remains, strung across with a tall thicket of razorwire, the kind of density necessary to hold an ork stampede-charge at bay. It looked as though the dangerous attempts the defenders regularly made to clear it had recently been abandoned – the barbed coils were weighed down with xenos dead, some sections sagging heavily.

'Four hundred yards,' Stryk said. 'Open ground. We need a break in the wire.'

'That way,' Wellend said, trying not to flinch as a shell went off nearby, and he heard the sound of shrapnel whickering past. He pointed left, towards where an undulation hid a stretch of the razorwire.

'There's a break in the line there, then you need to double back in this direction to get past the second line.'

'You heard the lieutenant,' Stryk barked. 'Hydras, on me!'

They were up and moving again, Wellend jostled between two of the armoured brutes as they abandoned fire-and-manoeuvre for the final sprint. Until they could reach the break in the wire they were running parallel to it and the trenches beyond, and that gave the xenos in pursuit a chance to close the distance. Wellend snatched a glance back in the direction of the knoll, and saw mobs of xenos flooding down the slope, the nearest pounding along what had once been a patchwork of fields fed by the stream, now reduced to a cratered moonscape of dirt and dust.

Stray shots from the oncoming orks began to zip past, twitching at the wire to the right. Another shell shrieked down – definitely Imperial this time – and ripped into the leading edge of the mob, but those not blown apart or bowled over simply charged onwards, their roaring growing louder and ever more frenzied. It made Wellend's skin crawl, grating at the primordial part of his mind and making him want to turn and face the threat, to draw his las-pistol and open fire. He knew that was madness – he'd be lucky to bring even one down before he was simply trampled by the onrushing tide of green.

Finally, they hit the gap in the wire. The Scions hustled through, the ones at the rear turning at bay and discharging their hellguns until there was space for them, the ones who passed through first then turning and shooting over the razorwire. Then they were moving again, forced by the off-centre nature of the next gap to double back the way they had come.

The closest of the trench lines were just a few hundred yards to their left now. There was no sign of the troops Wellend was sure were packed into them, no sign even that they were aware of the small Imperial strike team striving to reach them. He briefly imagined the horror of being shot down by his own side, his own regiment, the very men and women he'd fought alongside until just days ago. But the emplacements remained silent, and as the Scions reached the second gap, Wellend saw movement among the defences.

A figure, still too distant for him to clearly recognise, but identifiable as an officer thanks to the golden lace shining on his blue coat and the chainsword he was wielding, material-ised above the sandbag parapet, gesturing with his weapon. Wellend thought at first the Scions were the ones he was trying to indicate to, until more figures began to appear on either side of him.

Just a few seconds later the top of the trench section directly ahead had been replaced by a wall of blue edged with gold, a company of Mordian infantry arrayed in two ranks, lasrifles shouldered. Wellend had expected them to lay down covering fire from the firing steps and the parapets, but instead it seemed as though they were going to sally out.

Wellend panted thanks to the God-Emperor as they crossed the last few yards between the razorwire posts. He resisted the urge to sprint ahead to his old comrades, staying at Stryk's side and doing his best to catch his breath as the Scion lieutenant approached the officer who had first ordered his troops up from the trenches. Wellend recognised him as Captain Halden, commander of E Company of the 550th. The sight of him was a surprising disappointment, in amongst the surging relief – a part of him had imagined that his father would be here, expecting to oversee the link-up point between the relief column's vanguard and his own southernmost defences.

'Lieutenant Stryk, Eighty-Fifth Alphic Hydras,' Stryk said, saluting Captain Halden. 'We've just come from Kantu Collective. My orders are to instruct you that the relief effort is underway. The collective and the valley beyond is being secured as we speak. I would be obliged if you would direct myself and Lieutenant Felkin here to a senior officer, so I can pass on the news and make sure the breakout gets underway as quickly as practicable.'

'Understood. We've been expecting you, Lieutenant Stryk,' Halden said, though his eyes were on Wellend, and he nodded to him as he addressed him. 'Welcome back, lieutenant. It's good to have you back among the Five-Fiftieth.'

'Glad to be back, sir,' Wellend said, the words heartfelt. 'I'm here to help liaise between the pocket and the relief. Is Colonel Felkin at central headquarters, or is he at divisional command?'

A shadow seemed to pass over Halden's face, there and gone again as the Mordian captain's unflappable expression returned.

'I regret Colonel Felkin was killed earlier this morning during shelling of the northern end of the pocket,' he told Wellend. 'It was… instant. Colonel Gravitz of the Four Hundredth Ronarkian is now the ranking commander of Army Group Centre. I believe he's at central headquarters.'

Wellend's world seemed to suddenly become very small and quiet. He was vaguely aware of Stryk taking over, thanking Halden for the information and requesting he hold position with his company and the Scion platoon while Stryk and Wellend sought out Gravitz.

Wellend's father was dead. For some reason, it hadn't occurred to him that he wouldn't see him again, at least not in the past few days. He knew he had been in comms contact with Suchen. Just that morning he had stood in the strategium during the final operations briefing and listened to a recording of a message that had made it through the night before. His father had said that his command was ready for the relief column, that the pocket was still holding firm. Wellend had felt pride burning silently within. He'd thought of hardly anything else besides reporting to his father that he had completed the task he had set him, against the odds. That he had helped to convince Lieutenant General Havali, and that aid had arrived.

And now, suddenly, Wellend found he had to come to terms with the fact he would never tell his father any of that.

'Company will volley fire by ranks! Make ready!'

The sudden, familiar orders snapped Wellend back into the present. Sound and fury returned. E Company had formed up a little way closer to Kantu, about a hundred yards beyond the front line trenches and inside the wire, while the Scion platoon split into two squads that took to its flanks. At Halden's command, the Mordians brought their gleaming lasrifles to the poise position.

'Present!'

The lasrifles were levelled at the orks bounding in pursuit of the Scions, about to collide with the first of the razorwire hedges and the rotten remains decorating them.

'Front rank, fire!'

There was a series of *snap-crack* reports as the front rank of E Company gave fire in the Mordian style, a rapid triple-tap of shots, semi-automatic.

'Second rank, fire!'

The second rank did the same, each shot carefully aimed, sending red bolts of energy whipping into the xenos mob.

'Front rank, fire!'

Crack-crack-crack.

'Second rank, fire!'

Crack-crack-crack.

'Front rank, fire!'

The drumbeat of the Mordians at war had begun, and Wellend knew it would not end until ammunition was expended, or the enemy had closed to bayonet point.

He looked at Stryk. The Scion officer's face was unreadable behind his helmet's visor, but he gestured curtly with a gauntlet, into the trenches.

'You know the way to central command?' he demanded.

'I do,' Wellend said, finding the sudden numbness receding.

'Then lead on,' Stryk instructed.

Wellend made for the trenches, dropping down onto the firing step of the nearest. Other sections across the line to the left and right had started opening up as well, adding las, heavy weapons fire, and the thundering reports of Leman Russ battle cannons as a squadron rolled forward in support of E Company. If all went according to plan, it was the start of what would become the drive south, and the evacuation of the pocket.

And Wellend knew now that he would join it alone, without his father.

CHAPTER EIGHTEEN

'We need to get back up,' Vaughn snapped at Cass over the vox. *'We've been sitting here too long!'*

Cass suspected he was correct. The Harakoni company commander had reported that the remainder of the agri-collective hadn't yet been cleared – fighting was still going on amongst the westernmost grain silos and amongst the ork artillery battery on the eastern edge of the spur – but Cass had been closely monitoring the top cover comms while they had been grounded. A Lightning squadron leader from the 910th was reporting increasing aerial ork activity to the north, something seemingly confirmed by Suchen. The xenos were about to reply to the Aeronautica Imperialis strike, and memories of almost being caught by an ork air assault when they had been grounded in the pocket were still fresh.

'How's it looking up there, Cloud Knight Leader?' Cass asked Bix, managing to catch the Thunderbolt wing commander during a moment's reprieve.

'*We're still hitting ground targets,*' Bix's voice came back. '*That'll change soon once interdiction arrives. Now's as good a time as any to make a break for it.*'

Cass acknowledged and a moment later, to her relief, a transmission came through from Stryk, chopped up by static but still intelligible.

'*We've made contact. The southernmost brigade of Army Group Centre is on the move. Your Mordian is liaising just now with their command while I use the vox-hub. We're making sure the whole force gets a shift on. The rest of my platoon is helping the push south across no-man's-land to the collective.*'

'Copy that,' Cass said, wondering briefly whether Wellend was currently being reunited with his father. 'Do you need aerial support?'

'*Not for now, but I can't promise that won't change.*'

'Understood. You know how to reach me, lieutenant.'

It was time to get moving. She pinged Suchen and, as she waited for a response, checked in with the other two Valkyrie squadrons under her command. They had dropped their cargo of Harakoni Warhawks seemingly without issue – the only major loss so far had been one of Nemesis Squadron during the run in. That, and *Umbral Shade* from Shadow Squadron had taken a bad hit to the main starboard rotor fan. Marrand reported her pilot expected they'd have to make a run back to Suchen at the first opportunity. Other than that, they were all set. Cass informed the Harakoni they were pulling out for the time being.

'Nine-Hundred-First, prep for lift-off,' she ordered the three squadrons. 'Vagabonds will lead in echelon, Nemesis has the rear. *Ruffian*, take point. Once you're up, stand by for further orders.'

Her pilots confirmed, and they lifted back up above the collective. Smoke was pluming from a dozen different points amidst the embattled ruins, particularly to the east, where the Harakoni were torching the xenos artillery park that had developed on the flat ground just before the slope of the main valley side. It helped shroud the air above the settlement and offer the Valkyries some cover. Cass braced for incoming fire, scanning what she could see of the surrounding terrain, but there was little besides a few inaccurate blurts of small-arms from clusters of orks still fighting from the tops of the buildings under them, quickly dealt with by pinpoint heavy bolter blasts from the prow weaponry of the wing's Vulture trio.

They hung low, downdraught battering at the shattered roofs and dislodging scatterings of tiles from those few older structures still standing. Finally, the vox pinged with a response from Suchen.

Cass felt a surge of relief when she found herself speaking with Orlov.

'Stryk has reached the pocket,' she told him. 'Army Group Centre is on the move, and we're airborne again and awaiting orders.'

'How's the incoming?' Orlov asked.

'Just now, negligible, but we're still under fire. I don't want to hang around here if we don't have to, not with interdiction on the way.'

'Affirmative,' Orlov said. *'Command wants you back south anyway. The river crossing is taking longer than expected. The xenos are contesting it. They've reacted quickly. General Krannow of the Zenonians is in command of the vanguard, his command channel is five-three-five. I don't know if he'll want you for fire support, targeted strikes or transport.'*

'I hear you,' Cass said. 'We're on the move.'

The Valkyries made a break south. They flew hard, nose-down, through a valley filled with fire. While the top cover continued to circle high above, the other Thunderbolts and Lightnings of the escort were taking it in turns to stoop and strike at ground targets along the slopes and ridgelines.

It gave Cass and her wing the opportunity they needed to run the gauntlet. They took minimal incoming fire, and as they approached the southern end of the valley Cass was able to raise General Krannow on the vox.

'*Good to hear from you, Captain Elza,*' the general said, the sound of a heavy bolter and the cracking of lasguns audible in the background. '*It's hotter down here than we anticipated, at least this early in the day!*'

'My Valkyries are at your disposal, sir,' Cass said. 'What do you need from us?'

'*My lead elements are across the river, but they're holed up just north of the embankment,*' Krannow responded. '*We don't have a good target fix, but we're taking heavy fire from the base of the eastern slope, as well as directly along the valley floor. Need you to swing by and hit those xenos bastards so my boys and girls can get moving again. Otherwise, the whole crossing will stall and this operation will be a write-off.*'

'Copy that, sir,' Cass said. 'I'll see what we can do. Stand by.'

'Out,' Berrik's gunner, Jarn, shouted at her as hard rounds chewed the dirt around them, kicking up dust. 'Reload!'

Berrik began to heft a fresh belt from one of the ammo drums she had dumped next to the position, as Jarn let go of their heavy bolter's firing grip, flexing so his hand didn't cramp up.

They had not been anticipating the strength of xenos resistance this close to the river. They'd been under fire as they crossed over, and it had grown worse the moment they had hit the northern bank. Her Zenonian Free Company regiment and two battalions of Terrifern Light Infantry formed the assault vanguard, crossing the Eji in Chimera armoured personnel carriers before dismounting to engage. She'd been glad of the armour and the opportunity to avoid getting wet, but the briefings had all been run under the assumption that they'd be able to push at least five hundred yards up the valley before meeting serious resistance. Instead, they'd made it about a hundred beyond the north bank when the shelling began, and another fifty before one of the lead Leman Russ battle tanks was knocked out by a rocket.

They'd dismounted and set up in a ditch next to one of the withered rice paddies along the valley floor. Berrik commanded a six-strong heavy weapons section, giving fire support to C Company's Second Platoon, who were currently strung out to their left along the ditch. The disembarkation hadn't come a moment too soon – their Chimera had taken a direct shell hit, and was now a blazing wreck thirty yards to their rear. They'd been exchanging fire with increasing numbers of orks along a stunted treeline across the field, as well as higher up on the valley slope just to their east. The platoon commander, Lieutenant Gask, was dead, and the company commander, Captain Larn, was nowhere to be found. Berrik had no idea what was happening beyond her section, besides the fact that the advance was most definitely stalled.

'They're building up to a charge,' Olwin, the gunner for the section's second bruiser, shouted across at Berrik. He was right. She knew the telltale signs of an ork mob reaching fever pitch. The bestial roaring and bellowing was rising like thunder, and incoming fire was growing both heavier and more erratic as the aliens simply emptied their weapons in a frenzy.

There was a shriek that made her cringe, and another shell whipped overhead to detonate behind the ditch, sending clods of soil raining down on them. Someone started to scream.

'Waight, Waight,' she shouted frantically across at the gunner of her third weapon, who was currently slamming bolts across the paddy at the opposite treeline, the bursting of dry timber and brittle leaves marking the detonation of the explosive rounds. He eased up as the bruiser ran dry and his loader, Mikk, busied himself with the drum and belt feed. Waight looked across at her, hunched over the weapon.

'Hold your fire,' she shouted at him, waving her hand for emphasis. 'They're coming, and I don't want to risk two of us being empty when they do!'

Waight gave her a thumbs-up. She smacked Jarn's shoulder.

'You're loaded,' she shouted in his ear.

Jarn gripped the weapon's handle and helped brace it between the bipod and his shoulder with his other arm, squinting along the barrel's flat upside. Before he could open fire again, they both witnessed a surge of movement along the treeline.

With a roar of exploding battle-lust, the mob they'd been trading fire with came storming from its positions, a green tide that burst from the fire-shot timber.

'Here they come,' Berrik shouted left and right. 'Hit them!'

The trio of heavy bolters kicked in in unison, accompanied by a squall of crimson las bolts from Second Platoon. The resistance lasted only seconds. Over the ear-aching thunder of her section laying down maximum fire coverage, Berrik caught the howl of another incoming shell.

This one struck the rear of the ditch just back and to the left of Berrik's position. Her left ear burst and a torrent of dirt hit her. Briefly, she didn't know where she was or what was happening.

Jarn brought her back.

'Waight,' he was shouting in her face, yanking on her flak pauldrons. 'Waight!'

She looked left, still groggy, and recognised what Jarn was trying to tell her. The blast had staved in part of the ditch and hit Waight and Mikk in the process. Their heavy bolter now lay discarded, tipped over on its side.

'Shit,' Berrik grunted, realising in a heartbeat what was about to happen. Reduced to two heavy bolters, the section, probably the entire platoon, was about to be overrun.

'Jarn, keep hitting them,' she yelled back at her gunner before scrambling along the ditch to what had formerly been Waight and Mikk's position. Mikk was in pieces, definitely dead, but Waight was still alive. He was missing a leg and an arm, screaming horribly, writhing against the side of what remained of the ditch.

Berrik scrambled over him, reaching not for her fellow Zenonian but for his fallen weapon. She managed to heave it back upright and dig its bipod into the shell-ploughed earth, scorching her hands on its hot barrel as she did so.

Waight clutched at her with his one remaining blood-soaked hand, screaming his throat raw, but in a moment of panicked adrenaline she shoved him aside and clutched at the heavy bolter's grip, bracing it.

The xenos were practically on top of her already. They were throwing themselves through the brunt of C Company's firepower, big brutes that shrugged off the worst of the las fire. Only the heavy bolter rounds were sure of stopping them, blowing off legs and arms, cracking their thick skulls or gouging chunks from their torsos. And without all three heavy weapons in action, they weren't enough.

Berrik gritted her teeth and opened fire, the bruiser living up to its name and slamming her shoulder hard enough to make her grunt. It tried to buck out of alignment, but Berrik pinned it down and kept it broadly on target, whipping bolts into the knot of xenos that had used the gap in the company's fire arcs to close the distance. She felt a familiar, vicious sense of satisfaction seeing the howling beasts hacked down, bones splintering and flesh torn, innards spilled, the air misting with their foul, stinking blood.

She eased off for a moment to check the belt, knowing she couldn't afford a jam, not when she didn't have a loader. She noticed Waight had stopped screaming, but didn't have time to check him. She resumed firing.

There were too many of them. A sudden silence to her right announced that both Jarn and Olwin were dry. Reloading would take too long. The paddy field was carpeted with xenos dead and dying, but more were scrambling over their own slain, their brute features contorted with the desire to break and kill, to deal back the destruction they were suffering many times over.

A stick grenade arced into Second Platoon's position, its detonation heralding more screaming. Berrik heard what she had been dreading – the hollow click replacing the slamming report of her own commandeered weapon.

No time to reload. The nearest orks stampeded across the final few yards, the inhuman bellowing chilling Berrik as she snatched her lascarbine from her shoulder.

And then, as though at the behest of some conjurer or illusionist, the field before her simply disappeared. It disintegrated in a blaze of dirt and blood, as a wave of explosions ripped from left to right in front of C Company's tenuous line.

A shape rocketed through the debris, big and wickedly fast. It was a flier, but it was travelling so low Berrik felt as though she could have thrown a hand up and touched its underside. As it went, it spat two beams of high-energy las into the sudden wall of dust, half blinding Berrik. Then it was up and banking away, gone almost as quickly as it had appeared. Berrik watched it go, realising she was looking at a Navy Vulture gunship that had just unloaded its rocket pods and lascannons into the attacking mob.

As the noise of its engine continued to grumble across the riverbank, a short, deathly quiet settled with the dust. Then, someone somewhere started cheering.

The cry spread, and soon the whole company were roaring their defiance. Hailing their saviour, the airborne destroyer who had brought death and ruination to the xenos, doing honour to the markings on its prow – the hooded skull of Vagabond Squadron.

Grinning as viciously as that death's-head sigil, Berrik slung her carbine and reached for the nearest ammunition drum.

'Not as good as a warbird kill,' Cass heard Konstantina say dryly as *Ruffian* climbed up out of its attack run, leaving the devastated, burning paddy field in its wake. *'But still satisfying.'*

All along the southern end of Kantu Valley, the Vultures and Valkyries of 901st Wing stooped and struck. Cass had ordered them to split and pick their targets, and Konstantina had immediately zeroed in on a mass of orks breaking from cover towards the grunt vanguard pinned down just north of the river.

A horde of lightly armoured xenos on exposed ground – they were the perfect target for the rocket pods. Konstantina had ordered Straks to unleash the Emperor's wrath on the xenos, and he had complied.

Vagrant and *Rogue* were both higher up the slope of the valley's eastern side, peeling off with the Vulture and another Valkyrie from Nemesis Squadron. There were xenos entrenchments there, weapons systems and crude artillery batteries dug into the slope side. Las and heavy bolter fire lashed at the positions, wrecking enemy guns before they could switch from targeting the infantry and armour stranded below to the droning aircraft that had suddenly swung across them. Cass had her fliers hover in place as they raked the slope, then swing away just as anti-aircraft guns further north were brought to bear on them.

In just a few minutes the firepower of almost a dozen Imperial aircraft had decimated the orks massing around the relief force's vanguard. Cass ordered the wing to re-form its squadrons, doing another pass on the eastern slope as she did so and letting Zeke and the servitor drill more bruiser rounds into the wrecked, smoking emplacements there.

'Are they moving yet?' Cass called back to Korrie, meaning the Guard forces on the ground under them.

'*Looks like it,*' the navigator replied. A minute later, General Krannow came back in over the vox.

'*My brigade owes you a debt, captain,*' he said. '*The crossing is back underway.*'

'Happy to help, sir,' Cass said dutifully, scanning *Vagrant*'s fuel dial as she spoke. They were good for a couple of hours more over Kantu before having to turn for Barduk.

She was about to offer the use of her Valkyries to further expedite the river crossing when the news she'd been fearing most came through.

'*It's getting hot up here, Vagabond Leader,*' Bix's voice crackled in Cass' ear. '*Increasing numbers of xenos formations hitting from the north, east and west. A few squadrons running low too. I tried to stoop and sting, but some made it through. You're going to have company any minute now.*'

'Acknowledged, Cloud Knight Leader,' Cass said, looking to the auspex. At the same time, Korrie informed her that contacts had just materialised from the sea of returns the aerial duels playing out higher up were throwing back at them. A clutch of jagged red sigils, whipping south down Kantu Valley at a similar altitude to the Valkyries. They had just roared over the collective, seemingly without pausing to strike at the Guard now occupying it.

They were coming in too hard and fast to cut and run. The 901st was about to find itself in an old-fashioned dogfight.

She sent a terse warning to Orlov saying the 901st were engaging aerial targets at low altitudes over Kantu, then switched to the wing-wide frequency.

'Form up,' she ordered. 'We've got scrap-jets incoming. No time to disengage. We'll do a pass then draw them over the river and onto the relief column, where our anti-air can pick them up.'

The leaders of Nemesis and Shadow squadrons acknowledged.

'Got visuals,' Korrie called out. *'Five contacts, coming down the valley, low and hard. Less than two minutes out. Definitely scrap-jets.'*

That was bad news, insomuch as scrap-jets were razor fast and their pilots tended to fly like they had a death wish, even more so than most other ork aviators. But the terrain didn't suit them. Ork fighters had little to no hover capacity, prioritising raw, direct speed. They were incapable of matching the manoeuvrability of Valkyries and Vultures at low levels in terrain like Kantu Valley.

'The wing will split,' Cass ordered, making a decision on how to confront the oncoming xenos, knowing she had literal seconds to implement it. 'Latticework formation. Nemesis, go static on the eastern slope, low down, Shadow, do the same on the western. Off-centre, so you don't hit each other. Vagabonds, hold course. Cut them apart as they close.'

There was no debate, because everyone understood there was no time. Shadow and Nemesis squadrons broke left and right respectively and turned in on the valley, adopting hover mode up the lower ends of the slopes rather than surging forward with guns and engines blazing. That was Vagabond's job.

'Straight at the bastards,' Cass snarled as she kicked *Vagrant* forward, stopping just shy of going prow-down and risking ruining the lascannon firing arc. Suddenly she was racing along the valley floor, through the smoke and dust, the airframe vibrating around her.

She caught the glint of sunlight on metal and on cockpit blisters ahead, a glimpse as the smoke parted. Ork scrap-jets, coming right at them, down the valley, the scream of their engines echoing back from the slopes rising up on either side.

'Oh, *Throne*,' she heard Vaughn hiss. Konstantina had started laughing wickedly.

This was as brutal and desperate as it got, a head-on charge, both sides flying at one another. Cass intended to make sure the xenos lined up just where she wanted them. She could only hope her squadron didn't pay too high a price in doing so.

Shots lashed past. *Vagrant*'s cockpit shield shuddered with impacts. System warnings shrieked in her ears, followed by the even more urgent notification of a target lock.

A second to react. Cass knew she didn't need to tell Korrie when to hit them.

Las speared ahead of her, a constellation of half a dozen bolts whipping away as Korrie drained a percentage of the lascannon's power pack as rapidly as she could, the barrel turning red-hot. It was the necessity of dogfight firepower, undertaken when an aviator knew they had a few heartbeats at most to make their shots count.

One of the oncoming xenos aircraft was hit – Cass didn't know if it had been *Vagrant*'s las, or *Ruffian*'s or *Rogue*'s. But one of the scrap-jets combusted in a raging blossom of fire and debris.

What happened next was so fast Cass didn't have time to mentally register it until it was over.

The scrap-jets, the Valkyries and the Vulture met, and *Vagrant* almost collided with the lead. Some pilot's instinct, carved into her psyche by hundreds of operational sorties and thousands of flying hours, caused her to drive the stick forward, putting *Vagrant* nose-down and causing the Valkyrie to dip at the last instant.

Afterwards, Cass could see it so clearly – the scrap-jet, coming right at her, painted with warning markers across her visor, the xenos skull glyph decorating its front leering. Its airframe was a rusty red, with flame patterns daubed along its wings. Hard round cannons bolted haphazardly across its fuselage were blazing.

She actually caught sight of the pilot, a snapshot image of a hulking green brute hunched behind a filthy cockpit shield, its tusks bared in a roar that was lost amidst the fury of the engines. Coming right at her.

Then *Vagrant* lurched down and her view became one of the scrap-jet's underside, gouged down to bare metal by dozens of uncontrolled landings and streaked with rust. It rocketed just overhead with a roar that made Cass' ears ache, the closeness of its passing beating at the Valkyrie like the fumbling blows of some vast monstrosity trying to get a grip on them.

She clutched the flight stick in both hands, viced around her father's tags, feeling it buck violently in her grip as the wind shear threatened to cause the Valkyrie to spin out of control. Suddenly she was looking not at smoke or scrap-jets, but at the ground, rushing up to greet her.

The hard base alarm screamed at her. She hauled up, her whole body locked and rigid, making an animalistic whining noise as she fought back against gravity and the threat of annihilation.

Vagrant was one hell of a flyer. The Valkyrie came back up at the last moment, prow levelling off with a speed and precision that no other Imperial aircraft could have hoped to match. In an instant, Cass could see patches of sky again.

It was still closer than any uncontrolled descent Cass had ever experienced before. She felt a shudder as one wing actually grazed the dirt, and experienced an intense increase in lift and decrease in drag as ground effect kicked in.

She eased the Valkyrie back up, and finally remembered to breathe again. The entire moment, from the start of her instinctive evasion to regaining full control, had lasted less than five seconds.

Suddenly everything was demanding her attention. System reports, voices on the vox and over the intercom. She did a rapid scan to make sure the engines hadn't been hit and were about to give out, then checked the auspex in tandem with the vox-net.

Both *Ruffian* and *Rogue* had survived the pass. Konstantina was whooping with pure exhilaration, while Vaughn was swearing over and over again.

'Vox discipline,' Cass snapped, silencing both her pilots as she located their aircraft. Both had avoided head-on collisions and maintained their altitude. They were flying above *Vagrant*, their predatory shadows darting along the ground to Cass' left and right.

'Everyone still in one piece?' she demanded.

'Port engine took a hit, but the pressure looks fine and there's no sign of a leak,' Vaughn said. *'Also lost the prow las. A foot higher and I'd be missing my legs too.'*

'All good here,' Konstantina said, still practically panting with the feral excitement that gripped her in situations like these.

'Come to hover and turn about one-eighty, before we end up back over Kantu Collective,' Cass ordered. As the Vagabonds re-formed, she checked on Nemesis and Shadow squadrons, and found out if their gambit had been worth it.

It had. As Cass had hoped, the xenos fighter pilots hadn't been able to resist the challenge issued by Vagabond Squadron, the offer of a straight joust down the centre of the valley.

But scrap-jets weren't Valkyries. Their top speed was considerably higher, but in all the other measurements of manoeuvrability they came up short. Committed to a full-speed passage along the length of the valley floor, they had no room to turn or come about, and no time to react to the jaws of the trap Cass had laid – 901st Wing's other two squadrons, hovering like hawks riding the thermals above the slopes on their left and right.

The Valkyries and Vultures of Shadow and Nemesis squadrons opened up as the scrap-jets rocketed into their preset firing arcs. Las, heavy bolter rounds and rockets cut the ork aircraft apart, catching them in a latticework of death.

One managed to make it to the Eji before its las-riddled engine gave out and it plunged into the muddy waters, the splash it caused drenching the columns of troops struggling to cross to the north bank. The rest were all reduced to burning wreckage littering the valley floor ahead of the relief column's advance.

'Targets destroyed,' Marrand's voice clicked in Cass' ear, the calm tone a contrast to the adrenaline-charged exclamations of the Vagabond pilots.

'Good shooting,' Cass said, the thrill that her plan had worked rapidly swallowed up by the need to decide what happened next. 'Stand by for further orders.'

Vagabond Squadron came about and returned to the southern end of the valley. Cass hailed Suchen as they did so.

'Targets destroyed,' she relayed to Orlov. 'No casualties to report. Requesting permission to disengage and return to Barduk to rearm and refuel.'

There was silence on the other end of the line. She spent long seconds dreading the reply she might receive, wondering whether Orlov was at that very moment locked in a furious argument with Jakyra over whether the 901st should remain fully engaged.

Then, at last, the answer came.

'Copy that, Vagabond Leader. Permission granted. Turn for home.'

Cass closed her eyes for a second, feeling nothing but relief, then acknowledged and passed the orders on to the rest of the squadron.

'Oh, *thank the God-Emperor,*' Vaughn exclaimed.

'Maybe save that for later,' Cass warned, checking the auspex. 'We'll be back up again before dark.'

CHAPTER NINETEEN

Barduk was rife with semi-organised chaos as the 901st returned. The Valkyries were forced to use the secondary landing pads to the airbase's south due to the fact that a squadron of newly refuelled Lightnings were taking off from the primary runway that cut across the flight path to the squadron's hangar, while the secondary runway was being used for emergency landings by aircraft that had been forced to drop out of the dogfights still raging above Kantu.

They passed over one unidentifiable warbird that had crashed just short of the perimeter fence and was now burning, a plume of black smoke rising above Barduk and refracting the sunlight as the Valkyries swung by. Cass wondered if the pilot had made it out in time. It would be cruel, even by the brutal fates often suffered by Aeronautica aviators, to die just yards from safety.

There were more aircraft visible off the side of the emergency runway, wounded warbirds being tended to by ground crews while medicae teams treated their pilots. Several Thunderbolts were being hosed down with flame-retardant foam, while another was in the process of being abandoned as flames licked hungrily from its starboard engine.

The 901st passed by it all and came in to land. Zorn and the ground crews had made it to the secondary pads, accompanied by growling cargo-8 refuellers, just as the wing was completing its touchdown.

'Squadron leaders to me, everyone else remember to eat and use the latrines,' Cass transmitted before cutting the vox and popping the cockpit.

She dropped down without too much difficulty, relieved that her legs weren't threatening to give out this time. It was, she assumed, a by-product of the fact that she knew there was more to come.

She helped Korrie clamber down after her, noting the pained expression the big navigator was trying to hide.

'Have you got any morph left?' she asked her. Korrie just nodded.

'Then take it,' Cass said. There was no question any more that she needed Korrie when they went back up again.

'Damage report?' Zorn-Five buzzed as he clambered up onto the pad to join the aviators, his optics already scanning *Vagrant*'s hull. From the outside, Cass realised just how hard they'd been hit. The wings were holed in several places and the entire airframe looked as though it had been attacked with a hammer and chisel, dented, scraped and scratched by what surely amounted to hundreds of hits.

'Systems are reading fine and she's handling like a dream,' Cass told Zorn. 'Just get her patched up. No restarts or recalibrations.'

The ground crews moved in along with the promethium lines hauled up from the cargo-8s idling below. Cass descended to the hardpan with Korrie and Zeke.

To her surprise, she found Orlov waiting for her.

'I thought you'd still be at Suchen,' she told her wing commander.

'Not much use for me there if you're here,' he said. 'Besides, Jakyra is holding court, and I'd rather not play as one of her jesters.'

'Did she want us to stay up?' Cass asked, thinking back to when she'd requested permission to disengage.

'Yes,' Orlov said bluntly. 'I convinced her Valkyries weren't much use with empty fuel tanks and drained las packs.'

'Why are ex-fighter pilots all like this?'

'Because the ones with brains end up in the tactical wings. How was it?'

'Could have been worse. We lost *Divine Reckoning* from Nemesis. No other casualties, though *Umbral Shade* needs a rotor refit.'

'Well done for dealing with those scrap-jets,' Orlov said. 'I feared the worst when they showed up on the auspex.'

'Didn't have much choice other than to run right at them,' Cass said. 'They were on us. We got lucky.'

'Five kills and barely a scratch on you isn't luck, it's good flying, and good shooting,' Orlov pointed out. Cass took the compliment.

'I'm assuming you'll want us straight back up?' she asked.

'Yes. It's only going to get hotter up north as the xenos scramble in more and more reserves. We've already got a full-scale aerial battle on our hands.'

'Do we have reserves of our own?'

'Not in this sector, but both the Ushen and Torr fronts are monitoring things, and have a couple of wings on standby.'

'What's the play for the rest of the day then?'

'You'll go out with the Marauders. General Lushan is in command of the main body of the crossing, and he's requested a second drop along the ridgelines. They're struggling to secure them. Osprey Squadron have refuelled and taken on a new payload, and they only suffered a couple of aviator casualties in the last run, so they're the ones going back up first. You can keep them company. After that, it's just a case of being on-station and ready to react to the tactical situation as it develops.'

'You want us to run escort?'

'Nothing so formal. Kravitz from the Nine-Tenth has been pulled out of the melee up north to link up with them. But keep your eyes open.'

'Always do,' Cass said sourly.

'You ready to go back out?' Orlov asked, catching her tone.

'Do I have a choice?'

'Want me to take command? Say you took a hit during the first round?'

'A realistic choice, Orlov. One that won't make me a pariah back on board *Mandatum Divinum*.'

'We've always got a choice, Cass,' Orlov said. 'One day you'll be in my position, shackled to headquarters, and you'll damn the day you were promoted.'

Right then Cass found that hard to believe, but she kept her bitterness to herself. She didn't want to sound like Vaughn. The truth was the first sortie had gone well. It was just her nerves talking, the old fear that good luck now meant bad luck later. But she couldn't think like that. She was supposed to have conquered that sort of mindset.

Marrand and Sergios joined them, and Orlov told them what he'd already told Cass.

'It's been too easy so far,' Sergios commented. 'That can't be the entire xenos air strength along the Eji. There must be more of them.'

'The strategos back at Suchen are analysing it,' Orlov said.

'No official pronouncements yet, but I spoke with one before I left. He seemed to think the xenos air presence on this front has been hollowed out over the past month. We've made gains above Ushen and Torr, and the orks have responded to that by shifting forces there. Rather than continuous bombing of the pocket, the best ork pilots and their squadrons have been drawn to the more intensive aerial combat over the cities.'

'So they aren't massing to the north after all?' Sergios asked. 'Is there any actual hard evidence of these movements?'

'Not beyond after-action reports on enemy strength, no. But command is monitoring it. We've got Marauder Vigilants up and hunting for answers.'

'Whether they're really gone, or just sleeping, this presents an opportunity,' Marrand said. 'Havali's got lucky. It looks like he might actually pull this off.'

'Emperor willing,' Orlov said. 'But for now, we need to press our advantage.'

Cass spoke more with Sergios and Marrand, checking their squadrons were ready to go out again and running through possible contingencies in case they were engaged a second time by ork air power in the valley. Afterwards, she called the Vagabonds to her and ran through the same things.

'Everybody feeling good?' she asked, trying to sound upbeat.

'Ecstatic,' Konstantina said, seemingly without any hint of sarcasm. 'Another air-kill added to the tally. The record to beat is four in one day, so there's hope. We could do with more contacts though.'

'You sure that one when we were running head-on was *Ruffian*'s kill?' Cass asked, with a hint of mischief. 'Looked like it was *Vagrant*'s las that hit it.'

'Lies,' Konstantina exclaimed. 'We had a target lock, didn't we, Erik? You were too busy playing games with the hard base to tag anything, Chief.'

Cass yielded the argument with a wave of her gloved hand, and turned her attention to Vaughn.

'I'm fine,' the flight lieutenant said, looking at the rest of his crew. 'We're fine, aren't we, boys?'

Xijen, Holsten and Macks nodded.

'So far, so good,' Holsten said.

'Thought this was going to be a proper air scrap,' Macks said. 'So far I've only had ground mobs to shoot at.'

'I suspect you'll get plenty more of those, at the very least,' Cass said. '*Rogue* took some sore ones back there, what's Zorn's prognosis?'

'Las is being replaced just now,' Vaughn said. 'Portside engine is showing some issues but the coghead promises he can fix it.'

'Still airworthy then?'

'Yes.'

'Good. Has everyone eaten something?'

There was a chorus of yesses before Korrie added, 'Have you?'

'Once I've got you lot strapped in again,' Cass said. 'Turnaround needs to be quick. Let me know as soon as you're fuelled and armed and I'll vox the Marauders and air control. It's all still playing out up north, and they'll need the best before the day is over. That means Vagabond Squadron. Understood?'

'Yes, Chief,' barked the assembled crews, startling several nearby Munitorum menials overseeing the nearest fuel tanker.

'Dismissed,' Cass said.

Cass devoured a pair of ration bars, drained and refilled her canteen, and was looking for Zorn to check that his work was nearly complete when Zeke rejoined her.

'Do we have to take the dead-eye back up?' he asked. It took her a moment to realise he was talking about their new servitor gunner.

'Why, has it been malfunctioning?'

'I don't know. It babbles stuff. Sometimes words, sometimes numbers. Mostly gibberish.'

'It was shooting though, wasn't it? When ordered to engage.'

'Badly, yes. I don't trust it.'

'I don't like having servitors on the crew either, but as I said before, we need everything we can get just now. Unless you think it's going to go rogue and try and strangle you in the hold, we're taking it back up.'

Zeke's expression seemed to imply he thought it might well do just that, but he didn't want to suggest something like that out loud for fear of sounding foolish.

'It doesn't have a soul,' he complained instead. 'The God-Emperor is blind to it, and that means He might be blind to the whole of *Vagrant*. No good will come from flying with it.'

'I don't have time to debate servitor theology with you, Zeke,' Cass said. 'It's going to do its job. You do yours, and we'll all be fine.'

Zeke saluted grudgingly and went to check his bruiser's ammunition was being properly loaded.

Cass spoke to Zorn, who confirmed that he had done what he could to patch the worst of the airframe wounds with quick-setting plas-spread, particularly along the wings. The fuelling was also entering its final stages. Satisfied, Cass went to mount up, and found Korrie already in the aft cockpit.

'You get that morphia?' Cass asked as she climbed up in front of her.

'Yes, Chief,' Korrie nodded. 'I feel like I could reach out and touch the Old Mother up in orbit.'

Cass laughed despite herself.

'Better shake that off before we reach Kantu,' she told her. 'I don't want you any higher up than the rest of the wing.'

'I'm the best navigator in the squadron, I can maintain my altitude,' Korrie replied with a grin.

Cass pulled on her helmet, interfaced it, strapped in and sealed the cockpit. She made sure the rest of the wing was mounting up as well, then contacted the commander of the Marauder squadron they were set to fly north with.

'Osprey Leader, this is Vagabond Leader, we are going to be clear for lift-off in five. Repeat, clear for lift-off in five.'

'Vagabond, this is Osprey Leader, we are just completing our taxiing on runway primary,' came the response. *'See you up there.'*

'Fuel lines disengaged,' Korrie said. Cass saw the Munitorum ground crews scrambling clear with their long hoses. Their overseer gave her a two-thumbs signal, which Cass returned.

She hadn't actually had time to take off her flight gloves after they had touched down, but she pulled one off so she could touch her knuckles to her father's tags, then yanked it back on again.

She double-checked the fuel nodes were sealed and that the tanks were full and the pressure good, then ran through the rest of her preflight assessments, performed a visual scan of the airspace above, then checked in with Barduk Air Control that she was clear. Then, continuing with familiar routines that left no opportunity for the fear and doubt to surge up and drown her, she signalled to the rest of the wing.

'Nine-Hundred-First, this is Vagabond Leader, lifting off.'

CHAPTER TWENTY

The 901st got up again a little under an hour after they'd touched down.

Cass monitored comms as they flew north, trying to gauge how the air war was going. She eventually managed to tap into the channel of a Lightning squadron from the 910th, overhearing frantic scraps of in-action audio.

'Blue Dagger, they're on my six! I can't shake them!'

'Six, this is Three, bank right, bank right!'

'For Throne's sake Marawand, pull up!'

'Good shooting, Six, more at your four o'clock.'

'Marawand is down!'

'Do you see a chute?'

'Negative, negative! More contacts, twelve o'clock high!'

The audio sent a chill through Cass. She changed channels, trying not to think about what she was flying into the midst of.

Eventually, just south of the Eji, she caught up with Bix.

'The Nine-Hundred-First are inbound from Barduk,' she told her. 'Sounds like hell up there. You still in one piece?'

'Just about, which is more than I can say for my wing,' came Bix's reply. Her voice was shot with anger and adrenaline. *'We're going to need to break contact soon, or we'll be getting into Barduk running on dry.'*

'How's the ground offensive looking?'

'Good, from what I've seen. The vanguard is just a few hundred yards shy of reaching the southern slopes of the collective, and troops from the column are at the northern side. Most of the artillery and anti-air along the slopes has been silenced, but we're picking up a lot of ground movement to the east and west of the valley. They've worked out what we're doing. Another couple of hours at most and they'll be coming at the column from both sides. The pocket is under attack from the north, east and west as well.'

Cass hissed with frustration. They'd known it would be like this; in fact everything had gone more or less to plan, so far. But there was no doubt things would get worse before they started getting better.

'I can ask Orlov to clear us to engage air targets and we can up our altitude and join you,' she offered Bix. 'Perhaps cover you while you disengage?'

'Negative, Vagabond Leader,' Bix replied. *'We've got this tied up, just about. Offer your services to the ground-pounders first. There's still a good deal of column left to clear the river.'*

Cass acknowledged and wished Bix good hunting.

The rear of the relief force was visible below now, still south of the Eji. Ahead, a great thunderhead of smoke and ash hung over Kantu Valley, underlit by the glimmer of raging fires.

'Into the maelstrom,' Korrie said to her on the intercom.

'Just keep me flying straight, navigator,' Cass replied.

She contacted the column again, this time speaking to General

Lushan, who had command of the relief effort on the ground. He requested that the Valkyries provide close aerial support to the column higher up the valley – with much of the air cover returning temporarily to Barduk, more protection was needed for the infantry and armour now spreading out up the valley sides, securing the ork positions that had been bombed out by the Marauders and air-to-surface strikes.

The squadron of Marauders that had accompanied the 901st back up delivered their payloads along the valley's ridges, brutalising ork forces surging up and over them from the east and west. As the 901st flew in along the valley, Cass was relieved to note that the xenos air cover also seemed to be slackening.

'They'll be refuelling too,' Sergios pointed out when Cass mentioned it to the squadron leaders.

'If that was all they could put up, we're in a good place,' Marrand added.

Cass said nothing. It felt too dangerous to hope.

The Valkyries swung down as they passed the troops still struggling across the river, the Eji's flow interrupted by banks of Chimeras and reserve armour being used as a tide-break. They carried on into the valley proper, sweeping over the column, low enough for Cass to see the heads of the infantry turn at their passage and see mouths opening in cheers that went unheard by the pilots.

Explosions rippled along the crest of the ridges to their left and right as they went, the Marauders delivering their payload and adding to the great vault of smoke arching over the valley like the roof of some mind-defyingly vast, primordial megalith. Cass felt diminished under the canopy of destruction, small and inconsequential, but she knew she was doing herself a disservice.

They might not possess the capacity for raw annihilation that the bombers had, but an Imperial Navy tactical wing was never inconsequential.

They made a pass over Kantu Collective. Parts of the settlement were still smouldering, particularly on the eastern side of the spur, but it was all now under Imperial control. It had become a hub for the evacuation, with the first troops from the pocket now passing by along the valley floor below, headed south. Cass wondered briefly whether Wellend was down there. Was he helping direct the evacuation from within the pocket further north? Had he found his father?

The relief column had shifted from the valley floor up its sides, seeking to secure the channel through which Army Group Centre would pass on its way to the Eji and beyond, to safety. It was proving slower going than the evacuation itself. While the ork presence had been thinner than expected, and the work of the Aeronautica Imperialis had gone a long way to breaking their defences, the Guard were still having to deal with pockets of resistance, purging dugouts buried deep into the flanks of the slopes. It was a steep climb, and from what reports Cass could pick up it didn't seem as though the crest of either ridgeline had been taken yet.

General Lushan requested the Valkyries provide close support as the Guard continued their climb. Cass sent Nemesis Squadron to the western side of the valley and took Shadow and the Vagabonds up the eastern. They were given the comm frequency for a brigade of Varakian Deepers just north-east of the collective, clearing trenches and anti-aircraft positions section by section.

The Vagabonds moved up to add mobile firepower to the push, swinging by pockets of resistance and raking them with the heavy bolters. Cass warned Zeke of small-arms fire coming back at them in response, but the door gunner made no reply – Cass caught him muttering litanies from the Imperial Creed over the intercom, a sure sign that he was deep in the moment.

Vagrant swept over an emplacement buttressed with the junk orks built their camps and fortifications from. It had just been secured by the Varakians, who were pushing into the next section with *Vagrant* acting as their eyes in the sky, buffeted by the downdraught of the Valkyrie's engines as it switched back to hover mode.

Throughout the engagement, Cass split her attention between the ground contacts and the heavens, wary of ork fighters engaged higher up breaking off in an effort to stoop and sting them. Korrie was doing the same, and the auspex showed the nearest enemy contacts were a trio of fighter-bombers going at it with Thunderbolts from one of Bix's squadrons over six thousand feet up and away to the north. The only nearby threats were a mess of ground returns from the opposite side of the crest, a rising tide of ork foot-mobs moving in from the east and the west that were soon going to come crashing up over the crest and down onto the Varakians if they didn't reach it first.

Cass was considering offering to airlift as many of them as she could the last few hundred yards up the crest in an effort to help them win that race when Zeke spoke up.

'*I can hear something. Thudding.*'

'External?' Cass asked, knowing it was strange for any of them to be able to catch anything that wasn't part of the Valkyrie's systems while in full flight.

'*Must be. The hatch is open.*'

'Visuals?'

'*Nothing unusual.*'

'*I've got something,*' Korrie cut in. '*Individual contacts, small-scale, moving fast amongst the main body coming up the far side of the crest. Too fast.*'

Cass saw them too. Almost lost amidst the morass of infantry were shapes darting along the display. They weren't large or solid enough to register as an enemy aircraft on the powerful auspex systems used by the Valkyries. Cass had briefly thought they were just the scrap-vehicles and war buggies the orks used for ground transport, but they were moving too freely and erratically for anything with wheels and tracks. Besides, they were passing over the returns given off by the foot-mobs, so unless they were running them over, those particular contacts were in the air.

Zeke realised exactly what was approaching a split second before his crewmates. He had heard that thudding sound before. They all had. It had presaged death over Ushen, and now it had returned to haunt them, to hound and destroy them.

'Deathkopters,' the gunner barked into the intercom.

'Throne,' Cass hissed, immediately transmitting to Vaughn, Konstantina, and the pilots of Shadow Squadron. 'Deathkopters inbound, from the east. Climb! Climb!'

She pulled all available power, sending *Vagrant* surging skywards hard enough to drive her against her seat and make her grimace with the oppressive force of the Gs. As they performed a full vertical ascent, she got visuals of the contacts on the auspex, clearing the crest of the ridgeline just as the Vagabonds drew level with it.

Zeke was right. Deathkopters, dozens of them. They were small, single-person rotorcraft, all of them as roughly built and mismatched as any other ork vehicle, but all united by their use of jagged, spinning topside rotors to achieve flight, often in apparent defiance of their crude construction. Unlike most other xenos aircraft in the skies of Kanai Tertius, they were highly manoeuvrable – they could adopt a hover stance as easily as the Valkyries, and their speed and size meant they could pivot, ascend or descend even more rapidly. Their only disadvantages were that the Valkyries were larger, more heavily armoured, and usually more heavily armed.

Those factors were rendered moot by the fact that, in that

moment, Cass realised her squadron were outnumbered seven or eight to one.

The orks began firing as soon as they cleared the crest – Cass wasn't even sure if the xenos had locked on to them, or were just venting their deranged bloodlust at the first opportunity.

Rockets whipped from the jagged little rotorcraft, corkscrewing wildly. Cass had to stall the ascent and yank *Vagrant* to starboard, turning the motion into a banking manoeuvre as missiles streaked through the airspace the flier had occupied a moment before. One detonated, rattling shrapnel off the cockpit so hard a slight split appeared in the top-left pane of the shield.

'Keep rising,' she urged Vaughn and Konstantina as the first salvo screamed past, putting the engines back into vertical with a deft flick of one hand across the control panel.

'I'm hit,' came Vaughn's snarl. Cass realised his marker on the visor display was winking amber.

'Bad?' she demanded.

'Don't think so. Clipped the port wing uppers. Lost control for a moment, but it's responding now.'

'We need to gain height,' Cass urged. 'Maintain ascent.'

Korrie was already hitting the las, whipping bolts at the oncoming xenos. Cass kept one eye on the altimeter ticking rapidly upwards while trying to watch for more incoming fire, gravity still dragging at her. It made it hard to think, but she fought through it, doing her best to keep her body relaxed even as her heart hammered adrenaline through her system.

Deathkopters excelled in low-altitude engagements, but their smaller, single engines – regardless of how they'd been cobbled together by deranged xenos mechanics – couldn't match those of the Valkyries. Their operational ceiling was far lower, so the surest way of rendering them impotent was to rise above them, in a literal sense.

But ork pilots were rarely troubled by the limitations imposed on them by physics and engineering. Most of the rotorcraft tried to climb with the Vagabonds, and as Cass was forced higher, a different kind of warning alert pinged in her ear, demanding attention.

They were entering the engagement zone being contested by both sides' fighters. Even with the low numbers of ork aircraft still present, the airspace overhead was playing host to dozens of vicious dogfights, as the Thunderbolts and Lightnings of the 910th and 911th duelled the xenos for total air superiority. One ork fighter, its engines trailing foul smoke in its wake, squeezed off an opportunistic burst of hard rounds at the two Valkyries rising up into its sights as it pulled out of an evasive dive, sending several shots spanking off *Vagrant* and *Rogue*'s topsides.

'We can't go any higher,' Vaughn exclaimed. *'We'll be easy pickings for the fighters up there!'*

Cass cursed. She had trapped them between two different but equally deadly threats. But cornered, flying the narrow spaces, the deadly ones, that was where the Vagabonds excelled. At the edge of two engagement zones, where neither kinds of enemy flier excelled – that was where the Valkyries could still operate at maximum capacity.

'Hold this altitude,' she ordered. 'Split, and engage all targets.'

The Valkyries separated and drove into the maelstrom, armaments and engines blazing.

CHAPTER TWENTY-ONE

'At last,' Konstantina growled. 'A proper damned fight.'

'You've got that right,' Straks responded, sounding marginally less enthusiastic.

The deathkopters were the most immediate threat to *Ruffian*. They were rising in an attempt to match the Imperial fliers, still coming straight at them, the distance closing.

Konstantina hated them. She hated them not just because of the squadron's experiences over Ushen, but because they were challenging her and her warbird. Their very existence was like some kind of ramshackle, stunted parody of the holy Vulture STCs she had spent her life piloting, and it disgusted her. Their xenos blasphemies could not be allowed to live, certainly not in the airspace that Vagabond Squadron had claimed.

'Hit the bastards, flyboy,' she told Straks.

Ruffian ripped into the nearest rotorcraft. The Vulture's las-cannons speared a deathkopter charging straight at it, causing it to detonate like a flak burst.

At the same time, Konstantina tracked the prow bruiser from left to right, catching another two of the whickering contraptions in a hail of bolts. Both were wrecked by the explosive rounds and began to plummet towards the ground, tailing smoke and shorn debris.

Did these count as air-kills? No, Konstantina thought as she rotated the heavy bolter further left, attempting to track another of the xenos that had wisely broken off from its attack and was trying to swoop in under the squadron. She would not deign to grant any honours to these vermin and their parody, joke rotor-craft. Their extermination would not be recorded on the flank of *Ruffian*'s cockpit.

'*Incoming,*' Straks yapped in her ear. She caught the rocket coming a moment later, hitting a pedal and yawing sharply left. The missile passed right by the cockpit, underneath one wing, missing the Vulture by perhaps a foot. Konstantina swung back to level. The whole time, the heavy bolter hadn't stopped kicking out rounds, rotating to its maximum left-down position as it tracked and caught a fourth 'kopter. The xenos flier fell towards the slope, surrounded by a halo of sheared-off rotor blades.

Konstantina realised she was grinning viciously behind her resp-mask.

'You don't go head to head with *Ruffian* like that and expect to live, xenos scum,' she hissed.

Vaughn threw *Rogue* into such a vicious yaw it looked for a moment as though the Valkyrie was going to stand on its starboard wing. His harness yanked tight as he was thrown into the side of the cockpit, but he kept his grip on the flight stick and eased up on the pedals to bring the flier back to a flat plane.

The wild evasion had been necessary. A deathkopter, coming right at them, shot past in a hail of bullets and rockets, the fusillade wasted on thin air. Without the desperate manoeuvre, the two fliers would have collided.

'Get its tail, Macks,' Vaughn snapped as he swung *Rogue* hard to starboard, getting his gunner on that side of the aircraft an angle on the deathkopter as it shot away from them. Macks picked it up with a steady stream of bruiser rounds, the tracers among the belt whipping away like fire hornets after the ork flier. Macks was, in Vaughn's opinion, the best gunner in the squadron, which made him also the best gunner in the whole damned fleet. After a few moments, he'd connected the line of darting lights with the deathkopter's fuselage. It survived only a few shots before simply coming apart, the lightly armoured, roughly engineered construction blasted to pieces along with its xenos pilot.

Holsten was firing too from the other side at more of the ork rotorcraft hurtling past, while Xijen stabbed the prow las at another ork fighter that had dropped down from the melee above them. Those were the bigger threat, as far as Vaughn was concerned. Between the firepower and durability of the ork planes and the stinging manoeuvrability of the deathkopters, the Vagabonds were being bracketed.

'We need to drop low again,' he urged Cass, then cursed as *Rogue*'s systems screamed a warning in his ear, forcing him to evade another streaking rocket. He heard Macks yell as he was almost pitched out of the side hatch, only kept in the aircraft by his restraint harness.

That'll put us on an even footing with the 'kopters,' came back the squadron leader's response. *'Up here they can't swarm us as easily.'*

'We've got maybe a minute before one of those fighters starts tailing us, though,' Vaughn pointed out, frustrations rising.

Further protests were cut short by an impact that slammed him so hard against his own harness it almost caused his helmet to strike against the cockpit shield. He felt the flight stick fight against his grasp, followed in the same panicked heartbeat by the lurching sensation of a spinning free fall.

They'd been hit. There hadn't even been an incoming missile or target lock warning. He didn't know what exactly had struck *Rogue* or where it had come from, but he did know from the flight display that the port engine had just given out, and the airframe sensors were reporting damage to the same wing.

'Engine failure,' he grunted to Xijen through gritted teeth. 'Try to reignite while I get her level!'

He battled with the stick, working the port pedal at the same time and trying to adjust the angle of the flier's fins. His screens were lighting up red, warning of a loss of system pressure and a possible engine fire, but all he could do for the time being was stop *Rogue* from ploughing prow-first into the ridgeline.

'*It won't reignite,*' Xijen was shouting in his ear. '*Major system failure. We might have just lost half the port wing!*'

That news was about as bad as it came, but it was tempered by the fact he'd managed to haul *Rogue's* prow up. He cut the starboard engine, not wanting to run the risk of a fire spreading and knowing it might throw them back into a spin if it wasn't controlled.

Nothing was stopping them from going down now.

'Brace for emergency landing,' Vaughn snapped over the vox, both hands on the flight stick still as he fought to make sure they hit the crest level, rather than nosediving again and colliding head-on with the slope.

He just had time to glance at his sister's smiling face on the pict capture pinned to the cockpit shield, before *Rogue* slammed into the ridgeline.

'Rogue *has dropped,*' Konstantina said urgently over the vox.

Cass could see that. She had caught a visual of the Valkyrie going down through the port side of the cockpit. Vaughan had done well to make sure it hit the crest rather than the slope, and did so almost horizontal, but it still didn't look like the easiest of landings. Black smoke was pluming from one of the engines.

Cass lost sight of the crash as *Vagrant*'s systems warned her of another incoming missile, requiring more evasive manoeuvres. Orlov was in her ear, saying something about a major incident developing back at Suchen. She couldn't respond. She was barely even conscious of his words as she sawed *Vagrant* to port with more yaw and acceleration than she had really wanted. The shot from an oncoming deathkopter was almost point-blank, and even the evasion wasn't enough, but it did mean the twisting rocket glanced off the lower slope of the starboard wing and detonated in the air above rather than punching straight through and potentially into the hold.

'Hal, come in,' she said into the vox while swinging *Vagrant* back the other way to give Zeke an angle on the deathkopter as it whirred past. 'Hal, tell me you're still in one piece.'

Static was her only answer.

'*Ruffian*, do you have eyes on *Rogue*?' she demanded of Konstantina, the requirements of further evasion keeping her from getting more visuals of the crash site. She also realised that, in the midst of the frenetic aerial crash, she'd lost a good deal of altitude. They were back down in preferred rotorcraft territory, barely up above the ridgeline.

'*Affirmative, Chief, looks like they're still in one piece, but something's burning. I can see someone moving about, think it's Holsten or Macks. They haven't come down in a great spot, though.*'

Cass had no doubt that was an understatement. A little longer and the ork mobs climbing up onto the ridgeline from its eastern side would burst up over the crest and onto Vaughn's downed Valkyrie.

'Hal, get out of there,' she ordered into the vox, but there was still no response. For the moment, any of *Rogue*'s crew who had survived the landing were on their own.

Far above the carnage, where the oxygen was suffocatingly thin and the bitter chill of the void ruled almost wholly unopposed, eyes watched the battle of Kantu Valley unfolding.

A lone aircraft hung in the clear, perfect azure, circling high and slow, unseen by the many thousands fighting and dying beneath it.

It belonged to the 899th Wing, a Marauder, though it was unlike any of its kin. Not for it bomb bays full of explosives or extra armour plating designed to preserve its crew through hails of flak and the fire of enemy interdiction fighters. It did not even have a proud name like its fellow warbirds in the 899th, *Red Wrath* or *Hammerfall* or *Foe Crusher*. It was known only by its serial number, 76-42B, and though it was considered a pariah within its own wing, it did not mind, for it preferred its own company. It was a Marauder Vigilant, and its purpose was not to destroy, but to observe.

Vigilants were rare aircraft within the Aeronautica Imperialis, repurposed from a bombing role to provide surveillance instead. There were only six operating on Kanai Tertius, and 76-42B was the only one above the Eji Valley. Its fuselage was packed with heavy augur kit, blessed by the tech-priests of the Old Mother herself, those highest among the orders of the Martian priesthood that served on board the fleet. An array of sensorium spikes and dishes, pict capturers, vid-feeds and vox-uplinks allowed the Vigilant to monitor a dozen different engagement zones at once, from multi-spectrum target locking to pinpointing an object as small as a fallen helmet in a field of tall grass. It could transmit its findings to both the fleet and ground assets, be they high command at Ushen or, if required, the vox-set of a squad of front-line grunts. The Vigilants were one of the most potent tools in the arsenal of the Aeronautica Imperialis, and while other pilots might publicly scorn their lack of kill-power, in truth every aviator flew more comfortably if they knew a Vigilant was watching over them.

The commander of 76-42B, Flight Lieutenant Maximilian Crenn, had been monitoring the day's action since the Lightning vanguard flights had taken off from Barduk just before dawn. Unlike the other Aeronautica aircraft up above the Eji, it had not taken off from the airfield, and nor was it based there. It remained on board the *Mandatum Divinum* in anchorage above the valley, using the Marauder's capacity for void travel to translate from the great capital ship's flight bays down to its sub-orbital station, triangulated using aerial buoys that had been seeded in the upper atmosphere at strategic locations not long after the fleet's arrival.

Such methods offered the Vigilant the greatest degree of safety possible in such a fraught warzone. Orks made war anywhere and everywhere they could, and the limits of the upper atmosphere were not safe from their more extreme aerial experiments, or their warships currently in deadlock with the Imperial Navy in low orbit. Just as the Militarum were seeking to hold the line at the Eji, so Battlefleet Ajax held the space above it, and that presence not far beyond 76-42B kept it tolerably safe. But it meant it couldn't range further north.

That was a frustration for Flight Lieutenant Crenn, and had been for weeks. Just as fighter pilots relished aerial kills and bomber brethren in the wider 899th Wing prized each major successful payload drop, so the aviators who manned the Vigilants found worth in pinpointing and reporting on the enemy. Knowledge was power, or so the ancient maxim went, and aircraft like 76-42B acted as the font of knowledge not just for the Navy, but for strategos and Astra Militarum planners and generals. At their best, Marauder Vigilants saw all, reported all, located the enemies of man in their places of strength, and left them nowhere to hide, nowhere to recoup. The Hammer of the Emperor might sunder His foes, but it was the Marauder Vigilants who so often directed where it should fall.

But 76-42B had been able to do none of that, because the enemy's air strength was too great, and the Vigilants too precious, for Crenn to receive clearance from the air marshals to fly further north. For weeks now, rumours had been suggesting a major xenos build-up there, near the distant mouth of the Eji River Valley. Yet it lay beyond the range of even the powerful augur sensors of 76-42B. The xenos fleet likewise blinded the *Mandatum Divinum* and the other capital ships and escorts to what was happening planetside that far north. And so Crenn and his fellow observers had been forced to admit they had no solid data to work with, yet. High command was working off strategos supposition and a few Lightning scout pict snaps, and as far as Crenn was concerned, that meant they were working off nothing at all.

Such troubles had become secondary as the relief column stormed up Kantu Valley. Crenn, his co-pilot and vox-operator Naria, and the augur master, Volplex, had busied themselves with identifying the ork response to the powerful Imperial incursion, as well as monitoring the effectiveness of the bombing runs of their fellow 899th aviators. Smoke had soon started to shroud the narrow, craggy brown strip Kantu represented on their optics, but they had stripped out layers and switched to mixed filters, continuing to transmit updates to air command at Suchen Palace, to be rerouted where needed.

Crenn had just been about to address some unusual weather patterns that appeared to be developing further east when the calm, orderly flow of observation and data-relaying had broken down. Volplex had spoken to him via 76-42B's intercom, concerned that there was a malfunction occurring somewhere within the main array. Crenn realised what he meant when a mass appeared along the upper end of his main auspex chart, an overload of contact markers. Despite the nature of the advanced and fully sanctioned technology the Vigilant played host to, glitches were neither impossible nor wholly unheard of. Crenn ordered Volplex to briefly cut, flush and then reignite the necessary systems, while warning Suchen that there would be an interruption of the data flow lasting approximately three minutes, standard.

Most of the screens in front of Crenn subsequently went blank, but when they flickered back to life again, the distortion remained.

And that was when icy realisation, more chilling than even the frigid temperatures 76-42B had to contend with at such high altitudes, began to take a hold of the entire crew.

'Those are contact returns,' Naria prompted Crenn after he had sat for almost a full minute, simply staring at the outputs his aircraft was picking up. 'Hundreds of aerial contacts, moving down the main valley.'

'God-Emperor,' he muttered to himself, before finally starting to respond properly. 'Get me Suchen,' he told Naria urgently. 'Straight through to their primary comms, not just the air marshal. Patch Commodore Braizen and the rest of fleet command into this transmission too. We need to let as many people know about this as quickly as possible.'

'Suchen's on the line,' Naria said, hands dancing across the controls of the shared cockpit's vox-panel. Crenn adjusted his helmet mic and spoke, years of experience keeping his tone calm and precise despite the spike in his heart rate, the mounting panic as he came to terms with what he was seeing.

'Citadel Tertiary, this is *Spotter Six*. We're reading major airborne returns appearing across the scopes to the north. Routing a data packet canticle to you just now, over.'

'*Copy that, Spotter Six, we have the data packet on screen. Confirm not a glitch, over.*'

'Have flushed the systems and reappraised, contacts remain,' said Crenn, trying not to snap, trying to hold back the words he really wanted to say.

This isn't a damned glitch! There are hundreds of returns inbound from the north! Likely a thousand or more xenos aircraft, heading down Eji Valley. Dozens of formations. They're going to be above the pocket in under an hour.

The voice on the other end of the link to Suchen changed.

'Spotter Six, *this is Desert Star,*' it said. Crenn recognised the call sign for the commander of the tertiary front, Lieutenant General Havali.

'*Confirm what you're seeing up there,*' the general went on. '*Is this a new ork aerial incursion?*'

'Yes, sir,' Crenn said. 'It's… it's bigger than anything I've seen on Kanai so far. Half of the xenos air power must be up there right now. They're sending it all against Army Group Centre.'

'*Then the rumours were true,*' Havali said, his tone grim. '*They've been massing to the north for weeks. And now we've provoked them.*'

Crenn swallowed his dismay, and the urge to try and give advice to the general. That wasn't his place. His job was to watch, and relay. And if that meant watching, and relaying, the annihilation of both Army Group Centre and its relief column beneath a vast armada of ork aircraft, then it was a duty he would fulfil without hesitation. That was the lot of a Vigilant crew.

'I will continue to send data and updates as the augurs log them, sir,' he told Havali.

There was no reply. The general had already broken the voxlink. The voice of the regular operator returned.

'*Acknowledged. Throne be with you, Spotter Six.*'

'Better to pray for the troops in Kantu Valley,' Crenn said.

PART THREE

CHAPTER TWENTY-TWO

Vaughn groaned and sat up before undoing his harness. It had sawed into him in multiple places, and his back felt like he'd been bent over for hours, but he guessed without the straps and the helmet he'd be in an even worse state.

He looked around. There was no smoke in the cockpit, so that was a good start, though there was plenty outside. *Rogue* had shut down automatically post-landing, seeking to preserve system integrity, and Vaughn decided against kickstarting it again until he had diagnostics from Xijen.

That in itself could prove a problem. They'd come down along the crest of the ridgeline, and while smoke from what Vaughn assumed was the port engine was obscuring much of his view of the outside, there couldn't be xenos far away. That was without including the aerial scrap still happening low overhead.

He popped the cockpit shield and dragged himself out. The ground underfoot was a churned-up mess, and not just because of the force of *Rogue*'s landing. This was the area the Marauders had hit hardest, and now the twin ridgelines cresting the Kantu Valley's sides were a morass of craters and burning xenos wreckage.

He found Macks and Holsten climbing from the side hatches, both seemingly unhurt. Xijen was already up top. Flames were licking from the port engine, its rotors looking like a furnace grille. Xijen still had his resp-mask on, and was dumping foam from a fire-retardant canister into it.

'How's it looking?' Vaughn called up to him.

'I'll let you know when the bastard thing has stopped burning,' he responded. 'But it looks fried.'

'Like, "we're-never-flying-again" fried or "just-needs-to-cool-down" fried?'

'Pray for the latter. I'm going to fit a new capacity unit, we've got a spare. Then run the rotors without the fuel line connected, clear the spalling through it and see if it's cycling properly.'

'How long is that going to take?'

'I don't know! Fifteen minutes?'

'That's ten minutes too many,' Vaughn snapped. 'The mobs on the ground will be on us by then, assuming we aren't picked up by one of those bastard 'kopters while we're sitting here smoking.'

'We could withdraw down the slope,' Holsten suggested. 'Towards the Guard. They're still climbing.' He gestured past the mangled ground surrounding them. The ridgeline's edge hid the immediate slopes on either side, but the Varakian units they'd passed over on their way down couldn't be more than five hundred yards away.

'We're not leaving her,' Vaughn said.

Holsten looked incredulous.

'Are we even sure it'll fly again?' Macks asked.

'I can get her back up, I just need time,' Xijen reiterated from up top.

'Get on the starboard bruiser,' Vaughn ordered Macks. 'And Holsten, run down the slope and get those damn grunts up here to give us some support. It's about time they returned us the favour.'

He returned to the forward cockpit momentarily and reactivated the systems via the emergency reignition, then hailed Cass on the vox.

'We're all still in one piece, just about,' he told her. 'Port engine took a hit, but Xijen thinks he can get us back up again in fifteen. Not sure we'll last that long without support.'

He knew he was asking a lot of *Vagrant* and *Ruffian*, given they were still in the aerial equivalent of a knife fight with the swarms of xenos rotorcraft. He watched *Vagrant* as he spoke, the Valkyrie swinging low south-east, lancing beams of las ahead, scything another of the ork fliers in half and sending several of its short rotor blades thudding into the slope below.

'Copy that, Rogue, *we'll come in and cover you,'* Cass said without any hesitation. *'Shadow will watch our wings and topsides.'*

'Thanks,' Vaughn said, feeling a moment's heartfelt relief. 'Looks like we've got ground contacts incoming.'

He could hear them before he could see them, the bestial roaring and howling of oncoming ork foot-mobs. This wasn't the sort of tactical situation he preferred to engage them in. He scrambled up onto the Valkyrie's back with Xijen, using *Rogue*'s hull as a vantage point.

'We're about to have company,' he shouted to Macks, who was standing in the hatch now, heavy bolter braced. The angle *Rogue* had come down at gave him a half-decent spread over the eastern edge of the crest, but the presence of the wing, scarred and damaged though it was, would still impede a section of his arc. Vaughn would have to do his best to cover it, but he doubted his and Xijen's laspistols would be much good. He glanced back for

Holsten, hoping to see him bringing Varakian reinforcements, but there was no sign of the other gunner's return.

A few moments later and shapes came bursting up onto the ridge's crest, just a few at first but rapidly turning to dozens and then a solid wall of green muscle, ragged hides, leather and rough-forged metal.

Macks opened fire, slashing bruiser rounds into the mob as it caught sight of the downed, smoking Valkyrie and, with a chilling howl, charged.

Vaughn stood frozen for a second, almost unmade by a primal, ancestral fear. Then, he drew and primed his laspistol, and took aim.

Cass pulled *Vagrant* portside sharply, seeing a rocket from an oncoming deathkopter slash by so close it actually passed beneath the wing, between its base and the hold.

She kicked a pedal and kept the movement going, creating an angle for the servitor manning that side of the Valkyrie as the 'kopter attempted to evade by trying to fly beneath them, its spinning blades almost grazing *Vagrant's* underbelly. She had no idea if the semi-automated gunner hit anything.

Another deathkopter was coming at them head-on, but before either Cass or Korrie could react it was speared by a las bolt, tumbling away in burning ruin, its pilot's upper half reduced to a charred mess. Cass flashed a glance at the auspex just before she got a visual of Marrand's Valkyrie swinging past above them.

'We've got your topside, Vagabonds,' came the commander of Shadow Squadron's voice on the vox. 'We'll let you know if any-thing above starts stooping.'

'Copy that, Shadow Leader,' Cass grunted as she heaved *Vagrant* back to the horizontal and came around sharply, scanning the ground rather than the skies as she reorientated herself.

She picked up *Rogue*'s smoke plume, and realised just how precarious a situation Vaughn's downed Valkyrie was now in. Ork foot-mobs were surging up onto the ridgeline from the east, and *Rogue* had abruptly become their first point of opposition. Cass could see two figures up on the Valkyrie's topside, presumably Vaughn and Xijen, one of them stooped over the portside engine as the other began firing his laspistol at the onrushing surge. The port heavy bolter was also in action, but it was clear none of it would be enough.

'Hang tight, *Rogue*,' Cass said, knowing they probably wouldn't hear her. She flicked the switch to reroute the engine power to the under-wing rotors, hovering almost directly above *Rogue*, whipping at the smoke still broiling up from it.

She turned to starboard and hit the intercom.

'Blast them, Preacher.'

Zeke's heavy bolter added to *Rogue*'s, doubling the hits the orks were taking. It still wasn't enough. While those charging directly at the downed Valkyrie were checked for a moment, the mobs were almost covering the crest, threatening to lap around *Rogue*'s flanks.

'Em, could really use you over here,' Cass said, trying to spot *Ruffian* as she held station above the fallen Vagabond. Konstantina's indignant voice pipped in her ear.

'Coming, damn it!'

As was so often the case, the first Cass knew of *Ruffian*'s arrival was a shrieking passage of rockets, the small, lethal warheads whipping up a blizzard of shrapnel in an arc around *Rogue*'s eastern side. The next thing Cass knew, *Ruffian* was in front of her, face-on to the enemy so it could bring all its hardpoint weaponry to bear.

'How long is this going to take?' Konstantina demanded. *'We're having to conserve ammunition.'*

'I don't know,' Cass admitted, looking from the orks on the ground to the dogfighting still playing out above. The death-kopter air-mob had been gutted by the combined lethality of Shadow and Vagabond Squadrons, but there were still rotor-craft tussling with Marrand's fliers round about, and the clash of fighters above was ongoing. The Vagabonds were exposed, holding point in the midst of it all, caught static. Being so vulnerable felt anathema.

And even with their presence attempting to shield *Rogue*, they might not be enough. There was return fire hitting them now, and the numbers of xenos clambering onto the crest beneath them only seemed to be growing.

'They should abandon it,' Konstantina said. *'There's nothing more I can do for them when I'm all out of rockets and las.'*

'Just keep firing,' Cass said.

A missile arced away past *Vagrant*'s tail, almost clipping one of the fins. Cass grimaced.

'Come on, Hal,' she muttered into her resp-mask. 'Get the hell out of there.'

CHAPTER TWENTY-THREE

'We need to go,' Macks shouted up at Vaughn as he finished unjamming the heavy bolter. 'They're not stopping!'

'I'm not leaving her,' Vaughn barked back, emptying the last of his laspistol's power pack into the onrushing mobs. 'Xijen, for Throne's sake, give me some good news!'

His co-pilot said nothing, up to his elbows in the guts of the engine's electrical components. It didn't look like *Rogue* was going to be airworthy in the minute – or less – that they had before the orks hit them.

Vaughn had felt momentary relief when *Vagrant* and *Ruffian* had appeared directly above, like guardian spirits, slamming bolt rounds and rockets into the rising green tide as they held station overhead. It had bought them time, but still not enough – even the concentrated firepower of Vagabond Squadron wasn't enough to stop this xenos push.

'Just go,' he shouted down at Macks over the ear-aching buzz of *Vagrant* and *Ruffian*'s hover rotors whipping at them. 'Get out the other hatch while you still can and get down the slope!'

If the gunner heard him, he chose to ignore him, the heavy bolter's fire resuming.

Then came a different kind of gunfire. Vaughn heard a crackling noise and saw light, a sudden torrent of crimson slashing past *Rogue*'s airframe on either side.

Las bolts. The next thing he knew, Guard infantry in the grey flakplate and fatigues of the Varakian Deepers were charging past, firing as they went, meeting the orks just as they stormed the last fifty yards towards the grounded Valkyrie.

Holsten had made it back. He arrived, red-faced and breath-less, in the wake of the infantry rush, leaning against *Rogue*'s wing.

'Good job, gunner,' Vaughn shouted at him in a moment of exhilaration. Holsten just managed a thumbs-up.

The Varakians had succeeded in getting around *Rogue*'s prow and aft and interposing themselves between the Valkyrie and the oncoming orks, but the xenos still weren't showing any signs of faltering. Vaughn saw a Varakian sergeant waving up at him, and crouched on the edge of *Rogue*'s wing so they could speak over the chaos enveloping them. He experienced a moment's surreal recognition – the sergeant was the man he had punched during fight night at Camp Yuzen. The Varakian stared at him in turn, seemingly making the same realisation, before shout-ing and gesturing at *Rogue* with his idling chainsword.

'Can you lift off?'

'We're trying,' Vaughn responded. 'Hopefully just a few min-utes more!'

'The heavy weapons sections are still down the slope,' the Varakian went on. 'We need to buy more time! I'm going to charge them!'

'Do whatever you need to, sergeant,' Vaughn shouted back, wondering if he had misheard. But sure enough, the Varakian was turning and revving his sword, shouting at his men to fix bayonets.

Vaughn simply stood and watched as the Varakians bayonet-charged the oncoming orks. It seemed like the height of insanity, yet the Guard did it without any hesitation. Vaughn realised this likely wasn't even the first time they had engaged the xenos in close combat. It was simply part of the existence of veteran Guard units throughout the course of this war. It felt a world away from the experiences of Aeronautica aviators, and for all the dangers they faced in the skies, Vaughn doubted he would have had the courage to carry nothing but cold steel directly into the midst of an ork mob's stampede-charge. Yet that was what the Varakian Deepers did.

He was about to turn and remonstrate with Xijen when the navigator let out a yell that Vaughn hoped was the sound of triumph. He banged a maintenance hatch shut and mag-clamped it, then stood up.

'Get down in the cockpit and try and ignite,' he shouted over the sounds of battle and the ongoing wrath of the Valkyrie and the Vulture right above them. Vaughn scrambled to do so, clambering around the open shields and down, straining for the ignition switch in the forward cockpit.

To his utter relief, the engines ignited, and with them the primary rotors, both sets, vibrating through the plasteel airframe beneath him.

'Throne, yes,' he shouted, smacking his palm against his sister's pict before dropping down fully into his seat. He looked back to make sure Xijen was getting into the aft cockpit behind him, then lowered the shield, just as a wild spray of rounds clattered against it.

'Is Holsten in?' he demanded over the intercom.

'I'm in,' Holsten's voice came back from the hold, still sounding blown. *'Let's get out of here!'*

Vaughn switched to the squadron-wide comm frequency.

'Clear out topside! We're lifting off!'

He looked up, seeing *Vagrant* and *Ruffian* swinging away to their left and right, now firing beyond the front ranks of the orks, which were engaged hand-to-hand with the Guard infantry. The Varakians were being hacked to pieces, but they were focusing the orks' frenzy, and buying time with their lives.

A quick check of the readouts to make sure the engines were stable and Vaughn lifted, applying full thrust to the hover rotors. *Rogue* rocketed upwards, making his guts feel like they were being sat on and rearranged by one of the brutal xenos that had been charging at them. He grunted, but got the Valkyrie up to the same low altitude as *Vagrant* and *Ruffian* in a matter of moments, without any issues pinging up on the display.

'Z-Five is not going to like what I've done to that transistor coupling,' Xijen said.

'Dare I ask?' Vaughn said. 'What matters is that we're back in the air.'

'Well, no guarantees it'll stay that way… but I think it'll hold.'

That would have to do, Vaughn supposed.

He checked there were no immediate threats bearing down on them, then leaned across and tried to catch sight of the sergeant who had saved *Rogue* in the midst of the melee that was spreading out below them, but could not. More Guard platoons were arriving and storming into the fray, and he could see their heavy weapons teams setting up on the edge of the crest, preparing fallback positions for those already engaged.

'We're going to owe the Deepers after this one,' he admitted to his crew.

'Rogue, *status report,*' came Cass' voice over his helmet's headset.

Vaughn hesitated. This could be a means of escape, he realised. Other Valkyries from both Shadow and Nemesis Squadrons had already dropped out of the day's fighting because of damage suffered. *Rogue* had been hit hard. No one would argue against a return trip to Barduk.

He could sense the rest of the crew waiting for him to speak. He looked at Eleanor's smiling face, taped above his display. He took a breath.

'We're with you, Chief,' he told Cass.

CHAPTER TWENTY-FOUR

Vagabond Squadron poured fire down on the ork offensive trying to claim the crest of the eastern ridgeline. With the Guard line stabilising thanks to the heroics of the Varakian vanguard, the xenos were finally, momentarily pushed back.

'*We're clear up here,*' Marrand told Cass. The last of the deathkopters had been downed or driven off, and even the enemy warplanes higher up seemed to have dissipated. It looked as though the skies above Kantu Valley belonged to the Aeronautica Imperialis.

Cass was getting a transmission from Orlov, but ignored it while she checked in with Nemesis Squadron, across the valley, ordering them to re-form with the rest of the wing. Then she voxed Vaughn.

'Are you sure you're combat-worthy?' she asked.

'*I told you, I'm with you,*' came the reply. '*Don't make me reconsider.*'

Before Cass could continue, the transmission marker from Orlov blinked up again. She accepted it.

'*Cass, come in, damn it,*' he snapped in her ear.

She had never heard him address her with such indiscipline during an operation. A sudden, icy sense of foreboding pierced the heat of the moment, and she flipped channels to respond to her wing commander.

'This is Vagabond Leader, I copy.'

'*I know you're up to your neck in it, Vagabond Leader, but you need to hear this,*' Orlov said. His grim tone did nothing to alleviate her mounting concern. '*We've just had contact from* Spotter Six, *the Vigilant on station above the valley. I'm seeing if we can ping the long-range scan returns through to your auspex just now…*'

'Understood, standing by,' Cass said, her concerns only growing. As Korrie continued to monitor the surrounding airspace, she waited until finally the auspex chattered and whirred with an update, imposed across Cass' visor via the helmet hardwiring.

For what felt like an age, she looked at the returns of the ork air armada approaching from the north, and didn't know what to do. Then her years of training and experience took over, and an abrupt sense of finality gripped her.

This was where they would die, here, in this small, dry valley between the major fronts. It was good to finally know that for sure. Certainty, even grim certainty, was a blessing.

She routed the info to the other Vagabonds as well as to Marrand and Sergios.

'*I think there might be a bit too many of them, even for the Nine-Hundred-First,*' Marrand said. Cass was relieved to note the same acceptance she herself felt, tinged with bleak humour.

'*What has air command instructed?*' Sergios asked.

That was a good question. She put it to Orlov.

'*We have to hit the bombers,*' the wing commander said. '*Otherwise they'll level the whole valley and everyone in it.*'

'And how do we do that, sir?' Cass asked, trying not to sound too incredulous.

'You shoot at them,' Orlov said. *'We've got two fighter wings scrambling from Torr South and three from East Ushen, as well as every last reserve plane still on board the Old Mother. That might be enough to take the sting out, but those reinforcements won't arrive yet, and when they do it'll be piecemeal. We have to buy time. Every aircraft on this front is currently being instructed to meet the enemy head-on.'*

And give our lives to delay the inevitable, Cass thought, though she didn't say it.

'Understood. The Nine-Hundred-First is moving to engage.'

'Let them know they've been in a fight with the Vagabonds, Cass,' Orlov said.

'Front rank, make ready! Present! Fire! Front rank will retire one hundred paces!'

'Second rank, make ready! Present! Fire! Second rank will retire one hundred paces!'

'Front rank, make ready! Present! Fire! Front rank will retire one hundred paces!'

Again and again the repetitive orders were barked, punctuated by the staccato snap-crack of each blazing crimson volley. It was the sound of the Mordian Iron Guard doing what they hated most – retreating.

Wellend stayed with them. He didn't have to. They weren't his regiment, not even his division. But they were Mordians. Wellend and his father had been entertained in their officers' mess, and had several distant cousins among the regimental staff and the company subalterns.

Wellend wasn't going to abandon them. They were the last ones out, the northernmost division of Army Group Centre, the ones with the furthest to go to reach the partial safety of Kantu Collective and, down the valley, the Eji River and its drought-drained waters.

He had sought them out personally, knowing this would be the most dangerous section of the line, and knowing it would have been what his father would have wanted. Stryk and the Alphic Hydras had already withdrawn, orders fulfilled – instructions to retreat had been delivered to what remained of Army Group Centre's command, and many of the pocket's former defenders were now on their way south, past the collective, or at least drawing near to it.

But this section still had a long way to go. They had made it to the landing zone formerly at the heart of the pocket's defences. The agri-manor that had housed the headquarters was now a burning wreck, as was the deserted field hospital to the right. On the left, damaged Guard vehicles that had been abandoned in other units' rush to retreat were now providing cover for ork mobs seeking to outflank the steadily withdrawing Mordian line.

'Second rank, make ready! Present! Fire! Second rank will retire one hundred paces!'

The Mordian lines were leapfrogging one another as they pulled back. Their volleys were no longer triple bursts, but a full draining of the power pack. As one rank pulled further back and reloaded, the other would lay down a wall of las, only to retreat past them in turn when the other rank was in position.

'Your men make a fine showing, sir,' Wellend said to the commander of the rearguard, Major Beresford. Until recently he would never had dared address a superior officer without first being spoken to, much less offer a personal opinion, but things had changed. He was certain he was living up to his family's legacy. Sure that he was no disgrace. He was Iron Guard, and proud to be so.

If Major Beresford heard Wellend's compliment, he gave no sign, his steely gaze not leaving the blue-jacketed ranks in front of him.

'Damn it, Sergeant Reynard, dress that rank or I'll do it myself,' he barked. 'Watch your damned spacing!'

To someone not raised within Mordian military culture, the parade ground discipline employed during the retreat might have seemed surreal, almost deranged, especially when compared with the utter carnage unfolding all around. Orks were throwing themselves at the slowly withdrawing bulkhead, but so far they hadn't been able to break through. The Iron Guard's firepower was methodical and relentless, even in retreat.

There was a roar as another wave of orks came storming past the ruins of the former headquarters and into the open ground of the landing zone, which was now carpeted with xenos dead. They were cunning – they'd tried to time their charge just as the next volley had finished and what had momentarily become the front rank were sprinting back to the newly halted second rank. Worse, they were accompanied by several speeding buggies crammed with bellowing xenos, bouncing as they rode over and pulverised their own dead beneath fat tyres and wildly spinning treads.

The heavy weapons on the flanks of the second rank engaged. Part of the retreat's stately pace was to allow the teams manning the man-portable autocannons, missile launchers, lascannons and heavy bolters to continuously relocate and set up. With their arcs of fire largely unobstructed on the sides of the formation, they were able to send a hail of firepower into the xenos rush.

A rocket struck one of the war buggies in its forward left tyre, bursting it and sending it slewing onto the side and then its back, those orks not tossed clear in the crash broken brutally beneath it. A pair of lascannon bolts struck the second ramshackle transport, one scoring harmlessly off the side of its flatbed before the second punched through its engine block. Its unstable fuels detonated into a spectacular fireball, incinerating its cargo, igniting more xenos caught in the blast. Wellend found himself relishing the sight.

There was a slightly longer delay between withdrawals as the current front rank finished cutting down the last of the oncoming xenos, the second rank standing ramrod-straight, bayonets fixed and lasrifles shouldered as they waited their turn.

As long as the xenos were without armour support and the Mordians' nerve held, the rhythm of the retreat would continue uninterrupted.

As the retiring ranks reached the southern end of the landing zone and prepared to cross over the trenches to the south, Wellend caught a sound, rising above the regular backdrop of the battle raging across the valley. It was a deep, vibrating rumble, and it was growing louder.

Wellend looked around for the source of the noise, fearing it presaged heavier ork tanks, pushing through the abandoned trench lines to the north to break the Mordian resistance. But there was no sign of vehicles moving through the smoke and fire that shrouded the landing zone and the remains of the head-quarters building beyond.

He turned to Major Beresford, intending to mention the noise, but instead finding the officer looking not beyond the ranks but upwards, at the sky. Wellend did likewise, and found himself staring at impending annihilation.

There was a storm coming from the north. It was a gleaming black thunderhead comprised of brute metal, a flying wall of what Wellend assumed had to be over a thousand aircraft. And while they were too distant to discern details, there was no doubt that they were not the fliers of the Aeronautica Imperialis.

'Oh, God-Emperor,' Wellend breathed. The rising roar was the wrath of the coming storm filling the sky, engines great and small snarling like packs of ravening beasts, straining to be the first to taste blood. They were headed directly for the pocket, and over it, down Kantu Valley. And Wellend was sure that there was no force at the Imperium's disposal that could stop them.

The lead aircraft were nearly overhead. The sound reminded Wellend of being on board Captain Elza's Valkyrie – deafening, fear-inducing, vibrating through his whole body and crushing every other thought and consideration.

'All ranks, take cover,' Beresford bellowed over the thunder. It was all that they could do.

Wellend hit the dirt with the rest, while all around him, the world exploded.

CHAPTER TWENTY-FIVE

From east and west, Imperial wings threw themselves into the fight as they arrived, coordinated as much as possible by Jakyra and the rest of the air command element in the strategium at Suchen. It was an aerial battle in the old style, raw and vicious and razor-fast, continuously escalating and sprawling out not just over Kantu, but across the lower end of the wider Eji Valley and its river.

The 901st flew under it. They were moving too low and fast for the xenos fighter escorts and top cover to easily engage. The downside was they were soon almost beneath the approaching thunderhead, and in danger of being caught in the rain of munitions as it passed over the collective. That meant they would have to rise. It was now or never.

'They've split into two waves,' Korrie noted. Cass checked the auspex, and saw she was right. Whether by accident or design, there were now two distinctive thunderheads of ork bombers, one stacked up behind the other. Cass suspected they were simply racing one another, and the nearest formation consisted of the faster warplanes.

'Hit them,' Cass ordered. She heaved *Vagrant* up into a savage climb, teeth gritted, sucking oxygen through her resp-mask. Her point of view shifted to sky and shadows, to the vast shapes crowding the air almost above her, the lead elements of the xenos thunderhead.

She managed to steal another glance at the auspex via her visor, seeing that Vaughn was still airborne and managing the climb, seeing that the whole 901st – what remained of it – was still with her.

A fierce sense of pride gripped her. If this was how it ended, then there could be no better finale. The 901st would make these alien animals pay.

Shots cracked against the cockpit shield. Fire had started raining down from the defensive turrets studding the underbellies, prows and tails of the ork bombers. In moments the air around them was a latticework of hard rounds, ladders of shots spraying left and right indiscriminately. Cass ignored it. There was no point in trying to evade – doing so successfully under such a weight of fire would be impossible.

The ork bomber squadrons were flying far too close together. Kantu Valley was a narrow target, and the xenos aircraft were too numerous to be able to drop their payloads near-simultaneously along its length. A longer tail in the formation would have eased the problem, but each xenos pilot wanted to be the first to drop their beloved cargo and see it blossom amidst the Imperial forces packed below. They were almost wing to wing, the huge, flying menagerie of mismatched warplanes cramming the airspace and darkening the sky.

'*Target locked*,' came Korrie's voice in her ear.

'Fire,' Cass hissed.

Las bolts stabbed at the ugly, rusting pot bellies of the massive fliers passing overhead, piercing them. Two, struck by *Ruffian* and the Vulture from Shadow Squadron, *Reaper*, detonated spectacularly, and their deaths set off a devastating conflagration.

It was impossible to miss, and when just a few of the fliers were pierced by las, and their payloads cooked off, the consequences were devastating.

A chain of explosions ripped through the jumbled formation, some caused by the detonations themselves, others as nearby aircraft tried to evade the destruction but collided with their neighbours. Wings crumpled and airframes buckled as hundreds of tons of metal, fuel and explosives met cataclysmically above Kantu.

'Drop your prows and head for the slopes,' Cass shouted into the vox, turning *Vagrant*'s upward trajectory into a dive, wrestling against the G-forces and feeling as though her insides were being grasped and shoved forcefully downwards.

A hail of burning metal rained down on the Valkyries and Vultures of the 901st. Cass looked up, and saw the destruction they had helped initiate spreading like an apocalypse, a conflagration that felt as though it was presaging a final, total annihilation.

The 901st tried to outrun it. The remnants of the three squadrons split and threw themselves east or west, hoping to get out from beneath the firestorm falling across the valley floor.

'Jink right,' Korrie called urgently. Cass did so without question. A few heartbeats later and an ork bomber plummeted past on its way down, ablaze from cockpit to tail. One wing just missed clipping *Vagrant*'s port side.

More wreckage fell all around. *Vagrant* bucked and shuddered as it was struck by lesser debris, one burning length of fuselage crashing off the cockpit hard enough to scar its shield, the impact causing Cass to assume for a split second that she was dead.

'Right again,' Korrie called. Cass couldn't see where they were going at all now, and didn't have time to even glance at the auspex, flying blind and having to rely on her co-pilot's scanning. Even easing off on the acceleration would mean death.

Vagrant took more hits. Warnings sounded, shrill in Cass' ears. She expected at any moment for the flier to buck out of her grasp, thrown into a death-spin by a collision. She could do nothing but respond to Korrie's calls, reduced to acting on reflexes and instinct, flying with a desperate and reckless intensity.

'Left, left,' Korrie barked, and Cass had barely yanked on the stick before the fuselage of another huge ork bomber came ploughing past, wreathed in fire, so close Cass caught sight of burning grots flinging themselves from portholes and broken canopies in the heartbeat before it had gone past. One actually collided with the starboard wing and was whipped away in an instant. The wake of the downed flier rocked *Vagrant*, but just avoided clipping it.

Smoke engulfed them, black and acrid and shot through with flames. Cass felt a moment's despair, but then, suddenly they were through the choking pall. The eastern slope surged towards them. Explosions ripped across it as ork bombers not above the valley floor dumped their payloads.

Vagrant flew into it, and Cass was forced to pull up slightly as she was blinded again by a fresh wave of smoke and dust. She couldn't tell where the crest was, and in the split second chose not to switch to instruments.

They cleared it, and found themselves flying over a firefight raging between ork mobs and the Guard infantry that had occupied the valley sides.

That wasn't where they needed to be. Cass immediately began

to climb again, quickly reassessing. Beyond the ridgeline the ork air presence was less intense, but a hail of small-arms was soon beating at *Vagrant*'s underside from the xenos now below them.

'Form on me,' Cass ordered, her voice firm and clear despite how much the run out from under the debris storm had shaken her. 'Re-establish altitude at one thousand feet and prepare to re-engage.'

Ruffian and *Rogue* were both still with her, had both somehow made it through the maelstrom of fire and steel. The same couldn't be said of their sister squadrons. Sergios was gone, caught square by the remains of a falling bomber, according to his flight lieutenant. Shadow Squadron had lost their Vulture too, *Reaper*, brought down amidst the very carnage it had helped unleash. Most of Shadow Squadron had gone east with the Vagabonds, but Nemesis Squadron were now on the west side of the valley.

And for all the destruction their first run had wreaked, it hadn't stopped the ork air assault. The next wave was visible coming in over the pocket, above the pall of black smoke rising from its bombed-out remains. There was something truly monstrous in the midst of the ragged formation, mostly hidden by distance and the lesser aircraft around it, but looming like some mythical flying terror on the auspex.

'We're going again,' Cass urged. 'Under and up. Keep it tight.'

'*We've got aerial contacts closing fast from the north, down the ridgeline,*' Korrie said urgently. '*Rotorcraft. Big ones.*'

Cass snatched a visual and saw the impending fliers. There were three of them, like larger versions of the deathkopters that had attacked them earlier. They had fully enclosed airframes and two sets of rotor blades, one at the prow and another at the rear, whirling above them as they swept along the ridge's crest at a higher altitude than the Valkyries.

'*Transports?*' Konstantina hypothesised.

'Doesn't matter, hit them,' Cass ordered, swinging *Vagrant* to port. Whatever they were, they would bode ill for the Militarum troops battling across the eastern slope.

Vagabond and Shadow Squadrons formed up, but the rotor-craft were on them fast – Cass had expected them to stoop into an attack run and meet them head-on, in the tactic so beloved of ork pilots, but instead they maintained their course and altitude, threatening to overshoot the lower Valkyries.

Only *Ruffian* scored a hit, a hail of rockets from its pods hammering the underside of one of the xenos fliers. Its interior blew, belching flame, nosediving down towards the embattled crest even as the rotors continued to spin, scything up earth and bodies as it crashed.

Then the rest were overhead, downdraught beating briefly at the Valkyries as they passed, Cass snarling with frustration as she lost her angle.

'Come about and rise,' she snapped, unwilling to be out-manoeuvred by any xenos flier. 'Get on their tails.'

'*That might be a problem,*' Korrie told her, sounding as though she was unsure as to what she was seeing. Cass craned her neck as she looked up at the passing aircraft.

Suddenly, she understood exactly what they were doing.

The rotorcraft had side hatches, much like the Valkyries, and they were open. Shapes were barrelling from within their rusting holds, leaping with apparently suicidal fearlessness out into mid-air. And as they fell, the rocket packs strapped to their backs ignited.

'*Stormers,*' Vaughn barked.

The name had been given by Imperial strategos to those orks deranged enough to strap crude propellants to their backs, giving them the capacity to launch themselves skywards like parodies of the jump pack-equipped warriors of the Adeptus Astartes.

Cass understood the threat too late. Like the deathkopters, they had encountered stormers over Ushen, the creatures launching themselves at passing Imperial aircraft from the tops of the city's roofs. She had never heard of them mounting an airborne insertion though. Suddenly, dozens of bellowing ork warriors were dropping almost on top of the two Valkyrie squadrons, their rockets giving them the blaze of thrust they needed to reach the fliers. Both squadrons had bled speed to gain more time with the rotorcraft in their sights, and had then dropped off more as they prepared to use their ability to point-turn to come up on the enemy's tails. They were all but stationary. Easy targets.

'Evading,' Cass yelled, yanking on the flight stick and working the pedals. Too late. She heard a dire clang, reverberating through *Vagrant* as it was struck not by ork munitions or debris, but by spiked boots and grappling claws.

CHAPTER TWENTY-SIX

'*We've got visitors,*' Straks called to Konstantina as a flurry of impacts rang out against *Ruffian*.

'Bastards,' she hissed, feeling a potent surge of anger – outrage that these filthy xenos were physically defiling her warbird's hull, and frustration that they had fallen so easily into their trap.

'Hope you're strapped in, flyboy,' she growled to Straks, then, in a series of fluid motions, triggered the hover rotors, kicked the port tail pedal and yanked the flight stick to the right.

Ruffian lurched and upended. Konstantina had deliberately capsized her own aircraft, and for a second the world was upside-down, her harness straps were knifing into her shoulders, her stomach was doing loops, and the blood was rushing to her head. She kept the alternating pressure on the pedal and the stick though, turning the savage motion into a full roll and only switching as the starboard wing passed a clockwise two-hundred-and-seventy-degree angle.

The manoeuvre, conducted mid-flight in the midst of a for-mation, was outrageously risky, but Konstantina didn't care. She knew she had to shake their new passengers, before they started to saw and blast their way into the hull, hack at the wings or, worst of all, reached either the engines or the cockpits.

The roll did what she had hoped. She shook *Ruffian* from side to side for good measure, intending to throw off any last stragglers, and took the opportunity to peer down from the port and then the starboard side of the cockpit, catching glimpses of the ground below and, more importantly, the half a dozen xenos plunging, roaring and flailing towards the earth. Several managed to trigger their rockets as they fell, but they shot off erratically, failing to reach back up to *Ruffian* as Konstantina switched out of hover mode and shunted the Vulture forward hard enough to slam herself back into her seat.

'Think we're clear?' she asked Straks, hoping the quick, deci-sive action had ended the threat before it really began.

'*Looks like it,*' he replied, quickly switching auspex display to the external vidcorders showing sections of the exterior hull and the sur-rounding sky. '*Guess they weren't hanging on hard enough.*'

The same couldn't be said for the xenos attempting to board the other Vagabonds, Konstantina realised. *Ruffian*'s sudden hover-ing had left it out of formation, and now afforded Konstantina a view of *Vagrant* and *Rogue* ahead of them. Both Valkyries were beset by stormers, the xenos clambering precariously across the scarred airframes by way of claw gauntlets and grappling hooks. *Vagrant* was closer than *Rogue*, partly impeding Konstantina's sight line of the latter, and she could see two of the rocket-equipped brutes clawing their way close to the primary engine rotors across the flier's topside, while several others made to swing in through the open port hatch. *Vagrant* dipped its wings from one side to the other, clearly trying to shake them, but couldn't perform the audacious roll *Ruffian* had managed with the hatches still open and the ridge crest so close. The danger of losing control was too great.

'Chief, you've got to get your hatches shut,' Konstantina advised over the vox.

Zeke heaved the *Vagrant*'s starboard hatch closed, grunting as he was forced to slam the edge repeatedly against a grasping green limb trying to force its way inside. There was a wet snapping sound after the fourth attempt, and the arm vanished, allowing the Valkyrie gunner to finally lock the sliding door into place.

There was no time for relief – the port hatch was still open. The combat servitor acting as the gunner on that side was sending erratic bursts of heavy bolter fire down at the xenos mobs shooting up at them from the ground, but it didn't seem to know or understand how to swing its hatch door shut.

Zeke had known it was going to get them all killed.

Muttering catechisms his father had taught him as a child, he undid his harness and scrambled across the pitching deck of the hold, only his experience traversing it while airborne keeping him from being thrown from his feet. He managed to make it to the port side just as a shape loomed in the open space beyond.

The ork roared and swung a massive cleaver at the servitor blocking its way into *Vagrant*'s interior. Strapped in and with its grip firmly on the heavy bolter, the servitor was unable to defend itself, though Zeke wasn't sure it was even mentally capable of doing so anyway. A blow from the cleaver hacked down through its shoulder and into its torso, blood and oil jetting from the savage wound.

The ork bellowed again and kicked at it, trying to swing down from above, one burly arm still gripping the Valkyrie's topside like some great, enraged simian.

Zeke got his laspistol out and shot it, but it didn't do much. The servitor jerked, letting go of the heavy bolter's grip and actually snatching the ork's wrist, which only led to another cleaver blow. The xenos went feral, hacking with its weapon and kicking manically with its spiked boots, chopping the servitor to pieces. Finally, with parts of the restraint harness severed, the servitor toppled from its seat and out of the open hatch, leaving the way open for the stormer to swing fully inside.

By then Zeke had managed to get a grip on the port hatch's handle. He heaved on it, slamming it against the ork's flank just as it threw itself inside feet-first.

There was a crunch, but the alien's momentum was too great for Zeke to keep it out the way as he had the one on the starboard side. It was in the hold with him, sprawling on its back, the inactive rocket strapped there making it even more ungainly.

'Bastard,' Zeke bellowed at it, and it grunted back at him, flailing wildly with its bloody cleaver. He swung the hatch door shut and shot it, point-blank, but the las bolts did nothing but sear its craggy green hide.

It tried to get up, snagging Zeke by the ankle with its free hand.

Vagrant bucked. Cass was unaware there was a xenos on board, and was still trying to shake off the others swarming the hull. The sudden movement sent Zeke and the ork tumbling side by side down the length of the hold, slamming into the closed rear hatch together.

The impact knocked the air from Zeke's lungs and left him scrabbling. His pistol went off, cracking the remainder of its power pack into the port-side benches, leaving smoking, glowing holes in their frames. He could hear Cass shouting at him over the intercom, but couldn't reply.

The ork was on him, the hot, stinking butcher's breath and the fungal reek of its sweat seething through his resp-mask, drool running from its tusks as it bellowed in his face, its beastly little eyes blazing with violence. It managed to throw a leg over and pin him with one hand on his shoulder against the inside of the hatch. Zeke experienced its strength for just a heartbeat, but even in that short time he knew it had the capacity to crush his ribcage just by shoving against him.

Vagrant saved him. It jerked to the side again, pounding sounds ringing from the exterior of the hull as the orks still outside tried to hack their way in. Zeke and his assailant were thrown in the opposite direction, back towards the forward section.

He tried to snatch at something, anything. His arm was arrested, and he grabbed hold of a length of strapping that had once been part of the combat servitor's restraint harness, now trailing loose. He realised it was the litany scripts wrapped around his forearm that had initially snagged the main body of the harness.

He grinned manically. Divine providence. The God-Emperor was with him.

The ork collided with a loud clang against the other end of the hold, but shook the impact off and scrambled up at the same time as Zeke, panting and snuffling animalistically, possibly grunting something in what passed for its own language. *Vagrant* had levelled off momentarily, and Zeke snatched the railing overhead before he could be pitched from his feet again. He reached for his laspistol, realised he had dropped it, and found his fingers resting against the stock of the portside heavy bolter instead.

The ork came at him, roaring, before he could grip the weapon properly. He swung it down from where it had automatically returned to the stowed position after the combat servitor had been torn out, the heavy stock taking the worst of the ork's cleaver. It deflected off and down, and found the meat of Zeke's thigh instead.

He cried out as pain lanced through his leg. The ork wrenched the heavy blade free and Zeke's limb almost gave out, but he managed to hang on to both the bolter and the railing.

The Valkyrie bucked again, like a wild grox trying to throw its attackers. The ork was thrown back against the rear ramp before it could strike a killing blow. Zeke hung on, stomach lurching, his leg feeling like it was on fire.

The bruisers weren't designed to be able to swing one-eighty to point inside the hull, but at their maximum angle on the swivel, they covered about half of the near inside of the rear ramp hatch. And that was where *Vagrant*'s erratic flying had once again left the ork sprawling.

Teeth gritted, Zeke swung the heavy bolter left, as far as its frame would permit. Then, one hand still on the rail overhead, he fired.

The noise of the discharge in the confined space burst his right ear, and the recoil hurt his wrist and immediately kicked the weapon free from his half-grip, but not before it had spat a pair of heavy rounds down the length of *Vagrant*'s interior. One punched straight out through the rear hatch, leaving a fist-sized hole with sunlight streaming through, but the second hit the ork in the chest. It blew open the beast's upper torso with a thump and a shower of dark viscera. The creature's brutish expression changed from one of fury to shock, and it looked down at the smoking, pouring wound with something like disbelief. Its gaze returned to Zeke, and it tried to roar again and take a step towards him, but instead it choked on its own gore and toppled sideways before lying still against the raised ramp.

Zeke collapsed with a moan, finally able to clutch at his thigh. It was in agony, and his hands came away slick and red. Starting to shake, he managed to fish out the small medicae pack aviators carried in their flight suit's pockets and fumbled free a jab of morphia, which he stabbed home. He tried to tourniquet the wound and bind it, but the job was clumsy on the partially tilted deck. The pain made him hiss and shiver. The only blessing was that *Vagrant* didn't lurch again.

He slowly became aware of Cass trying to reach him over the intercom. It seemed to take a long time to grit his teeth and respond.

'I'm fine,' he managed eventually. 'We had an intruder, but the... the hold is secure.'

If Cass responded, he didn't hear it. He tried to get up, but cried out in pain, his boots slipping in blood – his own, the servitor's, and the ork's, intermixed. He forced himself to be still for a moment, to turn the agony into words of devotion.

'God-Emperor, witness your warrior-servant. God-Emperor, turn this pain into fuel. Enable me to do my duty to the very end. Do not forsake your warrior-servant. Do not forsake me. Please.'

He was able to drag himself up, teeth gritted, into his seat on the starboard side of the hold, and strap himself in. That was his post. That was where he belonged.

The Emperor would not abandon him, not while he still had a purpose to serve.

'There's still two on the starboard wing,' Korrie told Cass urgently as she worked the pedals in an effort to unbalance the orks that had landed on top of them. Systems had reported weapons discharges within the hold, blinking up urgently on Cass' visor, but apparently Zeke had it all locked down now. But if they didn't dislodge these last two boarders, it wouldn't matter.

'They're trying to saw off the wing,' Korrie said. Cass caught sight of a burst of sparks from the right, and heard a shriek of metal. The idea of trying to hack through a flier's wing while

simultaneously gripping on to it in mid-air was utterly insane, and exactly the sort of thing she knew an ork wouldn't think twice about doing. While the evasive manoeuvres had succeeded in dislodging most of the stormers, these last two seemed to be clamped on tight.

'*Cass, they're all over us,*' she heard Vaughn cry out across the vox. She'd lost visuals on *Rogue* more or less as soon as the stormers had hit them. The auspex showed Vaughn's warbird starboard aft of *Vagrant*, trying the same desperate jinking that Cass had been attempting. Before she could respond, Konstantina's voice cut in across the vox.

'*Chief, switch to hover, now!*'

Cass did so without question, then cursed as her visor lit up again.

Vagrant was taking fire.

CHAPTER TWENTY-SEVEN

Vaughn heard what sounded like Macks screaming over the intercom.

They were in the hold, topside, on the wings. He had shaken some off, but others were clamped tight with makeshift claws and spike-boots and rough mag-points. *Rogue*'s scream joined Macks' in his ear, the besieged Valkyrie warning him of electrical and pressure failures, of hull-point penetrations and what it construed as target locks.

'Can't shake them,' Vaughn hissed to Xijen. 'Where's Cass?'

Xijen didn't get a chance to reply. There was a thud as something impacted against the top of the cockpit shield. Vaughn twisted in his harness, and found himself looking up at a pair of xenos that had just used a burst of thrust from their rocket packs to leap from the Valkyrie's topside to its prow.

Vaughn jerked the flight stick left. One of the stormers immediately toppled off the shield, its bellow lost in the shrieking of the engines and the ongoing system alarms. The other clung on, a jagged gauntlet latching on to the left side of the aft cockpit's shield frame.

'*Throne, get it off,*' Xijen was shouting.

'I'm trying,' Vaughn barked back, kicking a boot against a pedal and heaving *Rogue* the other way.

The ork remained stuck fast. With its free hand it had started swinging a makeshift pickaxe against the shield of Xijen's cockpit. There was a crunching sound as the armaglass started to crack and split.

Vaughn felt totally helpless. He called out for Cass again, for anybody, but no one was answering him. Xijen was trying to draw his laspistol in the confines of the aft cockpit.

With a crash, the armaglass above Xijen caved in. Vaughn heard his scream over the intercom. He couldn't twist round to see what was happening, but a moment later the ork was scrambling forward onto his own shield, pickaxe drizzling blood.

Vaughn panicked. He flung the shield latch and heaved it upwards. The sudden movement caught the ork off-guard, and it bellowed as Vaughn slammed the top of the cockpit against it and pitched it, tumbling, off the Valkyrie's prow.

Its howl was lost in the rush of wind and the roaring of the rotors as Vaughn found himself with nothing between him and the world beyond his cockpit. He'd had to let go of the flight stick to fully disengage the shield, and *Rogue* now swung to port and down. Suddenly, the ridgeline was just beneath him. He clutched at the stick, trying to readjust, jaw clenched, as the ground surged up to meet him.

'Just hold steady,' Konstantina urged Cass over the vox. 'Hold steady, and trust me, damn it!'

Vagrant had swung to a halt just ahead of *Ruffian*. Despite its efforts to shake its attackers, there was still a pair of xenos on the near wing, trying to carve through it with buzzsaw-like weapons. A few moments longer and they'd likely cut the fuel lines to the starboard engine and risk sending the Valkyrie into a fatal spin.

Konstantina swept *Ruffian* in alongside with a combination of grace and speed that she had long ago stopped having to consciously think about.

'Hit them,' she urged Straks the moment she'd switched back to vertical hover and stabilised as a firing platform.

With only a few dozen feet between them, Straks swung the prow-mounted heavy bolter round and sent short, controlled bursts into the orks on *Vagrant's* wing. It was extremely dangerous. Explosive rounds at such close range were capable of puncturing the wing, penetrating the hold or, worst of all, damaging the near-side engine or primary rotors. But the orks were exposed and defenceless, and Cass was almost out of time.

Konstantina deftly pitched *Ruffian* to keep the fire arc open, and in just a few moments they had blasted the pair of xenos away, painting *Vagrant's* scarred starboard wing with alien viscera.

'You're clear,' she said, hoping she hadn't hit anything vital, and that none of their shots had punched through the hold. 'Everything okay?'

Cass' reply wasn't what Konstantina was expecting.

'We need to get to Rogue! *Hal's going down!'*

Vaughn let out of roar of effort as he dragged on the stick, the wind whipping at him. It briefly seemed as though *Rogue* wouldn't respond, as though it had finally had enough of their partnership, and had decided to end it all in a blaze of destruction.

Then, finally, the Valkyrie's prow tipped fractionally back above the forty-five-degree axis, and the flier was hurtling just above the heads of the ork mobs storming over the crest of the ridge below.

Vaughn whooped, adrenaline surging, the horror of the last few moments eclipsed for a few pounding heartbeats by the raw relief that came with survival.

He coaxed some altitude out of *Rogue*, feeling the Valkyrie struggle – the port engine still wasn't managing any kind of decent output, and he hadn't had a chance yet to assess the damage caused by the stormers. He hadn't even managed to close his cockpit's shield.

That was when he heard the last one, thumping onto the aft cockpit behind him.

'Throne,' he snarled, yanking the flight stick, making *Rogue*'s damaged port-side engine wail.

He didn't know if he had thrown the ork. He quickly realised it didn't matter. Something came arcing over his right shoulder, hitting the inside of the raised cockpit shield in front of him and bouncing off.

The stick grenade landed in the footwell, between the flight pedals and his feet.

In a surge of adrenaline, Vaughn reached down to snatch it and throw it back out of the cockpit before it could detonate. Instead, he found himself yanked back by his harness, not quite able to reach it. Held firm by *Rogue*. It was almost reassuring, as though the warbird was embracing him, and telling him not to worry any more.

Vaughn looked at his sister one more time and closed his eyes.

The grenade blew away both of Vaughn's legs and part of his stomach, gutting *Rogue*'s forward cockpit with him. The fatally wounded Valkyrie plunged the last hundred yards into Kantu Valley's east side, the remaining ork stormer still clinging to the flier's airframe leaping skywards on its rocket pack just before the flier fell.

Rogue exploded on impact, its twisted, promethium-fuelled remains a roiling pyre for Hal Vaughn.

CHAPTER TWENTY-EIGHT

Despite the sacrifices of the Aeronautica Imperialis, the first wave of the ork air armada devastated Imperial forces along the valley. Kantu Collective itself was razed, its knoll practically levelled. The area encompassing the south of what had once been the pocket was reduced to a moonscape of craters, ploughed dirt, burning wreckage, and the butchered remains of those Militarum regiments caught in the storm.

But the Imperium's ground forces were not destroyed. Few bombers made it more than halfway down the valley. Almost every weapon along its length was turned against them, a blizzard of shot, shell and energy beams that tore xenos aircraft from the sky and sent their wreckage hammering against the slopes.

Under the rain of debris, the relief force that had taken to the east and west slopes held their ground in the face of mounting ork ground pressure. The divisions chosen by Havali to break Army Group Centre out were the best at his disposal, and they proved it in Kantu.

Above them, the remains of the Imperium's air power re-formed. The second wave was inbound.

'Rogue's *gone,*' Korrie said.

Cass didn't respond. She'd seen it. Seen *Rogue* pitch forward, just after it had seemed to recover, the lurch too sudden to pull up out of this time. She wondered if Vaughn had still been alive when it struck the slope. She hoped not.

The last stormer that had brought down *Rogue* was arcing skywards on wildly twisting contrails, up and away before the impact. Cass barked at Korrie to hit it, knowing there was little chance of actually doing so, but knowing too that the downing of *Rogue* needed a reply. The las bolts twinkled away into the gathering gloom, streaks of brilliance, there and gone again, hitting nothing.

It had grown dark, Cass realised. Twilight was approaching, but it was still too early to account for the pall that had fallen across the embattled landscape below. The sky was overcast, more leaden than Cass had seen it since making planetfall. Cloud banks were rolling in from the east, obscuring the azure that had reigned unchallenged for so long.

'*Orders, Chief?*' came Konstantina's voice. Cass realised she was trying to prompt her. She snapped out of it, pulling *Vagrant* out of the dangerously straight line she'd been flying in, checking her positioning and that of the rest of the wing.

They had fresh incomings. The second wave, even greater than the first, sweeping down from the north like one of the cloud formations now ruling the sky.

Cass knew despair.

Bix's voice came in over the vox.

'*Still in one piece, Vagabond Leader?*'

It took a second for Cass to respond.

'Affirmative, Cloud Knight Leader.'

'We've got to try and delay that next wave,' Bix said. *'There are reinforcements still coming from Ushen and Torr, but they won't arrive before that hits the valley. If it does, at full strength, there won't be anything left of Army Group Centre to evacuate.'*

'Understood,' Cass said. 'I'm bringing together what's left of the Nine-Hundred-First.'

'We can pincer them. The fighters from above, and you from below. It's probably our only hope.'

'Agreed. Just let me know when you're in position.'

The 901st re-formed close to the river. The lead elements of Army Group Centre were over now, on the southern bank, but it wouldn't count for much if the xenos air armada was able to make it through. North or south of the river, they'd probably keep going all the way to Barduk and Suchen, obliterating everything along their flight route.

The wing was in a ragged state. Nemesis Squadron's Vulture had been forced to drop out with rotor problems and head back to Barduk. With Vaughn gone, all that was left were *Vagrant* and *Ruffian*, as well as two Valkyries from Nemesis and Marrand's Valkyrie from Shadow. Five warbirds against hundreds of xenos aircraft.

Best not to think about the odds. That was what she had told Konstantina, wasn't it?

'We're going in low, then climbing and stinging, right into the heart of them,' she told her fellow aviators. 'The fighters will hit them from above simultaneously.'

'Have you seen what they're shielding?' Marrand asked.

Cass had, albeit only on the auspex. A huge return, the most monstrous thing she had yet witnessed in the air on Kanai Tertius.

'Xenos aerial fortress,' Marrand said. *'A sky-gargant. It'll be packing enough munitions to level the whole valley.'*

'Then that's our priority target,' Cass said. 'Perhaps, if we can ignite it, we'll blow their formation, the way we did with the first wave.'

The other pilots confirmed that plan. Konstantina in particular sounded thrilled at the prospect of tackling such monstrous odds.

Word came from Bix that what remained of the fighter wings had formed up and were in position, preparing to stoop-and-sting from above while the Valkyries and Vultures slipped in under the enemy's guard and drove up into their guts. Cass' grim sense of foreboding was replaced by a sudden, vicious surge of determination. If this was it, they were going to tear the heart out of these animals.

'For Hal and Cobb, and Eleanor, and all the others,' she snarled over the vox to Konstantina. 'Let's get you a dozen more kill-tallies, Em.'

'Now you're speaking my language, Chief,' Konstantina responded.

The Valkyries swept back north along the valley, low, thousands of heads turning to watch them go as the remainder of Army Group Centre made its way through the valley of fire to the Eji. Cass tugged off her glove for a second and brushed her hand against the cold links of her father's tags. Just one more time.

'Good news, Chief,' Korrie said. *'It's raining.'*

To her amazement, Cass saw she was correct. She had been so focused on what was about to come that she hadn't noticed the first droplets as they came slashing down the side of the cockpit shield.

'Holy Throne,' she murmured. After months, it seemed like the drought was finally at an end. And that just might change things, but not in time to stop the xenos storm from breaking over Kantu Valley.

They were ahead and above now, a sprawling wedge of ramshackle aircraft, and in their midst, the monstrosity. It looked like a vast conglomeration of scrap metal structures given flight, the bestial madness of ork engineering in its ultimate form, studded with viewing ports, weapons blisters and the clusters of propellors that were somehow allowing it to defy Kantu's gravity. Cass hated the sight of it, hated such a flagrant disregard for the laws of order and engineering. Its very existence was a challenge to mankind's mastery of the galaxy, let alone the Aeronautica Imperialis' control of this world's skies. It had to be destroyed.

'*It's perfect,*' she heard Konstantina breathe. '*At last. The ultimate kill-tally.*'

Cass found herself smiling at her fellow Vagabond's bloodlust.

'*How did the strategos miss this?*' Marrand complained bitterly. '*They must have been preparing this offensive for months.*'

'Well, they're seeing it now,' Cass said. 'They had best get a good look before we wreck it.'

A terse message pinged through from Bix, stating she was engaging, drawing the xenos' attention towards the grey-clad heavens, rather than the five predatory, cruciform shapes darting along the depths of the burning valley. They were almost under the leading edge of the packed xenos formation, in danger of being struck once they started dumping their munitions.

It was time.

'Climb,' Cass ordered.

CHAPTER TWENTY-NINE

The 901st rose on wings of vengeance, screaming up out of the smoke and fire.

Las bolts spat ahead of them, claiming air-kills in a matter of seconds. Those ork fighters that hadn't surged topside to meet the charge of Bix's Thunderbolts and Lightnings were powerless to respond, unable to stoop sharply and quickly enough to pick up the sudden threat from below.

Cass was punched into her seat as she hauled *Vagrant* back and lined up for Korrie. Las beams arced away, tracking and then locking on to an ork bomber flying ahead of the sky-gargant. The bolts caught a starboard engine and blew it out, sending the ugly aircraft tumbling, passing *Vagrant* on the Valkyrie's way up.

Suddenly, the air was full of fire. The ork and grot gunners in the tail mounts and in blisters and hardpoints along the underbellies of the bombers had started to blaze away. A hail of hard rounds became a deluge to match the increasingly heavy rainfall as the point defences of the sky-gargant itself opened fire, dozens of weapons batteries studding its underside and stubby wings trying to track the Valkyries.

Damage was inevitable. Cass heard a strangled cry from Marrand over the vox, and saw her Valkyrie off to port suddenly pitch forward and drop, one rotor ablaze.

Something hit *Vagrant* in the aft cockpit shield, hard. The impact shook Cass and sent a crack shooting down through her own shield section, crazing the armaglass like a lightning bolt.

'Throne damn it,' she panted through the ongoing pressures being exerted on her by the steepness of the climb. 'That was a bad one. You alright, Mel?'

There was no reply.

'Mel?' Cass repeated. 'Korrie, respond.'

Nothing. Cass saw something red running along the inside of the cracked shield.

'No,' she breathed through gritted teeth. 'No, no, no. Korrie, come in. Answer me! That's an order!'

But there was no answer, only the scream of *Vagrant*'s laboured engines as they were pushed to the maximum, fighting with all their strength against Kantu's gravity.

Cass tried to raise Zeke, but he wasn't responding either. The intercom offered nothing but silence.

More shots hit the airframe. She felt a sense of panic, but rather than wrestling *Vagrant* out of its climb, she took manual control of the las and started emptying the power pack at the gargant towering above her, spitting fire and death down upon her like some primordial deity of destruction.

Then the port rotors gave way.

Cass had become oblivious to the warnings and damage updates she was receiving from *Vagrant*'s systems, but she couldn't ignore the sudden lurch, followed by the loss of altitude. Her charging ascent ended, and she did her best to compensate with the pedals as she yawed to one side, still under fire.

She could hear Konstantina in her ear, the words failing to register, warring with the sounds of *Vagrant*'s pain. Her stomach lurched, and they were going down, an uncontrolled descent threatening to turn into a spiral.

Cass fought the stick, fought gravity itself, stamping down on one pedal as she battled through what was about to become a death-spin.

Through, not against. The instinct was to try and counter it, but that had led to the deaths of countless young pilots. Even in a state of panic, Cass had experienced enough such nightmarish, dislocating spins to know to stay with the arc, then punch it, following through and regaining stability, and with it, control.

'Trying to reignite,' she managed to pant, beating at the port rotor's activation rune, her head beginning to ache as the spin worsened, pinning her against one side of her harness. To her relief, she saw the sigil light up on her display, followed a moment later by a coughing rattle as the rotor responded and began to turn again.

'Hold on,' Cass shouted and, as her vision began to grey and thoughts turned slow, dangerously dull and untroubled, she hauled on the flight stick and alternated the pedals.

Vagrant arced out of its spin with a speed and grace that belied the heart-pounding, skull-aching horror of its near destruction. Cass found herself flying straight south, dangerously low. There was black smoke trailing from the portside rotors, and they sounded far from happy. But she was still up and stable. *Vagrant* was responsive.

'Damage report,' she demanded from Korrie and, in the silence that followed, decelerated to hover, wanting to come about while taking some of the pressure off the upper rotors.

She swung around, twinning visuals with the auspex and doing her best to ignore the sickness curdling in her stomach in the spin's aftermath, trying to get a handle on the fight she'd just been forced to drop out of.

It was going as badly for the others as it had for her. She caught sight of one of the two remaining Valkyries from Nemesis Squadron plummeting to the ground, trailing plumes of smoke from both engines, fire wreathing its cockpits. Only *Ruffian* and the last flier from Nemesis were still climbing, up through the rain and fire, towards the monstrosity that was now close to passing over the smoking remnants of Kantu Collective.

A streaking rocket struck the Nemesis Valkyrie head-on, and it detonated in mid-air, a roiling fireball that became a smear of black smoke and tumbling debris, falling seemingly in slow motion back towards the valley floor. *Ruffian* alone was rising now, through the carnage. Unlike the others, it hadn't started to fire yet.

'Em, pull out, it's just you left up there,' Cass shouted into her vox-mic, knowing she wasn't going to be able to get *Vagrant* back up in time to help her, that the damaged warbird probably wouldn't even be able to make the climb.

'*That's good,*' came Konstantina's reply, her tone feral. '*This one's mine.*'

'Just a few seconds more,' Konstantina urged Straks.

He was desperate to open fire, and she shared his urge. It was anathema, not unleashing everything they had on the gargant filling the sky above them. But Konstantina mastered her need. She had to be sure. She had to make this count.

Ruffian was flying almost vertically now. The weight of speed and gravity pinned Konstantina to her seat, making her feel as though she was being inexorably crushed by the pressures of a vast ocean, squeezing her eyeballs, choking her throat, making every muscle strain and every vein pop, her gorge threatening to rise.

She held her grip on the flight stick. The target was dead ahead, and that was all that mattered. It was gloriously vast, a tribute to the insane capabilities of these relentless warrior-beasts who constantly challenged mankind's mastery of the stars.

Orks craved destruction, like a child that delighted in breaking and despoiling, but Konstantina would show them what true destruction meant. She would obliterate this freakish air-monster, would prove mankind's superiority amidst fire and steel, and claim one kill-tally that would eclipse all those that had gone before it. The thought made her shake even through the brutality of the Gs crushing her.

The target lock blipped. They had entered close range, the point where she could be sure of inflicting maximum damage. An erratic trail of shots from one of the monstrosity's belly turrets lashed over them, beating off the airframe like hail. They were under it and so close the rain was no longer hitting them, the monster's bulk shielding them from the increasing deluge.

Konstantina didn't even need to instruct Straks – the close-range target register did it for her. Her old lover let fly with everything *Ruffian* had, hard rounds, las and rockets.

They couldn't miss. Every shot hammered home into the underside of that rusting hulk. Armour plating was sheared through, huge landing gear systems mangled, defence turrets gutted in gouts of flame and showers of sparks. But the leviathan did not break. It shrugged off the wounds, like a vast cephalopod untroubled by the gnawing of a minnow. Konstantina gritted her teeth, and held her course.

'Focus fire, dead centre,' she managed, instructing Straks to use the tracers in the propellant of the heavy bolter rounds stream as a marker. They had to pierce it, to reach the bomb bays and the mountains of munitions she had no doubt were cradled within the monster's gut.

More return fire hammered them. *Ruffian* seemed to care as little as Konstantina – it offered none of the usual warnings, not even minor damage reports. It was as though the machine spirit knew her intention, and shared it. Damage did not matter any more, as long as the engines continued and the flight stick and pedals held the course true. Together, they would do the God-Emperor's work. Thanks to them, Vagabond Squadron would bear eternal renown, and all the good aviators these beasts had killed would be avenged.

There were tears in Konstantina's eyes as the sky-gargant completely filled her cockpit shield. Its ugly underside was streaked with explosive damage and fire, smoke scythed and twitched at by thousands of hard rounds. She could feel the whole of *Ruffian* vibrating with the power of the monster's engines, its massive propellers shuddering the air, rain cascading from them.

A shot struck and cracked the cockpit shield, crazing the view. *Ruffian* was being pummelled, struck blind, deaf and dumb, scarred down to silver plasteel by more shots than it could track.

It didn't matter. Nothing mattered any more, except the kill-shot.

The rocket pods were dry. Her beloved prow heavy bolter clacked empty. Only the las was left, barrels glowing white-hot, spearing beam after beam into the core of that scarred, scorched underbelly.

One last chance to try and change course, to heave on the flight stick, to force *Ruffian* back to the horizontal. Instead, Konstantina just held on.

'*Em*,' came Straks' voice in her ear, sounding tiny and distant.

'What?' she managed through the incredible pressure.

'*It's been fun*,' Straks said.

'It has,' Konstantina admitted, almost grinning. 'See you on the other side, yeah?'

If he replied, she didn't hear him. *Ruffian*'s starboard wing finally gave way, holed in dozens of places and shearing off under the extremities placed upon it. Konstantina felt the lurch to the side and compensated as best she could with the pedals. She knew she had a few seconds before they lost momentum and their climb was transformed into a spinning death-plummet.

She wouldn't let it end that way. She had always knows the odds of survival for a Vulture gunship pilot, and had known too, right from the very beginning, the sort of way she wanted it all to end. And the galaxy had conspired to give her that ending. It was just perfect.

She roared and slammed every ounce of energy from the engines and, with the last of her beloved, lethal warbird's strength, sent them surging up and into the fire.

Ruffian struck the underbelly of the xenos sky-gargant at full tilt, engines screaming, lascannons draining the remains of their power packs with one last overcharged shot.

The leviathan had taken worse bombardments than the one *Ruffian* had inflicted upon it, but the concentrated, increasingly close-range firepower had broken the integrity of one of its secondary bomb bays. Now, the Vulture gunship itself became the weapon that dealt the killing blow. It hammered through the scarred and beaten armour plates cladding the super-flier's bottom and ploughed on up, driven like a warhead by its over-taxed, ever-faithful engines. By the time it actually penetrated the hold, Konstantina and Straks had been crushed to death, but they had done what they intended.

The bombs within the bay detonated, igniting a chain reaction that ripped through the bowels of the massive flier. One section after another exploded, a conflagration that ripped irresistibly through the gargant's insides.

Slowly, the super-flier began to lose altitude. Its scarred prow dipped, starting to yaw to one side as the flurry of blasts knocked out a series of propellor struts. Not even the rugged power of its xenos engineering could keep it airborne any longer, could permit its continued flight in the face of such devastating damage.

The gargant came down just south of Kantu Collective. It was the largest artificial explosion ever experienced on Kanai Tertius. It levelled the northern half of the valley, obliterated the collective and created a crater that, when the dust eventually settled, was easily visible to the naked eye from high orbit.

Cass had watched with a plunging sense of despair as *Ruffian* had ridden into the fire. It was only as the sky-gargant had started to ponderously come down, wreathed in the explosions that were killing it, that she had realised what must follow. She turned *Vagrant* south, running hard.

The shockwave from the gargant's impact shook the Valkyrie like a child rattling a tin can. Cass lost her grip on the flight stick and, despite her harness, cracked her helmeted head off the cockpit shield's side. She experienced a strange moment of mental dislocation, struggling to think, finding herself not really caring what happened to her, what happened to any of them.

She came to with a gasp and snatched hold of the flight stick. All around was dust and smoke and a mist of rain vapour. She had only the vaguest idea of where the ground was. She managed to regain a fractional amount of altitude. The auspex was out. She was flying half blind.

'I need that damage report, Korrie,' she reiterated into the intercom, shaking, both hands on the stick now. 'Whenever you're ready.'

She craned her neck, hunting for something, anything, that

she could use as a landmark. The rain was seething down, combining with the airborne debris to create a choking pall. She wondered briefly if she had died, and had been condemned to fly *Vagrant* through eternity in some grim, stygian underworld.

Then she saw shapes under her. Not wreckage or bodies, but moving, struggling people. Guard infantry, trying to find comrades amidst the ruination. Trying to keep moving south, dragging their wounded with them.

And there was the Eji. It was foaming, churned up by rain and by the surge of water pouring from upriver, where the deluge had been coming down for hours already. Cass swung over it, tilting a wing, trying to form a proper view of what was happening.

The crossing was finished. The Eji was in full flow again, its banks swelling. The ford had been subsumed. The current was so ferocious she caught sight of several Leman Russ battle tanks and Chimera armoured personnel carriers being dragged like abandoned toys downriver. The fording point was gone, the chain of vehicles that had helped anchor it swept away.

Those that had made it to the south bank were consolidating, but as Cass came about through the rain, she could see a mass of troops still on the north side. Stranded now, cut off from the safety they had striven down the valley to reach.

Explosions ripped along the riverbank, kicking up water and dirt and blowing through part of a section of Guardsmen desperately wading out into the flow. Hydra batteries drawn up on the other side of the river had started to thud, ladders of shots streaking up past *Vagrant*. Cass saw that there were ork bombers overhead now, reaching the southernmost end of the valley and beginning to drop their payloads upon the greatest mass of Imperial troops. The death of the sky-gargant had taken many with it, and the ragged remains of the Aeronautica fighter wings were still engaging amidst the torrential heavens, but there were still enough xenos airborne to slaughter the packed remnants of the relief effort.

Cass tried the vox, attempting to reach the rest of the wing, then Orlov, then anybody, but she could hear nothing but growling static. There was a scrambled blurt, possibly Bix's voice, but nothing intelligible.

'Looks like it's just us,' she said. 'I'm going to put down on the north bank and start ferrying as many as we can across.'

Cass swung *Vagrant* low, ignoring how the portside rotors clattered and protested, and turned the Valkyrie back north of the river.

CHAPTER THIRTY

The destruction of the sky-gargant broke the efforts of the relief column.

Those troops north of Kantu Valley's midpoint, including the brigades holding the slopes, simply ceased to exist in any coherent manner. Worse, the valley's sides not only helped channel the blast radius farther south, but also shielded the hordes of xenos still mounting the crest from the east and west, sparing them the worst of the destruction.

In the stunned aftermath of the blast, a roaring green tide rose over the remains of Kantu Valley's flanks and came crashing down on the survivors.

Cass touched down on a stretch of sandy dirt next to the rising waters of the Eji, troopers scrambling to make space, whipped at by the downdraught of the hover rotors as she rerouted the engine's power. More bombs were dropping nearby, and there was a rush for the Valkyrie before it had even settled.

Cass kept the hatches shut. There was no point in opening them only to be mobbed and unable to lift off. She waved from the cockpit, trying to get the attention of the rain-sodden, panicked herd below, hoping desperately that someone would bring organisation to the chaos, before one of the falling munitions wiped them all away.

Eventually, Guard discipline reasserted itself. A Hyrkan officer emerged, barking orders and gesticulating with his drawn sword. NCOs and more experienced troops, understanding that trying to mob the Valkyrie would simply mean none of them got on board, formed a cordon, and soon even the most desperate were falling into line.

Cass disengaged the rear ramp, allowing it to drop. Wounded troopers were brought forward and helped on board.

'Let me know when it's full,' she instructed Zeke. 'No more than eighteen.'

She waited, watching the skies through the downpour, the fighting above her now indistinct, rain shot through with flashes of flame. She tried to kickstart the auspex again, but it was out, blank and unresponsive.

'Hope you know your way home,' she said to Korrie.

Eventually the officer waved up at her. She gave a thumbs-up, raised the rear hatch, and dusted off.

Vagrant was leaden, but the Valkyrie made it across the surging waters of the Eji, downdraught whipping at the river. Cass alighted as carefully as she could as soon as she reached the southern bank, troopers there rushing forward to help the wounded off.

'Here we go again,' she said as soon as they were clear. Hatches closed, she lifted off and crossed again to the northern side. The rain was forming a curtain all around now, and the port rotors were still protesting, but she knew she couldn't stop. Her father's words were loud in her ears.

We do our duty, and great or small, that is always enough. You can always rest easy, if you know your duty is done.

Wellend lived.

For a while he'd known nothing but the hammering devastation unleashed upon the pocket. He had been smothered by the destruction, cast aside like chaff in the wind. The concussion of nearby blasts had knocked him unconscious, and he had woken half buried, cut by shrapnel, his ears ringing and bleeding.

He had dragged himself out, slowly, painfully. The world that was waiting for him was almost unrecognisable, choked with dust and smoke and fire and the unidentifiable wreckage of human remains.

Then the rain had come. It had turned the dust to paste, the dirt to muck, and made his wounds sting. It had revived him, just enough so he could properly find his feet along with a degree of orientation.

There had been other survivors, equally torn and shellshocked. He'd led them, the discipline of ranks now gone, a stumbling retreat into the downpour as something vast had come plunging down behind them and brought further destruction to the northern end of the valley.

The beasts were almost upon them the whole way. Wellend could hear their roaring and howling over the thunder of the falling munitions and rattling engines, coming from left and right and behind, closing in. They were indistinct shapes in the torrent, and the only hope of evading them was to keep going, forcing his stunned, injured body to obey, trying to set an example for the others. If they stopped now, they'd be hacked to pieces.

Then he saw light, not the banished glare of the sun, but

beams of crimson brilliance that stabbed through the gloom on either side. Las bolts.

There was a crash, and something whipped overhead with a deadly whistle before detonating behind the Mordians. Wellend stumbled on, able to make out shapes before them now – the brute bulk of a Leman Russ, then a second and third battle tank, and figures strung out between them, their las bolts searing to the left and right of his ragged band of survivors, slamming into the half-seen ork mobs closing in around them.

The thunder of a demolisher cannon punched at his eardrums, and a second detonation ripped through the rain to Wellend's right, turning the leading edge of the xenos rush there to smoke and dirt and flying offal. The rest recoiled.

He heard a cry over the rain and the crack of the high-powered discharges.

'Watch your markers! Friendlies coming in!'

Relief drove him on. He wasn't sure if he shouted, or waved. He was conscious of the roaring intensifying all around, and the barrage of covering fire picking up as the Mordians managed the last few yards.

Only then did he realise just who was holding the line.

'Are there any more behind you?' Captain Stryk called out as the Mordians reached the Scion's firing line.

'I don't know,' Wellend admitted. He wanted to collapse at Stryk's feet, overcome with relief and exhaustion. Instead, he found himself calling out to the other survivors, shouting at them to form ranks alongside the Alphic Hydras.

The Mordians were almost unrecognisable, hats gone, once-pristine uniforms torn and drenched and caked with mud and blood. But those with weapons obeyed Wellend's abrupt orders without a moment's hesitation. In a few seconds, the weight of firepower being sent into the beastly shapes looming through the curtain of rain surrounding them intensified, as the Iron Guard ceased their retreat and joined the Scions.

Wellend fired off a few shots with his laspistol, and looked at Stryk, who nodded at him, the rain making his red carapace armour glisten. Steam was rising from the cowling of his hellgun.

'We're not planning on making a stand here for long,' the Scion officer warned him. 'The rearguard has collapsed. I'm trying to get any survivors I can back to the river. It's flooding.'

Wellend thought of his father, and emptied the remains of his las pack into the xenos, before reloading and replying to Stryk.

'We'll stay as long as you do, sir.'

'Understood.'

One of Stryk's Scions approached, gripping an auspex in one gauntlet. 'No solid friendly returns to the north,' Wellend heard him say, the words followed immediately by the thunder of another Leman Russ discharging its battle cannon, making the rain puddling along its armoured flanks leap and cascade down its sides. 'Just a lot of xenos.'

'Time to go, then,' Stryk said, and cinched his hellgun against his chest before scrambling up onto the flank of the Demolisher battle tank at the heart of the small formation.

'That's the last of them,' he shouted to the Zenonian tank commander, who was leaning out of her cupola. Like most of the Free Companies, she looked about as far from the Mordian ideals of discipline and uniformity imaginable, with a studded face and a shock of pink hair, matching the rough Free Company graffiti and stencil markings that decorated her tank. But Wellend had quickly learned, in the crucible of the pocket, that adherence to uniform regulations couldn't be used to measure a Guard unit's combat effectiveness, a fact that would have made his old instructors at the Vanandra Academy spit.

'Time to make for the river,' Wellend heard Stryk telling the Zenonian.

'We'll back up with you, but we're not crossing,' the tanker replied, wiping her rain-slick hair back from her face and over the headset she had on.

'You can dismount,' Stryk pointed out. 'Word on the vox is there's still a Valkyrie making shuttle runs across the Eji.'

The Zenonian shook her head. 'I've already spoken to the rest of the crews. We're not abandoning the tanks.'

Wellend understood. For many Guard units, the war machines they fought and sweated, bled and died in were the closest things to home they'd ever known. It made him wonder whether he should stand and fight as well. He tried to decide what his father would have done, and knew he would have ordered him to get the men out. It was what he had died trying to do. Wellend had to finish that work, make good that sacrifice. Otherwise, it would have been in vain.

'Emperor be with you,' Stryk said to the Zenonian. He dropped down off the tank's flank and called his remaining Scions to him. Wellend likewise shouted for the Mordians to fall in, noting with a sense of fierce pride how they did so with customary speed and efficiency, despite their desperate state.

Stryk spoke to him, calling out above the sounds of the Demolisher's heavy bolter sponsons opening up on the next ork wave.

'Let's move! If we're lucky, we can get out of this damned valley the same way we came in.'

CHAPTER THIRTY-ONE

Cass lost count of how many times she crossed the Eji.

The rain was continuing to worsen. She saw flashes of illumination dart across the heavens, and realised it was not the aerial war, but the wrath of Kanai Tertius itself, lightning transfixing the thundering clouds and acting as a snapshot silhouetting those warplanes still daring the heavens.

She swung *Vagrant* back to the north bank again. The Valkyrie was holding up, despite the weather, and despite the beating it had taken. Fuel was running low now, though. She was expecting Korrie to tell her any moment that it was time to turn for home.

The northern side of the Eji was continuing to swell, picking up the hundreds of bodies and abandoned equipment littering it and sweeping them out into the current. Explosions were still tearing at the last of those trapped on the far side, xenos artillery now brought up to pound the survivors. Counter-battery fire from south of the river was streaking away into the downpour, but the weight of the fire being directed against the Guard was only increasing as the cordon formed around the evacuation shrank.

Cass put down, a little higher up than she had before. Each time she landed she was forced to do so further away, as the river's edges continued to climb.

There wasn't much left for her to get out any more. Her own efforts and the relentless shelling and bombing had whittled the numbers down to a few dozen. They were taking small-arms fire now as well, and returning it, orks massing in the rain all around.

Cass dropped the rear hatch.

'Get on,' Stryk barked at Wellend as he fired, las bolts turning rain to vapour.

'What about you?' Wellend shouted back. The little cordon of Scions was rapidly contracting as they fell back towards the Valkyrie, laying fire down every step of the way. Through the curtain of rain, Wellend could just about make out the last of the Zenonian battle tanks, blazing as its ammunition cooked off. They had been overrun a few minutes earlier. The orks were practically on top of them now.

'We've survived worse,' Stryk told him, pausing to let his hellgun cycle back up on to full charge, maintaining fire discipline despite the overwhelming pressure of the situation.

Wellend doubted the Scion's claim was true. He wanted to stay with him. He wanted to fight. Not a backwards step.

'Go,' Stryk shouted. 'That's an order!'

Wellend looked towards the Valkyrie, recognising its markings. It was Captain Elza who had been continuously running the river crossing, single-handedly keeping the evacuation going. It didn't surprise him.

The last of the ragged Mordian survivors were climbing on board the flier. Orks were charging towards them from all sides, and though the Scions were dropping them with relentless accuracy, it was clear they were moments away from being overwhelmed.

'I'll make sure command knows what happened here,' Wellend promised Stryk.

'Just tell them we did our duty,' the Scion responded, putting a double tap through the chest of an ork fifty paces away.

Wellend mustered the remnants of his strength and sprinted for the Valkyrie, the last to clamber into its crowded hold. His final sight of Stryk was the Scion uncoupling his hellgun and drawing his combat knife, as a wall of howling xenos fell upon him.

A shell hit the Eji just upriver from *Vagrant*, drenching the Valkyrie. Another hit the embankment, rattling the port wing and the side of the airframe with shrapnel.

Cass barely flinched. She felt numb, exhausted. It was only the tick of the intercom that brought her round.

She expected to hear Korrie or Zeke, but it was another voice, speaking over the link from the hold.

'Captain Elza, it's Lieutenant Wellend. That's the last of us aboard. Good for lift-off.'

The young Mordian had made it after all. She acknowledged and raised the back ramp, then got *Vagrant* airborne again, barely skimming the top of the churning waters.

The south side was now hardly more organised than the north bank had been. Mortar platoons and heavy weapons teams had set up to try and provide covering fire across the river, but the foxholes they'd hastily dug had flooded, and the rapid rising of the water level had forced them back to extreme range.

Vagrant's upper port rotors let out a pained grating sound, and Cass felt the faithful flier dip momentarily, nose almost skimming the water. She brought the Valkyrie around and down as soon as she could, the river swilling around the landing points on the wings and prow, back hatch splashing as it dropped into the rising surge.

As they had done before, troopers on the bank rushed forward to help the occupants out. Cass had landed with the prow facing north, and she found herself peering through the rain and the scarred armaglass, trying to make out what was happening on the far bank, trying to see if there were any survivors still there, anyone she might still be able to get out. There were a few flashes of crimson that she thought had to be las fire, then nothing. The rain fell, and the water seethed and flowed, and Cass hesitated.

Having done it so many times, it almost felt like the natural thing to swing back over the churning river again. To cross alone, emptying the last of the las, flying into the fire the way Konstantina and Vaughn and Cobb and all the others had done. To end it all and be with them again.

That wouldn't be what they would want, Korrie told her. *Turn for home.*

She was right. The rest of the squadron might have finished doing their duty, but she hadn't, not yet.

'Maybe next time,' she muttered. She checked the rear ramp was clear and raised and slowly picked *Vagrant* back up, water pouring from the airframe. The rotors were turning, holding their familiar rhythm. They would see her safe home, she was sure.

She flexed her grip around her father's tags, and turned *Vagrant* south.

Far above, 76-42B watched.

The Marauder Vigilant was untroubled by the storm, hanging in the frigid, cloudless blue above and beyond. Its advanced surveillance systems stripped away the atmospherics, continuing to monitor events in Kantu Valley with only minor interference from the intervening storm.

Flight Lieutenant Crenn and his crew had watched as the battle had played out, as scrambling Imperial squadrons had thrown themselves against the vast, terrible bulkhead of xenos air power. Crenn took great pride in his duties as a spotter, but it was at times like these that the requirements of a Vigilant commander – to remain distant, aloof, and to transmit observed events clearly and impartially – became a great weight. He was an aviator of the Aeronautica Imperialis, and his first instincts were to be there in the thick of the aerial melee, flying in support of his fellow pilots.

Instead, he remained safe in his cockpit, tracking the planes of friends and family from the *Mandatum Divinum*'s atmospheric wings as they threw themselves against impossible odds. He watched as one Imperial marker after another blinked out of existence, reported their losses without audible emotion to command at Suchen. He sat helpless, waiting to see if all the deaths, all the sacrifices, would be enough.

The Aeronautica Imperialis savaged the ork air armada, and paid the price for doing so, but it was Kanai Tertius itself that ultimately turned the xenos back. Not even the orks' disregard for the dangers of flying in a thunderstorm was enough to keep the vast air forces they had amassed intact. Those that made it south over the Eji struck at the Imperial remnants there, but eventually even the most aggressive were forced to turn north and run for home, or risk being brought down by Kanai's long-withheld wrath.

Imperial airspace cleared too, the fighter and bomber wings withdrawing to their airbases, where they were grounded in the seething rain. Crenn watched one last aerial return, tagged on his displays as *Vagabond Leader*, seemingly passing back and forth across the Eji, time and again.

'That's Captain Elza's warbird, isn't it?' his co-pilot, Naria said, watching the same, strange phenomenon.

'It is,' Crenn confirmed. He had never met her in person, but all of the Old Mother's flight crews knew of Vagabond Squadron. Crenn had seen them in the thick of it throughout the day, had watched the signifiers belonging to the wing's other warbirds go out one by one.

'She's shuttling across the river,' Crenn said as he realised what he was seeing on the displays. 'Moving the last survivors across.'

Viewed from such a great distance, with a sea of returns indicating ork ground forces surging towards the river, it seemed like a tiny, insignificant effort. But Crenn knew it would be anything but that to those whose lives Elza was saving.

Eventually, the Valkyrie pulled away and turned south, the last Imperial aircraft to do so.

'All Aeronautica assets returning home,' Crenn reported to Suchen. 'Xenos contacts have also disengaged en masse and are running north. *Spotter Six* is tracking, will update on any changes.'

The Battle of Kantu Valley was over.

Vagrant put down on one of Barduk's secondary landing pads, the only Valkyrie to do so. Despite listing heavily, it made touchdown gently, eased onto the raised rockcrete with the deft care of an experienced pilot.

Cass shut down the systems one by one, the in-flight thunder dying, replaced by the near-silence of post-landing, with only the gentle ticking and creaking of the settling flier left to disturb the stillness. It was strange, and rare, to experience such quiet in the cockpit of a Valkyrie.

She tried to say as much to Korrie, but choked on the words. She made herself uncurl her grip from around the flight stick, her hand aching. Then she sat, perfectly still, strapped in, staring ahead at nothing.

She didn't know how long she remained that way.

A sudden banging on the cockpit shield made her jump and cry out. She looked through the cracks and scarring and blood misting the armaglass, and recognised Kravia Three-Six, Zorn's tech-adept assistant. He was sodden in the rain that was still slashing down, and his young, unaugmented face looked concerned. He waved at her, mouthing something she couldn't quite make out.

She raised a hand and unbolted the cockpit shield. It levered up with a crunch of broken armaglass. Suddenly, the downpour was hitting her, pattering from her helmet and striking, cold and stinking, against her lower face.

She slowly uncoupled her helmet from *Vagrant's* now-blank interface, then unfastened her harness so she could stand up. Her legs threatened to give way, and she was forced to clutch on to the cockpit's side before turning, and witnessing the ruination of her oldest friend.

She looked away. Climbed down, unaided. Heard Zorn, who was waiting for her with the ground crews, speaking as though from a great distance.

'Are you injured, Captain Elza?'

She made no reply, but walked around the prow, to the Valkyrie's starboard side. Found the hatch open and Zeke sitting there, held to his seat by his harness strap, slumped, the edge of the hatch sticky with his blood. The rain was beginning to wash it out in a pink cascade.

He was gone, like Korrie. Like all of them.

Cass pulled off her helmet, dropped it, and walked away, alone.

Vagrant remained, scarred and gleaming in the pelting rain, as torn and broken and lost as its crew.

EPILOGUE

'Here she is, the talk of high command,' Lieutenant General Havali said with an expansive smile, ushering Cass into the knot of senior officers he was presiding over. 'Allow me to present Captain Cassandra Elza, of Vagabond Squadron!'

Cass smiled, shook the hands proffered to her, and nodded her thanks as she was introduced to each one in turn.

'Thank you, sir, yes, it was nothing.'

'Yes, sir, just doing my duty, sir.'

'We did our best, sir. We couldn't have done it without your troopers on the ground.'

'Yes, sir, I'll be sure to pass your thanks on to the rest of the squadron. Thank you.'

The reception was being held in Aquila House, part of the planetary headquarters directing the full breadth of the Imperial war effort just south of Ushen. Like Suchen it had once been a palace belonging to the High Charag, but was altogether grander and more expansive than that provincial seat of power.

The chamber hosting the reception was made from timber and plaster, delicately painted with scenes depicting grand hunts and feasts, interspersed with high, slender windows that had been packed with flakboard and sandbags, the only concession to military necessity.

The evening was ostensibly to honour Havali and the efforts of the forces holding the Eji Valley. Cass was one of the centre-pieces of the event, and the general had been displaying her to everyone he could engage in conversation. She was wearing the dress uniform of the fleet's tactical wing, a navy blue coat with brass buttons and a peaked cap displaying the winged 'AI' badge of the Aeronautica Imperialis.

There were medals on her chest. One of them was new.

It had been a month, Terran standard, since the relief of Army Group Centre. One month since she had last flown. One month since Orlov had grounded her, had told her she was on rest and recuperation for an indefinite period. In that time, she had barely left the lines, barely spoken to anyone. Eaten little, slept less.

'Yes, sir, thank you. It was looking rough for a while, but I never doubted we'd get the job done.'

'Thank you, sir. Yes, we certainly reminded those beasts who rules the skies of this world.'

She felt hot and uncomfortable in her number ones, unaccustomed to the constricting fit, wishing she was back in her flight suit. Her features ached from the smiling. The faces, names and ranks of those she was being introduced to had started to blur hours ago, helped along by the drinks being pressed on her.

'Yes, sir, Lieutenant General Havali's plan was sound from the beginning. He put his trust in me, sir, and I can assure you there's no greater honour than when your commander does that.'

Orlov had forced her to attend. He had told her she would never fly again if she didn't. On the other hand, he said, he'd clear her for aviator duties if she came along and played nice. She supposed he could hardly avoid doing that, eventually. The most famous, most decorated pilot on Kanai Tertius, the hero of the Eji Valley, couldn't be left languishing in Barduk Airbase West, not while there was a war to win.

Havali claimed they were at least one step closer to that eventual victory. He had spent the whole night describing to a parade of senior officers how, by seizing the initiative and pushing the front up to the Eji River while simultaneously breaking Army Group Centre out, he had met what would otherwise have built up into an unstoppable ork offensive head-on, and checked it. There was some truth in that – the xenos had been massing to the north in far greater numbers than the strategos had anticipated, not just an air armada but a vast horde of warbands that would have surged south, crushed Havali's command and split the front between Ushen and Torr City the same way Army Group Centre had initially intended to at the opposite end of the valley.

It was not so much the Guard that had stopped them, though, but the River Eji itself, swollen by that long-overdue deluge. With the crossings impassable in the face of active resistance, both sides had dug into the opposing banks and spent the past month in desultory shelling. Concentrated firepower was what the Imperial Guard did best, and the orks had been unable to establish a hold to the immediate north of the Eji, instead being forced to extreme artillery range, making their new encampments amidst the devastated remains of the north end of Kantu Valley. Orlov had confided rumours that various xenos mobs were already breaking off to return to the fighting in the two great cities, where Imperial forces were making gains. It seemed as though the crisis had been averted, for the time being.

'Yes, sir, it's an honour. Not just for me, but for the entire squadron. This medal is for all of them, really.'

What Havali was barely admitting to, and what his superiors seemed to have decided to overlook, was the cost of his offensive operation. The numbers had been run and rerun again, and supposedly more troops had made it out with Army Group Centre than had been lost in the fighting to get them out, a figure that Havali was furiously spinning as a victory. From what Cass had seen, most of those present at the reception seemed content to swallow that claim, though from what she knew of high command politics, she wouldn't be surprised if behind the scenes the wheels were now in motion against Havali.

Orlov certainly seemed to think so. If the breakout attempt hadn't triggered the main ork force to the north to strike before it was fully amassed, the outcome could have been very different. For the Aeronautica Imperialis, it was bad enough as it was – the Eji River front had lost almost sixty per cent of its air power, and wings were being drafted in from both Ushen and Torr, a fact that Jakyra was apparently unhappy about. As far as Cass was concerned, the air marshal's discontent was just about the only good news from the past month.

'I'm sure you aviator types gave your all, but the Guard are the ones who held the line,' one drunken Ventrillian officer blustered, his face ruddy and sheened with sweat. 'You might win the skies, but we're the ones who have to take and hold the ground, isn't that right, Havali?'

'We do the Emperor's work in tandem, General Delanquet,' Havali said with a hasty smile. 'One is little use without the other. I'm sure Captain Elza fully appreciates the efforts of the Astra Militarum, don't you, captain?'

Havali received no reply. He frowned, looked around, but suddenly could find no sign of his prized Valkyrie commander.

Cass was gone.

* * *

Cass had a Munitorum groundcar drive her back to Barduk, ignoring anyone else who tried to speak to her. She made it back to the squadron lines, to the loud solitude of her own thoughts, thankful to be returning to them before she did anything she might later regret.

She entered the musty half-dark of the hab-tunnel, almost untouched since the squadron had last flown out together. She had wondered more than once whether this was damnation, whether at some point she had passed over and was now receiving the rewards of her failure, an eternity of anguish fitted to match the wagers of her previous existence.

For weeks she had despaired, alone and seemingly forgotten. She had heard that two other warbirds from the 901st, the Vulture from Nemesis and Marrand from Shadow, had survived the Kantu action, but with their crews still intact they had been flying sorties near constantly. The same went for Bix. Before tonight, Cass had seen no one but Orlov, and the dead.

There were bodies there, as Cass walked the tunnel towards her office. Bodies in all the bunks, where they belonged, each one clutching a scrap of litany script in hands that were cold and pale and hard, or burned into skeletal claws.

The sight of them comforted Cass. It was worse when they weren't there. When she found herself alone in the hab-tunnel, clutching at old bedding or sifting through abandoned belongings, shaking.

She reached her office and quietly shut the door, then sat behind her desk, the blinds half closed, still in full dress uniform. Her laspistol was lying in front of her, next to her helmet – Zorn had returned it to her, after patching the cracked visor. She had decided against taking the pistol to the reception.

She looked at it, then at the door. Was that movement she had heard, beyond it?

Cass kept still, finding herself imagining opening the door and being confronted by what she had wrought, by her dead friends. The Fledgling, half his face a red mask, the other half calm and pale; or Vaughn or Konstantina, blistered and burned. Or worst of all, Korrie, not as she had known her for years, but as she remembered her in those last moments, when she had turned and seen what the round that had punched through *Vagrant's* aft cockpit had done to her.

But what if it was Cobb? Not lost after all, not dead. Maybe he and his crew had made it out of *Pauper*, and had only just managed to reach Barduk? What if some of the others had survived as well? What if Vaughn had bailed out just in time, or if she'd been mistaken about *Ruffian's* final moments?

She stood up and walked around the desk, heart racing. There was no doubt something was moving there, just on the other side of the door.

She opened it.

Lieutenant Wellend stood poised, wide-eyed. The Mordian was wearing the starched blue uniform of the Iron Guard, though it looked ill-fitting, a hasty replacement for kit ruined during the fighting at Kantu.

'I'm sorry, sir,' he said, stumbling over his words. 'I didn't mean to intrude. I saw you back at Ushen, but you seemed busy and I didn't want to disturb you in front of the rest of command.'

Cass took a moment to gather her thoughts.

'You followed me back here from Ushen?' she asked.

'I assumed you'd return to Barduk. When I got here I just asked for where your squadron was encamped.'

'My squadron is gone,' Cass said with a sharpness she could not avoid.

'I'm sorry, sir,' Wellend said. 'I just… I felt I had to speak with you, and I wasn't sure I'd get another opportunity. I wanted to thank you, for everything you did. Not just for me, but for my father, and the regiment.'

'Did he make it out?' Cass asked.

Wellend's gaze dropped, briefly, before he answered. The pause was only small, but Cass had seen it enough times – too many times – to know its meaning.

'Not many did,' he said, 'but more than if you had let them shoot me at Suchen, or if you hadn't run that river crossing. I wanted you to know it mattered, to me and to others.'

Cass had been receiving plaudits all evening, but for some reason this was the first one that gave her any pause. She thought about bringing him into the office, sitting him down, and talking. But she couldn't. Instead, she nodded to him.

'Thank you. I hope command took note of you as well, back at Ushen. Without you the breakout wouldn't have happened either.'

She tried to make the statement not sound like an accusation. He shrugged.

'I've been promoted to brevet captain. My brigade is being amalgamated into a single regiment and redeployed with the Seventh Corps to Torr City.'

Cass almost grimaced. That sounded as much like a death sentence as anything she had heard recently.

'Congratulations on your promotion,' she said. 'Believe me, a captaincy will keep you busy.'

Wellend gave her a shallow, uncertain smile, then saluted her. She returned it as he spoke.

'It's been an honour, sir. Hopefully we'll meet again, but regardless, may the Emperor go with you, all your days.'

'And with you, Captain Felkin,' Cass said. As he turned away, she found herself speaking again. 'And, Wellend... he'd be proud.

Your father, I mean. It seems as though he was Iron Guard in the truest sense, and everything I've seen of you matches that reputation.'

This time Wellend's smile, though brief, was genuine.

'Thank you, sir. He did his duty, and so have I. He always said that's all that really matters.'

Several days later, Cass visited *Vagrant*.

It was late in the evening, and the dead weren't letting her sleep, so she went to the squadron hangar. It was deserted and locked down, and ordinarily not even a squadron leader would have been able to access it without permission from wing command, but it didn't take much for Cass to convince the Munitorum security clerk on duty to let her in.

Vagrant sat alone, under tarpaulins, surrounded by wide, empty, echoing space. Cass pulled the coverings off and paced slowly around her warbird, assessing the damage.

The final repairs had been completed by Zorn the week before – all that was needed was some fresh paint. *Vagrant*'s scars gleamed, a latticework of silver covering her, the plasteel still looking lumpen in places where it had been recently applied to patch over holes and wounds. In places Cass reached out and lightly touched the injuries, tracing them across the framework, remembering.

She climbed into the forward cockpit, into that well-worn, familiar seat, shielded now by a fresh, undamaged sheet of armaglass. She reached out with her bare hand and clutched the flight stick, and her father's service tags. Then she wept, and afterwards sat silent, the waves that had been crashing over her slowly settling into a cold, still, featureless expanse.

She slept in the cockpit, and awoke stiff and sore, to the sound of footsteps and angry voices. She looked down and discovered Orlov, gesturing at her to get out.

'I couldn't find you,' her wing commander said tersely. 'I should have known you'd be here.'

He looked as though he had aged a decade over the past month. Cass clambered down and saluted him.

'Smarten yourself up,' he told her. 'You've got visitors.'

'If it's more of the brass, I–' Cass began to say, but Orlov cut her off.

'You want to fly again, don't you? That's all you've been telling me this past month.'

'Yes, but if it means licking more generals'–'

'You can't fly without a crew, Cass,' Orlov said. 'That's why you've not been up. But that's about to change. At least tie your hair back, for Throne's sake.'

Cass felt a moment's confusion and Orlov waved towards the hangar's main doors, which were being heaved back by a few Munitorum drones, the new day streaming in.

'Their names are Harwel, Maynard and Keller, and they're all very excited to be joining Vagabond Squadron. They completed their final tests and checks on board Old Mother last week. This is their first time planetside.'

Cass felt herself starting to panic. Orlov read her expression.

'You've rebuilt Vagabond Squadron once before, and you'll do it again,' he said. 'But for now, you'll fly with the remnants of the rest of the wing, forming a single squadron. You'll have command, if I clear you for it, and I'm going to. The Imperium needs you, Captain Elza.'

Cass had always known it would come to this, and at times she had hoped for it. But now it was happening, she felt nothing but fear and denial. She tried to find the right words for Orlov, tried to tell him she wasn't ready, that the shades of her old crews, her old friends, weren't ready. He put a hand on her shoulder, and when he spoke again his voice had lost the coldness of command.

'I understand what you're going through. That may sound like grox crap, but I really do. It happened to me. Jora IX, against the Great Devourer. Your father was there, with Vagabond Squadron. It was a living hell, and at the end of it I was the only member of Nemesis Squadron still living. A cruel miracle. Afterwards, they promoted me. That's how I became wing commander.'

Orlov had never told her that. The surprise took the sting out of her panic.

'My biggest regret was not getting the chance to rebuild,' he went on. 'Throne, I've barely even flown since. For a long time, it was the worst thing I could imagine. But eventually, when I told myself commanding the entire Nine-Hundred-First was my way of paying back those good friends I lost, I actually started believing it. Now here I am, as whole as I'm ever going to be. You're at least being given the chance to rebuild.'

'And to suffer it all again, and again,' Cass pointed out.

'Welcome to the Aeronautica Imperialis,' Orlov said, the hand on the shoulder becoming a slap on her upper arm. 'You're going back up, Cass. All that's left for me to say to you is "Good hunting."'

Cass faced her three new crew members as they were permitted to set foot in the hangar. Three fresh-faced, wide-eyed youths in clean, regulation-issue kit. They saluted Cass, and she returned the gesture before speaking to them, her voice firm and clear despite the weight pressing down on her, despite the shades of fallen aviators she could sense all around her.

'My name is Captain Cassandra Elza. Welcome to Vagabond Squadron.'

ABOUT THE AUTHOR

Robbie MacNiven is a Highlands-born History
graduate from the University of Edinburgh. He is
well known for his Carcharodons novels *Red Tithe,
Outer Dark* and *Void Exile,* as well as the Warhammer
40,000 novels *Oaths of Damnation, Blood of Iax,
The Last Hunt* and *Legacy of Russ.* His work for
Warhammer Age of Sigmar includes the novel *Scourge
of Fate* and the Gotrek Gurnisson novella *The Bone
Desert.* His hobbies include re-enacting, football and
obsessing over Warhammer 40,000.

MORE FROM
BLACK LIBRARY

THE FALL OF CADIA
by Robert Rath

Cadia – a bulwark against the forces of Chaos that reside in the Eye of Terror. This proud world stood defiantly for centuries, until it was targeted for destruction by Abaddon the Despoiler in his Thirteenth Black Crusade.